Twine

Twine

MONICA DUNCAN

CROWSNEST BOOKS

Crowsnest Books

www.crowsnestbooks.com

Distributed by the University of Toronto Press

Edited by Allister Thompson

Proofreader: Britanie Wilson

Cataloguing data available from Library and Archives Canada

ISBN 978-0-921332-62-6 (paperback)

ISBN 978-0-921332-63-3 (ebook)

Printed and bound in Canada

Contents

For David

Pushing Past

It was supposed to be less comfortable at other people's houses, but Juniper loved Bethy's raised ranch. There was something complete about it. Complete in the décor, and that it seemed to have a full complement of appliances, electric can openers and whatnot. Juniper loved to just look around, feeling followed by the smell of dusky potpourri.

She looked out the slider as Bethy took the stationary bike for a spin in the living room. Bethy's rhythm wasn't even, and she was panting.

"Don't make a joke about being 'almost there,'" Bethy said as she pedaled.

"Really, do I look like your dad?" Juniper asked.

"I know, right? He says that, like, every time: 'You're almost there, girl, keep it up.'" Bethy lowered her voice to mimic her dad, but they didn't laugh over the tired joke. Bethy's dad was in the hospital with some heart thing. Her mom, Mary Ann, was there with him. Bethy was just home to feed the cats and had invited Juniper over to swim. She needed company. That's how Bethy was.

Juniper fiddled with the cord for the blinds. She was mesmerized by the whir of the bike's front wheel, and it was like Bethy herself was made up of circles. Breasts and cheeks, golden and rosy.

Bethy finished her living room workout and changed into her swimsuit. Outside, Juniper lay on the banana-yellow float and pictured what an aerial photographer would see: the aboveground pool, like a price sticker, in the middle of a sea of gray-green. Swaths of shape. An aerial photographer couldn't be wowed by Bethy's bikini, an extravagant strappy thing with gold hoops holding the triangles together. Juniper noticed the gap in her own emerald greenish one-piece where either the elastic had quit or the swell of her thigh just didn't. She shielded her eyes as she followed the old-school coconut scent, admired Bethy's goldness, and was pretty sure the sun treated different people, well, differently.

"You know, that date I had last week went great," Bethy said from the deck.

Juniper swirled her hands to think before she answered. "Mm-hm."

"He took me to Outback Steakhouse."

Okay, Juniper thought.

"You should try it," Bethy said.

"The Bloomin' Onion, or your date?" Juniper asked as she shielded her face again to look up.

"Ha-ha." Bethy stepped down the ladder with the finesse of experience and waded, chest high, to cool off without wrecking her hair. "Well, I just thought it could help you out, or whatever."

Juniper rolled off her float and felt for the bottom. She pushed off. There was just enough room to do underwater laps, bisecting the circle, like a tadpole. Underwater was a mini-escape so she could think for a second. She could feel her legs make a diamond then shove the weight of the water back, now more frog-like. She popped up and gasped. She wiped the water out of her eyes and felt Bethy close, waiting for a response, so she avoided eye contact.

Inside again, it was all Cheetos and Diet Coke shoved into their faces as if they were fifteen. As if. Twenty-three felt old to both of them, even though their afternoon almost seemed like a throwback to those easier times. When Juniper emerged from the bathroom in her shorts and t-shirt, Bethy offered to drive her home, which she declined.

"You don't always need to be so tough, you know," Bethy said. Juniper thought that was ironic. It was *her* dad in the hospital, and she seemed fine.

"I'm okay riding. Plus, how else would I get my bike home? I need it to get to work, you know." She was used to having to explain this to people. Her goal was to get a car by fall, anyway. She could tough out these next few months.

* * *

An hour later, Juniper was broken down on the side of the road with a dead cell phone. Every once in a while, a car would pass. She would stand taller and pretend she was fine and that she was walking her bike on purpose. She composed herself to look like she was just slowing down to enjoy the stunning day. Driving by at forty or fifty, no one could see her sweating from the exertion it took to push a bike that had jammed brakes. They couldn't see she'd been pushing and lifting her bike like this for five miles and hadn't even shed a single tear until mile four. And even then, the tears weren't because she couldn't do the four more miles it would take to get home. They weren't because she wasn't strong enough. She cried because she was the type of person to accept this kind of challenge as a matter of fact. It was written into her life that she would do this type of stuff stoically. There were times when she could have asked for help. Bethy most certainly would have smiled and waved for help by then. Or if she could have called, her mom would have driven right over. But her mom wasn't there that day, on the side of the road. And if that wasn't symbolic of growing up, she didn't know what was.

Anyway, Bethy would not have ridden her bike so many miles to a friend's house. She just wouldn't have. No one she knew rode a bike as a means of transportation. What with everything in that gridded landscape separated by stop signs at one-mile intervals, things were too far. Homogenous. Flat. At least it was flat, she thought, as the necessary positivity crept back in and she lifted and pushed forward.

Fuzzy Math

She was mesmerized by how the repeated rooms in the hotel super-imposed themselves upon one another and imprinted themselves upon her life. Daily, she thought of the math of Vacation Express as a physical space—stacked rooms, stacked numbers, infinity mirrors, fractals, perspective, the blankness of repetition and the possibility of getting lost within the sameness. Juniper was worried about getting lost.

There was, in fact, a "house of mirrors" aspect to the lives of people she had grown up with, marked by confusion about what they saw, what was real, and which direction was the right one. The people she knew just didn't make enough money to feel like they had choices. And it seemed like, with this new job of hers, she was in danger of feeling the same way.

As lean as a ten-year-old boy, Juniper was aware that her type of slenderness was not to be envied. Her hair was slinky and russet-colored, like a liquidy November leaf. Her pale ears poked out, elven. Her eyes, surprisingly dark for a near-redhead, were like tilled, wet, prepared soil. They were close-set, focused eyes. The clean lines of her structure were displayed by the perfect cross of her posture: a hipless plumb line from head to foot, set upon by level shoulders and punctuated by those dark brown, close-set eyes. Her knuckles mimicked a woodpecker's tats.

"Housekeeping!"

The heavy door clunked open. "Hey darlin'," a golf shirt greeted. "We were just needin' some extra pillows."

An older woman's voice from the bathroom clamored, "Two, Henry! Two."

Juniper and Golf Shirt Henry were standing in the dark entrance, practically shouldering the bathroom door. Bathroom Wife might as well have been visible. They both turned toward the voice that resonated cleanly in the echo chamber, and Henry said, "I've got it!" while Juniper overlapped, "Yes, I can do that," in her stage voice. Her voice also projected a deference that was fairly sincere. Not chipper and happy like Bethy, but quiet and clear, like a bow of respect. The folks loved that. The managers loved that. The businessmen went nuts for it. Sure, Bethy's perky butt and wet smile worked magic, but Juniper had her fans.

After she excused herself, she passed the front desk and said, "Yo, Manny. I thought 112 was checked out, but then they asked me for pillows."

"Huh? Lemme see that." He held out his hand for the log. "Oopsie. Mixed up 212 and 112."

She flounced to the supplies room. *"Got it."* She flung the words over her shoulder at Manny with his silky shirt and silky tie. Sometimes he even added silky pants to all that, stuck in his silky rut of Vacation Express management.

Back down the tube of darkness, tunnel of repeat. There was nothing about the feel of the place that didn't bother her. Number 112. Tat tat tat.

"Housekeeping!"

Golf Shirt Henry said, "Aha," with his arms outstretched. "Thanks, darlin'."

"Are there *two*?!" Bathroom Wife shrieked through the door.

"I got it!" Henry barked back. His hands were on the pillows, but he let go and said, "Could you just—" and gave a twirly gesture to the far bed. Juniper stepped all the way into the room and deposited the pillows on the second queen by the window. He said, "Hey. Who's that friend you work with? The one with the big smile?"

There was Karen, fifty-five, not smiley. Jo-Jo, thirty-something, a big girl, everyone said. As in 'she's a big girl.' Even though she wasn't a girl, and "big" was polite.

"Bethy," Juniper said and waited for more.

But then he pretty much seemed to forget she was there. Instead, he cupped his hands on the bathroom door. "I'm goin' out for a minute, hon. Be back." His wife was fumbling around and said something not clear. Henry held the outer door for Juniper, tossed her a tight-lipped "thanks," and seemed to beeline to the front lobby. *Unfuckingbelievable,* Juniper thought. *Who's your friend?*

Sure enough, not fifteen minutes later, she was carting over to 130, past the lobby, and Golf Shirt was already chatting up Bethy. *Unfuckingbelievable. You're on a trip with your wife!*

* * *

Juniper's afternoon bike ride home was on a country road that paralleled the highway. It was June, the sun was singing, and the wildflowers were out, purple on the right side of the road and soft yellow on the left. It was the wildflowers that got all the color in this town, she thought. As she pedaled, the smell crooked its finger, and she really wanted a bouquet. She turned her head full to the right and inhaled a swath of purple with a deep blink. Then she scanned the other side of the road to gather the yellow. While holding the wild violets tight in her mind, she blinked again and felt the glorious clash of an amethyst-butter bouquet. It lasted for two long seconds before she thought to do it again. With a swish of yellow across to the purple side of the road, she gathered an eyeful, as good as a real bunch in a glass vase filled with cool water perched on a whitewashed windowsill. To keep.

* * *

The next day, she greeted Manny as she went in to work through the front doors of Vacation Express. They weren't really supposed to do that, go in the front. But she wanted to pick up her check, and she secretly loved the grand whoosh of the front doors. It made her feel like she was back in Chicago again, back at the Art Institute. It really did transport her for a moment when she used that front entrance. But then the doors closed behind her, and the smell was all wrong. It was all bleach, new fake wood furniture, industrial textile smelling, instead of Indian food and spring hopefulness. Chicago was being reduced to these impressions, which she was pretty sure she was idealizing.

"June, Jo-Jo wants to take Saturday off, can you cover?" asked Manny. Juniper's instinct was to fuss and say she'd rather not. But she was on the hamster wheel of making just enough to pay her bills. Something niggled at her.

"Yeah, I'll do it," she said. Extra money. It was time to think about working a little harder. It was time to start thinking more about the next step. Chicago. Her art. Her future. She went to the storeroom.

"Hey, ladies." Juniper greeted Bethy and Jo-Jo. "Jo, I've got you covered for Saturday."

"Juniper, you rock. Thanks." Jo-Jo was sitting in a folding chair, testing it for all it was worth. "I got my sister's graduation."

Something about the word *graduation* made Juniper feel squeezed. But she said, "Glad to help," feeling good about that part at least. And the money. She looked down at Jo-Jo's tennis shoes, gray instead of white, strained at the outer edges. Juniper would take more extra shifts. She would start saving. She didn't have a specific plan yet, but moving out of Gobles, Michigan, would involve money.

"Hey, Bethy, what happened with that guy in the golf shirt who was hitting you up yesterday?" Juniper asked.

"Ew. No."

"I didn't think so. He was an ass to his wife right in front of me. And like, old, and polyestery," she agreed. The subtext of the conversation was the result of Bethy confiding in Juniper about what *she* did instead of taking more shifts. They had talked about the occasional businessman or hockey player passing through that Bethy did not find "ew" and that she treated as short-term boyfriends. She'd get a nice dinner, free drinks of course, and sometimes a little cash. Bethy didn't say they paid her, but it seemed the boyfriend business was becoming more lucrative and systematic as far as Juniper could tell. Everyone who worked there knew what was going on. Everyone was slightly horrified and fascinated at the same time. They didn't even think of the illegality of it. They could barely raise an eyebrow, let alone gossip about it yet, because Bethy was so cheerleadery and just not who you'd expect to fall from grace right in front of you. Yet there was a softness that passed between Juniper and Bethy, both understanding that Vacation Express and whatever they did there was temporary.

The Illusion

It was the illusion of country Juniper went home to. She was ten minutes as the crow flies to Walmart, not even driving, but walking across Eller's field. Despite the highways interrupting the gridded acres, she really could walk or bike anywhere. It did suck once the weather got cold, but she planned her trips pretty carefully. People were generally wimps about stuff, and she felt totally empowered not having a car.

She dug her keys out of her backpack and unlocked her trailer door. It was her own trailer, left to her by her grandmother the year before, 2003. It was actually willed to her. She was blown away after the funeral when her mom opened the letter. Of course her mom got Grandma's 1980 Olds, but the trailer was hers. She had been one semester away from graduation at the Art Institute of Chicago when Grandma got sick and passed away, taking Juniper's breath and sense of time away with her.

Home for a week after the funeral, she had stepped into the trailer and inhaled as deeply as she could. There was no permanence to be saved from smells or Grandma's voice or her touch. Juniper went room by thin-walled room, examining the stuff. Pictures—mostly of Juniper, knick-knacks, yarn creations, and quilts, and mugs and Tupperware. A nest of old-womanly comfort. But it was a little too scrubbed of its past, she thought. Grandma had been married for a long time, but you wouldn't know it to look around. Something about her trailer now seemed a façade to Juniper. The stuff seemed too normal, like Grandma Jezebel was trying to play the part. And Juniper thought, *Hey—wait a minute. Why is she giving me her trailer? Maybe she thinks I'm going to come back to Michigan. That I won't stay in Chicago after graduation. Does she think my art is just a passing fancy (as she would put it)?* Juniper spent one night in the trailer before heading back to Chicago to finish her last semester and wondered the entire time she lay in her grandma's bed—both awake and asleep, wondering, dreams morphing into conscious thoughts—if her grandma believed in her.

Because the love Grandma gave to Juniper was the realest thing. She was the giver of light in Juniper's life. Little Junie walked in the door, and Grandma's arms opened wide, and her smile and gladness at Junie's presence were real. That joy was there every time. Not her mom's exhaustion after working so hard, not her best friend's sweetness or boyfriends' lust, could ever beat that Grandma loved her with such freeness. Silly, joyful, warm, colorful love. It had been over a year, and that year anniversary, when things are supposed to get better, was bullshit. She'd been able to spend this past year privately with these things, thinking they would tether her to Grandma's life. But she was nagged by an insincerity that made her feel guilty. Well, maybe the feeling was a thread of anger. Grandma had left an unintentional legacy. People are supposed to leave their things, their genes, memories. But something had been locked and loaded into Juniper's psyche around the uselessness of a man's love.

Despite these complications, at least the main feeling still trickled clear like crick water: love was simple and welcome among the women in her family.

And now, after that year, she was just waiting to figure out what to do, what was next, and how to stop feeling so lonely.

"I got a friend in Michigan, little Ju-ni-per
'cross the lake and 'round the bend, little Juniper.

Oh little Junie, little"—Juniper stopped the voicemail. Ricky's guitar strum-strummed with the tune of "Liza Jane," his heart straining out his throat.

"There are five million girls in Chi-ca-go, Oh Ricky, oh. So don't waste your time on me no more, Oh no, no no." Juniper sang inside her empty trailer in a mimicky voice as she stirred her mac and cheese. But he couldn't hear her, so she was still just a lonely coward. Yesterday he had sung, "Junie, I've got your number, I wanna make you mi-ee-ine." He was stuck in some sort of song time warp. Even though he was still in Chicago and she was now in Michigan, he was still stuck on her.

Ricky. A slender boy, with that kind of sculpted face, turned-up eyes, and maroon lips. Despite the annoying pretense of his flat-billed hat and baggy pants, they had slept together a couple times. After she had led him on for months. During her last few weeks at school, it just seemed like she hadn't let loose enough. Like she should just be a little more reckless before the hourglass ran out. So she spent a weekend at his studio apartment, the whole time thinking, *Could this? Could we?* But it wasn't quite right. Sex was fine. He was nice, albeit too immature. She didn't see a future. But unfortunately, Ricky was giddy with her, and that weekend had cemented his illusions.

"J-dog. Junie. Fairy girl. When you moving back to Chicago? What's going on?" he asked the next evening over the miles. *See, that's what bugs me,* she thought. *I want him to ask, 'How's the art going? How are you? What are you working on?'* The art hadn't been going. But. *But,* she was on the cusp of starting again. She could feel it. It was important to recognize that feeling and how to harness it, then ride it out. When she started to feel like she was on a balance beam and about to fall off, and the feeling wouldn't go away, then it was time. A new project or something was about to start.

But she answered, "Just a regular day, followed by a regular evening, about to be a regular night."

"Like one of those sand sculptures you make at the fair, right? Layer of one color then another. Day, evening, night."

He did think like an artist, she'd give him that. A weird flow-of-con-
sciousness way of being in the world. But talking to him constantly
reminded her of the sadness she was feeling from being alone. The
view out the trailer living room window covered a large scope of
field that belonged to Tom Eller's oldest son. But he lived in Ohio,
so the land sat comfortably inert, not even rotating crops or hosting
oil derricks. It was lazy of him not to get some cash use out of the
land, but good for her to see the nice field grasses, wildflowers, and
shaggy pines throughout the seasons. She was appreciative to have this
chunk of land to herself, not be in some trailer park with regulations
and people blocking her views. She imagined the level she had in her
tool box set upon the horizon across the street, and how the yellow
bubble would center up with no adjustment. That was just the lay of
the land in those southern Michigan parts. Chicago may have been
flat, maybe not. The vertical obscured the topography. Honestly, she
had forgotten to think about any kind of wish for rolling landscapes
while she was in Chicago.

"I don't know, Ricky. Maybe I won't move back to Chicago. I don't
know. I need to think."

"Well, if you need a place to stay, I've got you covered."

"I'm thinking about stuff. I don't know. Hey. I need to go write down
some ideas, I'll talk to you later, 'kay?"

"I'll call you tomorrow," he said.

Juniper sighed. It was her own fault. "Okay, 'night." The sun had set,
so she was looking at her own face in the kitchen window. These kinds
of nights, when she was feeling suffocated alone in the aluminum,
she'd pick up when he called. It was like she could pretend it was going
somewhere, and he wasn't just obsessed. The thing that bothered her
most was that he didn't know her. She was an image for him. His
sylphen fantasy. Maybe Chicago was *her* fantasy.

When she thought about why she had left, it was clear. Lame,
but clear. And why she had come back to this Gobles trailer was
also clear to her. Because if not Chicago, then nowhere else but here
had meaning.

Tree Trunk

Juniper was pretty sure she was the only girl in her art school that had been unadorned. All those creatives she went to school with liked to decorate themselves. That's how she thought of it. Mostly tats, but also lots of colored, shaved hair. Piercings, of course. She really was not into all that. It seemed a little trite. If everyone did some version of body mod, how was that unique? Weren't they all trying to be unique? Which could get silly really fast. She had never even pierced her ears. Her hair was its natural color, her skin its pale pink self. A clean canvas.

Canvas. The bleached skin of watercolor paper. The quiet, brazen white grid of an oil canvas. Or just a board to slap some paint or fabric onto. She had two bedrooms in the trailer. The big one was for her supplies. Paintings leaned together, but not hung. Some of her work just hunched over in dark corners. Stupid trailer light was not even adequate. Last fall she had taken her easel outside and scooped up all that autumnal light as it fell down, decrescendoed. That was the last time she painted.

"Volume" could be a word used to describe the amount of someone's body of work. But for Juniper, volume was also something that accompanied her when she was creating. The process itself seemed to produce a constant buzz of white noise. It was so blank and persistent that she just thought of it as a white "volume." Sometimes up, sometimes down, and with a pushing weight of commotion. But that volume was now as black and silent as an empty hole. Was she getting sucked in? Sucked into nothing?

Painting wasn't a job, or a living. She did get her Bachelor of Fine Arts degree, which really was friggin' awesome because she was the first in her family to get any degree. Sure, it may have taken a "need-based" scholarship for her to get into such a good school, or any school, for that matter. And she may have been fulfilling some quota for all she knew. But now what? No one was impressed. The degree was useless. Just Juniper and the trailer. Juniper the maid. City costume shed, work clothes donned. Real life begun.

That's about how far she got with her soul searching—self-deprecation. She clocked in her time of wondering what she was going to do with her life. Ponder, ponder, oops, time's up. As good as filling out a job application somewhere. She was hungry and felt the pull of Subway. So she slapped on her jean jacket, climbed on her bike, and pedaled. She could hear Emilíana Torrini's "On the Sunny Road" in her head, scratching along with her as she cut through the field corner and bumped through the dirt, stones, and grass, which shaved off half a mile. She was always the only bike locked on the rack outside Walmart.

"Hey, Junie!" greeted Mrs. Dee.

"Hey, Mrs. Dee, how are you? How's Fred?"

"Oh, he's good!" Mrs. Dee jumped a little with glee. Even though she was like seventy and looked weighed down by her pink kitty sweatshirt (clearance rack $2), both feet left the ground with cotton-candy positivity.

"Awright, awright, that's good. Glad he's better." Juniper smiled slow and sweet for Mrs. Dee.

She got in line at the Subway, right past optical. It was not even its own restaurant, just a corner of Walmart. Even the fake brick—"frick," Juniper called it—was a picture of brick, not that molded plastic stuff, which would have been classier or something.

It was busy at dinnertime. The locals were out with their kids, and seniors were clutching their coupons. She liked to really debate what she was going to get in her head, but the line moved too fast, and she was up against the counter.

"Oh, hey, Ma. I can't decide."

"Junie, I got my break in twenty. Just wait for me. I'll get you my discount." Juniper pictured herself wandering around Walmart for twenty minutes, looking for something new, or maybe to see who was working.

"Okay, I'll be back," she agreed. Juniper's mom had worked at some part of Walmart for maybe the past twelve years or so. Walmart was near to their homes, so if there wasn't a car, it could be gotten to. It was steady, shitty work.

Juniper slid through two tight racks of beach towels for no reason but to feel the terry. She skirted the edge of Women's, where the clothes were too pastel. None of the clothes were for her shape. Things were too big or cut wrong. She found the most success at the Goodwill over to Benton Harbor. Old corduroys in shades of saffron and petite army blazers were more her liking. Plus the Goodwill was in a part of town that was not cool, and prices were tagged for folks who didn't have extra.

She wandered and watched. There was Gina, working in housewares in her orthotic white shoes, bangs cut too short, with the seemingly requisite sweatshirt, snowmen on pale blue instead of kitties on pink. And that's what made Juniper sad, that it wasn't even the right time of year for a snowman sweatshirt.

"Hey, Gina." Juniper brightened her face and nodded.

"June! Your Ma is here!"

"I know, Gina, we're having dinner on her break."

"Oh, good."

A kindness squeezed out of her pores. The place brought out her benevolence, a little joy at being known.

"Hi, James!" She waved this time. James was a good guy and had the most pronounced Michigan vowel sounds she'd ever heard. Even with her own Midwestern accent, she cringed a little at his incredibly strident "a's" and Canadian "o's"

"Oh, yeah. Hey, Juniper." He looked up at her over his glasses and waved back. She looped left again, past the bank of registers.

She always saw someone she knew, an old teacher or parent of an elementary school friend. The connections were always there. It was like a track with right angles, that broad outer aisle, racing her around a lap of memory.

"Juniper! I'm over here." Her mom gestured down to her booth in the corner. "I got you the number seven."

"Thanks, Ma." Juniper sat down and tore into her food, her weasely appetite hardly ever sated. She chewed and looked up at her mom. Everyone said she looked like Cora. She had her mom's exact same build, which Juniper thought was plain funny. But Cora's hair was bleachy, streaky. Her facial skin was stretched downward. Too many cigarettes. Her voice was rough and not sexy, just ragged. Cora had a full sleeve on her right arm and some kind of thorny rose nonsense on her upper back, and the *pièce de résistance*—her tramp stamp—was a snake, of all things, and also maybe the real reason Juniper was all clean and tattooless.

"How's Kevin?" asked Juniper.

"He's good, June. Don't be like that."

"I'm just checking." Kevin had been living with Cora for the past two years, and when Juniper noticed a bruise, almost perfectly camou-flaged beneath the butterflies and flowers on her mom's arm, she went nuts. That had been over a year ago. Cora and Kevin were still together, and Cora went to great lengths to hide any evidence that he was not a prince in a black t-shirt.

It had really thrown a wrench into their relationship, because Juniper and Cora were so much alike. They were close, and now Juniper felt like she needed to back off, or else she'd become intrusive and demanding. Like she'd hang around her ma's house demanding he leave. She had to let her mom make her own mistakes. As the only daughter of an only daughter, Juniper knew how to fall in line, keep the peace, be there, but not *too there*. They loved each other, Jezebel, Cora, and Juniper. Instead of expanding sideways and filling out in all directions like some family trees, the three formed a lineage that was strong. They were like the trunk of a tree, just not much for branches. Juniper had hated that stupid joke: You know you're a hick when your family tree don't fork. But now there were only the two of them, and Grandma was down there with the roots, nourishing them in memory.

"Okay, Ma. Is he working?" Juniper asked as she nursed her Coke.

"Yeah, June, I told you he's temping at Pfizer, it's good. We wanna take a vacation in September."

"Wow, nice." Juniper paused and was thinking about the paper wrapper on her meaty sub. Cora looked up warily. But there was nothing more to say. That was one beautiful thing about these intense relationships—knowing what the underbelly looked like without leaning down to see. Juniper knew that Cora felt trapped. She wanted love, and Kevin was a stand-in for what she felt she didn't have a chance in hell of getting. With Kevin by her side, even if it was only on the couch, she wasn't alone.

Overcast Showcase

One of the best places Juniper found to escape was the hotel pool. They could go when they were off work. There wasn't a lifeguard, just Gary skulking around doing his job, chlorining the water, along with everything else he maintained. She always had to say hi to him first. He would not make eye contact otherwise. She felt bad for the guy. He behaved as if he should barely be seen and definitely not heard.

"Gary, how's it goin'?" Juniper let her Michigan accent flare around certain people and softened it around others. She waited for his small talk, which usually came out in tiny chunks.

"Well," he said, and the word echoed off of the cement poolroom walls. "Well." It was like he couldn't get started. She stopped drying off and tucked the thin white towel under her arms and looked straight at him. She wanted to give him a chance.

"Things ain't too good."

"What's going on?" she encouraged, maintaining her stillness and attention.

"I guess I'm not doin' too good, got the big C." It took Juniper just an extra second to understand what he was saying. Her eyebrows tugged up in the middle.

"Oh, Gary, that sucks." She knew he would only say more if she didn't move or speak too fast. So she waited for him.

"Got some spots on my lungs. Surgery, probably, I don't know." He looked like his arms were tethered to lead weights. Everything except his oval name patch looked melted. Juniper thought of his life. He was single, kind of old, or at least old-looking. A job that gave him hours and hours alone. Cancer. The fogged up wall-sized windows showcased the overcast day. She looked back to Gary, wanting to hug him but not wanting to act like she felt sorry for him, not knowing what to say.

"Well, I hope you're feeling okay, Gary. Let me know if you need anything."

His saggy eyes, that might have once been vibrant, flickered. "Yup. Thanks, Juniper, that's nice of you." He said her name like *Jooonipr*. He stepped into the utility closet and started shuffling around the chemicals.

She found her flip-flops and squeaked into them, realizing that another man had been in the room. He wasn't swimming but rather walking the perimeter of the pool, slowly, wearing street clothes. As she was heading into the ladies' room to change, he asked, "Water warm?"

"Yeah, Gary keeps it nice." She was friendly toward any customer. He smiled at her with his lips closed. She noticed his wavy dark blond hair as she was shutting the bathroom door. She locked it, stepped into the little shower, and cleaned up for her shift. She tossed the towel in the bin on her way out and patted her slicked back ponytail. In the short hall leading to the lobby, he was there again.

"Hey," he said. She smiled politely. "Goin' to work?" he added.

She had on her cleaning smock with her fake brass nametag. And maybe because she was near Manny, she felt the attitude coming on, and couldn't help but do a TV hostess hand glide across her nameplate. "Yep!" she replied, too loud and edgy. *Rub it in, why don't you*, she thought. It was hard to not be a little embarrassed about her job sometimes. Not always, but sometimes. It was a thin line to walk—not being too big for her britches, as Grandma would say, yet also not wanting to get stuck in some rut. Not wanting to get complacent.

"I uh, am sorry, but I overheard you talking to that janitor." She turned around to face Wavy Blond Guy and to see what he might possibly say next. "I just wanted to say, I was impressed with your kindness toward him."

She didn't know what to say for the second time that day. That seemed a little patronizing, maybe. Why wouldn't she be kind to Gary? Because he was old, or a maintenance man, or what?

"Oh. Thanks. I think," she said.

"No, I didn't mean it in a patronizing way. I just, I don't know. You were patient with him. And kind. That's not super common." She guessed he was being somewhat truthful. At this, she let out her air a little and smiled at him.

"Well then, thank you." And he smiled back. She continued down the hall to the break room to punch in. Now she had this secret. She didn't know if Gary wanted anyone to know. So she just held on to the news like a clod of dirt in her hand.

* * *

The next morning, as she, Karen, and Jo-Jo were punching in, Gary was there, coiling the vacuum cord in the hallway.

"Ladies." All three smiled and greeted him. But Juniper was last with her hello, and glanced up at his eyes and demeanor. He almost looked regular, but then he gave her a sad, slow smile with just his mouth, not his eyes, and the fluorescent light didn't help. It was just an exchange from one quiet person to another. But it was heavy and hurtful to see him looking so sad. She wondered if he was being depleted by a thin life that was now unceremoniously dwindling.

Once they were all stocked up, a train of carts ready to dispatch to three floors, Gary held the door. Manny came out from behind the front desk and gave them their logs. Juniper was on the third floor, which was supposed to be very full that Sunday morning. In the elevator, she cringed at the smells that bugged her. It could never smell fresh with nary a window that opened. The elevators had their own little ecosystem of mirrored walls on two sides, brown tile, glowing buttons, and, oddly, a smell of new carpet that Juniper could never figure out, since the elevators had no carpet. The doors dinged open on three. She got a heave going so she could get the cart over the threshold before the doors moved in. She arced the cart athletically to shoot it down toward the end of the hall but had to pull back suddenly, as if on a horse's reins, so she didn't hit Wavy Blond Guy.

"Oh!" she said, startled.

"'Oh' to you too," he said.

"You're still here."

"Yeah, I'm here for a week. Family stuff."

"Sorry. There's not much to do around here. At all."

"I'm here for a funeral, so it doesn't matter, I guess," he said. She felt like a jerk.

"Oh, sorry."

"It's okay. My grandpa was sick a long time. Still sad, though. My family wants me around to help sort stuff out." Juniper found herself nodding, thinking, *I totally understand,* and wondering if he was close to his grandpa.

"I'm sorry for your loss. I went through that with my grandma last year, and I was pretty wrecked." She surprised herself by admitting something so personal to this stranger. "So it must be hard," she continued. "I know it was for me. I hope you're okay."

"See, you *are* kind," he said. He looked sad then, and the lines between his brows deepened. The elevator dinged again, and he just disappeared with a little wave.

* * *

Her morning work that day was laced with so many thoughts about Gary's condition and Wavy Blond Guy's comments. He must've been going down to breakfast, because she saw him again on his way out of the elevator, maybe half an hour later.

"Hey, what's your name?" she tossed down the hall, trying to sound casual.

"Kirk," he answered. *Kirk,* she sounded out faintly in the back of her throat, with its clipped ending.

"And you are...?" He turned sharply toward her when she didn't immediately offer up her name.

"Oh yeah. Juniper."

"Juniper! *Really.*" He was mulling it over, which she was used to. "That is one cool name."

"Thanks, Kirk." She was bantering now. Well, in her way. Maybe flirting. But he wouldn't know that.

"Would it be weird if I asked you to have a drink with me at the bar next door tonight? I'm stuck here for two more days, and, well, could use some company." She was bowled over that flirting actually worked. She was just testing it out, still wondering about the whole thing. She wasn't sure if she wanted to get a drink with this guy. She did find him attractive. It wasn't like she was hoping for anything *from* him in exchange for something from her. No. She wasn't Bethy, but the possibility lingered.

"Okay," she blurted.

"Okay," he said. "Eight?"

"Eight," she said and made sure to smile at him before she swiveled back to her cart. It was almost a great moment, until the sunlight that leaked in through the lone window at the end of the hall glinted against her "frass" nameplate, refracting its light into her face. She wormed her cart into the dark, narrow hallway of her next room to clean.

Redirect

It was a real big problem—what to wear. Should she dress regular, like she wasn't trying, or should she make a sincere effort and put on her one short skirt? She really wanted to call Bethy to ask. She almost did call her, several times. But she knew what kind of outfit Bethy would choose. And she didn't want to risk Bethy making any more gentle suggestions about how to ease a life such as hers, defined by worries and wants. Her thoughts glanced past what Cora would think. She made dinner and thought about the choices, and if it even mattered. If not spoken of, a transaction could be ambiguous. The intention could be tentative, even. Or denied. He seemed articulate and forward. She was about to clean his room. Why did he ask her out? She couldn't figure out whether to be more suspicious of him or her own self.

A slutty short skirt seemed too forced, she decided, but there was no real middle ground with her wardrobe. Jeans it would have to be. She did have a black hippie chick shirt that might be nice. As soon as she starting singing along with some Beck, her phone rang. Ricky! It felt like she hadn't talked to him in weeks. But she was busy. He would have to leave his song on her voicemail.

Something about Ricky's call made her redirect. It was six forty-five. She had time. She walked back to the large bedroom, first smelling the weight of oil paint that never really dried scentless.

Stacks of her past still leaned obediently. She reached over them to the sharp aluminum lever that would slide the window up. She wanted to let some of the weight out. Immediately, it seemed a ghostly mist rose up, dancing toward the ratty screen. "Shoo," Juniper whispered.

She went to the end of her closet and began to hum as she picked through her tools and colors. She rubbed papers and cloths, remembering textures while she sang recycled, tired melodies for company. Near the front door was her folded easel. It would be easy to take offense at its leaning, perched stance and see it as trying to escape. But of course she had placed it there herself. Her front door was aluminum, too, and made hollow clonking sounds as she propped it open. She held it with her butt as she found the little slidy piece down low that would hold the screen door open as well. Then it was possible to toggle the easel outside again, probably where it belonged.

She marched out tatters of paper and weighed them down beneath a rock on her stoop. She set out a cup of drawing pencils and added some clips to the tray of her easel. She sifted through her paper, mostly regarding the feel, but also enjoying the different flavors of white: eggs, cotton, evening snow. She relished how those assessments changed with the light that presented them. She chose a large paper that was torn on one edge, just a scrap to begin. She began to sketch a simple shape, like a butterfly. But then she ran into the house to get a medical book she had used for figure drawing and turned to the chapter on internal organs: lungs. She unhinged the screen so it slammed and shut bugs out then propped the book open to do an introductory sketch of a pair of lungs splayed like butterfly wings, but not so symmetrical. One side would be full of color and one side like a useless wing, shaped mostly correctly but heavy with spots rendering it useless for flight.

* * *

She left lots of time to pedal slowly so she wouldn't break a sweat. Her black shirt billowed like a little storm cloud. She had added a last-minute touch of black curl to her eyelashes and felt herself blinking carefully as pale yellow dust powdered the air. The inverted

umbrella bones of dandelion seeds made her look for little Mary
Poppinses floating by. Maybe she was a bit like the witch pedaling
through the storm to Oz. Black, billowy women. Behind her, the late
evening sun screeched orange like fingernails on a chalkboard. But
it was a real storm she was heading into, the cool scent of dark rain
up ahead erasing the mistful scents of sunny flowers and the contact
high of cut hay.

She could see the hotel up ahead, looming over the old shack of a
bar next to it. No artful landscaping could fence apart the visual irony
of the over-large "fucko" (fake stucco) siding of the grand Vacation
Express against the slightly leaning square hovel of the Side Bar. The
rain smeared the skyline, forcing her head down, and she had to work
hard to keep up her same tempo. No doubt the black eyelash curl was
doused out and the enchanting puff of her shirt deflated.

She knew she was early by ten minutes, so she stopped short of the
Side Bar and locked her bike at the hotel. She went in the side entrance
and paused to listen before quickly walking to the public restrooms,
just out of sight of the front desk. In the women's room mirror she
almost felt like crying at her streaked face and slopped-down hair. She
slammed out some paper towels and dabbed and pressed and wiped
until she looked better. There was also a hand dryer, and she pushed it
and ducked down to get her hair and shirt blasted. How dry could she
get in five minutes? She kept hitting the silver button for more hot air.
She also remembered the lost-and-found behind the front desk where
there were always umbrellas. How could she get there without getting
busted by the night clerk? It was either going to be Jo-Jo, who doubled
on the front desk some nights, or John, a lazy dude who occasionally
fell asleep on his shift. She combed her hair then tousled it to look
sexyish and found some old tinted lip gloss in her purse and figured
she could be lips instead of eyes. The coral glaze helped.

She stepped out of the ladies' room and walked with purpose up to
the front desk, not having a full lie at the ready. It was Doug.

"Hey, Doug, what's up. Can I borrow one of those umbrellas?" She
pointed to the box behind the desk.

"Oh, you still here?" he asked cluelessly.

But she didn't answer, just pointed again. He handed one over,
black, of course, and she said, "Thanks!" in an extra cheery tone and

was on her way. Back out the side door, she gauged the slats of rain before she dodged across the pavement to the dirt lot of the Side Bar and into the muggy front door.

There he was, in a booth facing her. Kirk's wavy blond hair stood out among the dark, bristly-haired crowd. He waved her over. It was her first good look at him, because she felt like she could finally stare, as she stepped closer and sat down. She expected more nonchalance, casualness from his expression or demeanor. But his eyebrows were zingy arrows, watching her. His eyes weren't just on her face, either. He was almost looking at her as if he didn't think she could see him. Assessing, approving. His shirt collar was open enough that she counted two undone buttons, plus the useless one at the top. He didn't do that thing when they arc their arm over the back of the booth, like they own the booth and the room. But he still owned the booth, just more subtly. His sleeves were rolled up and his forearms lined with quiet, resting muscle.

"Juniper." He said her name nicely, she thought, the back of his throat giving it a little rumble at the end. "Looks like you got caught in it." He smiled a little. She nodded and heard her phone ring again as she settled her purse next to her. She reached in to turn off the ringer.

"Sorry," she said. The waitress came by, and she thought, *That could be me. Bar maid, waitress, hotel maid.* He ordered a whiskey and Coke. She said, "Yeah. Me too, please." The span of table waited between them. She wanted to be something for him. Give something to him. She didn't have flounce in her repertoire and was briefly frustrated that she couldn't just conjure up a Bethy-ism. So she sat up straight and met his gaze. "How are things going with your family?"

He explained how his grandpa had been sick for years, and everyone expected his death, but he didn't have his affairs in order. The family was fighting over who got what and how to take care of his debt. His mom was a mess, and he was having to make decisions that weren't really his to make. Somehow he felt like he had been appointed de facto trustee, decision-maker, and fight mediator.

"But what busted me up most was having to make all the decisions about the funeral itself. I had to choose his suit and pick out his shirt and tie. I shined my grandpa's shoes that he would wear for the last time." Kirk was tearing up as he told these details, and Juniper felt her head grow tight as she was reminded of the wildflower bouquet on Grandma's casket that she had chosen. The conversation made Juniper want to run to her mom's house. Maybe Kirk caught that in her eyes.

"Hey, I don't mean to be dragging down the evening. I came here to be cheered up by your face," he said while finally unclenching his hands and raising his eyebrows hopefully. She had to focus on pretending to be relaxed. His face had a shape that she couldn't stop tracing, and he was saying too many things that caught her. None of this was like she thought it would be.

"Juniper, tell me about you," he said, which had the effect of a compliment. She loosened up a little and told him details about her life, skipping from one story to another, telling too much as he nodded for more. Thunder shook the shack. Drinkers laughed loudly. The sound of rain made them lean in farther to hear each other. They badmintoned across the table, him coaxing out her stories, and she was an effortless natural listener. She was that. Even when he said very little, she'd hit his off-handed volley.

She wasn't sure if she had succeeded at something, but things lightened. She joked about that day's angry hotel guest who wanted gel toothpaste and not the pasty toothpaste. He laughed. She went ahead and told the one about the kid who'd peed in the pool and freaked out trying to get away from the warm water. She knew that if she was earning something, she was doing a good job. Not that she was, but she could have been. She thought she could transform light and funny into sweet and suggestive if she wanted to.

Juniper was woozy from her second drink. The check was on the table. He grabbed it, which she liked. And while he waited for the waitress to bring back his card, he stood up and slid into her side of the booth. Like an animal, she stilled in wait. But his smell crept in. Some cologne or aftershave restarted her respiration, and his hand touched hers. His boldness thrilled her. He signed the slip, grabbed her chin, and kissed her deeply. His face like sweet sandpaper. He pulled her up and led her to the door. The neon Bud sign and green Heineken lights stamped an image.

"Wait," she said and opened her umbrella. He held it, and they ran for Vacation Express. She steered them toward the side door.

"Wait," she said again as she entered the hotel ladies' room for the second time that evening. She looked into her own eyes while rubbing her hands clean. She thought she still seemed damp-looking. Her jeans were not totally dry. She reapplied the coral glaze and noticed that she looked a bit wild; her eyes seemed bigger and darker.

In the hallway, she pulled him back near the side entrance and let him realize it was the stairs she wanted. She was light-footed and followed his sure and quick steps up to the third floor. As he walked in front of her down the hallway, his waist was discernible under his shirt, twisting a bit with each step. Inside his room, he held the door for her then excused himself to the bathroom. She sat on the bed that was made, likely by her, and waited in the dark until he came out. When he did, he grabbed her and pulled her to his bed. She did not say *wait* again that night.

He tugged hard on the button of her jeans so that the small of her back was lifted up off of the bed. And when her jeans were open, she felt the forceful coolness of the A/C on her sticky skin. The same low resonance he used to finish her name came out in waves as his mouth pressed against hers. His mouth pressed her neck and tasted her rain-damp breasts. His teeth grazed her hipbones, his face rested on her skin as he inhaled. He used his hands, grabbing and stroking her waist, cupping her ass. Then his elbows held her open as he kneeled on the floor in front of the bed. She could feel the heat of his bare chest as it touched her inner thighs. She gasped at his warm tongue, wet against wet, unable to form another thought. He kissed her and tasted her like he'd known her before. Like he knew what she wanted before she did. Her back arched into his face, her body with a will of its own.

She was still in her trance when he pulled away. He lifted her like a ragdoll and flipped her over. She was rattled and woken. But his force soon lulled her. His force into her. She didn't care. She didn't care about anything.

Afterward, she thought that she had been shoved down so hard into this bed of hers. This bed she made. Shoved down with this lovely man's desire, and that had lifted her.

A Drink

There were two more nights before he left. She spent them in Kirk's room. She would sneak out before morning and bike home in the mist—sticky, hot, sore, raw, recharged, and spent. Then she would turn around and come back, clean and with her secret knotted tight.

"Hey, Juniper," said Manny.

"What?" she asked, jumpy that someone might have seen her going in and out of 322.

"Nothing what. I forgot to tell you something kind of interesting. Sorry. But there was this guy looking for you like two or three nights ago." She held still like a rabbit, gauging whether to flee. She had the skill of a quiet person, of waiting out an awkward conversation. So she let Manny continue by not saying anything. Had Kirk asked about her before he left? Or when he checked out? Why was she so damn nervous?

"Do you want to know, or what?" He poked her. Damn that Manny.

"Yes! Tell me already."

"So this guy was talking to Jo-Jo, apparently, and stopped in like several times. At first he asked where you lived, which she is not stupid and did not give him. But then when he left, it seemed clear it was to check out your house."

"Manny, this is creeping me out. Who was it?"

"Oh, Jo got his name finally. Ricky."

Shit. Ricky. That first night she went out with Kirk, Ricky had called two or three times. Then two more times after that. She thought he had only left a message the first time, and he sounded normal. Well, maybe she didn't listen to his whole message. *Shit.* She pulled out her phone and said, "Thanks, Manny," while scrolling through her voice-mails. Uh-oh. There were four voicemails, not one. The first one was from when she was getting ready for the date:

"Juniper. Hey, girl. We haven't talked in a while. What's up. I was giving you some space, you know. But now I thought we should talk. Okay, call me." That was definitely not a song. Ricky sounded sad, which translated into Juniper feeling guilty. She didn't need to feel guilty. She didn't owe Ricky anything. She hadn't realized he had called five times and left four messages. Call number two, during the date:

"June. Just me. It boils down to I miss you. You must be busy tonight or something. I'll try again."

Third call:

"It's like midnight, and you aren't calling me or picking up, you must be out or something. Maybe a date for all I know. We should have talked. We need to talk. Yeah. You aren't that far. What, like two hours? Okay, see you."

Fourth call:

"Is this trailer your house? It must be, I see like a paintbrush on your porch. I'm looking in your windows, oh this is totally your place. But you aren't here, and it's 6:00 a.m., girl. I stopped at the hotel, they hadn't seen you neither." He mumbled something away from the phone, and it didn't hang up for a while.

Call number five was about eight in the morning. She would have been back at the hotel after riding her bike home to clean up, but he did not actually leave a message that final time. *Geez, what the fuck.* Maybe he'd seen her. How did all that happen? He was going psycho on her, peering in the windows of her trailer. *Not okay.* She had to call him to at least check on him. Maybe it was time to set him straight for good.

"Hey, Ricky, sorry I missed your messages, and um, apparently *you.* I hope you're okay. That's all. Okay, bye." When he called back immediately, she couldn't pick up. She was chicken to talk to him. She didn't owe him anything, she reminded herself.

"Yo, June. I give up. I saw you riding your bike home from the hotel. I don't know. You have just driven me crazy with everything, and I get I was crazy to drive out there, but I did it, and there it is. Now I know that you're busy or whatever. Let me know if that changes. K. Bye."

Juniper felt like shit. But relieved. Super relieved. She just wanted to call Kirk. But she had been stupid. She hadn't wanted to look needy and hadn't gotten his number.

Her lips were still stubble-burned from their days together. She was practically still gasping. They had talked so much as a gateway into bed. They communicated very easily, and he could make her open up with his questions. Like, "Have you ever met your dad?" Or telling her, "I'd like to see your paintings sometime." And he could silence her just as easily with his forthright desire. There was no transaction, just them both wanting to be together. But there was one thing. One thing that she might have been making up. The last day when they woke up together, she walked naked to the window and pulled open the curtain, letting him see her, even though she hid from the outside behind a sheer, she wanted him to have a drink. And when she came back to bed, he was sitting up against a pillow, and his hands were on top of the white sheet. His hands were curved in rest. It was so sunny, the bright enough to burn an ant through a magnifying glass type of sunny. She saw how the golden hairs on his hands curled and mimicked the shape of each finger. White and gold blared from sun and blond and sheets. And then she saw how a part of one of his fingers was indented skinnier than the rest. Maybe her memory was lying to her, but she thought it was his ring finger.

Having Someone

That thought snagged her fantasies for sure. It wasn't like she missed him once he was gone, exactly. But he was a sweet distraction, a sweet promise. The details of who he was and what either of them wanted remained unsaid. She was surprised she was okay with that, just as she was surprised that a small, weird part of her actually felt an attachment after knowing him for three days. There was no explaining it, and she didn't need reciprocity. The future would unfold it for her.

That last morning, she had slipped out of 322 and down the stairs. Gary was outside in the morning mist, tending to some patch of greenery. He went in as she unlocked her bike. She didn't say hello, and he didn't acknowledge that he saw her. Maybe he didn't see her. Or maybe he thought she was just like Bethy.

She tried to look Kirk up. But his last name was Jones. She couldn't find him listed in the Ann Arbor area, where he said he was living. He said he worked at the university. When she asked doing what, he said he taught a little bit. What? Oh, some humanities classes, he had said. She was scrubbing toilets when she thought about his evasive answers and realized she did care and didn't like his dodginess. At least she was pretty sure she didn't like it. *Ugh.* She stood up and looked herself square in the sheet of mirror that covered every bathroom wall. Her rubber gloves were too big, and she felt her sweat inside, sloshing around. She took them off to complete her final task of replacing the sample toiletries. One room was done. On to the next. She saw her darkness shine as she glanced once more to look for a clue in the mirror about what would come next.

Carding into the next room after announcing herself and waiting five seconds, she cleared her throat when she heard someone still in the room. What did people not get? Was using the "do not disturb" tag confusing? Sometimes people were asleep, okay, that she got. Or in the shower. But otherwise, if she walked in on them, it was their own fault. Checkout was eleven anyway. It was after eleven. She heard a man mumbling, then a giggle. A familiar giggle.

"Oh, shit! Sorry!" Juniper swooped out of the room with an image of Bethy on her knees following her out into the hall. Bethy's pretty blonde hair, swishing back and forth. *Okay, okay, I knew that could happen*, she thought. Nothing I didn't already know. Juniper was flushed and disturbed. The reality of it was not helpful to her being supportive. The guy was wearing a suit. She was really not trying to judge anyone, and Bethy was absolutely a great friend, but she had never felt so strongly that she needed to get the hell out of that job and that place. She went down the elevator with her cart, taking her break early. She needed to sit down.

Gary was in the break room. She needed to make sure he still wanted to talk to her, if he'd seen her sneaking around.

"Gary, how are you? Is there any news?" she asked.

"Oh, ya. They found more spots. Didn't Manny tell you? I go in for surgery in a few weeks. Ann Arbor." Juniper jolted a little, both at the place name and at the progression of Gary's cancer. But he seemed normal toward her.

"Oh, Gary. That sucks. But maybe they can get it all, make you better." She didn't know what the hell to say.

"I dunno. I'm goin' on chemo after surgery. I'm gonna be out for a bit."

"Is anyone going to be there with you?" she asked, nervous to hear his answer, thinking *please, let him have someone.*

"Ya. My sister'll be there. So that's good. I'm stayin' with her after the surgery. She's gonna drive me to chemo appointments. But first, she'll fix me my favorite lasagna before I feel too crummy to eat." He smiled at his self-deprecating joke. She could see a bunch of missing teeth on his right side. That made him seem more vulnerable than the cancer, seeing him smile.

She exhaled. "Oh, good. I'm really glad you'll have someone there helping you." Juniper wondered why he would talk to her, specifically. Was it that she simply asked how he was and paused long enough to listen? It didn't matter. Now she cared, and his story haunted her enough.

She realized she was going to sit there in the break room until Bethy came down for lunch, just so they could pave the day over. They had been hanging out at Bethy's a lot, where her parents had the good cable. Bethy's dad was recovering fine, and there was relief at that. But they had fallen behind in any kind of meaningful talk. Juniper hadn't even mentioned Kirk. And they both clearly had stories to tell.

Bethy finally came in, but Karen was there too, doing her crossword puzzle, so neither of them said a word. Bethy fumbled around in her cubby for her lunch. She hung up her smock. Juniper was sitting across from Karen, licking her yogurt spoon, following Bethy with her eyes. Juniper always felt the fluorescent lighting could scour away at a person's soul. Karen finished up her own lunch and folded up the paper. Hard to tell with Karen's gruffness if she noticed the tension in the room. Karen said, "See ya on the floor, ladies," as she stepped out of the room.

The sound of the vending machine was obnoxious. It buzzed and let off mingled smells of peanut M&Ms and Fritos. The colors were flat, the textures were flat. Juniper didn't need to taste the junk for all five of her senses to be offended. She wasn't impervious to the lure of junk food, but something about that machine got on her nerves, like it was a person she just couldn't get along with.

"Let's go outside. It's so nice out. Let's picnic, this room sucks," Juniper suggested and stood up. Bethy packed up her lunch bag, and they walked silently through the hall, out the back way. They found the only tree with some shade and an overthrow of dandelions marching up to them.

"Are you okay with all this stuff you're doing?" Juniper asked right off the bat. "I mean, is it weird with these guys you meet?" She didn't want to shame her friend in any way, but she also wasn't sure that what Bethy was doing was such a good idea.

"How do you know if a guy is safe?" Juniper continued.

"June, you're such a worrier! I just have a good sense about people and steer clear of the weirdos. And hey, I really am sorry about that earlier." The wind chose a few strands of Bethy's golden hair and flung it in her face, while it slapped Juniper's smock like a sail.

"Well, I've known a few weirdos, and you can't always tell," Juniper said then took a bite of her peanut butter sandwich.

"Oh, *please*, you have not known weirdos. Have you?"

"Not in the way you're thinking." Juniper said, and she took another bite and chewed, thinking about how much to tell.

"What do you mean?"

"For me, it was my grandpa. He hit my grandma, amongst other things. He hit my mom. He was a nasty drunk who hurt them both really bad. But he had slicked-back silver hair, looked like an older Cary Grant. People loved him. He was so fucking charming in public too. So you *couldn't* tell." Juniper looked right at Bethy for emphasis.

"June, I had no idea."

"Yeah. When I was real little, I think four or five, he was outside raking leaves, Mom and Grandma were in the house. And I guess I was getting in his way or something, jumping in his piles. All I remember is him starting to yell at me. He started yelling and grabbed my arm hard and was dragging me back toward the garage, and I screamed. Both Grandma and Mom slammed outta that house so fast. They saw that he had come for me, it was gonna be my turn. Couldn't control himself." Bethy was quietly listening.

"That was the night Grandma left my grandpa. Well, she kicked him out and saved us all. The three of us formed a perfect triangle of support after that..." Juniper trailed off.

Bethy reached over. "I'm sorry about all of that, Juniper."

They had a view of most of the parking lot from their shady tree. They watched a delivery truck unload linens and Manny go in with some takeout from the burger place. A blue Subaru pulled in. A man got out and walked around to his trunk. Juniper's eyes opened wide.

"What?" Bethy asked, following her focus. Juniper grimaced. The trunk blocked him, but there was a glance of that hair. She thought he was gone, but the jolt she felt was confirmation as he swiveled his car door shut and swung into the front entrance as glass parted like a concierge's arms in greeting.

"*What?*" Bethy asked again.

"Our lunch break is over. Let's go," Juniper said. As they stood and brushed themselves off, she added, "I know that guy."

"Oh, really?" Bethy raised her eyebrows.

"I wanted to tell you. I had a thing. That guy was here a couple weeks ago."

"June. Shit!"

They had only a moment before they opened those back doors and lost all their privacy, so Juniper said, "We had a thing. It was amazing. I think he might possibly be married."

Bethy tied her hair back into a quick ponytail. "Okay, Juniper. We can handle this. Do you want to run into him or not want to run into him?" Her kind response and judgment-free understanding made Juniper lean in and hug Bethy, surprising both of them.

"I don't know," Juniper said over Bethy's shoulder. She stood straight, pulled open the back door, and took a big breath.

Beneath

Juniper felt like she was being punched, of all things. Maybe it was the conversation she'd just had with Bethy. Her stomach was cramping and spasming, and she had trouble figuring out what to do. She had to admit, she was somewhat mad at Kirk for not telling her he'd see her again so soon. For not being in touch. She was hurt. And yet she couldn't wait to see him. Couldn't wait to run into him.

She snickered to herself at how, all of a sudden, Vacation Express seemed bright and sunny inside. The aqua and tan décor seemed fresh and not catalog-y. The three floors bristled with the excitement of guests coming and going. She was spinning like a pinwheel, suspiciously vibrant to everyone but Bethy, who understood her exuberance.

"Juniper, you seem a little frantic, hon," said Manny.

"I'm fine," she said. "How are you?"

"Okay, so-so, ho-hum. Jay is being a bitch to me. So, whatever."

"Ugh. Drama again?" She forced her eyes to lock onto Manny's.

"Yes! He doesn't realize we are fantastic together and just creates problems where there are none."

Juniper nodded sympathetically. "Hey, we should all go out soon. Bethy and you and me and whoever."

"Yes, I would totally love to drink, I mean vent." He winked. Okay, she had been paying attention to Manny, being a good friend. But she was really on the lookout for Kirk. She was going to be obsessed if she just hung out in the lobby. She needed to go about her work until she figured out how to approach him. What to say. Maybe he didn't want to see her. No, that was stupid. If he didn't want to see her, he would have stayed at the Red Roof Inn up the road.

She made herself walk up and down that first floor hallway and finish her rooms for the day, but she was nervous as all hell. She wrestled the fitted sheets and billowed the flat ones. She lined up the pillows. Cornered the toilet papers. Wiped the TV cabinets. But then every time she stepped out of a room, she felt antsy, anticipating running into him. When she was finally done with all her work, she marched to the lobby. She couldn't wait any longer. Her pulse seemed to be outside her body, booming. She was going to put away her cart, take off her smock, and find him, even if she had to sneak a look at the logs to find his room. She glanced over at reception and was steering through the lobby, and poof, there he was, leg crossed in a tan chair, reading *USA Today*. She rolled the cart next to him and stopped. He looked up and slowly smiled at her, like the moon coming out of an eclipse, full, mysterious, lovely.

"Juniper." She stood there in her smock, holding the handle bar of her cart with both hands. She did smile, but the intensity of the day crashed in on her, and she felt shaky. *Jesus.* She could barely say hi.

He said, "I was wondering when I was going to run into you." *Hopeful.* "I was going to sit here until I did." *Super hopeful.* "I had to come back to my grandma's to help out with her house. She decided not to sell." *Neutral.* "And I felt like we had unfinished business." *Super hopeful.* All she could do was stand there and wait for him to say more. To say something that made it clear that he wanted to hang out with her again. To be with her, or whatever.

"So, ah. Are you free tonight?" he asked. Her hopefulness burst open into some unrecognizable, multicolored harmony of sound and light. She actually felt like something was wrong. Her vision was closing in on her, dizzy, blinking, pulsing, speckled vision, a closing black circle like the end of those old cartoons. She flopped down in an empty chair and inhaled slowly. She could push through this, she thought as she exhaled in a controlled stream. Her vision opened up a bit.

"Yes, I am." She was incapable of decent conversation. But she had the awareness of Manny behind her, listening to every word, no doubt.

Kirk folded the paper and stood up. "Can I maybe pick you up? So you don't need to ride your bike?" He stood in a way that seemed confident of his control over the situation. "Six good?"

She nodded. She gave Kirk directions to her place. He walked away, and she turned to watch his torso twist down the hall toward the elevators. *Well, the jig is up now,* she thought. *Go ahead Manny, soak it up.* Manny was almost laughing at her. But then he paused to really look at what she saw, the stripes on Kirk's shirt undulating.

"Mm-hmm," Manny said. "We'll talk later, girlfriend." She was embarrassed and excited, happy and freaked out. She looked for Bethy. It was a short skirt kind of night. She knew that much.

* * *

It was just growing pink out. He knocked. She had burned a vanilla candle and cleaned. She had interrupted the random catalog of her leaning artwork to create a hierarchy of best works in front. They looked like they were randomly leaning, but she had debated for a half an hour about which pieces should be casually facing out. She was dressed but barefoot. It was so deep into summer that even her shag carpet seemed wilted and moist. The days had been holding so still. The breeze had been paused. The trees had stopped their swishing. The days had seemed to be individually framed and set apart from each other, until he showed up. His knock rattled the old aluminum frame of the screen door; it rattled more than that. When she opened up, it was his scent that filled the room and mixed with the vanilla. He brought a chaser of evening gravel and grasses so that all the smells mingled to create some thrilling "your date is here" scent.

He wrapped his arms around her. She leaned in and turned her head against his chest. She couldn't look down at his hands, at his finger. Not yet.

"I'm happy to see you," he said in his low way. She felt foolishly struck dumb. She had an inkling to apologize for her shabby trailer, but she told herself that she had nothing to be ashamed of. It wasn't shabby to her.

"I'm happy to see you too. How's your mom and grandma?" she asked.

He pulled back. "It's been rough. That's why I'm here. They need my help doing some more repairs on the house, fixing a ramp for her, stuff like that. I meant to tell you I was coming, Juniper. I meant to call you."

Family was shoved aside, though, as he stepped closer to her again. He leaned down and pulled her face up to his. "I meant to call you." His words were hollow, but his kiss was not. They were still standing right in front of her door, but now he was holding her. Almost lifting her with his strong arms. He did then, lift her lightly, to the couch. He reclined her head onto the pillow with the cross-stitch alphabet. He was being gentle, as you would be with an object that is delicate. He was watching what he was doing, not rushing, but clear and firm as he leaned all the way down to kiss her again, deepening his stance. But then he pulled up, pulled back, as if he remembered something. He looked down and unzipped and presented himself to her, to her face. And he pried open her mouth like she remembered him prying open her legs. He slipped and pushed, and she somehow felt left out, because his throaty moan sounded like it was coming from a treetop outside. Abruptly, though, he stopped and came back down to her. He stepped out of his tan shorts completely. He angled out of his t-shirt then hovered over her in the most delicious, menacing way. Her face flushed with the functional perfectness of her little green skirt as he separated her bare legs with his. He moved aside the last piece of cotton separating them, and while maintaining his push-up form and eye contact, he pushed himself again. Onto her, into her. She let out a murmur of pleasure, the liquid in her eyes rising. Like he just wanted to push and push and push everything. Her neck bent back over the armrest of the couch. She couldn't feel discomfort. Her bare feet clung around his back as his movements churned them like a coupling rod on a train wheel. Movements completed, then erased, the rest of her thoughts. He yelled out. Yelled in a voice she didn't recognize from before, and in an overlapping of moments, she began to control their momentum. Her momentum was all that was left, and she felt her smallness grow, as her thoughtless core, her wet pulse, drove her insistence. Then sounds, like a cat beneath her trailer at night, came out of her. She came out of her.

Her screen door was the only thing between them and everything else. They looked at each other and laughed at the wetness everywhere. Her little white jacket that had been waiting for its moment was hung from her dinette chair, now like a flag that had given up. Her tank top was still on, askew, showing her shoulders with a sheen of sweat. She could feel her raw lips swollen.

Now the moments had slowed even more, from framed days to film squares being moved by hand. She reached up to touch his hair as he sat beside her. She remembered his tsunami right in front of earthy gold. Her fingers dug into the thickness and squeezed just a little.

"Ow!" He flinched.

"Oops, sorry! I didn't mean to pull. I just... like your hair."

He stood and zipped. "So this place was your grandma's?"

"Yeah. Her house, her stuff. I miss her." In the hallway, she glanced at the photo of Grandma with her three girlfriends against the ruddy background of a spring rush at Canyon Falls in the U.P. She didn't usually stop to look anymore, but Grandma's eyes met hers. Kirk moved toward the back room. Juniper followed. They had talked about her paintings. He had mentioned he'd like to see them someday. She did notice anew that the smell of art clung to spaces in her trailer and became prevalent as you inched toward that room. The small, east-facing window meant that the room was dulling by that time, and there was a gray film of removed light. She thought to turn on the switch, but that would have tainted everything with a butter yellow. She decided to let it be, as nerve-wracking as that was. What did this guy know about painting, anyway?

"Juniper. This is nice stuff. Wow." He leaned over to pull up one of her portraits of one of her exes, Rob. He tilted it toward the window. "Realism like this is certainly not trendy, but there's always an important place for it. Especially now, with its rarity, depicting our digital life with this perspective, it almost holds a nostalgia of purpose."

She coughed. "Um. Thank you?"

"God, what are you, like twenty-three?"

"Twenty-four," she said.

"Well, SAIC is a great school. Great school." He picked up another painting and leaned it. Although she was now even more skeptical of who this guy really was, she had regained control of her thoughts enough to really respond to him.

"Yeah. My intention is not to use realism exclusively but to incorporate it into larger concepts. I just knew I had a lot of learning to do, to be able to tackle that genre before I used it within other works." At this, he nodded and smiled.

"So what are *you*, like, thirty-five?"

"Thirty-seven," he answered. This replaced her shock over his comments with a flood of questions. Married? Kids? Divorced? *Married?* But instead of launching into questions, she told him about Gary. She took her sketches and color thoughts off her easel and showed him the lungs.

"I wish I had real lungs to look at, but that's not possible."

"Yeah, it's not like we use cadavers at U of M."

"Kirk! What do you teach? Specifically?"

"Okay, I'm an art history professor. Adjunct."

"Why didn't you tell me that? Especially after you found out where I went to school?"

Kirk exhaled loudly. He handed her lungs back to her and gave a weird little grunt. "You know, I just wasn't sure how much I wanted to say right away. Can we leave it at that for now?"

Juniper's head yelled, *Hell no!* But she didn't really want this to end just yet. She was weak. She just wanted to *incorporate* realism into what was happening. She was always funniest in her head. "Yeah. Okay. For now," she said.

One of the few real restaurants in town was a burger bar. She knew the owner, Nina, would recognize her and see she was on a date. But whatever. There was hardly anyone there, since it was a weeknight. They sat down and ordered their burgers and beer.

It was another booth, and they were seeing each other in the relatively unmagical light of the place. Lionel Richie was singing about dancing on the ceiling, establishing that Gobles really was independent from the rest of the country. Their beers came in large plastic mugs. He held his mug up. "To unexpected happiness during a tough time." Their plastic thunked, and she drank. Up at the bar was Nina, and she looked over and her face lit up. She set down her rag and came around straight to their table. *Oh boy,* thought Juniper.

"You don't happen to be Kirk Janoski, do you?" Her face was still alight. "Oh, and hi, Juniper!" Kirk's face was filled with consternation. "Peggy's boy?" Nina continued.

He looked embarrassed but held out his hand. "Yeah, that's me."

"Oh, look at you! You wouldn't remember me, but my sister Ann used to sit for youse when you were kids. So sorry about your grandpa. You and Juniper musta known each other from the good old days, huh?" Nina seemed to laugh ironically about "good old days." She must have also been a little foggy on their age difference. Just as well, thought Juniper.

"Yeah," Kirk and Juniper nodded in unison.

"Well, I hope your ma and grandma is doin' okay, send them my best, so good to see you here! You were always a good boy. Still got that nice hair too!" Nina said as she backed away. Juniper worked on her burger, wanting very much to be done with this part of the evening. They did need to talk now. But obviously not there. They were alone in the booth, and it was squeezing them together and not allowing them freedom to speak, what with the walls having ears and all. Juniper finally said, "Janoski. I do know your family."

"Yeah. I thought maybe," Kirk said, obviously uncomfortable. "Let's finish up here, then go talk." She could handle that, she would have to handle that, even though her head was spinning. Soon, would there be anything left to say? When she swallowed the last fry she could eat, all she tasted was the squares of salt. They were magnified into cubes, cutting her tongue. To her, the salt was a foreshadowing of the tears she would be tasting soon.

Kirk's Confession

"Do you want to go to the hotel or your place?" Kirk asked. If they went to the hotel, he would have to drive her home. If they went to her house, he would have more control over when he left. *She* wanted control over when he left. What if this didn't go well? But ultimately she wanted her own cross-stitched, pot-holding comforts.

"Let's just go back to my place." It was still in that lightest time of year, and Michigan was perched on the farthest edge of the Eastern Time Zone, which meant deep summer stayed light until after nine. They drove Juniper home into a sunset that was more awesome and important than anything that was happening in their lives. It held more wisdom than any conversation they were about to have. Kirk's windows were open. There was the persistent stillness in front of them, and the expected August haze. But beyond that, the colors were so saturated, that they nearly created a sound to Juniper. She hummed a single pitch into her open window. Combined with the sound of his tires, she etched a chord with her voice upon the wind. She tried to match the ephemeral bloom of the drive-in movie she was about to crash into.

When she opened her trailer door, she could taste the dirty metal of her key. This happened to her sometimes when she was scared or nervous—her senses would get all jumbled in a synesthetic mess. She dropped her keys on the table, and the clangle was felt as a sharp fingernail down her spine. She went right back to their couch, tucking her legs and skirt under her. She gestured for him to sit too. But he said, "hold on," and went down the hall to pee. She waited and looked around at her wood paneling, and hoped he was looking right at "God grant me the serenity" on her bathroom wall behind the toilet. Anything to nudge his conscience.

He came back and sat down next to her, and she was sad that the couch had been so beautiful less than two hours before. She was not about to speak first. She was not about to ask for some explanation.

"Okay, so look. I'm married," he said. Her jaw clenched, and then it released. "Aw, *come on!*" she said. Of all the ridiculous things, that's what popped out of her mouth. Her disappointment burst out quicker than obvious anger. "*Come on, Kirk!*" She said again. She felt defeated by the circumstance.

"I know." He was holding his hands together in a clenched prayer position. The heat of the room was on him. It was his burden, and he was sweating. She flipped through a Rolodex of possibilities: He did this all the time. He never did. He had kids. Or not. He was happy. His marriage was awful. His wife was in a coma. He had several wives. Dammit. She wasn't going to start guessing out loud.

"I felt so guilty about last time. It's why I couldn't call you. I don't do this Juniper. I don't." At that, she looked up at him. She looked up to hear more.

"But you came back," she said.

"I was riveted," he said. She shook her head. She was thinking about him being riveted. She was thinking about the times they were together. She thought they fell under the category of fucking amazing.

"I mean, I don't know what it is about you, actually."

She deflated a little at this reverse compliment.

"Things aren't great at home. They've been bad lately. I don't know what she and I are going to do. I've been lonely, and then I come out here, and bam. There you are, Juniper. You know. I thought you were beautiful." That did it. She started crying. He went on. "So I'm sorry I lied about my name, and didn't tell you what I did. In a panic, I wanted to cover my tracks, make sure you couldn't call me at home or something." His words sunk like lead. Except the beautiful part, that was like a kite.

"Do you—" she started. He finished, "I don't have kids." Something about that definitely relieved her. But then filled her with something else, like dread, but different. If they didn't have kids, somehow this opened up possibilities to her, and she wasn't sure if she liked that. She looked into his eyes, and tried to memorize them. "Look, Juniper. I know we come from different worlds." She bristled at that, at him setting her apart with his words like that. Because she had thought they came from the same world, the art world superseding any socio-economic roots. It was a real shocker, that her nice degree didn't equal some kind of ticket here. Not in Kirk's eyes, anyway.

She clearly hardly knew him. But she felt something. Something like a quiet stream beneath the surface of the forest floor. Some kind of compassion or kindness. Out of this feeling for him, she said, "Kirk. I think you should go now." And he said okay.

* * *

Juniper knew he was still booked at Vacation Express for a couple more nights. She knew he planned to be over at his grandma's first thing for breakfast. She left for work early that next morning, thinking a swim would at least feel good. Exhaustion could help. Her mind couldn't obsess when her body was chugging so hard. The pool would be quiet. She unlocked the door, and could smell an abundance of chlorine. It reminded her that Gary would be leaving soon, and she worried about him ever returning. What was his life? She could imagine what his life was to others: maybe a side note or afterthought. That's how she saw others treat him. But what was his life to him? That's what she found almost terrifying. What if he himself felt his life was a side note or afterthought? He did not live carefully. Was she mean to think that? Living with care was being open. His life was passing in front of her, nearly passing away in front of her, and to think it might disappear like a raindrop in a pond made sadness well up. Was it okay to mean nothing? Being without want was supposed to hold some purity. But was that any different than a rock? No giving and receiving? No sense of self or worth. This was an anger-inducing thought, and maybe unfair to who Gary really was. She wouldn't know. But a need to place blame was human. She blamed this culture of place for creating a boy turned man that withered on the vine. This culture of careless living, careless eating, careless learning and way too much careless loving. Gary was about to fall off his bike into an abyss, and he didn't grab the brakes or steer his wobble. He was just letting go. Breeze would whistle, and Juniper was watching.

She felt so guilty about her thoughts. But guilt, guilt was right up there at the surface though, easy to access. The sensation in her core mixed with feeling the cold poolroom air swoop around her. After shedding the clothes atop her suit, she did an illegal dive, and began her back-and-forths, her splashes scribbling all over the silence. The water was the perfect temperature. The brand-new sun streaked in the plate glass. She had only done a few laps when she swore she saw Kirk's figure pass by the poolroom window. She thought maybe it had even paused for a moment. But she was doing her flip turn, and by the time she stopped and rubbed the water from her eyes, the peripheral ghost was gone.

That day marked the only time she ever felt like becoming absorbed in her work at Vacation Express. The textured wallpaper had a redeeming quality, she appreciated as she wiped a splotch of wine (she hoped), off the quiet sage color. She felt quiet with observation, and gentle toward the moderate thickness of the carpet, the stance of lotion bottles. She felt serene about the glisten of clean glass on the prints of flowers or villages. The images themselves were still absolutely sucky, but the glass was nice. She even dared to inhale deeply, the chemical-laden air, just to siphon out the clean molecules, and to feel them expanding. She imagined the intelligence of her human body separating the wheat of good air from the chaff of bad. The intelligence of her lungs. How could she differentiate herself like that? Again, the guilt. With her quiet being, she truly dwelled in her place of work that day. That one day.

Despite the sadness of Gary, and even though she had also met *him*, Kirk, there, at work, she considered it the place that could get her through this time. Past Kirk, through Gary. She let the elevator's gravity pull her down to the lobby, where it was real and bustling.

She was relieved to feel the crowd of a full house. It was Saturday, and Karen, Jo-jo and Bethy were on. Manny of course up front. The place was lively with guests. Juniper was depressed about Kirk, but honestly, oddly, also giddy about Kirk. She didn't want to feel giddy, but knowing he was still checked in, amped her up all over again. Juniper had figured out which room was his on the first floor, and it had the 'do not disturb' tag. She walked by it only twice. Knowing he was still there felt like hot waves echoing the sensation of his weight upon her.

She uncharacteristically piped up at lunch while everyone was in the break room.

"Hey guys, I need a distraction, who wants to go to Side Bar tonight?"

"Duh, me!" said Bethy.

"You owe me a shoulder to cry on. I'm in," said Manny. Karen said, "I want a darts re-match from last time." Jo-jo sat in her seat, her face turning red. Juniper felt like Jo-jo wasn't sure they meant her too. "Come on Jo, you can't be the only one," Juniper encouraged.

"Um, I have this thing to do for my ma."

"Come on!" Juniper said—a phrase she was clearly using too much.

"Okay, I'll come after," said Jo-jo. Juniper was happy to have these people around her, and realized she had forgotten someone. She scurried down to the pool thinking she'd find him. "Gary!" She startled him in the utility room. Before he even stood up all the way she said, "We're all goin' out to Side Bar tonight. Come with!" It was her turn to be startled—it was his face. Like coiled Edison light bulbs, his eyes lit bright. Then followed his lips curling up. He had some white junk in the corner of his mouth, and his whiskers were growing in patches all up his cheeks. But he smiled one of those smiles old people give that make you see what they used to look like.

"Everyone's goin'?" He asked.

"Except John. Someone has to watch the shop," she said.

"Good, I don't like that little shit anyways."

Juniper laughed. She was struck by his strong reaction to the whole thing, and how easy it was to get him to open up. It made her think of all the times people walked by him without saying a word, or stopping to just listen for a moment.

* * *

They all showed up at Side Bar that night. They took over the big table in the middle. It wasn't until they'd been there an hour, chatting and drinking, that Jo-jo showed. She entered the smeared glass door, done up in a dark blue blouse and had flat-ironed her hair. She had on a whole face of color. But it wasn't that. It was that Gary whooped out, "There she is!" and slammed his hand down on the table with a chuckle. Everyone else paused what they were saying and bust out with laughter. Good-hearted laughter at Gary's joy, and Jo-jo's flattered face. It was a good night already.

They ate chicken fingers that had been thawed by the deep fryer. They played darts and pool, and siphoned down pitchers of beer. Juniper had ridden her bike, just so she didn't have to worry about a ride home from one of her drunk friends. After a while, it was just Manny, Bethy and Juniper at the table while everyone else was playing or watching a pool game. Bethy said, "I feel so bad about what you told me about your grandpa. Your grandma never got remarried, right?"

"No, but she was my hero the day she left Grandpa." Juniper leaned back, with her large mug of beer snug in her hands.

"Jesus, you're positive about the whole thing."

"I never thought about it like that but. Yeah, maybe." Juniper was aware they were having this conversation in front of Manny, who may or may not have caught everything. But she didn't care anymore. It was her story, but it wasn't her doing. The whole night was feeling like a release.

"What, June, you're grandpa was abusive?" Manny asked.

"Just a drunk hitter."

"Oh, girl. I'm sorry. We have that shit in my family too." See, everyone was so damn nice.

They all got up then, to give Karen her real darts tournament. Juniper waited until everyone was caught up in the first round to lean into Bethy and say, "I saw him last night." Bethy turned her head so fast, she slopped a little of her beer. She stood and faced Juniper with her eyebrows up, "Well?"

"Well, everything. It was awesome. But he is, you know. Married. So it's over." Juniper realized whom she was talking to, and that married did not always equal *over* to some. Bethy scooped her arm around Juniper, and said, "Aw sorry, hon. Too bad he was an asshole."

Well, that made her feel defensive. Bethy was trying to be supportive, but it pushed Juniper in front of him, wanting to both hide and defend him.

"Naw. It wasn't like that," Juniper said. But Bethy wasn't paying attention. She was watching Karen sweep everyone in that damn darts match. Juniper watched the side of Bethy's face. Beth's face. Her easy face. She got a little mad in secret, thinking Bethy didn't seem to understand. He wasn't just some guy passing through. Okay, maybe he was. But he was her only guy passing through. She didn't know how to say that without sounding like an ass herself, so Juniper just left it at that. It didn't matter. She didn't think he was an asshole exactly. Although he did lie. She'd probably get angrier and angrier after he left, but it hadn't sunk in yet. Jo-jo did a big ole pirouette after she nailed a bull's eye. Everyone laughed, and Juniper joined in. Tonight, she was going to bask in the glow of sympathy and company from her friends.

They drunkenly ordered one last pitcher. Jo-jo wanted to leave first. And everyone, *everyone*, noticed that Gary seemed to get tired after that. And it wasn't a sick tired. He left minutes after Jo-jo. Manny was crying about his sometimes-boyfriend. Bethy was oddly quiet. She was waiting for another round of her dad's test results, and was just listening to everyone else that night. Juniper had said enough, and needed to go home and crash. She said her good-byes, and went around to the side to grab her bike. She figured if she kept her eyes and ears open, she could stay out of the way of any late night drivers by pulling into the fields to let potential drunkards pass. She loved the smell of late night combined with late summer. It was a nighttime dewy fog that stacked the smells of sweet clover hay, wild flowers and happy dirt. She pedaled onto the gravel shoulder and watched on her right as Vacation Express ruined the beauty of the night. She passed the second entrance, and stopped with one foot on the curb. His blue car was right there. She thought she could see his first-floor room light on. She was pretty sure which window was his. In a trance, she hopped off her bike and walked it, tink, tink, tink, into the lot. She laid it down in the wet grass and walked to his window. His curtain was open a crack so that she could see him, the curved shape of him against his pillow, the tv flicking. She couldn't be blamed for what was happening, as she was in a trance. She knocked on the glass softly. He seemed to jerk his head up. She jumped back. He slid off the bed and took a step toward the window. She leaned forward and knocked again. He pulled the curtain and sheers aside. She stood there looking sad. She didn't mean to look sad, but she was nearly crying again. He turned around quickly and went out of his room. She met him and the side door, *their* side door.

They barely said hello as he held it open for her. She followed him down the fluorescent-lit hallway to his room. His shirt was off. When they got inside, and the heavy door sealed them in, she reached up to hug him. Even though his smell brought her back to their slipping bodies, their hug was filled with compassion. Gentle regret. Maybe a loving goodbye. He sat her down on his bed, and they looked at each other. She wanted to ask him questions. She wanted to jump ahead to where he left his wife. But there was no arguing with the heavy pebble of dullness in her stomach. The wrongness was a dead-end. Yet some parallel Juniper sat there quietly while he tucked her hair behind her ear, exposing her neck. This other Juniper looked at him with scared eyes. Scared at the momentum that swooped her aside like a riptide. This is how it was with him though, a loss of self that was so welcome and thrilling. It was being allowed to set time upon a shelf for later. It was not needing to know who she was, because that was being redefined by giving herself up to him. And that is what she did. She lay back on those white sheets that she might run through her hands later. She passed through a sensation of heat, like when she might pull those sheets out of the dryer, clean and fresh.

End of Summer

Something was different. A sprinkle of sweat on her upper lip. Something in the wet part of her guts. Her lightness was betraying her. It was gone. This was her persona—a huge part of her identity—her effortless lightness. Sometimes she felt a warm pulse in her fullish lips when they were closed. But her waist was like a whip of willow branch. Her arms, dandelion stalks. Her skin, fair and smooth. Her ankles like bird beaks. She could be air. She counted on it.

But now something felt awkward, and it was making her disoriented.

"Manny, I feel sick, I need to go home." Juniper marched up to the front desk like a demanding hotel guest.

"Um, okay, just call me about tomorrow, 'k?" He didn't ask what was up. She was too reliable for those kinds of questions, and she was only leaving her shift two hours early. No time to think about tomorrow, yet, anyway. She rushed out of the automatic doors and unlocked her bike. Riding home was filled with the sense of wanting just to be there already. Sweat emerged anywhere a limb attached. She was about a quarter mile from her trailer when she realized she couldn't stop. She realized/admitted to herself that she may have missed her period. She needed to keep riding. A wet tendril stuck to her forehead. She thought quick about who might be at Walmart. It was the only place. Her mom would likely not be working. The gray brick loomed ahead. She focused on just getting there, one pedal at a time.

She locked her bike and saw Mrs. Dee with her back turned, organizing circulars. Almost running, Juniper flitted deeply into the aisles by the time Mrs. Dee could turn around. She zigzagged her way over to Health and Beauty, found the tampons, and stopped to look past them to the little section of other womanly needs. Lube. Ovulation kits, spermicide. Pregnancy tests. Walmart brand. She palmed it and thought about how to check out. *Okay, try to find someone I don't know, but if I can't, then try to find someone who will keep my secret.* She zigzagged back near the front, just to scope it out. *Thank god for high turnover at this joint,* she thought. There was a new guy all the way in checkout eleven, practically across county lines. She zipped up to the conveyor, plunked down the box and a twenty, and waited out the seconds. He mercifully bagged her purchase, instead of just handing her the box. She carried the bag through the double doors, waved just enough at Mrs. Dee to imply being in a rush, and shoved the bag deep into her backpack. The ride home was the longest she'd ever taken. Worse than that January storm that overtook her last winter. Her mind was just about at a hard boil.

She propped the screen door with her butt, unlocked the aluminum door, pushed into the living room, and was nearly flattened by the smell of yesterday's falafel. She waded through the heavy odor to the bathroom, yanked down her jeans, but realized she forgot her backpack. She waddled to the living room, grabbed the pack, and waddled back. Tore open the packet, the stick, sat down, and realized she'd never done this before. It struck her in the heart. Through tears, she read the instructions, peed, set the stick down, and let the sadness come. She looked at her watch and knew she had ten minutes to cry hard while she waited.

And she knew. Like you were supposed to know the first time you fall in love, *you just know,* they say. Well, she just knew. She pulled up her jeans, washed her hands, and swallowed some air. She rubbed her eyes dry so she could face the lines. She almost laughed when she glanced over the toilet and reread for the gazillionth time her grandma's plaque: "God grant me the serenity to accept the things I cannot change..."

Two dark pink lines blinked up at her, innocent as a baby rabbit. She felt one explosive moment where she gasped and wanted to yell, *What the fuck?!* But she struck the thought, and calm settled through her. Calmness speckled what felt like rain on her head. Or like a breeze that touched all of her skin. She fell still, but the birds continued. For a moment, she felt like Cinderella, where the blue birds pick up her ribbons and tie her bow, and the music starts. But those thoughts fell to the floor like changed clothes. She breathed in and felt a layer of weight at the end of the inhalation. There. A weight at the bottom. Thoughts dropped farther down, submerged. And she felt overwhelmed not by panic, but by calm. She was overcome with, of all things, peace. She stepped outside to find it was still summery. She sat down on her stoop with the birds, in the sun, alone. Wait. Not alone. Not alone ever again.

Old Dog Tavern

"Let's go *out*, girlfriend!" Bethy begged. They had the following day off together. "Let's go into Kalamazoo!" Bethy always wanted to get away. Juniper tended to want to put her head down and plow ahead, thinking if she didn't look up, this part of her life would be over sooner. Like it would magically jump to the next part, the better part. But they both had the next day off, and Juniper had nothing else to do. Bethy fake pouted while she waited, tapping her foot, which was clad in a ridiculous silver slipper-type shoe. Juniper sometimes felt like the tomboy next to Bethy. Juniper just *was*. She didn't bother to garnish what she was. She worried she was too plain, bordering on frumpy. She often liked Bethy's style and flair and colorful drama. She felt like a moth battering against Bethy's light. But even so, they worked together.

"Oh, *alright.*" Juniper said.

"Yay! Maybe we can stay with my ex. Let's stay over. Let's go crazy!" Bethy jumped up. Juniper wanted to be excited. She wanted to drink fun drinks in plastic cups, but it was just that she had maybe run out of time. But Bethy was an expert at this type of college fun. Juniper still hadn't had enough college fun, and now it was certainly too late. Maybe she could just pretend.

When Bethy picked her up that late afternoon, Juniper was wearing a tight white jean jacket and the now infamous slightly flouncy and short light green skirt that deserved a last hurrah. She only had flip-flops that would work with such an outfit, but she was complete and dedicated at least to trying to be cute.

"Oh my god, you little slut!" Bethy squealed with delight and approval when she got out of her car. "I don't recognize you, Junie."

"I know, I know. I needed to at least try. Plus, if I didn't, I would just disappear around you."

"Oh, please. You have that annoying natural beauty thing going on. Now it's just amped up."

They drove through the straight back roads of Michigan with the windows down. It was a slingshot down Route 40, then a left elbow into Kzoo. The afternoon was warm, the radio songs were perfect, and the sense that this day was a part of a fated future filled with the scent of lilies made joy creep into Juniper's heart. Almost simple, Popsicle summer joy.

Kalamazoo would always be exotic to her. It was a portal where the world opened up into possibilities. Even though she'd lived in Chicago, Kalamazoo was "the city" from when she was a kid. It was encouraging how the off ramp just rolled you right into town. Though she was always a little reluctant about fitting in to a place more broad than she was used to, Kalamazoo was big enough that it welcomed everyone and small enough that she knew that meant her too.

Once they slowed down on the side streets, they could feel the smell of wet brick enter the car. Juniper pictured how the city lights at night were a little hazy and not that impressive. But it was bigger than Gobles. Sometimes things are more impressive if the comparison is fathomable. And the maze of it was mostly what had captivated Juniper's sense of wonder all those years. You couldn't see the edges. Bethy zigzagged through the apartment complexes overshadowed by the crushing loveliness of late August.

On the street where they had parked, the sidewalks gave a little, like they were lined with felt. But it was just the moss. It was just a city where nature interrupted constantly. Not glorious, mountainous, rivery nature. More like dandelions gone to seed that speckled the low air, impervious maple trees like cockroaches, pushy, demanding space, and moss and crooked weeds arguing with the asphalt.

They climbed some deck-like stairs to a third floor apartment where the door itself was an omen of dirty.

"Hey there, Beth." A young man opened the door, reached for Bethy, and pulled her into a deep hug. He lifted her off the ground and rocked her while smelling her hair. Juniper stood there bowled over by this display of what was clearly a history of adoration and hot love. Bethy's eyelids seemed heavy when she looked up at him and kissed him. Jesus, thought Juniper.

"I'm Scott." His voice was deep, his eyes silky blue, and Juniper felt a little pressure in her sternum from where his handsomeness hit her.

"Juniper." She smiled, remembering to try.

"Come in, ladies. What can I get you? A beer, water, tea, a toke?" At that everyone in the room laughed, Scott, Bethy, Juniper, and the other two guys who were enveloped in the cushions of an old striped couch. Juniper's vision closed off a little from the newness and nerves. It was thrilling to be there, and not know how the night would unfold. Bethy looked at Juniper and smiled, reassuring, excited, sheepish (from that display by the front door), and happy.

One of the guys scooted over and said, "Sit, ladies."

The girls sat, and Bethy chatted in her easy breezy way. There was some old Led Zeppelin playing, and the guys segued back to their spirited discussion that had been underway. Something about mixed meter they were debating. Plus Zeppelin had that sexy edge that was filling the room like wafts from a joint, and it was the sounds that loosened her first. The pulsing, then how the melody slipped all around.

The guys did, in fact, smoke up a bit before they headed out to one of their favorite bars. And even though she shook her head when they offered her the roach, she could feel the scratch and burn at the back of her throat as she leaned back into the sloppy couch, her back forced to curve too much, her legs consciously held together. It felt like if she kept her legs crossed, she could hold in her new secret.

Once they got back into Bethy's car, Scott was up front, and Juniper was squished in the middle of the backseat between the other two guys, who were each a little weird in their own way. The tall one with dark hair seemed led by his Adam's apple. The other guy's face was soft and a little cherub-like. But she decided she was going to enjoy being squished and their boyish pot smells.

Juniper stepped last through the front face of the Old Dog Tavern. Indeed, it had pale brick skin, black-rimmed windows like eyes, and a bright red curved door mouthing *OPEN*. She stepped up into the welcoming gape and was swallowed into the wonderland. These are the kinds of places that reset your buttons, tip your angle so you have a fresh perspective, she thought. She immediately wished she could drink herself to the place that would show her what to paint next. And like twisted magic, a pint of something appeared before her. She wrapped two hands around her glass and looked around to see where it had come from and was greeted with a wink from Scott. Jesus, she thought again. *He owns that shit.*

She wore her waiflike identity with some womanly intent that evening. It wasn't just sex or wanting to be desired, but before those things. A fresh start was on her mind, even through the impossibility or improbability of it, now. It was the mindset that holds a woman's hand then nudges the small of her back into wanting to be wanted. The feeling that makes a woman's mouth fall open just a little when her tongue is pushing forward behind her teeth, when she is quiet with it. Juniper sat like that in her tight little jacket. That night, maybe she was straddling the worlds of what could have been with what was.

A rockabilly band was going to be playing that she was looking forward to. But before they came on, was an hour or so of karaoke. Bethy was sidling close to Scott. The other two guys were doofusing around the pool table. But Juniper didn't feel alone or uncomfortable at all. It was just right. Some big, burly older dude grabbed the mic and started some preparatory bouncing up on stage. The first strains of that synth and drumbeat from "Born in the U.S.A." started, and the whole room came together in hoots and clapping. Encouraged, the burly guy dug in like he was gleefully grinding out a cigarette on his shitty day. He was off-pitch, endearing, and hilariously awesome.

Scott's tall friend Jason got up next and did some very rhythm-free cringy Eminem. The boys heckled him good-naturedly, and he flipped them off, which garnered boos from everyone. He schlumped back to the pool table. Some girls sang a love song together. Everyone seemed happy, mellow.

Something about the night made Juniper want to let her secrets out. She set down her untouched beer. Bethy said, "You're not gonna drink that?"

Juniper said, "Nah, not yet," and walked up to the stage. She had a song in mind that she'd belted since she was a girl. She knew she always came off as quiet, but quiet people hold the biggest secrets. She sat down in the chair next to the machine and clicked around till she found it, and not that Fugees one, neither. They barely knew she was up there when she started in with the soulful intro. She was Roberta Flack for just a moment, until Juniper herself filled the space as she sang about strumming pain. With triangle hits turning the pages, she cast a net over the room as the groove began. And here she stood up and started to sway. She could feel the cool green against her light legs. She could see her friend looking up at her with new eyes. Cherub-faced Mike over at the pool table stopped with his cue. She continued her gritty, smooth sweetness by flinging out the phrases like twisted streamers of herself. Scott smiled and caught every word. When she got to her favorite verse about "him" finding her letters and reading each one out loud, it unplugged a round cork that had been stopping up her heart. The power she felt at letting herself be beautiful was indeed like a man's hand on the small of her back, pushing her, thrilling her. The room whistled over her last phrase. They hooted her down the stage stairs, and she squeezed her eyes shut while she sat down and Bethy hugged her and said, "Shit, girl. Just wow."

They all danced to the rockabilly boys, even Scott's goofy friends. Everyone bouncing, stomping, sweating. Scott saying, "Juniper, you are something!" Her song still echoed with everyone at the bar. She didn't want to let on that she hadn't even had a sip of beer, so they decided it was Scott who was sober enough to drive them back to his apartment. He dropped off the boys. He set Juniper up on his couch with a blanket and throw pillow while Beth waited for him in his bedroom. Juniper was spinning and happy, and the blinds to the slider in Scott's living room were wide open. The screen invited the night into his apartment, and through the filter of parking lot light, through the sieve of screen, she could see wires and neighboring vinyl villages. She could see outlines of all those whispering trees. And she could smell dumpsters and lilies. The smells killed her softly to sleep.

Back to Work

They drove home the next day. Bethy left flinging promises up to Scott, but Juniper was self-contained. When she opened her trailer door with the evening alone ahead of her, she thought she knew what was coming next. She was off balance from her shifted perspective from the night before. It was the tipping vertigo that made her hopeful. But maybe it was the weight in her abdomen altering her sense of balance. She made some wholesome beans and rice and ate alone at her dinette, where her Grandma had eaten, but rarely alone. Friends, Cora, and Juniper had been frequent guests. Lately, the trailer had never heard so much quiet. But there was the volume again. She was beginning to paint regularly, and with that shift, the timbre of her days and nights changed. She was working on the lungs, and it was Gary depicted in the composition. But was it him, or just his sickness? Was she creating a version of him, or was his presence reminding her of something? She wanted to make sure it was from a place of openness, this question.

She had also started several new sketches and was doing a whole color study, just to get her oil painting chops back before she started the details on the lungs. This focus at home left her unlonely. Her secrets left her unlonely. And everything became lifted in the light. Her friendship with Bethy meant more. Her acquaintance friendships with Manny and her coworkers meant more. Even before her news, she was going to visit her mom more, simply out of wanting her company. Finding joy in her artwork, her real work, colored everything.

* * *

"Hey, Ma, how are ya?" Juniper asked as she let herself in Cora's house after her shift the next afternoon. Her mom still lived where Juniper grew up: a two-bedroom ranch that was old, worn, and simple, a mile past Walmart in the other direction. Second-hand oak tables and a mishmash of chairs. A detached, leaning garage.

"Juniper!" Her Mom greeted her effusively with a hug as she stepped into the kitchen.

"What, Ma? What's up?"

"You know."

"I know what?"

"You were right."

"Kevin?"

"Aagh. Yes." Cora gave a grunt and sat down on the blue vinyl dining chair. She lit up and started in. Juniper went over to make coffee. It was still early, three o'clock.

"First he lost his temp job. So he was here *all the damn time*." Cora added an eye roll for emphasis. "You know me. I like my space." Juniper was counting days. She just saw her mom a couple weeks ago at their last Subway dinner. A few weeks was a long time for them to be apart. But a lot had happened to keep Juniper away. So had he already lost his job?

"When did this happen?" Juniper asked.

"The day I saw you. He comes home, tail between his legs, case of beer. So I'm adding up what we won't be getting. We fought. I know he felt bad, he was tryin'. Turns out he's a delicate flower. Soon as he was a little bit lost with his direction, no job to go to every day, he starts feelin' bad about himself." Juniper gave a "tsk" of appreciation for Cora's story.

"Guess what low self-esteem does to a man?" Cora asked rhetorically. "Nothin' good. Beer and the couch are one thing. One annoying thing. But when he starts takin' it out on me, I had it. I been down that road before. June, I was good this time. He shoved me once, which coulda been misinterpreted. But then the next day he gave me a fist right in the shoulder." Cora pulled up her t-shirt sleeve, and sure enough, there was a bruise. It was hard for Juniper not to explode with anger.

"Jesus Christ! What is *wrong* with people!" she shot out. Most people didn't know Juniper's fiery side, but Cora did. Juniper's judgment often landed squarely on Cora, but she took it. It was meant with love. Even though Juniper was criticizing Kevin, they both knew that it was Cora's choices that were questionable.

It reminded Juniper of the artsy guys in high school that had seemed to use her. Then college, on and off with a math major from Chicago University. It was her most serious relationship to date. Robert didn't look like a loser at first. He was beautiful and sat for her to draw him many times. Together, they loved Radiohead and Dirty Projectors and Indian food. But he was both angry and dull. He got stuck in these repetitive OCD-type behaviors, which made him exasperating sometimes. When they left his apartment, he would lock and relock his door. She couldn't figure out what the heck he was doing; it seemed to be he did it differently every time. So she asked him, gently, nicely, "Rob, what is up with the door-locking thing?" He pulled a sheet of worn and folded notebook paper out of his jacket that had a chart. Whether he started right to left or left to right depended on whether it was an odd day or even day. And the number of times he relocked was connected to some algorithm he'd created based on what day of the month it was.

Here he was, trusting her with this secret, and she judged him for it. It was too weird and no way to live, she thought. She both bristled and cringed at the thought of an algorithm creeping into the bedroom with them. Just, no.

Besides, when he got stressed, he would kind of flip out. His anger had already made her nervous. He was twenty but had seemed like an immature kid to Juniper when he lost control like that. It came off as whiny and entitled and like he needed his mom to calm him down. Juniper never wanted to play that role in his life and pulled away from Rob and his angry numbers, ultimately surrounding herself with a more comfortable blanket of art friends.

And then Ricky, which didn't last long per se. But somehow between the preamble of a year of flirting (or her stringing him along) and what happened last month, Ricky may have accidentally turned into her longest "relationship."

And now her secret, Kirk. She had to count him. He was leaving the most lasting impression of all. There was a lot to think about. Not just Cora's mistakes, but Juniper's too. Neither Cora nor Juniper would even get into Jezebel's mistakes anymore. That was a pain that squeezed their hearts too tight. They were just glad to be safe and together, albeit just two of them now, but safe and together.

That was the thing. The women were real. Soft, hard, gritty, sweet. They were real. But the men were all some kind of folklore. And it wasn't that they told like a fairy tale, all simple evil and mystery. It was that they were reduced to some two-dimensional story. This was the part that scratched like nails on Juniper's chalkboard. This was what left the shadow of angst.

She pictured Grandpa's rounded belly and the shape made between each strained button. The off-white of an old t-shirt peeking out, eye-like, between the straining tan button-down—the only shirt she remembered on him. She thought it funny that she remembered his belly and buttons. That was her eye-level back then. She had an impression of his slicked-back silver hair and his gruff commands. Also, her memory slid around his eyes. That memory was stolen from photos. His eyes were an icy blue, too recessive to show up anywhere else in the family.

And her dad—she never called him that—was someone who frustratingly sounded nice. He sounded quiet, like her. He sounded like he was smart and serious. She wanted to know him, what he smelled like. Motor oil? Beer? The woods? Flannel? He probably smelled like a black t-shirt and cigarettes. But how could she know for sure?

Cora made him sound kind of great, until the part where she found out she was pregnant. For some reason, when Juniper pressed Cora to tell the story, Cora always included what he was wearing. Cora had taken him out to White Castle, which they still had down in Benton Harbor. Cora seemed hung up on his Pink Floyd shirt with the triangle that he was wearing that day. Cora was kind of happy she was knocked up, she said. Scared, sure. But with no real plans and an honest love of Jeff, she was excited. She saw the three-sided prism on his t-shirt as an omen. Cora's seventeen-year-old self thought it represented the strength of them together as a new threesome. Jeff, Cora, and this baby.

But apparently he had choked on his burger. The manager had to come over and hit him on the back. Cora said she wondered why he had stuck the whole thing in his mouth, anyway. They weren't *that* small. But Jeff kind of was. Small and wiry. Skinny. Cora thought they fit together beautifully, she told Juniper. But turned out he was smaller than Cora knew. He was pseudo-supportive for the last few months of school/the first few months of her pregnancy. But then Cora dropped out, and he graduated and *enlisted*. He left her without saying goodbye. Now, when Juniper thought of the horror of that, she tried to understand. She knew how it felt not to know what to say, so you say nothing. But what he did was, of course, unforgivable. He left them both. And the worst part was that he made the same decision every day since. Well, maybe he had visited her early on; her mom had said he came by once. And there was one picture. Then there was that evening that he crashed her choir concert. But other than that, he chose anew, every morning, not to show up or reach out. The betrayal would be more easily overcome if it was in the past. Everyone, including Grandma Jezebel, had wanted Juniper to get over it, because it was so far in the past. Cora seemed over it. Sort of. But Juniper couldn't get anyone to understand that it wasn't in the past, if he was still rejecting her, twenty-some years later. Because each day was new. Each day he chose. Why was she the only one who saw it that way?

In general, Cora's philosophy on men waffled. On one hand, she acted like she needed a man like a fish needed a bicycle. And on the other hand, she just couldn't help herself. Like men were a plate of cookies, and if you were left alone long enough, you would pick one. Except where the cookies are assholes. And you pick the worst one because you waited too long or weren't able to see the other plate of good ones across the room. You pick the one someone else already took a bite out of.

"You want some Hamburg Helper here for dinner?"

"I thought you'd never ask!" Juniper gently put her arm around her mom's shoulder. It'd be Hamburger Helper and Cokes in front of *American Idol*. Cozy and familiar.

"Hey, Ma, I started painting again," Juniper said as they were getting out the sour cream and burger meat.

"There you go, hon. I knew you'd get back into it."

There was no good way to poke through the hamburger plastic. Your finger could stretch through the cellophane, into the center well. But when it finally broke through, you'd likely be touching raw meat blood. You could use a knife, but then it, too, would be contaminated. What to do with that annoying sheath protecting something that could be sacred or toxic? It was a twisted luxury, when your luxuries were modest, to be able to ponder such things as the plastic and Styrofoam encasing your food. The trappings of sustenance and the pools of pink that were more reality than anyone really wanted. She threw the garbage away and dumped the chunk of meat into the warming pan. Cora tore open the packet for the sauce. They were comforted by the promising smells of powder in torn paper and cardboard and settling meat. Cora opened a can of mushrooms and drained the liquid. They waited.

Forest

Juniper had been obsessing over *him* for a few weeks before she gave in. Janoski. She now had his name and could get in touch with him. August had fallen down with this feel of sadness. It wasn't emptiness without him, just hot sadness. The trees were heavy. Juniper and Bethy went to a farmer's market in Benton Harbor. They went over to Rocky Gap park and spent a day at the beach. The water was dark aqua, the sky was flat gray.

By the end of the month, she pictured him preparing for school. She looked up his email address. She wrote to him. He wrote back within two hours, but from a different account.

Juniper, he started. *It was wonderful, but I can't.* Then he wrote again: Let me call you. So she sent her number, and he called. She was sitting in her trailer, and when that phone rang, she dropped the pot she was washing and barely dried one of her soapy hands well enough to press "talk."

They talked the stars out. He answered everything without her asking, but they were not the answers she wanted. It was like she was watching him dissolve. He dissolved a little each time she could feel his love for his wife. Sure, he told Juniper that he was angry with his wife and frustrated at their impasses. He talked about his discontent

74

and even talked about leaving her. But Juniper felt this woman in the present tense.

Over the next couple of weeks, they talked many times. He would call her, and she would run with sudsy hands or carelessly set her paintbrush down, like painting didn't matter as much as what he might have to say. She didn't like the way that felt. He did ask about her painting. There was even some very off-handed mention about "hey, why don't you think about grad school?" But it did not come with a "hey, I'll put in a good word for you here at U of M." She was a little miffed at one point that he'd casually suggest grad school but not offer to even give her a recommendation or introduce her to someone or *anything*. He had seen and appreciated her work. And it was really striking her that maybe her work was better than she had given herself credit for. She had gained some weird objectivity with her trailer gallery greeting her every day. The juxtaposition of trailer and hotel and Gobles against her work gave her this skewed perspective. Well, really, it was a *fresh* perspective. Fresh in that it was free from all that elitist bullshit that scared her away from Chicago in the first place.

He talked about his wife more and more. He was extracting himself with his talk, and Juniper was trying to put the whole thing in a place. They never mentioned meeting up. In her mind, she never lessened the fact that she might now love him for what he had unintentionally given her. It was the strangest sense of love she would know. Like that for a stranger, really, yet with an undeniable connection not only to that person but also the earth that they stepped upon. The air they had shared, more than their bodies, became spun into love. What they created was no doubt being spun into some kind of love.

But then, like opening her hand to release a lightning bug, she let the school year start without picking up his next call.

She spent the entire day in bed feeling her booming pulse. Sure, she cried. She didn't know what to do except lie around with the sad irony of simultaneously losing and gaining.

It was early evening that finally called her out. Her trailer felt too confining. She was still in her large white sleeping t-shirt, but she wiped off her teary face and stepped outside. Crickets and toads that hung out at the remainder pond across the field expanded her in a moment. She tucked the trailer back with its screen door. She was barefoot and stepped off the small porch. As a girl, she had prided herself on how far, and over what surfaces, she could not just walk, but run barefoot. She still walked the gravel drive to the mailbox and back with no shoes, weather permitting. She couldn't let herself get completely soft. Besides, it was end-of-summer. (Really it was start-of-fall, but she was clinging.) Moss pads and abundant greenery were everywhere. It hadn't rained for a week, the ground would be dry enough, and the late sun reached through the trees. Her front yard was a poky and matted field, like a little girl's messy head. It was tamped down in the places where deer had lain. Her backyard was a dense clump of trees. She had thought of the backyard as a forest when it had still been Grandma's.

She stepped like a giant among crabgrass, stopped at a patch of unbelievable wild strawberries that surprisingly hadn't finished yet, and avoided mole holes or vole holes, she didn't know which. Beyond were electrical wires. Highway that could glint a speeding light from miles away. She reached down to pick two strawberries that had been inexplicably left. They were full with miniature red juice, as perfect as the inside of wax bottle candy.

She walked around her neglected and loved yard. Each step shored up her resolve to feel the prickly grass and bright cold spots of mud. To pay attention, and not just see—she always saw—but to listen. Feel, taste, smell. The sky settled with her as she stood at the edge of her unruly carpet square of a yard. She stood at the edge of the little forest, feeling like she should knock. It had been too long since she'd visited the mushrooms and the lichen on each northern tree face. She spread the branches like a beaded curtain and stepped inside.

The forest darkened with the mood lighting of a pot-clouded living room. The missing light pulled a cover around her. The curtain swished closed. She wanted to see how far she could step into her little forest toward the middle without stepping out. How far into the middle could she get? How dark would it get? At first, the ground inside had seemed covered only with a layer of dry pale orange leaves, dead for more than one season. She crunched along until a stick poked into her foot. Her calloused soles were like nature's moccasins, so she only paused, didn't wince. Her footing followed the way that was thickest with leaves. Something flat, metallic, and silver glinted up ahead. When she got to it, she saw it was just a 3 Musketeers wrapper. She didn't have a pocket. But she picked it up and smelled for any remnant of chocolate, then wadded it into her fist.

She couldn't see the forest edges anymore. She was somewhere in the middle. No light was visible through the trees, but the glow from above lit her way.

A white Pay Day wrapper was next. She snatched it too. Then a Styrofoam Big Mac shell. She wished she'd brought a bag. This wasn't a trail of breadcrumbs, but it was a trail made up of flares of silver, neon reds, and blues. Her patch of nature, this forest, with its illusion of isolation, was littered with these interruptions. These careless signposts of people. Surrounded by open farmland, yet feeling framed in by roads that led to her cultural destiny, she turned and ran. Ran with the weight in her belly. She fled the forest with the 3 Musketeers wrapper still stuck in her hand. She ran with her hair streaming behind her.

A Swoop of
Exhaust

She had never heard anyone talk about the secret-keeping that is early pregnancy. She figured she might be a couple months along, because she had been with him four weeks before, but she was supposed to do the math from her last period. Her belly would look flat to anyone else, but with her shirt off, looking at herself sideways in her bedroom mirror, she could see a softness that was new. She wanted to tell no one for as long as possible. The news was such a shock. But even more shocking was that she had known immediately and irrevocably that she would keep this baby.

She dressed for work in her baggy jeans and green t-shirt. Brushing her teeth, she looked into her own eyes to see if she looked different. Not really. Until she caught a glimpse of her chest.

"Holy!" Her eyebrows shot up. The tops of her breasts were pushing out of her shirt. They were round. Forget the belly. The roundness of her newly fullish breasts just about made her choke on her toothpaste. And her veins did this crazy weave across her front in a shade of green that pulled from her shirt. She laughed at herself in astonishment. Greenish bluish veins are not supposed to be beautiful, yet she was struck by the colors and fullness she was exuding.

She was going to be late to work, but she rushed into her room to find another shirt. There, a button-down thing to put over the t-shirt. She felt like she was going to throw up as she swung her leg over her bike. But she rode to work with the biggest smile, feeling pukey and hot and full, and like crying. She was so fucking happy. Also, she would stop swearing.

She was incredulous, not only about what was happening to her, but also how it made her want to run to Cora. Would her mom be able to tell she was different? Maybe. Juniper needed her.

After work that same day, she called her mom, and they agreed to meet up at Subway for Cora's break. Cora was already waiting with the food on the table when Juniper got there.

"Jeez Junie, I haven't seen you in a week again. That's not right."

"I know, Ma."

"What, you meet someone?" Cora teased.

"No!"

"I got you the seven, which I knew was a safe bet. You meet someone?" Cora asked again and looked at Juniper through squinted eyes.

"Thank you." Juniper ignored the comment as she grabbed the paper-wrapped sandwich. "I started painting something new. I'm doing this set of lungs. I guess I can tell you. There's this guy at work." She lowered her voice and leaned across the Formica, aware of being top-heavy. "He told me he has lung cancer. I was so overwhelmed by him being sick all of a sudden, it just made me want to start painting again, like I had something to say finally."

As she said that, she had a flash of her mother as portrait, chewing her salami. She considered using the fluorescent lighting too. That would be strident and revealing, she thought. Once the ideas started, they often sprayed like an outdoor spigot that had a secret tap she was unaware of and was certainly not in control of. The well sprayed ideas like water, full of minerals, dirt, and scrum from the inside of old lead pipes. Messy ideas. Plus today was about a distraction. She wanted to be with her mom but didn't want Cora to know why. Not quite yet.

"Of course you have something to say, honey. You've always been so creative." Cora munched her chips.

"So, anyway," Juniper floundered. Cora squinted at her again. Juniper had an unusual awareness of her number seven. She unwrapped the sandwich filled with salami and ham and pepperoni, and she felt like the white grease nodules of the processed meat looked up at her. The ham was too shiny, covered in a pomade of slickness. The color of ham reminisced pink fur slicked down. The lettuce and tomatoes were clearly trying to be reasonable, but the wetness by association tainted their cause. Juniper turned her head so that she could inhale something beside the scent of her food. That mayonnaise was up to no good. She could anticipate the feel on the roof of her mouth, everything all slippery and slimy with mayonnaise and wet animal fat. And she felt a nausea that made her let go of the paper wrapping and put her hands on her thighs, palms down, gripping. She let out a small mewl of discomfort. But no one could hear such a subtle sound in that waterfall of white noise.

Especially because at that moment Mrs. Dee sidled by and greeted them with an over-large smile. Juniper saw the blackened parts that outlined each tooth of Mrs. Dee's smile while she was eyeing their food. She asked Cora about how she was liking it over at Subway compared to housewares, because she was thinking about making a switch. Juniper closed her eyes momentarily, hoping the sick feeling would pass by before Mrs. Dee was finished. A swoop of exhaust from the main entrance knocked Mrs. Dee into remembering her greeting duties and took Juniper for one more quick little spin around the nausea merry-go-round. Holy Jesus. This was not going to work.

"Ooh, I gotta run. See you ladies!" Mrs. Dee scurried to the front, and Cora busied herself with her own sandwich. The nausea passed, and Juniper took a couple hummingbird sips of her Coke, imagining she looked like the cardboard cup, all white and beaded. She exercised all of her willpower to finish her meal within an inch of its life and act normal.

"Hey, who's the guy at the hotel that's sick? You know I know half of them over there." Cora continued where they had left off.

"Okay, but don't tell anyone. I don't want him thinking I blabbed."

"Sealed."

"Gary Shepard."

"Aw, shit. I went to school with him. He's only a year or two older than me. He was real sweet, but like a hurt puppy."

"Yeah, so. That's him," Juniper concurred but now felt guilty again that she was using Gary's illness as some diversion from her own big news. And she was hit, as they sat for a moment of quiet, like on a front porch, watching folks stroll by, she was hit by his withering life. And her growing one. The equal exchange seemed horrific, maybe not beautiful at all. Had she done something wrong, had she taken something? Well, kind of. She was growing, he was dying, and she was going to mark it down for others to see. How wrong was that? It frightened her. What was coming out of her was frightening her.

She had thought she would feel a comfort at being with Cora, but that was not the case. No comfort, and slight astonishment that her mother couldn't see through her lie by omission. She felt hot and self-conscious. She realized the comfort would likely only come once she reconciled the feeling of this life for a life. And once she told her mom the real news. And the time was not yet.

Juniper Blossoms

It took her a couple of days to realize the real reason she didn't want to tell anyone. It was because Kirk himself didn't know.

She spent her bike rides to work thinking about how to avoid chemicals while cleaning the rooms. She figured she could easily talk Jo-Jo into pairing up for their shared shifts—once she told everyone. Jo-Jo was very vocal about hating vacuuming and the physically demanding stuff. Juniper thought she could handle those duties for now, if Jo could handle the toxic stuff.

Her mind circled back to the logistics of what to do. Tell him? Don't tell him? These were the two branches of the flow chart that followed her everywhere. If she told him, then all of these life-altering things would result. It would tear apart his life, no doubt. If she didn't tell him, she would carry the weight of that by herself, forever. It was a tag-along with claws. She wanted to hide.

She even felt like she had to skulk around Gobles, including the library, which was one of her favorite places. She wanted to look at the pregnancy book section but was afraid of someone seeing her check something out. Instead, she used the computer there and looked up "pregnancy oil paint." She read: "Some studies...exposure to solvents...increase the risk...miscarriage, risk of birth defects and learning problems—so using oil-based...not recommended." She cleared her history. The words hurt.

But she couldn't pause to cry over that; there were real tears to be shed. It was fine. It would be fine. She'd draw, she'd watercolor. She'd make it work.

Like many artists Juniper knew, she had talent but was maybe a bit weak in areas such as ambition and determination. The sensitivity that made her good also led her to being easily derailed. She had been attracted to creating, because that was who she was. But the rest of the stuff needed to be successful was a mess. So here she was, with an edict in writing telling her not to do what she was doing. "Miscarriage" and "birth defects" weren't words that she could pretend she didn't see. And for the first time that she could remember, instead of losing momentum and stopping because of an obstacle, her instinct was to reroute. *If I can't paint in oils, I can do something else.* The impulse to create was stronger than the impulse to succumb to inertia. Sitting in the shellacked library chair, amongst old things and those little teensy red bugs that surprise you in old books, she was filled with intent and purpose. She was creating a person. The creation was happening without her consciousness, and that flow could be a flood, a tidal wave that continued a genesis of an idea into a work. She could let that physical wave of creation spill over and push her artistic momentum.

Juniper held out her fingers and did the math again. This little person was going to show up around May, maybe? She had to get to a doctor. This was real. She sat a while longer with the exhaustion of it. She had probably created a pair of ears today. Maybe some teeth. She was tired. She rode her bike home. September folded in upon itself as Juniper blossomed.

* * *

The very last day of September showcased morning frost. She figured she was about a month away from her second trimester. She knew she would need to tell someone. She would need to tell Bethy, or her mom, or him.

She talked Bethy into a shopping trip in Benton Harbor, and they'd spent over an hour at Goodwill. Juniper secretly riffled through a whole new category of blouses and elastic waists.

"Hey, Beth, how's this hat look on me?" Juniper raked a brimmed beanie down over one eye.

"Very cute. And very perfect with your coloring."

As if an eggplant-colored hat would hide Juniper's lower truth. Wait, higher truth? For fifty cents, it was worth a try. She threw one of the roomy blouses onto the counter with her hat and they checked out with their loot.

"Pull over here," Juniper said for their last stop.

"What? The library?" She suspected Bethy wasn't a huge fan. How to explain getting a couple of books as a necessary errand?

"Yeah. I really want to see if they have *Girl with the Dragon Tattoo*." It seemed plausible and cool enough to be urgent. "They don't have it in Gobles."

"Oh. Okay." And as if following the script Juniper had written in her head, Bethy said, "I'll just wait out here," as she pulled into a spot and cranked her Coldplay.

Juniper brought her backpack into the Benton Harbor library and found the expecting mother books she was looking for. The checkout girl was either kind or indifferent and didn't comment. Juniper hid the books in her pack.

"Well, did they have it?" Bethy asked as Juniper eased back into the car. She even had to pretend to be as agile as she used to be. But now she always felt bloated and crampy and certainly not agile.

"Nope." Juniper was tired of lying already. How did some people do it so effortlessly?

At home alone, she ate up the information about pregnancy and would sometimes feel brave and read things about babies too. But the reality for her was about the pregnancy itself. That's what was real. That was what had changed her. A baby was very, very abstract. It really was going to be time to tell, so someone could take her to the doctor. She was just gathering her mental strength.

She sat at her dinette with her hands curled around a hot tea. She felt cocooned in the trailer, safe with her secret. She wore a dark blue cardigan around her like a blanket. The tea was blueberry, the smell like snips of the summer that was behind her. Michigan summer berries.

It was all becoming more amazing with each passing day. She was just so sleepy and thought about all the short cuts she had to take at work now. She vacuumed lazily and only wiped what looked dirty. No one would know. She refilled the toilet paper and sample soaps. She found herself peeing in every single bathroom she cleaned. No one would even know she was having to go, like, twelve times a day. She was sure no one knew and that no one could tell. She just wished she could keep it a secret the entire time. Her tea warmed all the way through to the back of her hands.

She went to her stereo and turned on the saddest music she could find. She put "Hurt" by Nine Inch Nails on replay. It wasn't the words. She liked how his voice choked in and the instruments released. The tightness of sound was what she needed. She realized this lonesome afternoon in her trailer was to be a last hurrah. She would cry and hear the music. She would think about her past and gently close that door with a click. It was time to walk into the next room.

* * *

She heaved her leg over her slanted crossbar. Something twinged in her right pelvic area. Like a pull of muscle. Her bike seat pressed on her pelvic bones and soft nether region as she forced the pedals forward, past Walmart, to her mother's house. She immediately started sweating.

She kind of knew her mom's schedule and knew she'd be home. She should have called first. But she couldn't wait any longer and couldn't risk a loss of courage. Wind had started, and a little slanted rain had begun. It was cold and the cardigan flapped open, but she didn't want to stop to button it. She didn't want to lose her momentum. She couldn't shake the sad, which seemed to tug at her pants and sweater. But she had to stay focused and keep pushing the pedals down. She had to tell her mom. She needed help now. It was time to tell. She tried to match her crying to the streaky pace of the rain, just so one didn't overwhelm the other. It was going to be okay. Pedaling was at least good for one thing, a nice steady rhythm. It was. Breathe in. Going to. Breathe out. Be, pause, o, pause, k.

Telling

She saw her mom's car. She simultaneously knocked and swung in the kitchen door.

"Well, Juniper! Why didn't ya call? Scared the jukebox outta me!" Cora was on the couch fiddling with her CD player. She was swearing in frustration but didn't even ask Juniper to look at it. Neither were good at that kind of stuff.

"Sorry, I just decided to bike over after I was already out," Juniper lied. She was dripping wet, and Cora went into her bedroom to grab some dry clothes for her. Juniper had a little panic that Cora would choose something too tight. But she came out with a big t-shirt and sweats.

After Juniper changed, she slumped on the couch next to Cora and grabbed the remote, just to look casual. But she didn't turn the TV on.

"What's up, little girl?" Cora asked. *Did she really just call me that?* Juniper wondered as the tears, barely held back as it was, threatened anew. She closed her eyes and felt her heart start to bounce around. This was hard. It was just her mom. But she felt the significance of it. What if Cora wasn't happy about this news? Little girl. Juniper's bottom lip jutted out, and she felt stupid, just like she was eleven, or five, and just little. She'd always been little. Little girl.

She cried, "Mom!"

"Honey! What?" Cora was alarmed.

Juniper could see she was worrying her mom. "No, it's okay. I'm okay. It's just." Juniper hunched her head down and let the tears out. Cora wrapped her arm around her. "Okay, you just take a minute. I'm right here."

"I did *not* meet someone," Juniper said. "But I *am* pregnant." At this Cora bust out with a laugh. Her teeth arced up and down, and Juniper could see all her broken and filled teeth. Her eye rays spread out.

"What! Those two things are mutually exclusive!" Cora laughed some more. "Oh, Juniper! Oh, Juniper. It's gonna be okay." She petted Juniper's hair and kind of rocked her on the couch. Probably nothing more she could have asked for. It was exactly why she came home. Was her mom okay? Was *it* okay?

"Now, honey, I know you're upset, but I need to ask you a couple questions." It's like she was a professional with this kind of news. Cora sank back into the couch and tucked a leg under so she could turn and see Juniper's face. She kept a hand on Juniper's thigh. "Do you know how far you are?"

"I don't know exactly, but I think like three months."

"Okay, you have to tell me then what you're thinking about doing. You know what I mean."

"I'm so scared, Mom. I'm so scared 'cause I know exactly what I want, and you can't change my mind."

"I won't do that."

"I'm *keeping* this baby." Juniper made herself say the words. She had to be brave here.

"Well, I won't lie either. I'm a little shocked. I thought you was gonna be blowing outta here any day now. But you know, honey, this is not unknown territory to me." And then Cora also started to cry. "I'm not too thrilled at this tradition we've got goin' here. But—" Then she reached all the way over and grabbed both of Juniper's hands in hers and looked straight at her until she looked up. "But I am going to help you. And a little part of me, maybe a huge part of me, is just plain thrilled." At that, both girls, both women, burst out anew, crying and hugging and just watering that tree trunk with the sunlight of their little family.

* * *

Cora made goulash to nourish her daughter. The perforation of the tomato cans mingled smells of aluminum and acid. The oniony meat was a warm umami. The bleached white soft tubes of elbow macaroni cradled everything, which was then knitted together with salt and pepper. Juniper was raised with the sentiment that red meat was an iron-giving life force, and she ate with a gusto that was equal to the love that Cora put into the meal. They were nearly animalistic in their wordless care and response.

Then they spent the night quietly talking, trying to make plans. But Juniper deftly dodged direct questions about "the father" and said she wasn't ready to get into all that yet, and they weren't together, and he was likely completely out of the picture.

"But is that what you want?" Cora asked. "Do you want him involved?" That knocked the wind out of Juniper. What kind of question was that? Confusing is what it was. She knew not telling Kirk was cowardly. What was she avoiding? There had to be some powerful inertia at work here. Because not telling him would cement how difficult this was going to be. Every month she didn't tell was a month he wouldn't be helping. But what if he didn't want to help out? What if he refused? *Could* he refuse? She felt some anger creeping in, but with nowhere to actively direct it, she just shoved it back down into her secret anger stash. Juniper was sitting on the couch, feet up on the old ottoman, not saying a word in response to Cora. She was thinking. But Cora didn't go for that.

"Juniper, you have to answer me. Do you want him involved or what?" Juniper envisioned a ballooned belly in this exact same spot. In a relatively short span of time here, she wouldn't recognize herself. She was unintentionally holding her breath, which added to the slowly rising panic.

"Look at me," said Cora. Juniper looked up, but her mouth was shut tight. New tears burst her open. She cried but still couldn't answer.

"Oh, hon." Cora sighed. "Look, we can talk more tomorrow." At that, Juniper's eyebrows pinched upward in worry. "Or later, whatever.

We'll figure it out." Juniper nodded a little. "You must be tired. Sleep here." She nodded again, and Cora got up to put clean sheets on the extra bed.

That night, Juniper slept in her old bedroom. She had a dream that she was wearing an umbilical cord as a bracelet. She was wearing it as part of an outfit, so it must have been deliberate. It was so weird that she could feel the softness of the bracelet and see its color, a transparent whitish pinkish. That meant the bracelet was healthy. She skimmed the surface of consciousness enough to wonder how she was feeling. Was this a positive image? She slipped back into sleep thinking at least it wasn't a necklace. At least it wasn't a choker.

As weird and disturbing as her thoughts had become, she was enveloped in comfort as she opened her eyes to a late morning sun. For her it was color and tone that determined the time of day. A little color usually leaked away as the morning pushed ahead into day, but the brightness usually ramped up. Gray days tended to throw her sense of time flat on the ground. But today was bright and clean, maybe ten o'clock.

She had gotten up to pee three times overnight and felt comfortable enough to just lie there. She was proud of herself for sort of planning ahead and dropping the news on her mom when she didn't have to work the next day. Everything had unfolded with Cora, mostly as she had wanted. She could begin to rest. She could stare at her covers. The blue blanket was outlined to look like a quilt, and it had squares of varying blue flowers. Big, purple-blue hyacinth balls, little teeny blue bells, morning glory vines, bluebonnets, all patched up into blocks of memory. It was her quilt from childhood. Its comfort was infinite.

Juniper came out of her room renewed into the new day, thoughts and nausea swirling together. "Ma, do you have any old pictures of Great Grandma Carol?"

"Somewhere, yeah," Cora said while she scrambled eggs for both of them before she headed into Subway.

"I'm just gonna stay here today, 'kay? I'll make supper. Spaghetti and garlic bread. I'll cook for us. It'll be ready when you get home."

"Oh, June. You're the best. The old photo album is in my bedroom closet."

The pictures and albums were in the box where they'd always been. It was obvious to Juniper that her baby was making her want to look back. Look back before her only job would be to look not ahead or behind but to live fully in the moment. She imagined having an infant involved the most immediate kind of living known to humankind.

There was a sepia portrait of Great-Grandma Carol from the early 1900s in a cardboard sleeve. She was Grandma Jezebel's mother. The portrait seemed to have been done in a studio. She wore a dress with a gigantic collar, and her hair was artfully coiled. Her face did remind Juniper of Grandma. Their close-set eyes and very pale skin. There were photos of other relatives in the box too, including Great-Grandpa Walter. But it was Great-Grandma she gazed at, looking for history and clues, and some kind of sentiment in her sturdy, unsmiling face. She remembered the high school graduation picture of her Grandma, and she rummaged around for that. In 1957, she looked smooth and nearly effervescent. From that image, that image that Juniper loved—Grandma when she was young—she patched together an idea. For all her anger at the men in her life, the women remained a source of love. With the women she felt safe. Safety in a relationship is knowing you can screw up and they will still love you. And knowing if they screw up, you'll still love them. That feeling is an especially magnanimous presence in a person's life. To know you will always love someone is a very complete feeling.

She stood up next to her mom's bed, strewn with photos, and placed a picture of each of her grandmothers side by side. Then she went back to Cora's closet and rummaged for yearbooks. Gobles High School 1981. Seniors, Cora Kowalski. In the back of the yearbook were loose photos of her, posed with her head turned over her shoulder. Juniper got a thrill seeing her mom so young and pretty. She'd seen the picture a hundred times. When Juniper was in high school herself, and about to get her own senior picture taken, she felt a jolt to realize that *she* might have been a part of this picture. Her mom would have been pregnant by the time that photo was taken. Her mom had graduated with a GED, because she had to leave in May of her senior year to have Juniper. The yearbook had been printed before Cora had to leave school, so there she was, included. Something in Cora's black-rimmed eyes had a "fuck you" quality, there was no doubt. Her hair was flipped back, her sweater an innocent pale yellow. Juniper knew she was projecting, but she felt the softening haze created in the photo lab was just from wafts of smoke encircling Cora in a frame, choking her future.

Now there were three. Three photos marking time and family. One more to add. Juniper found her senior picture and regretted her asymmetrical jagged cut. But then she figured if she too had a granddaughter one day who laughed at her, it would be okay. She put her photo next to the other three. Wow, she really saw some family resemblance. The eyes for sure, and the sharp bones of their cheeks and chins.

She took the four portraits outside and set them on the plywood table. She had found her nice digital camera from her institute days, still stored in her childhood closet. Under the grubby November light, she started taking pictures of the pictures. There was no glare, just a filtered sun. It might be perfect.

She thought of this life in her belly. She felt this life as new growth on an old tree. A fifth portrait would soon be added to this lineup. She could scarcely imagine its perfection. It would be too pure. It would represent everything to come.

Drippy Heinie

She would tell Bethy her news next. She knew she was still dodging telling Kirk, "the father." When her mom had called him that, it was too much. He was just this guy that she was now tethered to, some guy who gave half to make a whole. Some guy that didn't even see her as equal. She didn't even know if she *wanted* to be with him anymore—at all. When they had talked on the phone, his realness unspooled in front of her. She could hear him in his kitchen one time, and could hear him doing his normal things. But they were things in a grown-up kitchen that seemed odd or irrelevant to her. Like using a dishwasher. Everyone had a dishwasher. Well not her mom, or her—or her grandma. But he was loading the dishwasher and putting things away. He was putting a lot of things away around his house. Like tidying.

They had also talked about art. It was fascinating and intimidating to hear him talk. His depth of knowledge was intense and impressive. He had so many facts and dates and quotes, like the historian that he was, she supposed. But she knew her mind. Even if she were thirteen years older, with that much more education, she would not think in that linear fashion. Maybe that difference was a balance. But something about this talk made her inwardly cringe. She nodded to herself as she remembered.

Juniper had fixed herself up that day, for Bethy. She had blown her hair dry and smoothed it. She had curled her eyelashes and added a touch of lip color. Enough to draw the eye upward, but not enough to draw suspicion right away. She had two pairs of pants left that fit, and one of them was stretch pants. Today she wore her hip-hop pants that were now not stylishly revealing her perfect little hipbones. They were now rubber-banded at the top button. She *could* button them, it just didn't feel good. It hurt. She felt constantly full and yet constantly hungry.

"Hey, Bethy!" she said as she was putting on her smock, newly relieved that it never fit her well.

"Hey there, Juniper, what's up?" Bethy nudged her playfully. "We haven't hung out in like, weeks. I want to tell you about stuff. Let's go out."

"Yeah, you read my mind." Juniper nodded and smiled and thought about the drink she wouldn't be having. Bethy had met someone passing through town, so they hadn't done the bar thing in a while. Bethy was busy chasing down this guy. At least hers was supposedly single, Juniper thought.

She counted the minutes of work that day. She thought about how strong she was and that she could push through the new feelings of sweatiness and clumsiness. She could clean and vacuum and fit sheets and wipe mirrors. She could do it. But it was getting harder, and she never thought she'd be the kind to need so much rest. Karen had called her to bring an extra case of paper towels to keep in the third-floor supply closet, and Juniper thought she could just take it up the back stairs, like she always did. But she had to pause after one flight, heaving and sweating, like she was on an air-strapped mountain instead of below-sea-level Michigan. The baby needed her oxygen. The baby needed her blood. She walked slowly and felt her hips sway anew. Each stair was a thought. That was how it was going to be.

"Thanks, hon," said Karen, not looking up. "Tough workout, them stairs?"

Juniper couldn't answer that. So she didn't. "Need anything else?" she insincerely offered.

"I'm good. And you rest if you need to," Karen said, looking up into Juniper's face. *What the? Why'd she say that?* This day couldn't be finished fast enough.

* * *

Bethy didn't want to go to Side Bar. She wanted to go into Benton Harbor. So they did. They hit a pizza place, then the closest thing to a hip little joint they could find. Bethy said, "two Heinies, please," the second they sat down, so what was Juniper supposed to do?

The beers came, and Juniper said, "And a water, too, when you get the chance," to the very young-looking waitress. She let Bethy start in on whatever. A little bit about Scott, a little bit about a master's degree. Bethy was in her usual chatty mood, which Juniper normally found entertaining. But she was seriously getting sleepy, and it was only eight o'clock. She needed to talk.

"Hey, Beth. Can you keep a secret?" Juniper asked, knowing full well Bethy was a horrible secret-keeper. She knew that Bethy would tell everyone, which would relieve Juniper of the duty herself.

"Um, maybe," Bethy said, sipping her beer.

"Seriously, this is big," insisted Juniper.

Bethy giggled but then stopped when she saw Juniper wasn't smiling. "*Okay*, what is it already?"

"Look, remember that guy?" Juniper asked.

"Yeah, I remember the *one* guy," Bethy said.

"Well. Look. I'm pregnant."

"Jesus fucking Holy Christy shit bucket! Wait. Are you kidding? You're kidding." Bethy ran through a rapid series of reactions. Juniper sat there and waited for her, as still as her untouched golden Heineken.

"You're not saying anything. You're not kidding." Bethy got serious. She glanced at Juniper's drippy full glass, which was obviously worth more than words.

Bethy said, "Oh my god, oh my god. Wait."

Juniper laughed this time. "It's real. It's true."

"Well, don't just sit there, tell me everything!" Bethy yelped and comically grabbed Juniper's beer for herself. Juniper took her time, telling everything, and felt a little heavier with relief, as heft was her new sense of being in the world. She was weighted with purpose and, well, weight.

"Bethy, can't you *tell*? Don't I look different?"

"Stand up!" Bethy commanded. And Juniper slid out of the booth and stood.

"Oh my god, I'm such an asshole! Look how fat you are!" They both laughed so hard. Juniper was practically crying, weeping from emotion and sweat and just a general sense of leaking.

"I know!" she agreed. She had really only gained maybe nine pounds. But on Juniper that was noticeable.

"Okay, now Karen made me promise I wouldn't tell you but," at this Juniper rolled her eyes, "she *told* me she thought you were knocked up. She said she could tell by how your hips were rocking when you walked."

"Really?" Juniper asked, embarrassed.

"Yeah, weird, huh?" said Bethy.

It was late November, and the sky wasn't even trying. The lights in the bar were intentionally dim, but Bethy just stopped and stared at Juniper in the saggy light. She stopped talking and looked at her hard. "Yeah, your face is fuller. And your face is just different. You're different." Bethy made the last statement with a hint of puzzlement and possibly a teeny twinge of jealously, which was not even vaguely what Juniper expected. Bethy scooted around to Juniper's side of the booth and put her arm around her.

"Junie, this is amazing, and I am so happy for you. You're gonna have a beautiful baby. Especially with all that thick blond hair," Bethy said. They laughed again. What a beautiful thing, Juniper thought, to have this secret and someone to share it with. Bethy paid her bill, and they gathered their things.

"You know I'm gonna tell everyone, right?" Bethy asked as she held the door for Juniper.

"Ugh, I know. Okay."

"Plus, I hate to break it to you, hon, but this secret is about to tell itself." Bethy poked at Juniper while looking her up and down, fully taking in the nine pounds.

"Ha-ha," said Juniper as they stood next to each other on the sidewalk in front of the bar. "Ha, frickin' ha," she said as she rested her very tired head on Bethy's shoulder.

Kinko's

A few weeks later, her belly had popped, and she smiled at the crescent moon of skin that showed between her t-shirt and stretch pants. She was waxing larger by day. It was with defiant pride or surprising joy that she didn't want to be modest. She kept pushing the limits of her t-shirts, bursting and stretching both the top and bottom of her extra-smalls.

All the pictures she had taken at Cora's were waiting in her camera. She had scrolled through them over and over, admiring and mulling. She had so many pictures, and they had morphed into a couple of really good ideas. She was trying to figure how the ideas could become a full concept and the separate faces could unite in purpose. She drove to the nearest Kinko's, thirty minutes away, with her camera's memory card. She entered the store and saw there was no line. The guy at the desk looked competent.

"So, I'm wanting to crop and resize these photos to 12x12, then just print them, matte, on photo paper," she said as she approached the counter in back. He nodded. "And are you also able to print the last four of them on some type of canvas, also 12x12?"

He was still nodding and said, "Sure, no problem."

Juniper slid over the memory card. Instead of looking at the card as he took it from her, he looked at her stomach, showing its small bump of roundness, which he could likely completely see from his taller vantage point. This attention was new enough for her, that she didn't quite know how to feel about it—exposed? Proud? Shy?

"Okay, great, about how long?" she asked.

"Tomorrow, okay?" He smiled at her with something like appreciation. And now she definitely felt a little exposed by her blossoming belly.

She was blushing. "Thanks, yeah. See you tomorrow." She bustled out of Kinko's empty-handed, aware of her possibly waddling behind.

* * *

The next day, he was there behind the counter, like he'd never left. He was eating a candy bar. He smiled again when she entered, crumpled his 3 Musketeers wrapper, swallowed, and said, "Hey there, how you doin'?" as he tossed the wrapper out. He had Juniper's order waiting and slid the prints out of the sleeves. "Do these look good? Like you wanted?" He set each of them out along the counter, like a dealer in some revealing, personal card game.

She loved how they looked. She was nodding and smiling and saying, "Oh, that one's good," and "maybe that's too dark," as he continued. Deftly, he stacked them back up and slid them into a large flat Kinko's envelope for her to take.

Next, he brought out the four canvas prints and lined those up on the counter. Even though she had narrowed these down to just four, she was sweating the cost. But that's how it was with art stuff. Cost be damned, credit card to the rescue. She was really excited to see the effect of the photos on canvas and told him so.

"So, would you like these canvas ones mounted on frames?"

"Well," she answered, "I would. But it's gonna be too much for me, I think."

"Naw, just hold on." He gathered them up gently and went into the back room. They were the only ones there.

"Can you hold on for like fifteen minutes?" He poked his head out from the back room to ask.

"Sure," she answered, wondering. The music was mingling with the smells of the place. Both seemed under a sheen of plastic.

He came out with a stack of four canvased portraits all wrapped on frames. "Okay, you're all set," he said. She was stunned at the stack, now three-dimensional, and how it seemed to bring her idea to life. Great-Grandma Carol's eyes right there on top, taking it all in.

"Wow," she said.

He likely saw her worry, because he added, "The frames are no extra."

She didn't know if it was her belly that spurred his generosity, but she was so grateful. "Wow, thank you so much," she said. "I really appreciate that."

"Seems like you have a pretty cool project going there," he explained. It felt like such a gift to Juniper.

Sharing Duties

"What's it like?" Jo-Jo asked. They were alone together often now that Jo-Jo agreed to share duties with Juniper. They were in their third or fourth room of the day. Juniper had been doing the bathroom but had to come into the room to rest on the corner chair. Juniper had caught Jo-Jo staring at her many times. But she knew she was up for public display, and it didn't matter. It was just curious to Juniper, Jo's fascination. She didn't know how to explain feeling huge to a large person.

"Well, I feel my heart all the time. It's working so hard. And my lungs feel like inefficient paper bags. And I feel a stretchy-pully weight down low in my belly. Like there's a lot going on down there, like a little factory of baby being built."

Jo-Jo was nodding. "It sucks you have to keep working like this."

"Well, I do just need to sit back for a minute, 'kay?" Juniper asked as she put her feet up. She could get a little reclined rest while she watched Jo-Jo shove the vacuum around. Of course, it would be nice to have someone feeding her grapes. Of course, she wished she didn't have to be a pregnant maid.

She periodically had to shimmy her butt around to get comfortable. And the zig-zaggy noise of the vacuum held off conversation. It was five or so precious minutes of sitting. She was in her second trimester, and her belly was a perfect round little ball. Everyone kept telling her how cute she was, except Jo-Jo, who now wound up the vacuum cord in silence and seemed generally more reverent and respectful of the miracle. She billowed the white sheets. It was Juniper's favorite part—when she got to watch someone else billow the sheets. Juniper's arm span was so short, she always felt her bed-making was clumsy and hummingbird-like. She scurried around the bed too much to be efficient. But Jo-Jo was big and billowy herself, and Juniper felt a satisfaction at all the snip-snap flups. She closed her eyes as Jo finished the pillows and felt like she was being taken care of somehow. While she was still, the weight in her belly seemed to bubble. Like an effervescence from within, she felt little popping bubbles in her stomach.

"Jo-Jo!" Juniper said. "Jo-Jo! Stop!" Jo stopped her business and looked at Juniper for explanation. Juniper took a slow gasp in. "It's my baby. My baby kicked!" Jo-Jo walked over to Juniper and sat down on the bed. "There, again!" Juniper had her belly in her hands, but it was something on the inside. She could only feel it from inside. A moat of time surrounded Juniper, isolating that moment. No tomorrow or yesterday. Juniper and her baby, and Jo-Jo representing the rest of the world. Life.

It was Jo-Jo who cried. Not just a tear, but full-on crying. "I'm just so amazed. I'm just so blown away, Juniper. I mean, wow, there's someone in there." Juniper nodded with a maternal serenity, and she thought of her baby as a person. A sweet, soft person that would define and redefine love.

* * *

Juniper was pretty sure that Jo-Jo marched right out of work that day and over to Gary's house. He had come home to rest for a couple months. They were letting him gain some strength after his surgery, before his chemo. Well, it seemed that Jo-Jo had gone into his house to steal what she could. To steal some of his precious vitality for her own. Juniper did not know if that was fair. Maybe she was giving him some of her own strength and vitality with her womanly intent. But Juniper had thought about it a lot. Because it wasn't long before Jo-Jo was also knocked up, ultimately just a trimester behind Juniper.

Juniper would always remember that day feeling her baby kick for the first time, and Jo-Jo's awe. Jo-Jo must have been chased by time that day. It must have chased her out of that hotel room into Gary's home to steal his seeds, like a modern fairy tale. Thirty-some-odd years behind her pushing her to a man who saw her beauty, a man that could give her something forever, a baby. Jo-Jo must have wanted to jump into Juniper's moat of timelessness before it was too late.

Train

Cora came with Juniper to her appointments. This was her five-month ultrasound. She always got so excited and nervous for the baby's heartbeat. It was a chugging train, fast, and going to last a hundred years without cease. Cora was sitting in the father seat, and Juniper could always tell when she was nervous, because she hugged her big purse in her lap. She actually held on to it with a grip like a football. They were waiting for the ultrasound person.

"Ma, don't be nervous," Juniper said. "It's me that's going through this."

"You're kidding me right now. It's not just you. This is *us*, Juniper. This is my grandbaby. Our family." Cora seemed sweaty with nerves. She crossed her leg and bounced it all over the place.

"Ma! Take a breath."

"I know, I know. Sorry." Cora crossed and bounced her other leg, and Juniper noticed her acid wash jeans with the knee holes. It was for sure that roles got mixed up in their family. Like for instance, right then, Juniper felt more parent-ish, trying to calm Cora down. But how weird, because she was there as a new parent herself. Old parent, new parent, old child, new child. And they missed Grandma/Mom/Jezebel. It was fated then. What passed over the next while as the technician spread the jelly and waved the magic wand, squishing sounds. The darkened room in anticipation.

"Do you wanna know the sex?" the tech asked. Her nails were outrageous works of yellow and gold, studded with fake diamonds. Juniper watched the tech's hands buzzing around her belly like bees. She had been clicking down measurements. Every time she typed, it was loud with those yellow gold clackers. And Juniper's mind buzzed with wonder, worry, and unsureness.

"Juniper!" said Cora. "We want to know, don't we?" Juniper was creating an awkward gap of silence in the room. She didn't know if she wanted to know. But then she did. Who was this baby?

"Yeah," said Juniper. The tech squished around some more, and click. Click. What looked like Polaroids were coming out of a printer thing. The tech turned the computer screen to face Juniper and Cora, and the whole world fell away as Juniper saw her baby's big head. The fuzzy black-and-white image of a belly and arms. Arms! Her baby's arms and little finger bud things. And the legs, they were moving, kicking! She felt the bubbles inside of her synchronized with what she saw on the screen, kick, kick, kick. At this, Juniper and Cora laughed.

"She's a feisty thing, of course!" Cora exclaimed.

"You don't know it's a 'she,'" said Juniper. There was so much joy in the small, dark room. The tech ticked her pointer finger at the screen, clicking somewhere on the baby's middle.

"Your mom is right. You're baby's a girl." And with that confirmation, fate was satisfied.

"Oh! Oh!" said Cora.

"She looks healthy. I'll let the doctor come in and talk to you." Juniper wanted to grab her arm to thank her for everything. But that's not how it was. The bees quietly buzzed out of the room.

"Thank you," Juniper said to her as she left.

"Sure hon, congratulations." The tech turned around and smiled at her before shutting the door.

Urges

So this was the next part where everything was real, and she would be buying miniature clothes. Her mind continued to alter, along with her body. She remembered so many of her dreams that she was convinced she was simply dreaming more often. And her dreams were nuts. Rampant sex, underwater sex, immaculate sex (which only made sense in the dream—it was an intention by two people to have sex—which in her dream was the culmination of the sex act itself). She was so full, and all the lines in her body were continuing to unstraighten. Her vision was becoming wavy too. Lack of focus, she thought. She dropped things. More lack of focus.

When she passed an angled three-way mirror near the Target fitting rooms, she stopped. She was not a stop-and-looker, but now it was voyeuristic, for this certainly could not be her body. Seven months pregnant, she could turn her head and see her ass in that mirror, larger, flatter, and frankly unbelievable. It was shocking, and she looked up to see if anyone was paying attention, and when she was alone enough (Bethy was looking at shirts), she took both her hands and tried to wrap them around her left thigh. She could not connect her middle fingers, which she used to be able to do. She pictured the girl that turns into a blueberry in *Charlie and the Chocolate Factory*. Juniper had never asked this question in her life, but as

104

Bethy walked up with her armload of shirts, she knew that there was no one who would accept the question more sincerely.

"Bethy, do I look fat?"

Bethy snorted. "That's hardly a fair question, June," she said as she riffled through the bras next to the changing rooms. "I mean, you've defined the word 'lean' since I've known you. Slender, twiggy, et cetera."

Juniper stared at her, waiting. "But?"

"Butt!" Bethy snorted again. Juniper laughed too.

"Shut up!"

"*But*," Bethy continued, "you're somehow skinnier than me still, I think. But for you, you're huge. You have blossomed, girlfriend, and you have curves. Now, look at me, 'cause this part is important." She waited for Juniper's eyes. "You're beautiful like this. It's changed you, and it's amazing, and you are beautiful." It was like when the doctor told Juniper that the baby was healthy. Hearing she was beautiful sunk in slowly and deeply. But also, hearing she had changed pelted her with its truth. She wanted to ask how she had changed, besides the obvious. But then, no. She wanted to figure it out herself. She *had* changed. No doubt that change wasn't finished yet, either.

At Target, the aisles of baby things were there to create very strong consumer urges, and Juniper stepped down the first aisle with skepticism. The cuteness felt like stitches of needle and thread going in and out of her being. Touch the cute things. Squeeze. Pick up the cute things, they smell like puffy clouds of lovely love. Juniper was suspicious, though. This wasn't real. She could hear snippets of Bethy squealing all up and down the aisles, skittering from one thing to another, rubbing the soft, fuzzy stuff. What was real was the unknown. Waiting was real. Being in between one reality and another was real. And the secret blossoming love, of course, was real, creating a pain of grasping, protective needing. A longing to touch and hold.

She stopped on one of the random red squares in the sea of off-white linoleum, inhaled the store scents, and let herself find the fabrics that had nailed baby pastels. If done correctly, it could be innocent and joyful, and not cloying. She stood on her square and pondered wants versus needs. What would her baby *need?*

Juniper bought some pink and purple onesies. She bought a tiny aqua jumper that had buttons made of bunny heads. She was skeptical, but she wasn't immune.

* * *

Juniper leaned into her door for the forty-five-minute ride home. She was sleepy but kept herself awake enough to daydream. Her night dreams were indicative of some wack ideas. But recently it was like her subconscious had been invited to the table. She had random memories from childhood that played out as they drove through hallways of trees, then flats that invited you to find the horizon. A new windmill looked modern with its whiteness slashing past. It reminded her of making "God's eyes" out of popsicle sticks at Sunday school with her second cousin Sherry. They had woven in and out with rainbow yarn. She must have been five and hadn't seen Sherry since that day.

She had new fears of irrelevant things. For example, she worried about choking on cotton balls. What the hell was that? She also worried about her feet getting bigger, which was probably a legit concern. And she worried about liking the taste of baby food, which shouldn't matter, right? She sometimes, rarely, remembered Chicago. But when she did, it was fantastical. The colors were luscious, unlike the reality of southern Michigan, which truly washed everything in shades of gray. It was not meant as a slam on her home place. The observation was still astonishingly true, a lifetime later, how the grays seemed to emanate from everything. Anytime she thought she could nail down the taste of the grayness, the fresh air or car fumes would lace her impression, washing it away like a wave.

But Chicago. She closed her eyes to ease the transport. There the weather seemed so sliced beautifully into a pie of seasons (she was always hungry). Uncomfortable Christmassy sleet. Light green yellow strident spring breezes, still a little uncomfortable, but full of hope. Smelly summer hot stickiness with wishes to be somewhere cool and swimming. And magazine fall. Plaid wool leafy perfume, pipe smoke, new fabric, new paints and pencils, and unwritten paper. Her first month of school, she had walked everywhere, saying hello to the city that was bejeweled with new color, culture, and food. Architecture replaced pole barns and ranch houses and trailers. On the side of a building erected with cinnabar-colored bricks, a low corner had caught her eye. On the bottom of this glorious building was a chunk of bricks that had gotten knocked out. The corner had been replaced with blue, yellow, red, white, and clear Legos. The spot was no more than a foot or so wide, but the Legos went around the corner and were perfectly integrated into the structure. It was a little un-reality and likely a comment on nothing. Someone had actually glued them in somehow. It was art for art's sake, primary joy. All those things felt like a beaded necklace of memories that looped around her, as real as if she had bought it at Goodwill. She opened her eyes just as Bethy tipped them over the gravel threshold to her trailer.

After a quick nap on her couch, she turned on all the lights in her house then went to the back room. She stood for a while looking at Gary's lungs and decided that multimedia would be okay. She needed to finish. She was going to create some texture for the lesions, like little dust bunny ghosts of life-destruction. She was using pastels to create a glow of health around the other lung. He was fading in real life and coming into focus here in a back room of Jezebel's trailer.

She had been sketching more. She'd draw at breakfast, eating toast clumsily with her left hand while she scratched an idea out on paper. She'd rush to her back room after a day of work to experiment with etching out a thought that had come to her while putting towels in the washer or wiping down sinks. Juniper just thought she had her head down, working. Working at what didn't matter to make money for what did. She was using every scrap of paper and every stub of pencil she had left. She found herself considering colors that weren't her first choice in order to make use of her dwindling supplies. Supplies cost so much money. She had to ration.

In Chicago, during her senior year, she had actually begun her application to the graduate program in fine arts. She had always thought about staying. Her only close girlfriend, Kat, had gotten into the ceramics studio for her masters with an offer of an assistantship. It seemed Kat's destiny was preordained, since she was uniformly admired by students and faculty alike, hip, beautiful, and as calm and curvy as the programmatic pots she threw. They'd even talked about getting an apartment together.

But before Juniper got too far, she had struck up a conversation about the graduate program with Professor Quinlan, her favorite, the one she thought she could trust. She knew she'd need several letters of recommendation and wanted to gauge his reaction. She felt like she could confide in him.

"What do you think about the grad program here?" she asked him one day after class. He was zipping up his laptop, gathering his coat, and clearing the crinkly wrappers off his desk. Trader Joe's cereal bars and Odwalla bars had likely been gulped untasted. It was funny what the mind clung to with a bad memory. He was so nice to her, always. And he stopped what he was doing. She saw his curly gray hair, and he shoved up his glasses with his big hand that always looked too sausagey to hold a brush with such finesse. She remembered the line defining his bifocals.

"What are you thinking, Juniper? About next year?"

"Yeah, maybe," she said. She stumbled a bit in her response. Fact of the matter was, she just wasn't confident. There was something about her work that was decidedly "uncool." There was a uniformly positive response to art that was new and trendy, and Juniper hated that. It was true, all the students liked to be simultaneously surprised by a novel idea and pissed that they themselves hadn't thought of it first.

But Juniper loved realism. She didn't *want* to love realism. She knew she had an edginess in what she chose to depict; she wasn't all cityscapes and portraits. But she wasn't cool, like some of the other students. And she felt like she was one of the masses, head down, working and learning. She knew she hadn't really stood out in her four years there.

"Well, that could be good," he said. "But it's pretty late in the year, and the applications have flooded in. You should see this one kid we're getting from Japan, holy shit. Woo, the talent." He exhaled loudly, puffing out his cheeks and shaking his head to show just how much talent. "If you were thinking of money, we've given most of the scholarships out by this point."

He knew a little of her situation and that she didn't come from Lincoln Park or anything. But that wasn't totally uncommon. She wasn't special in her need. But his lack of enthusiasm struck her like a brick. She wanted some twinkle of reassurance that she was good enough even to get into the grad program. But she would never know if it was his preoccupation with packing up, or if he had somewhere to be, or if there was nothing meant at all by his answer. His lack of enthusiasm struck her hard enough that she never got up. She never finished the application. She was ashamed at her lack of resilience.

Kat had pushed. "Come on, Juniper. Let's get a place together. You can wait tables or whatever."

"But I'm not even going to be in school with you guys." "You guys" had consisted of what seemed like all of Juniper's friends and acquaintances.

"You can try again next year," Kat said.

But Juniper's shame grew like a fungus in a Petri dish. She almost lashed out at Kat during their last conversation about school. "I clearly suck and don't belong here with you guys," she had said.

But Kat called her out. "Juniper! You didn't even apply!"

"How could I, after Quinlan practically shot me down?"

She could tell that was when the rift happened. Kat didn't think she was being reasonable. Kat knew the truth about what Quinlan said—virtually nothing. Certainly not enough to count as a rejection. Kat wouldn't heap Juniper with praise. She didn't believe in that. As friends, they had been mutually supportive of each other's work. And Juniper actually believed that Kat wouldn't have been her friend if she didn't admire a lot about what she was creating. Kat didn't separate the art from the artist. But she smelled Juniper's desperation and neediness and stepped back. Kat couldn't heap the praise high enough for Juniper to stand on.

Juniper couldn't face the next year as a self-declared outcast. She had to move away. Honestly, being home in Gobles had likely allowed her to open up. Maybe time had allowed her to unclench and not feel like she had to protect her delicate ego. It had taken over a year, but here she was, creating again. And all that doubt she had been nursing, doubt about whether she even loved it enough, could fall away. Beneath it all, she was still driven to create, and that part of her identity stayed intact. In fact, away from any scrutiny but her own, she continued to open up. Her head wasn't really down and focused. It was more up. Eyes wide, keen. Seeing things, absorbing things, letting feelings roll through her.

She was seeing the mundane and domestic world through a lens of what else it could be, what more it could mean. The prints and canvas photos of the Kowalski women were also staring at her in wait. She saw the potential ideas just stacking up. Her life was pretty much stacked up with possibility.

Wall Mart

She waited for Bethy after work outside near Bethy's car. It was early spring, and like ripping a Band-Aid off cold. She leaned against the stucco wall and pulled a pencil out of her back pocket. Even her maternity jeans with the big elastic band had pockets in the back. The wall was so blank and off-white. She turned around and just scratched it with the gray, back and forth, etching, following the splattery lines of the gloppy dried cement until a face appeared. She loved to watch her subconscious doodle out the end of a pencil. Attached to the face that was becoming sad was an arm pointing. She had just finished the grooves around the knuckles on a hand when Bethy popped around the corner.

"Sorry to make you wait." Bethy was juggling her purse while putting on her coat. "Hey, what are you doing?"

"Nothing, I didn't mean to make it so big." In the rippled eggshell there was now a hand pointing and a seeking face right at eye level.

Bethy said, "Hm. That's good," and got into her car. Juniper's bike was locked in the tin shed.

Bethy dropped her off at Walmart for dinner with Cora. Walmart had felt like a second home in a way that comforted and disturbed Juniper. Because of her small family, it likely broadened her sense of being connected to folks in town. The characters were important.

People who knew her. People she knew through a depth of time. People who had quirks that defined them, maybe acquired through a tough life more than a genetic tic. Others' quirks stood out so obviously to her. She wondered what characteristics in her life were the result of more than genetics. Or the quirks she exhibited that everyone quietly noticed.

The Walmart employees seemed to form a display board of off-kilter behavior. Some folks had a volume control that was set too high, like Mrs. Dee. Juniper was never sure if they were hard of hearing or just not used to being heard. Some folks stood too close and talked right up into your face. Some exhibited a delicate anger and flinched at an assumed slight, like James with the OCD. There was often a real undercurrent of anger in these types of places, Juniper felt. People were just angrier here than Chicago. They were angry they'd lost their job. Or that their job was crappy. They were angry they didn't quite make it to college because no one helped them. And defensive as all hell. Not everyone, and not all the time, but there was an undercurrent of indignance and a culture of being sure to perceive normal things as an affront. It was truly almost like a psychological epidemic in these parts.

Of course, with all of these observations, the folks that seemed "normal" stood out in the oddest way of all. Their very normalcy begged the questions about why they were there in the first place. Something must've gone wrong. Something not obvious in their congenial, intelligent ways.

Were these even two different kinds of people? Juniper wasn't sure if she was connecting dots or just adding some pointillism to her impressions. But parallels lined up in her mind. For instance, she had been silenced by her own sense of what was right, or fear, or utter confusion. She had not spoken up about something as monumental as a new life that had been created. The father of this baby girl did not know he was. Every once in a while Cora would ask, gently, "June, what's up with baby daddy?" Just to open up the conversation. But as everyone knew, Juniper could be infuriating with her silence, and sometimes she would just not answer. Cora was not a pushy person, so the question scurried into a corner under the couch.

Bethy had asked her early on, "What did he say when you told him? Is he coming back? Is he going to leave his wife?" Juniper just shook her head. Most of the time she could put the thought away in a secret compartment. She was not at peace with her decision. She thought of Ricky quoting Rush in a high falsetto, singing about how not choosing to decide means you still have made a choice.

So she had been silenced. And something was going to come out, 'cause that's how these things worked. Balance. So she had to let her subconscious rise up to draw a finger pointing over to Side Bar, in defiant remembrance of a love that should have been. A love that wasn't. It wasn't going to exist as she had wished it might, but it rose up in her belly as a life of its own.

"Juniper, we need to talk about your job and stuff," said Cora over the Formica. "I mean, how are you doing it? Aren't you exhausted?"

Juniper had been going to Walmart or Cora's after her shift more and more. She'd been going to Cora. Her mom was now cooking for her multiple times a week while she lay sideways on the couch or napped in her old bed.

"I forgot to tell you, Manny said I could start doing some admin stuff. I'm going to cover the front desk for a while. Me and Jo-Jo both, I guess." Jo-Jo was already in her second trimester, bigger than ever, and not willing to clean at all anymore. "The other girls are going to pick up extra shifts. Karen wants the money. Doug is doing some of Gary's stuff. We're all just swapping roles. Poor Manny," Juniper said.

"Yeah," said Cora, "but what about when the baby comes?"

Juniper did realize that was an issue. How long she would need off of work. Her due date was early May, and she was constantly counting months. How long she had left plus how much money she would make equaled not enough. It was easy to be good at this kind of math when the answer was always the same.

"I don't know about when the baby comes," Juniper said.

"Yeah, well. That's why I'm bringin' it up."

Juniper sat down heavily. These conversations made her more tired than climbing the back stairs at work.

"June, you're gonna need time off. That means no income. We gotta figure this out. My pay ain't gonna cover the three of us." Cora was fittingly sitting at the Subway table surrounded by ads and coupons, snipping deals. "It's likely you're gonna have to go on WIC." Juniper closed her eyes against the thought. "Or you could...call the father," Cora said. "He has to give you money."

Juniper got a little flamed up at that. "I'm *not* calling him. It's not going to happen. No."

Cora set down the scissors and squinted at Juniper, like she did when she had almost figured something out, when she was so close she could almost catch Juniper in a lie or whatever it was.

"Okay," said Cora. "But why not? Just tell me, why not?"

Juniper let out a little groan. "He was a nice guy. He was. *Is*, I'm sure." She fiddled with the glossy ad packet from Babies R Us. They didn't even have a Babies R Us anywhere near them. "But he's married." She dropped it like a dirty sock.

"Yep. Okay, I figured somethin' like that." Cora jumped on it. "Okay, well." Her gears were turning. "Wait. Does he live in town?" She leaned into the table and whispered, "Shit, June, please tell me I do not know this guy."

"No, you don't know him," Juniper assured her, not totally one hundred percent sure but figuring it was a better answer.

"Okay then. You tell me if you change your mind, because here we go, doing things the hard way. *Again*."

* * *

Juniper picked up a case of doll-sized diapers before she left. Little baby Mickey and Minnie Mouses would be stamped all over her baby-to-be's butt. What a racket. She had never bought a case of anything in her life. There was something about babies and consumerism that was getting to Juniper. She had to buy stuff, she had to have stuff. Her baby needed baby things, but she wasn't sure her baby would need a mesh baggie to put food in so she could chew it while she was teething. Or shoes. An infant couldn't possibly need shoes? Cora had helped her buy a crib at the beloved Goodwill, along with some other "hold-the-baby" devices: rockers, shakers, wigglers. But she just wanted to hold her girl in her arms. Eight months was real. Baby girl rolled around. Her hands seemed to think Juniper's ribs were monkey bars she tried to grasp, then frustrated, kick. Feisty little sweetheart.

Once Juniper was home, all of her subliminal simmering led to an idea that was weird, but she did it anyway. She tore into a bag of diapers and carefully pulled out just one. So little, with a baby powder scent certainly manufactured chemically wafting out of the plastic bag. She actually thought it was so adorable, the sweet tiny diaper. She held it and opened it, listening to the crinkling. The powder scent overtook her living room. She opened the tapes. She didn't want to waste one; they cost money, but she began to fill the diaper with things. A garlic peeler, a chip clip, a collapsible cup, a free sample of scented baby lotion, all things united in their extraneousness.

The next time she was in Walmart, she took the filled diaper out of her cart and set it conspicuously on a shelf, open and offering its criticisms. On the absorbent part she had written: "Don't buy what you don't need."

What the hell was happening to her? She couldn't just think it, she had to say it? She pushed the shopping cart down the aisle, leaving the diaper offering its stuff, hoping this new need to share was a phase that would pass when the baby came. But there was something new in how she felt about her family, about the men in her past, that was on her mind lately. She spent her whole life not talking about it, not speaking up. She wasn't sure what it would mean to start now.

Swing Low

She told Bethy about her shopping expeditions while they were on break at work. Bethy had listened as she was eating. But she stopped chewing while Juniper explained how it was going to be impossible to pick a stroller when there were fifty gazillion choices, each one more expensive than the last.

"Geez. This baby stuff is more complicated than I realized," Bethy said.

"I just keep asking myself, 'What's this baby gonna *need?*'"

Bethy nodded.

"Not what do I want. But *need.* And it still amounts to more stuff than I can afford. I'm a little freaked out, to be honest."

They were in the lobby of Vacation Express, Juniper behind the desk to answer phones, Bethy leaning against the counter. The automatic doors were opening and closing, and people were coming in with rolly suitcases.

"Hey. I think I'm a shitty friend," said Bethy.

"What? Don't be ridiculous," said Juniper.

"Yeah, we don't know how to do this baby thing, do we? You need a shower!"

"Oh," said Juniper. "That didn't occur to me. Or my mom either, apparently."

"No, I don't think your mom is supposed to do it. Lemme ask *my* mom."

* * *

Bethy's mom, Mary Ann, couldn't wait to open up her lovely raised ranch to all the ladies they knew. There were pink balloons and a chocolate Oreo pie, proud with Cool Whip. Mary Ann presented Juniper with a wobbly slice the second she walked in. Mary Ann knew what was up. She clearly remembered how it was to be pregnant. Karen and Jo-Jo were there. Mrs. Dee and a couple more ladies from Walmart. Two of Cora's cousins and their daughters had driven down from Muskegon. Mary Ann had two of her church ladies there helping out. Juniper held her chocolate-smeared plate printed with pink baby rattles and her pink fork and teddy bear napkin because they were so sweet. She didn't want to set them down, even though she was finished.

And then Mary Ann said, "Juniper, would you like another slice of Oreo pie? You must be hungry." She winked. And Juniper almost cried for real.

"Really? I can do that?" Juniper asked both sheepishly and with lusty hunger. Mary Ann laughed while handing her a new plate filled with the whipped goodness.

"Oh my god, thank you," said Juniper.

Cora came inside after a needed cigarette in the car. "Thanks so much for this Mary Ann. You didn't have to do all this." Cora too was not used to being given things, let alone in excess.

They played games and drank some lemonade punch concoction. They all sat around Juniper as she opened one present after another. A car seat, fuzzy blankets, stuffed sheep and duckies, packs and packs of diapers, and pretty mini-dresses with ruffle butts. More onesies and a baby book to mark milestones, and an overly generous wind-up swing that played lullabies. Juniper was moved at the outpouring. She just then figured out why they were called showers. She didn't want to love the stuff, but at that moment—she loved the stuff. And although Bethy was beside her writing down all the gifts, Juniper would remember who gave her what for years to come. She was overwhelmed at the *things* that were entering her life. And at that moment it was gratefulness that rose to the top. Presents were being loaded into Cora's car, and Juniper went over to Mary Ann once more.

"Thank you so much. I don't want to cry, sorry," Juniper said as she started to cry, "but this means so much to me." She leaned over herself and gave Mary Ann a hug.

"Oh, sweetie, I love this kind of stuff. And you're a great friend to Bethy here. We're so happy to do this!"

Juniper laughed inside at the chipper talk, like mother, like daughter. She hugged Bethy too. As they pulled out of the driveway, Juniper's eyes rested on the nice shrubs and black shutters and Bethy's lacy curtains.

* * *

Besides the gifts and food, the thing Juniper was most grateful for, the thing that made Mary Ann the most amazing hostess ever, was that no one asked. Not a single church lady mentioned. No work friend of Cora's, or cousin, asked about "the father." She could have cried with joy and relief at this generous kindness. This benevolence would linger in her heart.

It was not Kirk's fault he didn't know about the baby. But it was his fault he was married when she was created. It took Juniper a while to realize that he wasn't totally an innocent bystander. It was neither of their fault that the birth control failed. But he shouldn't have chanced becoming a father when he was not free to become a father. Juniper did sometimes think she wasn't fair in not giving him any choice or awareness. But there was a worse part—she had an inkling that the fact that her own father had not been around had shaded her decision not to invite Kirk into their lives. Her grandpa had deeply and painfully betrayed the women in their family by physically hurting them. Her father had really done the same by hurting them with his absence. So the basis of Juniper's decision was suspect—even to her.

She was recreating the family pattern. Did people do that? Did smart people recreate the discomfort they were used to? She could have reached out to Kirk sooner and more. She could have insisted. He could be there at her trailer, waiting to load the generosity out of her car, into their home. But he wasn't the good man she wanted to be with, because he wasn't good enough. She realized she wanted a great man. And this kind of great had nothing to do with accomplishment and everything to do with the choices of showing up.

Greatness. She started crying, feeling like she was mourning something not meant for her. Poor Juniper. Why was she crying now, after the nice party? It was probably hormones. Just some hormones and outrage.

"Oh, June, hey. Don't cry."

Juniper was struck at the image of Cora's head barely above the top of the wheel.

"Where are they!" Juniper was getting mad, then she was mad that she was mad on her beautiful day. Cora was listening, so Juniper went on. "Why aren't they doing their part! Stupid assholes." She punctuated the thought, then felt like she shouldn't talk like that with a baby in her belly.

"Hon, we didn't invite them." The car got quiet with Michigan and what Cora said. You couldn't not see it, out all the windows, making sure you remembered that the sun wasn't going to come out.

Since the get-go, Cora and Jezebel had been fueling her tank with stoicism about things that were done that hurt them. Things by people, yeah. But also things by this sucking place. Dammit, why did it have to be so hard. Images of pinkness and fuzziness—joy from the day—laced through these thoughts, which felt like they were burning her. They had made it clear that she should just get over herself all those times when she was upset about her dad. And *they* were not just Mom and Grandma. *They* were the other kids at school dealing with the same thing. They were her teachers, the grandmas pushing carts at IGA.

And the other "they," the people on TV isolating themselves from her, and the people keeping wages down, her professors at school, and people not valuing the factories that kept folks producing. It was like Juniper and her people had been gerrymandered. She simultaneously scoffed at the thought and patted herself on the back for remembering that high-school word of jiggering things to get what you want and keeping the power of certain folks contained.

Cora rolled up onto Juniper's gravel drive, the Pop Rocks of home. She wasn't going anywhere now. Juniper had dried her tears. Cora let her be and began to haul stuff. With one hand, Juniper held the storm door, with the other hand, she held her achy hip. She was thinking about men and blame and percentages.

She reached back into an imagined time and place when her dad was a boy. He was a product of the same environment as Cora. So at what age was he innocent, and what became his age of reason, his age of blame? Okay, she was focusing on her dad maybe a little too much here. He wasn't Kirk, and Kirk's absence was her own fault.

So at what age was *she* innocent, and what was her age of reason?

When she was eleven, Juniper had a choir concert at school. It was an evening concert, and it must have been spring, because the trees were swaying and bright green, like baby membranes that the light could still penetrate. The evening was exciting with pinkness and a secret she had. Mom and Grandma were both there with shiny purses, clasped with brassy ball hooks. Juniper begged her mom to French braid her hair. Her outfit was lavender. Juniper was sucked down fully into the memory, and the details popped out, one by one. She had on white tights, which were a bit little girlish, but she felt so pretty, she didn't care.

Juniper remembered warming up with the group in the bright classroom and Mrs. Welch's arms swooping in and out. Juniper's throat was clean and cleared from the bubbles of Pepsi she'd had at dinner. The fluorescent lights poured down on their shiny braids and bows. The thought of being nervous was unknown, and her sole intention was to radiate their songs, and especially her solo. She thought she would outstretch her hands and give the music to everyone in the audience, and surprise her mom and grandma, who would be so proud.

Mrs. Welch guided them down the hall to the back door of the stage. Juniper was giddy and kept bumping into her friend Jessica and giggling, trying to share the excitement.

But Jessica was more mature. "Junie, stop!" she remembered her scolding. They stepped up onto the risers, Juniper so small she was in the front row where everyone could see her dress. She remembered searching for her mom and grandma while Mrs. Welch was talking, trying to find their faces in the dark. She could see Grandma's glasses with their particular oval shape and Mom's goldy hair that always reminded Juniper of guitar strings. Those things glinted.

She remembered singing everything with clear diction, just like Mrs. Welch had taught them. The audience flashed and clapped. It was finally her turn to shine, and she stepped down off the riser, next to Mrs. Welch on the piano. The microphone had been lowered to just her height. And the choir began with their swing lows, then they would fall away for her. Her hand went up to shade her eyes in gesture as she sang, "I looked over Jordan and what did I see." She peered over Jordan, to the back of the auditorium, and saw the daddy men in the back, Jessica's daddy with a video camera. "A band of angels coming after me," she sang louder than she should, but she felt the angels coming. And together with the chorus for the next verse, they sang, and she had a chance to inhale and exhale the sounds and her surroundings. The daddy men watched their girls, and she saw a man who suddenly looked familiar. Her voice got quieter like a spun sugar thread. "Well, I'm sometimes up and I'm sometimes down, *comin' for to carry me home.*" Then she started to cry, because she saw that man in back with his slightness and reddish hair and black t-shirt. She saw his dark eyes glinting right at her, glaring back at him with a despondency she didn't understand. She sang-yelled the last verse with the choir: "Swing low, sweet chariot, comin' for to carry me home! Well now they're coming for to carry me home!"

It wasn't the last song, but through the rain shower of clapping, she fled offstage. Her tears were streaming because that man looked just like the man in Grandma's photo album. A man with her on her second birthday. And plus that man had waved at her. While everyone was clapping, he was waving. He knew her, and she cried a rageful sadness at this daddy man in the back of the auditorium who ruined everything she had to give that evening. He ruined the surprise that she had for Mom and Grandma—her big solo. He ruined everything by not showing up until then.

They found Juniper in the field behind the school, up in a crabapple tree. Her white tights had a ladder snag. Dirt mixed in with her tear tracks. Her mom explained that they thought it would be okay to let him come. He wanted to see her. They thought she would be *happy* to see him, both Grandma and Mom pleaded.

"Happy to see who?" she yelled in the dark at the two of them. "I don't know that guy!"

"Honey—" Her mom reached up to help her down from the tree.

"No!" Juniper was still yelling. "No!" she yelled again as she threw off her mom's hand and turned to jump, probably ten feet down from the tree, into the weeds. She thought she might trample a garter snake, so she ran out of the field quickly to the edge of her school's playground. She waited in the mowed grass until her mom and grandma made their way over to her so she could yell one last time.

"*He is too late!*" There was nothing more to be said. They all nodded at that one, collectively, in the dark, in unison. Yep. He was too late.

Task

The next time she went back to Walmart, it was to visit the outdoor section. She had ridden with Cora to work and was going to hang out and eat Subway then go home for a while and drive her mom's car back to get her at the end of the dinner shift. The Outdoor department was celebratory with displays of seeds, plastic fencing, and colorful pots. She wandered the aisles heavy with the smell of mulch. She knew she was close to what she was looking for when she saw sandbags and pavers. She was disturbed by what she was looking for. And there was a sadness defining this particular shopping trip.

She came upon an array of natural-looking paving stones, some like granite, some rectangular. It didn't have to be too large, just believable. She found a realistic slab and lifted it, shimmied it, really, into the bottom of her cart. The kid checking her out leaned over to scan the little stupid sticker on the single slab. He didn't ask why she had just one. It wasn't that heavy, but he didn't even offer to help her load it into her car either, so she eased it, end over end, up into the trunk.

After an early dinner with Cora, she drove back to her trailer. She carefully hefted the slab back out of the trunk and laid it on her front step. She went in to find some tools. She found a flathead screwdriver and a couple of paint scrapers that might work. Then some pencils, a metal T-square, some sandpaper. Outside, she got to work, standing next to the stair with the slab horizontal, facing her. First she drew guidelines and then started shaping her letters. It took a few experiments to see what would work best. She scraped. She tapped the screwdriver with a hammer like a makeshift chisel. She did have some luck kind of scraping out the lines, drawing and scraping simultaneously with a sharp paint scraper. It was helpful that the stone-like material was actually synthetic. She worked for an hour before she needed some water. Then she went straight to her bed and set the alarm for eight, an hour before her mom's shift ended. She fell asleep thinking, *I've got to focus on getting the baby's room together. I have to pick a name. I have to store my paintings so there is room for the crib.*

But when she woke up, she went straight back outside to gather her things in the dark. Her sadness was morphing into something edgier as the project emerged. She was energized. She was excising a hurt. She turned on her weak porch light, and the shadows that sank into each letter she had completed were sinister and perfect. She added just a hint of black paint to clarify the letters. Then she felt a little guilty. But she wasn't about to stop. The black was a smoky, morphing feeling. She hated to name anger. It was never a comfortable feeling for her.

The next day, she chiseled before and after work. Some of the letters were a little uneven, and the spacing wasn't as exact as it could be. But it was clear and good. Clear and right. She did not mean to be vindictive or slanderous, but she did want to voice this wrong that defined her life.

When it was finished, she backed her car up to her porch and carefully loaded the slab into the trunk again. She drove out to Gobles Cemetery, where her great-grandparents were buried. And her great uncle Fredrick too (their son, and her Grandma's brother, childless, unmarried and died at the age of forty-three). And Grandma. Jezebel Irene Kowalski, 1940–2003. Even after she had left Grandpa, she kept his last name, because Cora still had it. And Juniper.

She stopped the car next to her family's plot and rolled down the windows. She wanted to sit and think for just a moment before she got out of the car. The windows were the crank kind. This old car was Grandma's, after all, and it had lasted longer than Juniper had been alive. She popped the trunk and tilted the slab onto the rubber edge. She slowly eased it to the ground. She grabbed the trowel she had brought and stabbed it into the dirt, meeting resistance, popping through grassy roots, barely being slowed by the small stones and their grating sounds. The slab wouldn't fit at first, so she'd have to dig a wider trench. But this was a mission, and it was laden with a need to say what she came to say. She turned the trowel so she was piercing the ground with an overhand stab and that gave her the force she needed. The aggression of that movement allowed the tears to come.

She slid the slab back over and tilted it into place. The exertion or sobbing were giving her cramps, so she slowed down. She pushed the dirt back and patted it down, nestling the stone tightly. It was secured by at least eight inches of dirt. It stood on its own. She wiped her face with the back of her arm. She wiped her eyes.

The evening was reaching out by then. It was a battleship gray and overcast, a little too cold to be comfortable, as typical as Michigan could be. The stone seemed to sit obediently straight and proud with its hand-scraped message:

HERE LIES THE FATHER
THAT COULD HAVE BEEN
(AS GOOD AS DEAD)

Having Her

Juniper had done the tasks of heart and mind in preparing for her baby. She was finally ready, and she showed up at work to pick up her last check for a few months. Manny came around the front desk and gave her a big hug and a wrapped present.

"I should have given this to you when you had your shower," he said sweetly. "We're going to miss you, Juniper doll."

"Thank you for the gift." Juniper reached out. "But Manny, I'm only gonna be gone for a few months."

"I know, but you're going to be a different person when you come back. *If* you come back."

"You know I'm coming back. I'm going to need to work. And I will *not* be a different person."

"Alright, alright. Bring baby in so we can see her, okay?"

"I will." She was teary again. She turned around and waved before she moved through the front doors.

It was time to wait. She went home to her trailer and saw the piles of stuff everywhere. The large room was overflowing with mess, but Gary's lungs perched on the easel. They were nearly human-height, and she imagined his face atop, with its holey smile encouraging her.

What had begun as outlines of an idea would now be finished into the piece. The lungs were in color, but the edges were not, just charcoal and pencil. She knew that she needed to finish the work before her baby came and continued, both sitting and standing, as her body would allow. She ate and rested and worked some more. But all the baby things still crowded her living room. Hanging her paintings would free up floor space in the art room. She hung one painting over the couch, replacing a yarn wall hanging of a sunset. But then something about the latch hook evening gave her an idea about how to put the final touches on the thickened layers of the lung/wing. This wasn't exactly typical nesting, she suspected. But after two weeks of cleaning and organizing and finishing her last work before she became a mother, she felt complete. There was a nursery area in her bedroom, a clean home, and a finished piece of art.

She took the lungs on the easel outside to see the final textures and colors and glows of shape. They were so real to her that she felt the air from her yard and oxygen exhalations of the trees from her little woods giving a last breath to them. Breathing last breaths *for* them. As unrealistic as the lungs were, with the colors too bright to be real, she could almost sense a movement of thanks, a pulse of leaving. Gary's lungs, respirating as he coasted into the next place.

* * *

Juniper started staying at Cora's. Four days past her due date, she got up in the middle of the night, and water from between her legs splashed on the bathroom floor. She stood, legs more than shoulder-width apart, and saw the water was clear. She waddled to the linen closet and grabbed an old beach towel. She shoved it between her legs and thought about where to sit. Her adrenalin had begun to spin, and she just stood there. Cora must have sensed something, because she burst out of her room, saw Juniper with the towel, and said, "Finally!" Sweat popped out of Juniper's upper lip as she braced herself through the first few contractions that had begun with Cora's exclamation. They timed her. "Fast and furious," Cora said.

They loaded her into the car and drove to the hospital. The sun was rising. Juniper said, "I know this is weird, but can we roll down the windows?" Cora cranked her side and Juniper hers, just like they were jointly pedaling Juniper's old bike. The day strode into the car, whipping and cracking. Juniper's hair had gotten long over the past year, and she held it in her two hands like a rope over her right shoulder. The air was rife with dancing pollen, and she could smell the first cut hay as they hurtled through space. Fallow fields no less important than the seeds of corn bated to burst through impending summer. And the microcosms of wet dirt, like her womb. Those smells held answers. She held on to the farmland smells as they entered through—what else—automatic double doors into the maternity ward.

Then, with the vinyl seating and white sheets, for a moment the hospital reminded Juniper of the hotel. But there were beeping and tubes. And a real bracelet. Cora was talking to one person, then another. Juniper's muscles tightened and pulsed. Her belly hardened. No one had warned her that she might feel a trickle of grief at the thought of her baby leaving her body. It was as if the baby inside and the baby coming out were two different people. She anticipated meeting her little girl with excitement and joy. It was all pull and release. She could feel her water still leaking. Her mouth opened, her jaw unhinged, and she cried out. Her throat clenched as she let go a self-conscious cry of pain. The nurse paused the Velcro around her arm and looked at her, intoning seriously, "Let it out, don't hold back. You can breathe deep and release your sounds. It will help the baby."

Yes. Juniper needed that. She wanted to yell, not out of weakness, but from the strength she felt rising up. She felt like a well of strength. The only sounds she heard were the ones from within, her heart whooshing and her head beating. She cramped again, and her belly rose up in a hard ball. Her voice was a low moan that scooped the energy out of her. Her noises like sex, her sweat and salt like a tide going out. It was a falling away, and a giving up, with an emotion reserved only for life giving. They had lowered the lights in her room. Day never crept in.

Until she pushed. They told her it was okay now, she was open. Her eyes gripped her surroundings. Her hands tasted the metal rails of her bed. The cotton gown, like papier-mâché, formed her shape. She pushed the tears out of her eyes, the redness out of her skin, all the air out of her lungs and insistence out of her belly. Maybe her green skirt fluttered away like a leaf as she pushed with her soul.

The doctor turned to the nurse. "There's the head. Here we go."

Strong pushes, and the baby slid out. Juniper was terrified, completely terrified, for the several seconds it took to hear her baby cry. But she did cry. And Juniper cried with her. She reached out. It seemed like it took them so long to give her baby back to her and fill Juniper's arms. "My baby. My baby. My baby."

Juniper could smell blood like iron and dirt. When she held her girl, she felt a connection to her place and home, Michigan summer and her own mother. The smell of the drive that day. The first-cut hay had cast cones and rods of golden green scents through the unrolled windows. Juniper whispered, "Clover," then, "Clover," in the baby's ears and skin and her fuzzy back and right into the baby's mouth. Then they took her so that her mom could cut the cord. Cora cut the cord, but she left the twine. Everyone talks about the cord, the severance. But all Juniper felt was the twine of them together, the connection that would knot and rope and pull them together forever.

Baby Home

Clover took to Juniper's breast what seemed like all day and all night.

"You know you could supplement," Cora said.

"No," said Juniper.

"It'd give you a break."

"I will not purchase artificial breast milk in cans. That is ridiculous. Who came up with that idea, anyway?" Juniper's mothering instincts were strong, so she sat on that chair in Cora's living room and nursed and held and sweated. She had all the time to gaze at Clover. The baby had a shock of corn silk hair, like she'd been plucked right out of the fields.

Cora would come home with groceries and Subway and news from the outside world.

"Look at that pretty girl!" she would coo randomly. Her delight fed Juniper's strength. Babies needed joy at their arrival, and Cora was wonderful for that. Juniper had digested too much *People* magazine and random paperback smut. She didn't want to crank up the TV while she was nursing, because she thought that the noise wouldn't be ideal for Clover. It was important to try not to mess up something that was perfect. Her eyes rested on the beauty of her daughter.

In her old bedroom, she found some art books from school. She liked to perch one open to a single painting on the arm of the chair while she was nursing. She would take in an old and lovely Renoir while Clover was on the right side. Two sisters that maybe looked like mother and daughter. Then they'd switch left, and she'd flip to some rust-and-blue Rothko chunks.

Cora came home from her shift one day and said, "June. I have some news." Juniper was bouncing a swaddled Clover up and down the dark hallway connecting the bedrooms. Cora had brought in blinks of summer. Juniper had been secluded in the dark cave for what seemed like months, but it had just been four weeks. She waited for Cora to go on. Cora set down her purse, kicked off her Nikes, and reached for her plastic lighter with the little red pout lip, an icon of Juniper's life and childhood.

"Ma! Not in here. *Please.*" They'd discussed Cora's smoking, and she was trying. She could go outside and had promised to be quit completely by the time it got cold. But now it was June, hot and shifty, with lots of time left.

"Okay then. Come outside with me." Cora slid her shoes back on. Outside were woven folding lawn chairs set up next to her ashtray atop a garden table made up of an old plank on top of two buckets. Juniper sat down while peeling Clover out of her cotton husk. Cora stayed standing, lit up, and walked around the corner of the house to blow out her dirty air. She came back and moved the ashtray with lit cigarette to the ground near the maple tree. She paced and talked.

"I was talking to Janine, who's friends with Gary's sister over to Ann Arbor." Cora seemed uncomfortable inhaling the fresh stuff from beneath the maple leaves. "Juniper, Gary passed a couple days ago."

Juniper had already felt like her emotions were barely stopped up by a dam made of balsa wood, a flimsy fence. Like not much was holding her together. She handed Clover directly to her mom and made sure Cora had her head. Then she sat back down in the plastic woven chair and leaned over and cried. She covered her face, because she worried that Clover would see her crying. She was so stunned by the news. It was so sad. It was so soon. What about Jo-Jo and the baby? Juniper kept picturing Gary in the pool utility closet next to the buckets and jugs and mops. She could see his wizened face and shoulders that had given up.

That night they all had at Side Bar, the memories surrounding that time sunk deep enough to create permanent grooves. Gary slamming the table with joy as Jo-Jo made her entrance. Their sly exit together. Juniper's magnetic pull to Kirk's room, likely the night that Clover was conceived. It was all woven together.

Juniper felt as sad as if she'd known him a long time. It didn't make sense how Gary had gotten to her. It was just moments of understanding that passed from her to him, but likely not even the other way around. Yet in paying attention to him, she had cared about him. That damn plastic from the basket chair strained its impression against her bare legs. The physical sensation played a trick of switching her attention to the discomfort of sweltering and chafing. The sadness, too, was physical.

"Jo-Jo, it's Juniper." She was hit by the cool house smells as she went inside to call.

Jo-Jo was crying when she answered her phone. With no preamble, she said, "The baby is due in less than two months," and kept crying into the phone.

"I know, I know, Jo-Jo." Juniper felt wise with experience. "You just have to take care of yourself no matter what now."

"Yeah," Jo-Jo said. Her voice settled down. "Do you know he was so happy about the baby?"

"I did hear that," Juniper said.

"Yeah. He didn't care that we weren't married or nothing. He knew it was a boy. I'm so glad he got to know it was a boy. His son. He's a good man, Juniper." Jo-Jo caught herself and paused to acknowledge the wrong tense. "You know, I love that man for what he gave to me. He was happy to do it too."

"I know, I know," Juniper tried to soothe.

Jo-Jo said, "The service is over to St. Jude's Parish on Friday at ten."

Juniper said, "Okay, I'll see you there. Jo?"

"Yeah?"

"Do you need anything? I'm so sorry things happened this way."

"Juniper, will you come shopping with me next week? I need all this stuff still."

"Yes, of course." Juniper thought about Jo probably not getting a shower. Her ma was on disability in a real shabby old trailer where Jo lived with her. Gary didn't have any family except his sister around. But they were going to be new single mothers together. That was glue right there, and she wanted to help. She felt horrible about Gary, and cried, really for Jo-Jo.

Back in the cushy chair with Clover, Juniper had her first truly selfish thought since her baby was born. She wanted to go home and see the lungs. Gary had flown away. His soul was gone, his body was gone. But after some time away, she wanted to see if she still thought it was good. She was ashamed. She felt like a jerk.

Cora's living room lamp wasn't enough light for the room. The brown carpet and paneled walls were stifling. But Clover's golden eyelashes curled up, flicking the sixty watts all over the place. Juniper pulled her onto her breast, and Clover's fingers splayed out, open, concentrating on her nourishment. Cora tiptoed in and leaned over the chair, checking on her beautiful granddaughter. Juniper looked up at her mom and smiled with heavy eyes.

* * *

The funeral for Gary was filled with the Vacation Express people. Gary's sister and Jo-Jo were in the front on the end. Bethy sat next to Juniper and was upset she hadn't brought Clover. Already, Bethy didn't understand you couldn't bring a baby to a funeral. The first two rows were full of their people, and behind them were strict varnished lines of empty pews, like Scrabble tile holders.

The priest was cloaked and swung incense around. Again, Juniper was ghosted by the scent of chlorine. The incense was a burning sweetness that seemed inappropriate, like someone had lit a bong in celebration of Gary's life. But maybe that was just because Juniper wasn't used to the Catholic ritual. It was the smell of cleaning and hotel carpet, and, of course, chlorine, that stuck with Juniper. And maybe a little tiny hint of oil paint.

False Marker

Juniper wore this long strip of cloth the color of a fuscia flower. She wrapped it around, over-the-neck, and crisscross to hold her Clover. The uproar she created when she strolled into Walmart for the first time. Clover was five weeks. Mrs. Dee was there. (How was it she was always there?)

"Oh, oh oh! You come right here Miss Juniper! I have not met this pretty little one."

"Clover," said Juniper.

"Oh, now that's different."

"Yes," said Juniper. She had walked the mile and a half from her mom's. She was beyond tired. Beyond. But she was with this new person, this sidekick that was more charming and cute, and created goodwill at every turn. It was fun. Mrs. Dee, James organizing, and Gina white-shoeing across the floor. Everyone wanted to see the baby. And watching the face of Bucky, old Bucky, like sixty-five and in Sporting Goods for half his life, completely melt at the sight of this little sweetness in Juniper's wrap. Over the sound system of total junk music, Juniper could hear her favorite, Emiliana Torrini, in her head. "Nothing Brings Me Down" strumming, uplifting. The place was certainly a new set of colors. It could be harsh with the yellow and blue smiley-face logo, but on this new day her eye was drawn to the softness of a smear of mud that had gotten tracked onto the floor. Someone's hand that gripped a mug of coffee from the back. And behind her, the porthole of light from the relatively small bank of front doors, reached in and grabbed dust motes and people's hair, like a filter of glow. Walmart became a stand-in for someplace new. Like she was wearing a headlamp, Clover lit her way. It was a new time, and time to go new places.

Juniper walked home with her bag of diapers and random snacks to keep her going. It was July, she could already fit into her cut-off jeans shorts, unbelievably. They were tight across her middle and thighs. Her hips had expanded, and maybe would stay that way, but those shorts buttoned, dammit.

She'd heard things of people being young and in love, but what about being young and a mother? She felt beautiful, so beautiful. The sun came to her and shimmered through her copper hair, streaming. The two girls plodded through the fallow Eller's field. Fallow meant unlined, unprescribed by sugar beet greens. It was field grasses of high summer, Juniper's absolute favorite. The undulation alone was mesmerizing. And the smells, life and death simultaneously streaming and weaving about. Grass drying into the end of its life. Butterfly wings everywhere, attached to living butterflies. Clover's sunbonnet, a picture unto itself. Yellow. Juniper blew a stream of cool air into baby's face. Clover pursed her lips and blinked rapidly.

The rhythm they formed was clunky and consistent, bobbling across the field, then onto the edge of the road. No cars passed. Up ahead on the right was Juniper's trailer. Their home. The key, the doors, the living room, moist again with so much summer. The hallway smelled of oil paint and diapers. Powder did not cover the reality of sharp sweat and sour honey warm milk and the oddly not-too-bad infant poop.

Home may have to be a passing fancy. Home may have to change. Maybe this trailer was a container of memories. There was too much to say, and too much to stay. It was the first real time she had that feeling, of moving on, and it was just a little niggling. She could swat it away like a fly about to land on her baby. Cora called that evening.

"June."

"Hey Ma, what's up?" she answered sleepily.

"So I was getting gas today, and saw Shelly and them."

"Yah?"

"They was over to Gobles Cemetery, visiting Grandma and Grandpa Kowalski and saw this weird thing." Of course Juniper did not say a word.

"There was this, I don't know, fake grave stone or something," Cora continued. "They tried to explain it to me, but it didn't make no sense. I couldn't figure if it was vandalism, or what. I kind of want to go check it out."

"Well don't go now, Ma. It's getting dark."

"Will you come with me tomorrow?"

"Clover needs a bath first thing, I'll have to nurse her, and I need to get her napping in her crib here. I don't know if I can go tomorrow." Juniper made excuses.

"Oh come on, you hardly get out," Cora said. What was Juniper supposed to say? Plus her vanity about what she had done crept in, and the part of her that wanted some credit, said, "Okay, let's go."

The next morning the three of them went out to the cemetery. Cora pulled up next to the Kowalski plot, and right away, before she was even parked, said, "Hm." Juniper watched her mom get out and go over to Great Grandma, then Great Grandpa. Then Grandma Jezebel, like a beacon. Cora went to her knees and cried immediately upon seeing her mother there. The wind seemed to be communicating something with its cool voice. It hadn't been that long Jezebel had been gone, and talk of her always brought a lot of laughs and tears, but seeing her grave was a jolt. If Cora had looked behind her, and seen Juniper bouncing around with Clover, she'd have noticed that Juniper wasn't crying. It's not that Juniper wasn't struck by being there, seeing Grandma's grave. She missed her like everything. But, Juniper had been there recently, and the shock this time wasn't about seeing Grandma's name like that, all etched in stone. The shock was over to the right, her stone, still standing. She hoped it didn't desecrate the sanctity of the place. She meant only respect—to those that deserved it. A loose strand from her braid blew into her mouth.

Cora wiped her eyes, and turned to where Juniper was standing. Followed her eyes down to the statement.

"Well, what the hell?" Cora said. She stood there a minute, thinking through the breeze. Finally she read it out loud, seeming to process it, "Here lies the father that could have been?" Cora stood there for a minute longer. Then she turned to Juniper. Juniper stood facing forward, staring at the stone, not wanting to engage Cora. But she'd either have to act incredulous right quick, or it would seem odd. Juniper busied herself with jiggling Clover, fussing over her socks, wishing she had a hat, tightening the baby wrap that held her. Clover's hair was short clear lines of twinkling gold, and it was undulating slowly, like a tv-top fiber optics display.

"Juniper."

"Yeah." Juniper was a *mother*. She felt like a kid. Being questioned.

"Do you know anything about this?" Silence. "Do you know what it's supposed to mean?" Juniper was startled at the shallow depth of her anger just then.

"Of course I know what it means! Think about it. The loss of fathers who choose not to be present for whatever reason, is like a death to the kids they leave behind. Abuse, neglect, absenteeism, our family knows a little bit about all that."

"You seem to know exactly what this means."

"I know what it means to me."

"Is that 'cause you possibly put this here, and you wrote this?"

"I'm not taking it down."

"June, this might be a little disrespectful to the other family that comes here, ya know. Shelly didn't know what to think."

"When I think about Grandpa, or my mysterious disappearing dad, I'm still crushed. Crushed." Juniper's face crumpled, and she started to cry. That made Clover cry. "And now, *now* with Clover's father out of the picture," Juniper continued through her jerking voice, "I just felt this overwhelming sense of wrongness. This isn't how I wanted things to be." Juniper bent her face to touch Clover's. She smelled her baby and felt the savior of endorphins surge through her heart. She rubbed the divot at the base of Clover's neck, absently, like a good-luck charm.

"I'm sorry Ma, if this is controversial in any way, but I'm angry. This is how I'm dealing with it." Cora, still pissed herself, but always supportive of Juniper's creative way of taking on the world said,

"Okay, let's go." Then she turned around and put a kiss on her hand that she touched to Jezebel's stone. "Bye, Ma. Love you." Cora's eyes stayed straight ahead, and her lips shut, for the entire drive home.

* * *

It was like someone had seen them drive out there, have their conversation about the stone. Maybe a graveyard caretaker had been lurking behind one of the big trees. Or maybe Shelly had just tattled. But either way, Cora must've said something to Shelly, who said something to someone, who said something to someone else. That would be about the extent of the chain in small place like Gobles. Because two days later, the *Paw Paw Courier-Leader* showed a picture of Juniper's stone with a caption. Cora marched over to Juniper's. Well, she zipped down the county highway, pulled into Juniper's dirt driveway, and *then* marched out of her car, waggling that newspaper right in front of her. Cora knocked loudly, then must've realized she could wake Clover, and knocked again, softer. But it was too late to take back. Clover was up anyway, and the rat-a-tats were loud and clear at any volume. Juniper was bouncing and wiggling, trying to get Clover settled into some position where she wasn't crying. Juniper was sweating, as usual. It was rising July in a stifling trailer, worse from the shared body heat, and likely the pounds falling away from Juniper, disappearing into evaporated sweat, heating the rooms further.

"Ma, what?" Juniper asked when Cora strode into the little living room with uncharacteristic urgency. She waggled the news in front of Juniper. *"What?"* Juniper had no patience for games.

"Did you see this?" Cora waved. When she saw Juniper was in the dark, she opened the paper, and flattened it on Juniper's dinette. It was a skinny little paper, with one section. But right on page two was a quite nice shot of Juniper's stone. Someone had cleverly gotten a blurry "Gobles Cemetery" behind the very in-focus sentiment. "Here lies the—" Cora started.

"I got it." Juniper interrupted her mom as she read the paragraph:

Someone's idea of a statement or prank was left behind in the Gobles Cemetery this past month or

138

so. A false grave marker, made by hand, with the statement "Here Lies the Father that Could Have Been (As Good As Dead)" was erected next to the Kowalski family plot.

Discovered by former Gobles resident, Shelly Wurtz, as she was visiting her family's plot to lay flowers and pay her respects with her two daughters, Becky and Jill, the stone left her and others wondering how it got there, and what it really means. Although Jerry Little, caretaker of Gobles Cemetery, did say it was certainly against cemetery policy to allow markers that were not directly linked to a specific body, he left it there upon discovery two weeks ago, saying, "I didn't think it would hurt nothing," and "Maybe it was a message to the Kowalski men." The stone is technically outside the Kowalski family plot, and is at this moment, being left in place until further facts and information can be gathered.

"Juniper, you know this is not what I wanted, this attention." That was the thing about Cora, she was small, she felt small, and wanted to stay that way. She didn't ask for much, or expect much.

"I know Ma. I'm sorry. I never intended to make you, of all people, upset." Cora was nearly crying, and seemed to be working hard to hold it together.

"I know you're talking about your dad, your grandpa, and now Clover's daddy too."

"Don't call him that," Juniper said.

"Okay, but I know you have all that pain and betrayal. I get that. I don't even expect you to not be pissed off. I'm still pissed off."

Juniper was reaching over to her mom's purse, and peeked inside to grab Cora's pack and lighter. "Here, Ma. Let's go outside and talk." Cora lit up on Juniper's stoop. Juniper was bouncing around the yard with Clover, who was edging toward hunger. "I've been quiet, Ma. In fact, I've felt stifled at times. And something strange happened when

I got pregnant. I started wanting to say something with my art. Not like before, with a nice drawing, but literally say something." Cora was sucking deep on her vice, blinking through the smoke. "I feel like I'm on the cusp of finding my voice." They switched places. Cora got up and started pacing the yard. Juniper sat on the stoop, lifted her t-shirt and began nursing Clover. After a minute Cora stomped out her butt so she could come sit beside them.

"You know I'm just used to shutting up about stuff. So it's hard for me to see you spilling all these beans. If I'm real honest though, I wish I coulda spoke up a time or two." It was so quiet that they could hear Clover smack and swallow.

"June, go take a shower when you finish up there. I'll watch Clover." They were Mother and Daughter again. Mother-daughter/mother-daughter. Like before, but different.

Sub-rural

She felt like a kitchen timer, ticking down the seconds until Clover would be three months. That's when maternity leave should be over and she should go back to work. Should. She hadn't really thought enough about it before Clover was born. But now she heard the ticking getting louder. And it drove her nuts, because three months—twelve weeks—was total bull. What man or person without a baby in their arms made that shit up? How did this culture not see that Clover needed her all the time? Clover did not need daily, eight-hour breaks from her mother. It wasn't like Juniper had an important job, where work was piling up with her gone. And she wasn't receiving pay or partial pay while she was out. It was just Manny holding her job for her. For how long, she didn't know and was sure Manny himself didn't know.

Time sluiced together duties of love and caretaking. Or time became irrelevant as it passed. Clover grew rounder and more beautiful. If she just kept her eyes on Clover, she could keep her focus away from the stressy thoughts and into the dirt of ideas.

Juniper had been receiving WIC and other financial assistance from the state of Michigan. There was still talk about them moving in with Cora, just to combine household expenses. There was this arbitrary cultural pull to be back at work and a very real financial pull to be back there. But if she went back, it seemed likely most of her measly income would go to child care. That made her feel trapped and upset.

But she couldn't let herself be immobilized. Juniper packed up the diaper bag. Clover's head was warm and wafty. Juniper inhaled over and over with her lips pressed on the silky threads as she carried Clover out to Cora's car. She had the CD player that she left plugged into the cigarette lighter. She cranked up Red Hot Chili Peppers and drove them over to Vacation Express. Manny was right there in the lobby, arranging the free newspapers. She watched him for a moment, remembering what he said about her being different when she came back. But it was his being the same that struck her.

"Manny!"

"June bug!" He whirled around. "Ooh, you bring her here right now." He hugged Juniper and cupped Clover's little hand curled up like a ball of yarn. They made small talk while Manny held Clover in the lobby love seat. Juniper flung herself back into a chair, baby carrier empty but still attached, and felt the lightness of about twelve less pounds. "Hon, you look tired. But skinny! I mean good-skinny. You come to visit or work?" He winked at her.

"Thanks. I don't even know, Manny. I just felt like I should come. I mean, of course, it's nice to see you. But I thought I was coming to figure out work. I don't know."

Manny was nodding. "Look, you don't have to come back now if you don't want. You know we got that new girl cleaning, and actually two more desk people. I have got to train another manager. I am working too much here." He shook his head.

Juniper said, "I need the money, but I hate to leave her, you know?"

"Honey, I *don't* know." He leaned his head sideways to make good eye contact with Clover. "But you should do what you think is right. You're her one and only."

Juniper was thinking. She just needed a little more time to think. To be ready.

"Can I have another month or two? Will you still have something for me then?"

"If you don't mind part-time, Juniper, I'll always have something for you. Anytime." Manny touched Clover's face with the back of his hand. "Can you get me one of these? I want one of these."

"I can't. Well, I could, but that'd be weird." They laughed, but his eyes were sad.

"Manny, thank you so much for giving me some time. It makes me feel a little better, less stressed, you know?"

"Good, I want to help you. Now please, for the love of Dios, let's go out soon!"

Yes, yes. She smiled and nodded and said how happy she was to see him and that she looked forward to going out with the crew. She plucked Clover out of his arms and carried her out to the car. The doors closed and the Chili Peppers continued their thonking bass. She walked into her house and set Clover in her crib. She still thought she could hear it. Tick, tick, tick. Maybe a little softer, but not gone.

Jo-Jo had her baby boy and named him Garret. He was big and healthy and was a chunk of joy. But she was poor. And she was practically alone, living with her own mom in a trailer not even close to as nice as Juniper's.

But Juniper didn't compare herself with Jo-Jo. She almost didn't see that their situations were exactly the same: baby, no partner, barely adequate job, mother helping with childcare. Well, their situations were *almost* exactly the same. Juniper had a college degree, for what that was worth. But that wasn't the real thing that made her feel different.

Juniper was an artist. She didn't always feel like she deserved the title. But she knew it was true because of how she saw the world even more than what she did or did not produce. She might not be successful or even close to fully developed, and she might never be able to make a living creating, but she was an artist, and it gave her everything. It gave her hope. And aside from Clover, it gave her direction, purpose, and joy. Some days she felt like she had it all, which she knew was wrong. She knew that wasn't true. But when she looked at Jo, the struggle looked so much harder on her.

Juniper had been sure to share any baby stuff she wouldn't need with Jo-Jo. And Cora had also scouted some excellent clearance items, which they had wrapped for the new baby. They went over to Jo's trailer to meet Garret.

That morning had the kind of summer heat that stole. They all tried to move slowly as they stepped into the living room. Jo's sick mom, Sue, was there to greet them from her living room chair. No one knew exactly what was wrong with Sue, some fibromyalgia-type thing Jo never talked about. Sue seemed bewildered by the influx of babies as they all crowded the living room. But she was sweet and seemed slightly happy for the company. It was as hot inside as it was getting out, and the trailer had a smell like soggy particle board. Juniper also detected the classic cigarette-laced upholstery combo.

Juniper held Garret while Cora held Clover and they all chatted. Juniper was sure she could see a sag in the living room floor. There was tape around one window. The place was the reverse layout of hers. There were dust-lined fans whirring everywhere.

After everyone was done admiring the little ones, Juniper said, "Jo, go get a shower. I got Garret."

"You sure?" Jo-Jo asked.

"Go. You might not get another chance today." Juniper was admiring Garret's heft and trying to get a handle on him like a sack of potatoes.

Jo-Jo's eyes looked grateful. "Ma, get them some lemonade at least."

"Of course, you ladies want somethin' to drink?" Sue pushed up out of the recliner.

Cora and Juniper both demurred. "Our hands are full," Cora joked. But the tone of her voice didn't quite get it right, and the joke fell flat. Juniper had it easy as Garret conked out for her after a few minutes. But Cora was toggling Clover, who was drooling and shoving both hands up into her face. Maybe a tooth? Likely hungry. Juniper wondered if she could just lift her flap in Sue's living room.

At the other end of the couch, she could see Cora was fretting about Garret. Sue didn't seem as agile as one needed to be to lug an infant in and out of a car seat or crib. Sue wasn't old; she just had trouble getting around. She was still busy getting herself some kind of powdered shake thing as Jo came out from the shower. She looked tired still but was smiling. She reached out to take Garret.

"I feel so good!" Jo said.

When they left, Juniper's anxiety over feeding Clover had amped up. She was very ready to relieve Clover's fussing with her milk. They zipped across town to Juniper's trailer. Juniper relaxed as she settled on her own couch with a grateful baby guzzling away. Cora did some dishes, and they could rest in the comfort of Grandma Jezebel's home. Cora brought Juniper a glass of ice water, which she swilled then gestured for another.

Juniper kept finding herself thinking about motherhood, and life and art, and what they all meant together. In the harsh climate of subrural Michigan—the harsh cultural climate of scraping by with little and feeling like you deserved less—she was surprised at what folks missed right in front of them. The joy that was theirs for the taking, or change that could be had for the cost of some courage. Moving towns, getting a degree, going on birth control so you didn't have your kids too young. Yeah, but look what happened to her. She unlatched Clover and flipped her around to switch sides. Well, barring unforeseen circumstances, these things could be had. Too many women seemed saggy and disempowered, and despite her journey that was beginning to look typical, Juniper felt like she was looking at it from the outside in. She knew her time spent away in Chicago had given her a different perspective. Motherhood was different in ways no one had mentioned, and Juniper was quietly grappling with that. Her own grandmother and mother had taught her that motherhood was a burden. Of course, there was distinct love and presence from the women her family. She wanted to pass that along. But she had been shown that motherhood was exhausting and troublesome, and expensive and constant, and lonely. For Juniper, it was all of those things.

But no one mentioned what else motherhood was. It was also what catapulted her into womanhood. She felt newly voluptuous in body, yes. She also felt voluptuous in creativity. She was surprised by her recent bursts of inventive thought. Since her pregnancy, her mind had reeled with artistic intent and perspective. Her visual intake of the world was growing louder. The humming volume was accompanying her everywhere. Her caretaking duties did not allow her to constantly create, but how she was experiencing life and earth and people had shifted into a constant heightened awareness. The genesis of this new human had pushed forth an afterbirth of creation. She was told that motherhood taketh away possibilities and freedom. She heard women say they had "lost themselves" when they became mothers. Then why did she feel so completely whole and expressive? Why did the love she felt for Clover span over the fields and trees and sky and the people at Walmart? Beauty was bombarding her. Truth wasn't always beautiful, and that was bombarding her too. Was motherhood affecting her differently than it was supposed to? Was there something wrong with her?

She was so exhausted. Clover was wet-faced and asleep. Juniper righted her so she could lean back with her feet up on the ottoman. Cora quieted out the door with a wave and air kiss. Clover's head nestled into Juniper's neck, and they were belly-to-belly. Juniper fell away, concentrating on their rhythm, two of her breaths for every three of Clover's. She remembered the word "hemiola" from class as she fell asleep.

* * *

Late that night, Clover woke in a fit of crying. The windows were all open, lamely gaping for wisps of breeze. They were hot and uncomfortable, and Clover's sweet hair was stuck to her forehead. She had an odd long tendril that reached down her cheek in an ess shape. Juniper felt a gut pull to pick her up. It was a feeling she got many times a day but could be intensified by worry or concern. The feeling of needing to hold her baby was like a string sewn into her gut that was pulled by an outside force. A painful tug released only by her arms being filled. Clover was screaming and sweaty, and Juniper bustled to the bathroom sink to wet a washcloth. She wrung it and wiped Clover. But Clover was too hot and screamed more.

Juniper was nearly in tears over the urgency of Clover's cries. She turned on the second light in the bathroom and saw a welt on Clover's temple, red and swelling as she watched it. Still gripping Clover, she rushed back to their room and the crib. On one of the slats of wood was a dark, meaty-looking spider.

"No!" Juniper yelled as she reached out with her hand around the crib slat and gripped and squeezed the large spider until she heard a crunch. She squeezed again, making sure it was dead, and flung the wetness of dead spider into the trash in their room. Clover was still in Juniper's left arm, alternately whimpering and screaming. "Shh, baby girl. Shhh," Juniper begged.

She wiped her left hand clean on a towel. She felt panicky about the welt and went to call her mom but then stopped and dialed the clinic that had given Clover her vaccinations. Each time they had been there, the nurse had so kindly taken Clover's height and weight and checked her heart and lungs to make sure she was growing well. No one in her family had hardly ever gone to the doctor. She had in fact figured this lack of care was the reason her grandma died too young. She was sure Grandma could have gotten better, or at least lasted longer, if she'd gone to the doctor on time.

She would not take care of her baby in the family tradition. *No.* She left a message on the office's emergency line and let herself freak out a little while she waited for a callback. It was only a couple of minutes before some lovely, kind-sounding angel of a nurse asked her questions about the welt and Clover's behavior. She even waited while Juniper took Clover's temp.

"It's 101!" Juniper said, so worried.

"That happens with these little ones, no cause for alarm yet." Juniper nodded through her shakiness. "There was this spider." She described the spider. Its image was clear in her mind, the ugly brown black chubby sinister shape.

"Okay, now. That might likely be the problem there. You want to put some ice in a cloth, then see if you can get that swelling down a bit. Now, you should give her some baby Tylenol if the fever doesn't go down in an hour or two, 'kay hon?"

Juniper whimpered a little assent.

"It's gonna be okay now. You call me back if you're still worried. I'll be on all night." Juniper felt like an addict needing the nurse's motherly salve as fortification so that she might have the strength to mother as well. The angel nurse didn't hang up until she had both bolstered Juniper's sense of capability and gotten assurance that she was okay.

Juniper got ice and sang to Clover. "Twinkle, Twinkle," and "Row, Row," and "Old MacDonald." She held the soft cloth with its lump of cold to baby's head. Clover's crying subsided. She inhaled jaggedly, like a soft breeze over washboard gravel roads. Her face was wet from tears and heat, but her crying had fully stopped. As Juniper got to the duck sounds on "Old MacDonald's Farm," Clover's eyes locked onto her mouth. Juniper quacked passionately. Clover laughed! Her silky wet lips turned up, and her round, soft belly bounced with puffs of air.

Juniper stopped singing, amazed. "Clover!" Clover looked up at her mother's eyes. "Quack, quack!" Juniper squawked again. And Clover let out the tiniest little grunt of joy. Then Juniper mooed, and Clover thought that was hilarious and squealed. Juniper laughed at Clover's laughs, then they were giggling up a storm.

Juniper was pretty sure she had loved Clover from the second the pee stick had two lines. But what she felt then was more than she had ever felt in her life. Juniper continued to sing and played with Clover's hands and face and belly. She set the baby tub up with cool water and washed and dried Clover. It was after midnight. Her baby was soft and clean, and her welt had gone down a bit, and her fever too. Clover was going to be okay. But Juniper's heart was in the shreds of irreversible love.

Hospital Visit

She saw the way Clover looked at her, and the way she looked at everyone else. It had taken Juniper a while to realize that Clover did not yet separate mother from self. Juniper's breasts belonged to Clover's hunger. Juniper's arms and love were taps with spigots. But Clover was turning from a needy infant into a jubilant baby, eyes bright, easy laugh, grabby fingers, sticky with spit and reconstituted Cheerios. Four months, Five months. Hot days, then cool days and cold days were irrelevant, they rolled together and away.

The happiness was against a backdrop of poorness. It was frank poorness, that Juniper was so used to. It was okay. She was used to worn things, or wearing flip-flops even if the weather was cold. But Clover needed what she needed. And they needed a car.

When she and Cora went over to Mike's Used Autos for her first car—it should have been an enjoyable experience, a happy experience—they fought over the cost, and needs versus wants. Juniper didn't like that the '91 Toyota Corolla didn't have airbags in back. And it had a cassette player like Cora's car, so she'd have to rig up that stupid disc player still. She had survived Clover's first months without a car, but only with the constant help of Cora, so really she was happy for what she got. Cora was putting $100 down so they could drive it off the lot. Its taupe color nearly tortured her, but obviously, those kinds of things didn't and couldn't matter. She hugged her mom in thanks, and crawled into the backseat to figure out how to install the car seat.

It was maybe time for Juniper to think about working again for real this time. Cora had been taking care of them, bringing groceries, diapers. But late fall was whirling around the trailer, and the heat bill was going to be high for both of them. Juniper worried again, that she'd have to move in with her mom. But there were practical solutions to problems. No clothes? Juniper was extra inspired to lose those last few pounds to fit into all her old clothes. Thank god nursing was free.

* * *

By November, winter hit a pause. Apparently, Cora's dad had called. Grandpa. He was in the hospital over in Allegan. He had been living in South Haven with a girlfriend and her jumble of grown children this entire time, and no one had looked him up or asked after him. Now, he's thinking he might die, and he reaches out.

"Ma! You don't have to go see him."

"June, I know, but." Cora took a deep hit off her cigarette. "I just can't believe he wants to see me. Can't believe he's sick."

"Yes, well he is mortal."

"Hey. He's still my dad. What do you expect? I'd just forget about him completely? Well, I'm sorry, but I didn't. I'm upset, okay?"

Juniper softened. "Yeah, no. I get that this would bring stuff up for you. But going to see him won't change anything. It'll likely just suck. What does he want anyway?"

"He just said he's in the hospital with a blood infection, doesn't know how long he's got left, and wants to see me one more time."

"That's how he put it? See, even that sounds selfish to me."

But, there was nothing Juniper could do to stop her. She couldn't stop Cora from driving over—in Jezebel's car no less—to see her fucking Houdini of a grandfather. He had hit and fondled his way out of their lives. Wasn't too bright either, so it took him a little longer than some to escape. Juniper kept it casual, when she asked Cora exactly when she was going.

"I've gotta go now, June. Who knows how long he's got. I want to say something to him, at least."

"Well don't expect a damn thing from him," Juniper said.

"I know, I know. It'll be hard, but I'm doing this. I'm going over in the morning."

And when morning came, Juniper was waiting a quarter mile down Cora's road, sweet Clover buckled in back with a book and sippy cup of water, ready to follow Cora when she took a turn toward the highway. There was no way in hell she wanted to visit the bastard herself, she couldn't bear to see him. Cora knew not to even ask. But she also could not let her mom go in there completely alone. She had called the hospital and found out his exact room number, just by saying she was his granddaughter. She parked after Cora had gotten out of her car. She gave Cora a good head start into the hospital, buckled Clover into her stroller, and they followed her on up to the second floor.

Watching Cora from a distance was disconcerting. Cora's shoulders nearly folded in on themselves, and Juniper tried to think whether that was her usual stance or not. Cora stepped into her father's room, and Juniper snuck closer and closer, until she was standing right outside his door and could hear them. His gruffness was immediate.

"Oh, well you did decide to show."

"Hey Dad," Cora said.

"Well, at least gimme a hug if you come all this way," he said. She must have hugged him. She wouldn't have dared not.

"How you doin' Dad?"

"Well, hell. I'm doing bad." In his voice, Juniper heard no concern or regret. He was doing bad, that was his sole perspective. Cora had to have heard it too.

She leaned and peered around the door frame into the room. His slick Cary Grant hair was thinner, but still abundant for a man his age. Juniper wanted to see wisps of oldness, she wanted to see him fully reduced. He looked okay. He didn't look small and shriveled. There was nothing to be shocked by in his appearance, which was not what she wanted to see. Horrible, she knew. But she at least wanted the justice of time. Hard old bastard couldn't feel or succumb to a thing. Well, not yet anyway. She realized there had been silence, and leaned again, to see.

"Well, give your old man a hug," he said.

Cora must have thought the same thing as Juniper: He already said that. Maybe he was diminished in some ways. Juniper angled in to see his face once more. She saw Cora lean over obediently, and his hand, with a clear tube stuck to it, reached down and around until it cupped her mother's ass. His fingers deftly and expertly reached up between her legs, and his fingers seemed to disappear in that crease, in the searing hot moment before Cora yanked away. Cora let out a sound of whimpering anger, or something like that. Maybe a cry, she couldn't tell. Cora snatched her purse up off the chair and walked out with horror in her eyes.

"June!" Cora said as she approached the elevator and realized who she was looking at, that it was her daughter right in front of her. "What are doing here? Why are you here?"

Immediately, Clover reached out from her stroller and whined for Cora to pick her up. But Cora waited for the elevator while looking straight at the doors. The doors opened. They stepped in together. All of a sudden Juniper didn't know what to say. What she wanted to say was: *I didn't trust you. I never trust him, and I don't trust the two of you together.* But that was a useless thing to say. No use piling hurt up like that. Juniper was there to put her arm around her mother, and guide her down the elevator, and to the parking lot, and out of that fucking horrible, horrible place.

But when the elevator doors sealed them in, Cora opened up. First of all, she started to cry. "What did you have to come here for? What's your problem?" Cora's voice was like chunks of chalky gravel. Then louder, she said. "I hate him so much! I hate him, hate him, hate him." Cora was rocking and hugging her purse in the corner of the elevator when it dinged open. Juniper collected her mother's arm to move her out, but Cora yanked away. "Just go! I don't need your help, Juniper." And it was the way she said her entire name, with each letter enunciated, that stung Juniper.

They walked out to the parking lot separately. They drove back to Gobles, each in their own car. But Juniper tried to keep Cora's car in her sights, while they suffered the length of highway. She hurt for her mother. Juniper pulled in at Cora's. Cora had left the door ajar, knowing full well Juniper would be right behind her. Juniper came in and closed the door, and walked over to Cora, curled on the couch. She was facing the back of the couch and crying.

"I'm not crying because I hate him no more. I'm crying cause I miss *her.*" Juniper sat down next to her mom while she cried. She sat and they stayed like that, hoping the pain would settle back down to where it had come from.

Jezebel. They both missed her all the time. It got worse, not better, when Clover was born. She wasn't there to hold her great-grand-daughter. And it would have been an easy joy because she was another girl, and Clover was as light-filled and easy as Jezebel herself had been.

Grandma Jezebel practically had a sign nailed to her front door "No Boys Allowed." Their story included hatred toward men, pure and simple. Jezebel was the prophet of this Kowalski truth. Jezebel had been abused by her husband, maybe her father, the way she hinted. Things like, "Well, he was an angry man. Youse don't need all the details. That was a long time ago," came out when she talked about her own father. She'd always pave the past with platitudes. But her eyes would be wet and downcast when she did this.

And then Jezebel discovered her husband laying with her daughter. Their clothes were on, laying on the couch. But his gaze and caress of Cora's hair made Jezebel screech. Cora felt horrible, like she'd been a bad girl, and she'd cried for days. But for some reason, this was a story Jezebel and Cora both talked about more freely. He was even allowed to stick around after that episode. But when Jezebel saw him grasping for Juniper next—it was years later, but memory is real short with that stuff—she snapped. Thank god, she snapped. And they were all safe because of it. Safe from further damage if they just stayed away from all that was bad about them asshole men. Of course, something was creeping into Juniper's mind about staying away from all that badness. Of course. That meant staying away from all. All that might be good. And if you were a woman who loved men, as Cora did, as Juniper might, (no one was really sure about Jezebel), then you might have to do without love completely if you didn't take that risk. Jezebel's spirit was crushed by men, and so she touted and protected with her false prophesies. Juniper was now wondering and thinking maybe that is what they were. False prophesies: Juniper would be a damaged slut if she loved them men. And to think, Jezebel was just named after that Bette Davis movie from 1938.

Cora was crying on the couch after that hospital visit. She was crushed once again, and was also being mad at Juniper, which made some kind of sense to both of them. Then, Cora's anger turned up a notch.

* * *

Cora was known for not using tools. So when Juniper noticed a sledge hammer—something that had always leaned against a wall out in the garage from Grandpa's days— standing on the thin layer of snow next to the front door, she paused. Like a lover that wants to get caught, it was not only perched, but seemed laden with crushed grey dust. Juniper thought, *no.*

She had been coming around, checking on Cora the past week. Cora didn't seem fine, that was true. Instead of going inside to have coffee with her that morning, Juniper got back in her car, rebuckled Clover, and drove out, yet again, to Gobles Cemetery.

The morning was filled with a smoky-looking fog and new cold. But she knew what she was going to see. This was between her and Cora. As Juniper twisted her headlights off, she saw it. The crushed grey dust against the sloppy snow showed like blood in a black and white movie. A textural difference more than color. She saw her stone was gone. She got out of the car, and went right to the place to interpret what she saw. She didn't know what. If she was horrified or mad or hurt. The thing was in crumbles. The way that synthetic stone crushed and crumbled was something to behold. The segue from snow to cement powder gave her pause, and she connected the subtle colors to the sky before she chastised herself to focus. The stone left that powder everywhere. Ghost powder. The morning sounds were sparse. Bird, car passing. Room to hear imagined guttural yells, and sledgehammer cracks. Cora would likely have had trouble yielding the thing. But a person wouldn't care about difficulty. It would only add to the moment. Juniper bent down on her knees and touched her hand over the few inches of ragged top that was left of the stone. Like a miniature mountain scape. Surrounding it was her crushed words: AS THE DEAD FATHER LIES HERE AS GOOD THAT COULD HAVE BEEN. The words were unrecognizable, but she imagined them tumbled, out of order like that, as she was crying. Her work was crushed. But the meaning behind her words, the sentiment, could not have been celebrated more brilliantly. This was not lost on her for a moment, even as her anger seethed. And her sense of betrayal. Her own mother. Her stone became truly a piece of art for Juniper right then, as her fingers bumbled over the rubble, and generations of hurt tumbled out of her.

The Key

She needed a break. She needed to feel a little reminiscence, a little reminder of being young and childless, of feeling a little frivolous. She wanted to laugh with a grown-up and hear about irrelevant things. She wanted to just flash back, nothing permanent. She called Bethy.

"Look, I'm gonna come over, and we'll find you a cute outfit. You probably fit into all your old clothes anyway," Bethy said. She walked into the trailer, bringing sunshine. They were going to drop Clover at Cora's and spend the entire day in Kalamazoo.

"Oh, where's my blondie?" Bethy sang as she walked around the living room, teasing Clover in her play yard.

Bethy scooped her up, and Clover smiled with four teeth and said, "Bababa."

"Two blondies," Juniper added, looking at the two of them, so natural. Bethy was born to be a mom; she just hadn't realized it yet.

"I am so excited I can't stand it. I miss this!" Juniper said. She felt like she was about to start talking and just not stop.

"I have so much to tell you," said Bethy. "But first, let's find you a shirt that shows off your royal largeness."

Juniper had been the embodiment of constant change. She had mostly recovered from puffs of thigh, padded ankles, and the big,

156

round belly. But her breasts were still like a new person in the room. Before all this, they had clearly been an afterthought, as in, "Oh yeah, she's a young woman, she'll need a couple dabs right here." But now. Now she understood Steve Miller. Somebody was gonna want to shake her tree. Oddly, the men down in Benton Harbor really seemed to see her large ass and ripe peaches and had even seemed to overlook the whole "with child" thing. She had actually gotten a catcall when she had been down there in her last trimester. Some men had seen her as big and luscious, and all she could do was waddle around and take it in and laugh a little.

But something now was retained from that feeling of fullness, of ripeness. She had no idea she would love feeling like a woman this way. She wanted to have fun. Bethy knew the way. Juniper didn't feel like she used to. Her hips were rounder, her ass still bigger. Getting dressed that day made her realize that she had a figure like she'd never had before. It was okay, maybe better than okay. They were going to Kalamazoo, and they were going out, and she realized that the little girl in her had been totally left behind.

The trip reminded Juniper of the one they'd taken a year and half before. Even though it was too cold to have the windows down, they were singing and talking and laughing about the sad-sack dudes Bethy had been seeing lately. Juniper didn't need to talk about the wonders and moisture of motherhood. But by the time they got downtown and parked, she was getting a strong urge to talk about Kirk, of all things. She was probably just desperate to really talk to the only other person in the world who knew her story. Clover's story. They began strolling, window-shopping, sipping the fancy lattes that Bethy had bought them both.

"I never should have let it get as far as it did," Juniper said as she pulled her corduroy jacket tighter. Bethy turned sideways as they strolled. "I should have told him, maybe. Probably."

"June, you never really talked about what you wanted to happen. By the way, that scarf looks great on you. Did you want him to divorce his wife and come be Clover's daddy?" There was that word again that Juniper kind of hated.

"Thanks. No. I guess I didn't. I mean, I know I didn't. We talked on the phone a lot after he was back in Ann Arbor, and something wasn't right for me. He had this way of being, I don't know, precise, that I kinda disliked." The mulberry of her scarf flapped around like a cartoon tongue. "He seemed particular about too many things, and I found myself wondering if he'd be kind of controlling. Plus." Juniper stopped walking. They were in front of some toy store with an oversized jack-in-the-box in the window. "Plus, he kind of crushed me."

"Huh? What do you mean. Besides the obvious?" Bethy asked as she blew into her mittens.

"Yeah. So I was thinking of going to grad school before all this happened." Juniper gestured to her flat belly.

"Oh?"

"Yeah. I was. And he's like, this art professor at U of M."

"What! Really?"

"Yeah. So he came over, saw my paintings. *Liked* my paintings, and never offered to help or give me a letter of recommendation, or shit. I don't know. He didn't offer *anything*."

"Well, June, that's complicated. He can't be writing his mistress letters of recommendation."

"I know, I know." Juniper knew. "But he could have done something, right? Anything?"

Beth tilted her head side to side in acknowledgment that the bastard could have done something. "Yeah."

"It made me feel like I wasn't just younger. I wasn't just poorer. I wasn't just less educated. It made me feel like I was just *less*." Juniper started walking again. She took a sip of her cold latte and finished it. "It helped me let go of the wish for him. And then like, the next day, I found out I was pregnant."

Their outing was going to culminate at the Old Dog Tavern. There was something about that place that Juniper had just loved, and she begged Bethy to go there with her again. Once inside the red-rimmed front door, they unwrapped themselves from their layers, sat down, and tucked everything behind them on their chairs. There'd be some guy singing soon, and it seemed nice to settle in and wait for the cozy wood and warmth of the place to settle their chattering teeth and bring comfort. Juniper wrapped her hands around an oatmeal stout. The singer climbed up the few stairs to the stage platform. She witnessed his movements in stop-motion. She saw him as a sort of 'Clothed Ascending a Staircase'.

"Beth, do we know him?" Juniper asked just as she realized who he was.

"Mm, no?" said Bethy. She was checking out the room, looking for people she'd like to know.

The singer with guitar sat down on the wooden café chair, and he took up the whole stage. He was that kind of man. The café chair held him like a cupped hand. His guitar. His beer. His eyes. He pushed up his Buddy Holly glasses. But she was able to remember his face without the glasses. His gentle handling of her portraits was reproduced in his gentle tuning of the guitar strings. It was the Kinko's guy. He looked younger than she had thought before. His competence and generosity had made him seem older.

It wasn't that the stage was small. It was that he was a presence. A big man, with a little decorative beard and hairs curling up out of his orange checked shirt. He leaned down to take a sip of his pint as he was tuning the strings, his glasses hiding a little of his countenance. Could she smell hops from where she was? Like a grapefruity brightness? He sat up and sighed, still twisting the tuning pegs. His exhale must have jiggled the molecules in front of his face, which tickled through the space, which whispered right past Juniper's nose, and triggered her to inhale. Yeah, it was grapefruit, she was sure.

And then his voice as he warmed up. "Hey everybody," he said to the room, and the corners of his eyes turned up like he was smiling, but he wasn't. Like cats' eyes. "I've got some songs for you," he strummed some sad notes, "and the first one goes like this." He segued into a briny shanty with a heavy beat he was kicking into the floorboards. She could barely hear the words because his voice had the warmest timbre of liquid mahogany. She had never, ever, heard a voice like his. She couldn't move her head to look around. She was struck still by his sound. His guitar was an agile foil to his warm, liquid voice. He sang a couple more songs of his own, soulful and sad. But then he switched gears and did something playful and kind of raucous again. It was like he had run backstage and put on another costume, of someone light and joyous, and he smiled while he sang that one. It was an athletic tune, and he leaned back with a "Haha," of satisfaction to himself as the last strum died away. He sipped his beer again, like he was unaware of the hoots and clapping. Modest. Beth elbowed Juniper, "I'll be right back."

"All right now. I've definitely got a soft spot for old stuff," he continued, but then curled over for a moment in the privacy of tuning. After a few peg turns and strums, he seemed satisfied and sat up and looked around. "'So in Love.' Cole Porter." He poured out his version. Just poured and poured, and it fell over her, melted into her with its taunting and deceiving. And after he finally got out all the words, he opened his eyes and looked up. He seemed to look around and notice there were people there listening. She leaned on her elbows and sat forward to fix her gaze on his hands, then his face. His hair was dark with sweat. His eyes were light with what he was doing. He seemed to look at Juniper. Maybe he had noticed how intensely she was locked onto him, or maybe he recognized her. "So in love," he sang again and again, and here she swore she saw a sort of smirk, or was it a wink? Or her imagination? He finished, "So in love with you, am I." Then he did; he looked at her. She smiled and looked down into her lap, so caught at the possibility of being recognized. And it was like he threw away the key.

At intermission, he set his guitar on its stand, wiped the wetness from his forehead, and reached down to sip his beer. He stood up and walked down the stage steps straight toward Juniper's little table. He was looking right at her, and it was like the roller coaster ticking up to the top, knowing it was about to plummet.

"Hey there," he said. Whoooosh.

"You sound great," she managed.

"Thanks. Good enough to get you to stick around for the second half, I hope?" She blushed. Then he saw someone else he knew just as Bethy sat back in her seat. He tipped his head toward her again and waved to his buddy. She watched him walk away in slow, measured steps, not hurrying, but even and sure. Time overlapped itself when she recalled that night she sang karaoke. On that very stage she sang of him killing her softly with his song, and the coincidence was too much. Or maybe it meant nothing. As he sat back down for his next song, her intense feelings about that song pushed up onto the dais with him that night.

She clapped and found herself murmuring her appreciation to Bethy. She ordered another beer and let the vinyl seat console her. He sang all night. She was sure that was how long it was, precisely. Bethy made her leave. It was late, and they had to drive home. And when they got up to go, her body turned to the door while she put on her scarf and jacket. But her head swiveled back toward him. He wiped sweat from his forehead again and finished his second or third beer, leaving what looked like foam from the sea he had been singing about. He stood, and his thick legs flexed in a stretch. Sweat was dripping down his neck. She had to follow Bethy out the door as the crowd was still doing their happy yelling, but she turned all the way to face him one more time, and with her fullish lips closed loosely, she smiled just a little right to him. And his eyes curled up and pierced her again.

"We didn't do much, June. I hope you had a good time."

"It was perfect, Bethy." Juniper watched the night fall behind her in the side mirror. By the time they turned north on M-40, Juniper felt her breasts tingle with milk let down. Old Dog Tavern faded. Despite the cold, she rolled down her window for a minute, just to check if she could smell any new brightness, or if the citrus was all in her mind.

The Next Project

Something about the ruined gravestone made Juniper unexpectedly excited to move on. Or move ahead, or say more. And right there in her back room were the four canvas prints bolstered on frames, everybody looking at her. She had decided that she wanted to paint on the prints themselves. The idea had become clearer. Juniper propped the photos in her living room up against the old plaid couch, making it obvious. Of course. Now one photo was missing.

Clover woke from her nap, and she felt intense happiness as she dressed Clover in a soft jumper the color of hyacinths. She gathered her up with the diaper bag and drove over to Cora's. She knew the perfect backdrop. She dropped her keys on the front table in Cora's entry and plunked Clover down on her childhood quilt in the old bedroom. Clover was sitting up all by herself, holding her feet. The cliché of blond hair set off by the blue of both Clover's eyes and the flowered quilt was the prettiest thing Juniper could imagine. Clover smiled like a lighthouse beacon, blinking and almost too bright to take in. Through the high bedroom window, a last-minute shaft of light teased Clover's hair into a spectrum of glossy threads. Her portrait would not be serious, like the others. It was impossible to take those spitty lips and rounded cheeks with anything but a giggle. It was possible that Juniper's

happiness was magnified by the realization that she'd need one
more canvas print bolstered on a frame, just like the other four.

* * *

Brazenly, she was going to drive to Kinko's. Clover was buckled in
for the adventure. Juniper was actively embarrassed on the drive,
embarrassed that she was now officially chasing this guy. Chasing
him based on what? That she loved his voice? She did, though, she
loved his voice. And just the way he was. His intensity.

She slapped in a disc of Radiohead and grooved her shoulders to
the beat. As the whir of flat scenery passed by her, she started singing,
and Clover sang too, "Aaahhh!" Juniper sang with gusto, right along
with her backseat backup singer, to "Creep." At a stoplight, she put
the song on repeat so they could sing the weirdo refrain over and
over. That got them to the Kinko's strip mall.

The parking lot was like the lobby of a concert hall (her ex, Rob,
had taken her to the Chicago Symphony that one time, and the
grandiosity never left her). The plate glass of the shop was like
the edge of a stage, glaring with the hot lights of nothing, signs
advertising and the slanting streaks of reflection blocking her view
of what if. *What if he's in there?* Her heart floated to the top of
her throat, pulsing like roiling lava lamp bubbles. Ridiculous. She
buckled Clover into the baby carrier, facing front, legs dangling.
She walked in with a sense of purpose and was hit with the smoky
smell of burning copies, burning plastic, carpet made out of recycled
six-pack holders.

Clover reached out her arms, Frankenstein-like, and started
squealing. Juniper started doing her mama bounce but was quickly
distracted by the fact that he was there, as big and burly as she
remembered, his hands flat on the counter, leaning into the room.
As she approached, she had time to take in his beard and blue eyes.
She hadn't remembered them as blue, but there it was. The room fell
away for a moment, at least for Juniper, when he said, "Well, look
who it is."

Her own smile hit her so spontaneously that she had trouble
returning a simple hello. But Clover had no trouble and kept

squealing. The squeal was usually delight or curiosity. But today she was convinced Clover sensed her mama's discomfort, and it was just plain sassiness. Before Juniper got a chance to apologize for the noise, he shifted his gaze from Juniper to Clover and said, "Is that right?" in a sing-songy voice. He crouched to her level and made a funny face, and of course Clover squealed again.

"Hey. You're smaller than last time you were in here."

"Yeah," Juniper said.

"Well, she's adorable."

Juniper smiled at that, smiled at him, and said, "Well, I'm back. I have one more. Photo, I mean." She was still bouncing, probably looking ridiculous.

"Do you want a print, or canvas, or—" He waited for her to elaborate. But did he actually remember she had other photos printed on canvas? Did he remember mounting them on frames? It had been about a year since she started her project.

"Yeah. I do want this one printed, and on canvas too. Like the others I did? If you remember?" *Ugh.* This was starting to be excruciating.

"Canvas one mounted on a frame, 12x12?"

She looked up at him, sheepishly maybe, and nodded. He slipped into the back room while she wondered how much he would do this time. Would he mount it for free again? Should she accept the gift?

"You were at my show last week," he said, leaning out and around the backroom door. *Hoo.* This was awkward. But she had to push through.

"Yeah. You were kind of awesome." She said more than she meant to.

"Well, thank you. It was really cool to see you there, actually," he said, still leaning back to look at her. Clover screeched. He laughed. Juniper nodded while bouncing and trying to calm Clover. He disappeared again, and she waited, bouncing and flustered, but happy.

He came out with Clover's face on the three-dimensional square. The fifth "Kowalski woman."

"Does this look good?" he asked.

"It's perfect," Juniper said. "I'm actually going to be painting on these canvases, so—" She fumbled around for her credit card. This time he took it. As he was handing her card back to her, he said, "So it's Juniper?"

"Yeah."

He reached out his hand. "Dahl. Dahl Iverson." She shook his hand, because what else was she going to do? And he said, "Wow."

Wow to her name, or wow to what? That she was stalking him? That she was a horrible conversationalist? She couldn't think clearly, she felt like an idiot. *Creep.* So she said, "Wow yourself."

His face lit up, and he heaved out a big laugh. He was so expressive. Kind of beautiful. His face got suddenly serious and he said, "Coffee sometime?"

Her internal lava lamp was just a-roiling. She grabbed a nub of pencil and scratched out her number on the edge of the bag that her print was in and tore it off. "Yeah. Sure." She handed it to him and focused, trying to sound calm. "That'd be fun. Thanks." She continued to smile as best she could. She couldn't remember the rest. Clover's silky hair. Driving home. Radiohead. She sang her heart out. Juniper and her backup singer.

* * *

They were at Cora's for dinner. Juniper had just changed Clover and felt freedom enough to pick up her cell when it rang. A man's voice said, "Is this Juniper?" It couldn't be him yet; it was just a few hours later. Her heart jumped a little.

"Wait, who is this?" she asked.

"Sorry. Yeah. It's me, the guy with the copiers and guitar, Dahl." Cora's ears were perked like a bobcat's nearing a hidden field mouse.

"I'm just calling about that coffee?" Again like an idiot, she paused too long. "You know, I like to keep my fans around."

She finally said yes. They would meet Sunday. Cora had inched to the basement with laundry. But the second. The *second* Juniper hung up, she heard Cora yell from downstairs, "Juniper! You meet someone?"

"Oh jeez Christ," Juniper said with a laugh.

Coffee Date

She saw Dahl through the glass of the coffee shop. From her perspective, it was like he was always on a stage. He was standing near the counter in a blue sweater and black scarf. Her entrance was more grand than she intended. The door whooshed behind her. The morning air pushed her up to the front.

"Hi!" she said. They stood face-to-face, and she had to look up just a bit. She realized she might be standing too close and pulled back a little. He laughed. At what, she wasn't sure.

"Hi Juniper," he said. His eyes rested on her. The blue with the golden halos around the iris. But they weren't talking. Was the conversation stalled already? No, that wasn't it. He was smiling, and she found herself looking at his face too long. She shifted her gaze to the menu behind the counter. He ordered then gestured for her to go ahead. She thanked him. They waited at the end for their white mugs then picked a table in the front window. She set down her purse. She had worn a necklace, a delicate string of raspberry-red beads she had loved in college. The exact color of Swedish Fish. She hoped it was pretty.

"So you're an artist?" he said. She was so happy he seemed interested in her art. She couldn't wait to get into it with him. See what he thought. He was a musician, he had to have some ideas. She wanted to talk about Chicago. She didn't even know where he was from. But the conversation took a hard turn.

"And a mother," he said. She felt herself deflate. What was she supposed to say? *Ugh.* How to address this. He couldn't have been completely freaked out; he asked her to coffee.

"Yeah," she said. What? He was looking at her with such a question mark. "What?" she said out loud.

"I'm curious about that," he said.

"Her name is Clover."

"I thought that's what I heard," he said. "Cool name." He was still clearly wanting more information. "She's darn cute."

"Thank you. Yeah. I adore her."

"So what's the deal? If you don't mind me asking. You're not married, are you?" He cut right to it.

"Oh, no!" She was surprised at what was obvious to her, needing to be addressed. "No, I was never married. Just found myself pregnant and obviously wanted to keep her. I wanted to be a mom." She surprised herself by spinning it that way. His shoulders visibly relaxed, and it was her turn to laugh. He even looked a little shy for a second. But they dug in after that, their lives, their art. She could focus on his words better when he wasn't distracting her with his singing. But then, well, his face was distracting to her too. Forthright in its joy. Open. She liked his beard.

They talked about their names. Everyone thought "Dahl" was some affectionate nickname, like "hon" or "sweetie." But it was a family name, he said. She practically blushed when she thought about how he was such a buck of a man, he more than carried the name. And Juniper explained how her name came to be.

Apparently a young Grandpa Carl Kowalski had gotten stranded in the woods one night in the U.P. on some logging job. The snow was so fierce, he lost sight of his truck. He was mostly surrounded by chopped-down stumps that provided no safety or protection, but he managed to find a bushy thicket of juniper. The snow came so hard and fast that night, he ended up sheltering in place as the snow created an igloo over the flaps of flat leaves. He became hungry and found himself nibbling on the plentiful juniper berries. As night and the howling winds wore on, the shelter and the berries were all he had. His own breath recycled warmth to keep him alive in the frigid air before dawn. He barely slept, but the turpentine kernels and flat branches were both his company and salvation. The sun didn't really start melting him out until late the next morning. And family lore had it that was how Grandpa became an alky who loved his gin and how Juniper got her name.

Dahl's sepia hair had a reddish hue when he was backlit by the meager November glow. He nodded at her story. They were northern folk, the two of them. His Norwegian roots held both an exotic and comforting appeal. Her deep Michigan soil.

She drank her coffee slowly and felt the caffeine zip around her insides. The conversation paused, and they gazed at each other. It was an oddly long pause for two people who didn't know each other very well. It was odd not to look away. But they didn't look away, and his familiarity sank into her like rain into earth. They continued talking, but the air was charged with them, by them. The coffee shop got smaller and smaller until it was just their table. Just their hands around their mugs, and his eyes. Then he took in a breath and said again, "Wow."

Normally someone would ask, "Wow, what?" But Juniper didn't need to ask. She didn't need clarification or reassurance. She was there. It was becoming wow. So soon.

"You really are beautiful," he said. He was looking right at her, and she absorbed his compliment with stillness and joy.

She could feel the sun glowing through her hair, and how her necklace had settled into the vee in her neck. She was looking down at her hands but looked up into his eyes when she responded. "Thank you," she said. She didn't have the courage to say what she was thinking. That he was beautiful too.

She noticed the white sky out the window and had the good sense to realize a natural pause. She had the good sense to leave him wanting more, or at least she hoped. She took the plunge and said, "Well, I have to go get Clover at my mom's." That brought them up for air. They stood.

At the exit, he reached up over her head to hold the door for her, and she could smell him. She swooned. Holy son-of-a-bitch, his smell was a place she wanted to be. This wasn't like the bar, when she felt his hoppy beer breath glide past her; that was just infatuation. This was nuts. This was some kind of chemistry match. Outside, it was threatening sleet or something that made the air heavy. She inhaled deeply, really so she could get one more hit of the air that was laced with him before getting in her car. He gave her a big, enveloping, not polite hug.

He called her the next day.

"Juniper. I'm a horrible guy," he said by way of greeting. "I have to tell you something crummy." She hadn't had time to do anything but repeat her favorite scenes from the coffee shop over and over in her head. Beautiful. His smell. Blue eyes with golden halos. She almost didn't welcome this interruption of her reverie. But he waited like it was her turn to talk. At first all she heard was the word "guy," and his rumbly, warm voice. The manliness of him was lodged in her mind. But she was brought into the moment by the word "crummy" and his tone.

"What?" She asked.

"Yeah. I have a girlfriend," he said.

Come on! She yelled in her head. *Just come on already.*

"Juniper? You there?"

"I'm here." She didn't mean to sound frustrated. That wasn't gonna win anyone over.

"I know, I shouldn't have even asked you to coffee. But I was just so impressed with your art, your ideas, just you." He said. "So I did. I was bad."

"Why is that bad?" she said. "It was just coffee. No biggie."

"Yeah. But no. It wasn't all innocent for me." She thrilled at this. "Juniper?"

"Yeah."

"If I didn't have a girlfriend, would you go out to dinner with me?"

She smiled. She was worried he could hear the wet crinkling of her mouth, a dead giveaway. "Yeah."

"I know I have stuff to sort out. I'm sorry if I misled you. I'm gonna go now. But hang on, okay?"

"Okay." She was tentative and had no idea what he meant. She did hang on. She hung on for weeks with no word. She had Clover and her mom, she had her work. She had the meaning of her portraits churning around in her mind. The last thing she needed was a confused guy. Maybe it was the kid thing. Or she was too weird, or not hot enough, or dressed dumb. Or didn't talk enough. After the silence of Kirk, the repeated, inappropriate silences of Kirk, she had zero patience for that again. But she had so deeply thought Dahl would be different. She was more hurt than she should be. She just stayed busy and kept going.

Mind Your Place

She moved the coffee table so she could just look at the faces for a while. Five in a row. They'd greet her as she passed them on her way to the bathroom or when she was stirring some pasta. She also had all the flat prints as well. She messed around with those in a grid-like pattern on her floor. She stacked them like a flat totem pole, Great-Grandma Carol on the bottom. It was her family tree again. But that was too obvious. She thought about her mom's reaction to the gravestone. How Cora wanted anonymity. Juniper saw that as part of the problem, not even feeling like you deserved life, liberty, and the pursuit. Like someone was doing her a favor. Cora always acted like someone was doing her a favor. Juniper had been slowly welling up with the entitlement to be heard. This was no direct political statement, but socioeconomic for sure. She lined the prints sideways again. For there had been no perching upon one another's shoulders. All the propping up from one daughter to the next had just held them even. There. They were all even. In a row. You lend me a quarter, I pay you back. But that's not how it should be done. You give me a quarter, I get educated. I start a business. I improve my life, which improves yours. This is how other cultures did things. Doctor lawyer engineer cultures. But theirs was a blue-collar, minimum wage, mind-your-place culture.

So she thought of including one element from each photo and incorporating it into the next. Their legacy.

With paint she would alter each photo. Great-Grandma Carol could be looking toward the left, away from the others, back in time. Grandma Jezebel would be wearing Great-Grandma Carol's large triangulating collar. Stifling social norms easily represented by ridiculous style trends. Cora would be altered to share some of Jezebel's naïve exuberance, the rah-rah of midcentury middle-classdom. Juniper would line her own eyes fiercely in black rings, hemming in her view with rebellion, and Clover would be marked with the asymmetry of change. Clover would be moving out of the frame and only partially visible.

The sepia flesh of her ideas spilled and filled out into facial expressions and colorful shading. The movement of her concept allowed her some real movement in her life. She felt ready to go back to work part-time. With Christmas a few weeks away, she more than needed the money. A facsimile of a winter coat could be made by layering enough sweatshirts and sweaters. But she could really use a pair of winter boots. Her tennis shoes now had a little hole near her pinky toe that let the slush in. Her driveway was gravel, and the puddles were just about unavoidable. She finally had that car, which was a bonus, but her needs and Clover's were overflowing. The thought of selling the trailer to move in with Cora was upsetting and seemed too much like a lazy solution, and a betrayal to her grandma. Any anxiety about going back to work was overshadowed by the bills staring up out of her mailbox. Cora would take Clover for three days a week; they could do opposite schedules for a while. She would make some money.

"I'm so relieved to hear your voice!" Manny said. "But you know, right now, I only got housekeeping. You okay going back to that?"

"Manny, that's fine. Honestly, I could use the exercise." And Juniper meant it. It wasn't that she was enthusiastic about working as a Vacation Express maid again, but this time it was different. This time it was with a clear view toward something in the future. A means to an end, they called it.

"I won't lie and say I'm not relieved," Cora said that night after dinner. "We can do this. I got her, June. I can do those three days. We'll make this happen." So many times like that, Juniper's life was filled with this kind woman who seemed to see life through splayed fingers covering her eyes and her beauty. Her scratchy-throated, dried-flower beauty. Her mother.

"Mom." Juniper stopped washing dishes, dried her hands on the towel, walked over to Cora at the table feeding Clover rice cereal with mashed banana, leaned down, and hugged her from behind. "I love you, Ma."

"Well, you are my pride and joy, and I ain't afraid to say it." Cora choked up. "Now I got both of you I'd do anything for, and this is gonna be the best Christmas in a long time." That moment was like a present with a bow. And like it wasn't pretty enough, it seemed someone had come along with sharp scissors and curled up the dangling ribbons too.

* * *

She had once heard that it took three weeks to make something a habit. Just a myth, maybe, but it was a useful goal. She had spent two weeks and six days pushing Dahl out of her mind. They'd had a magical Christmas, buying Clover toys and dresses and getting swept up in the decorations that triggered everyone to celebrate with purchases. And she was almost there to the habit of not wishing for him. But then her little chunk of connection buzzed. Her phone, his number, not even entered into her directory. But she knew it was him. It was weird how something you were waiting and wishing for could seem abrupt.

"Juniper, it's me, Dahl." He was out of breath, like they were in the middle of a conversation.

"You sound excited," she said.

"I am!"

Argh, she hated cryptic conversations. But she had grown to the point where she kind of masochistically loved awkward silences. *Bring it on*, she thought as she waited for him to say more, to explain. Also, she was a little pissed. It was too reminiscent of Kirk and his being with her without being available. Nuh-uh, not that again.

"I'm calling to see if you'd like to go out to dinner with me."

"Seriously?" she asked, her will immediately weakening.

"Seriously."

She wanted to ask him to explain himself. She wanted to see the broken contract. She wanted to see his whole heart before she even ordered an appetizer.

"Okay," she said.

Their evening was made lovely by the fact she was eating a pasta dish with artichokes, which she had never had before. The artichokes were brighter-tasting than she thought they'd be. The lights were a low-slung amber, and there was the requisite dark red accents of an Italian restaurant. Juniper and Dahl were talking and happy.

"Wanna try my ravioli?" he asked. They were settling in. It was an intimate request. He actually cut a piece for her and held out his fork. Not her fork, but his. She knew it would taste great as the bite came toward her mouth. She opened her eyes, after fully enjoying the feel and taste of his food, to see a girl with long, dark-brown, glossy hair blow into the restaurant. She had on a short black skirt, and Juniper had that microsecond of jealousy over her prettiness. But they were safely tucked into a dark back-corner booth, and Dahl's eyes were on Juniper.

The girl was standing near the front lobby, snagging the periphery of Juniper's good time. She heard this girl talking to the hostess, then their server. Then she marched. Glossy Girl marched, in that stupid short skirt, over to their table. And her high-pitched voice growled like a baby animal.

"You son-of-a bitch!"

Juniper dropped her fork. Dahl wiped his mouth, but his teeth were still purple from the nice wine they were drinking. Glossy was facing Dahl, more than Juniper, like Juniper wasn't there. And Juniper's heart wrenched when she heard the girl's shrillness crumble.

"*Why?*" Glossy started crying.

"Come on now, Melissa, we talked about this."

She hit him. Just a swat on Dahl's big shoulder. But he grabbed her wrist, which made Juniper both relieved and uncomfortable. With Glossy's wrist locked in his grip, he managed to slide out of the booth and pull her back to the bathroom hallway area. Juniper could hear their heated exchange and didn't know what she should do. She tried to listen but still took a bite of her fusilli and chewed slowly, hearing Glossy Melissa's crying voice. She swallowed and leaned out of the booth to watch them. Even though she had never experienced this particular kind of drama from this particular vantage point, something about it was wearying. She wanted more innocent, oblivious goodness before being forced to watch this kind of reality. She didn't want to see their reality.

Dahl had control over the situation, and Juniper felt his voice sounded firm and not unkind. She took another bite and washed it down with some wine. The wine was so good, and she just wanted to keep eating in case the meal would be ending soon. Juniper alternately took bites and craned her neck to watch their progress. Finally, Dahl and Melissa walked back through the dining room and out the front entrance. Juniper was momentarily crushed, thinking they were leaving, until she realized that Dahl hadn't taken his jacket. She was grasping on to hopeful when he came back in the jangling door by himself and ran his hand through his hair, pushing it back, maybe clearing his mind in a very literal way. He looked so flustered and tired when he slid back into the booth, but Juniper admired the cornucopia of emotions she'd just seen him display. This little maelstrom of events had resulted in a realization that she liked seeing all those emotions. It made him full and three-dimensional, and kind and present. He pushed his glasses up to where they belonged and said, "You're still here."

She smiled softly and sincerely. "I am." She sipped the last of her wine as slowly as possible while he finished his cold food. Then they ordered dessert.

It was a gentle conversation, from both of them, about his newly ex-girlfriend. He eased Juniper's anxiety over this beautiful girl by the fact that his attention effortlessly refocused. With his kind yet firm dismissal, Juniper became the beautiful girl.

Her cannoli was crumbling all over her shirt, and the powdered sugar felt like it exploded on her hands and lips and cheeks. She wondered if she was supposed to be having this much trouble with her dessert. He laughed, watching her grapple with her napkin and the crumbs.

She was uncomfortable, and she was aware of this uneasiness. She was trying to decide if she liked mouthfuls of ricotta cheese when she realized her unease wasn't really with him. It was discomfort with her own feelings. She was entering some kind of new territory, parting some kind of beaded curtain into a place that had maybe been there, but was new to her.

Dahl dropped her off at Cora's that evening after their dinner date. He parked the car, turned it off, unbuckled, and angled himself toward her.

"Hey. Sorry tonight got weird."

Juniper shrugged one shoulder. "It's not your fault," she said, not sure if she meant it.

"You know, I really thought about things between our coffee and asking you out to dinner. I mean, I thought about them so much, I broke up with her. I realized that she wasn't what I wanted."

Juniper was able to look at him and take in his earnestness. It was dark out, and there was a bluish cast of light filtered through his car windows. A little mix of random country street light and moon glow. She couldn't help but notice. She was trying to decide exactly what she thought, looking at him. She flashed back to his singing voice. The color of his eyes would match the light with its blues and golds, if she could see them in the dark. His shoulders were thick and broad, his stomach almost reached the steering wheel, his beard was trim, his lips looked soft. His brown hair made her want to reach out to find out if it was rough or smooth. Nothing was objective anymore. She found him utterly beautiful. His hand was draped over his gear shift. She reached out to touch it. He raised his eyebrows and smiled. He then took her hand and pulled her toward him. She helped by leaning in. She closed her eyes and let her lips fall open just a little. Their lips first touched, then their tongues. She took a sharp breath in, then leaned in for more.

Juniper's Now

She started the new year trying not to feel like she wasn't taking a big ol' step backward. Her first day back at Vacation Express depressed her a little. It didn't help that she was a heartsick for Clover as soon as she left Cora's driveway. But she had to stay positive. That was her duty. For her girl, for her mother, for her art.

She had come in through the side door, eager to see everyone. Manny still had the lobby all decked out with a tree and colored lights. The first person she saw was a view of Bethy from behind. Bethy behind the front counter, fiddling with the fax machine. She wasn't wearing a smock. Her hair was loose and flowy, and she had on *dress pants*. Juniper wanted to reach out to her and grab her by the blouse and yell, "No!" But Bethy was not Clover. She couldn't constrain or attempt to control Bethy's behavior. They'd certainly established that much. Bethy's hair twirled like a tea-length dress as she turned around. Juniper only had a swift moment to compose her face from alarmed to friendly.

"You're here!" Bethy said, looking glamorous, of all things.

"Yep." Juniper felt divided by the front desk and her own smock. "What's up?" she said by way of greeting and by way of saying *what the fuck happened to you, are you giving everything up, you are going to get stuck here for the rest of your life.*

"You're surprised, huh?" Bethy said. Juniper knew that Bethy knew what she would think. They'd talked about this very thing. She wasn't sure if this meant Bethy would only be making money the traditional way.

"Good pay, I bet."

"Better than before," Bethy said, then blushed realizing her faux pas, that her "before" was Juniper's "now." Right then, Juniper's consternation kerklunked to the next square of the slideshow. Past alarmed. Acceptance. She had a baby. Bethy was going to be a manager. Totally divisive things had never stopped their friendship before. But she made extra-sure that when she got Clover from her mom's after work that day, they went home and Juniper turned on some music, loved her baby, and worked on her project. She had to keep her purposes right in front of her. Her eyes ahead.

Well, mostly. She couldn't deny that he was on her mind. He had given her a CD of his playing, a demo with five songs he was using to get gigs. She would listen to his voice like she was absorbing the lush color palette of an adored post-Impressionist, or the direction of an Andy Goldsworthy stack of rocks or trail of leaves. The quality of his voice often distracted her from his words and guitar sounds. She had to doubt herself, that she wasn't falling in love with him, but his voice.

He invited her to one of his gigs. It was at a coffee shop in Kzoo on a Tuesday evening. She brought her sketchpad and asked if he'd mind if she drew while he sang. He'd look up and smile at her between songs. The warmth of a room seemed to easily overtake him. And she could hear his sweat when it sprayed, when it dripped. He brought out that sensation in her, not just of seeing the world, but hearing it and the synthesis of the two.

Of course, she was amazed. At first she thought it couldn't possibly be love, because she was too in lust to see straight. Right away, after their second date, he had driven her back to her trailer. Even though he knew Clover was at Cora's, his car crunched over her gravel. He said he wanted to see her place. They both knew why. As she unlocked her door, she didn't feel like he would think it was shabby. She had cleaned it just on the chance something like this could happen. Right away, she looked at her plaid couch and thought of Kirk there, hovering over her. Kirk had never been inside her bedroom, which was where she led Dahl.

They stood in the doorway of her bedroom, kissing deeply, then pulling away to look in each other's eyes, then going back for more. His big hands nearly enveloped her waist, like he was eating her up with his grabbing. His hands moved down to her ass and squeezed, and she moaned.

They had talked about art and music. They had talked about the pace of life and how they both liked to take it all in, slowly and deliberately. They were artists' lives, messy and rambling, and slightly dysfunctional, maybe. She didn't *really* know about his. But she knew enough to let herself be completely taken when he lifted her up onto her own bed. He lifted and kissed the underside of one arm, then the other, and pulled her sweater up over her head. He too hovered over her. But she and anyone else could see that this was different. It was so different this time.

She unbuttoned his shirt. Another plaid shirt, exactly the same as the first plaid shirt she saw him in, but a different color. His chest full of curly hair, exuding a smell that tugged out her most primal wishes. She kissed his chest with her eyes closed, inhaling, breathing him in, knowing she had been right as they left that first coffee shop. She had been right about the chemistry of them together. She was overwhelmed as their clothes came off. It was a blur, the grasping and pulling. They were sweating already as he looked into her eyes to ask before he pushed himself into her and groaned with that first entry. He groaned and tilted his head back. He slid easily. He told her she felt amazing. They kissed again and again. When he came, all she felt was joy. When she came, she felt like she was falling in love. The pulsing had never been so bright.

* * *

So it hurt in her gut, the pulling. After they had been together, she was obsessed with want for him and remembrances of him. Feeling so good and warm all the time tormented her, like when she was just trying to buy some cereal, and Prince with his cream came over the sound system, and looking at Wheat Chex got mixed up with wanting to go home and close her bedroom door and eyes and smash out her desire, picturing him.

The lust just squashed her, squeezed the breath out of her, and not just when he was on top of her, although that was a little perverse thrill in itself. The mahogany of his voice hot-pressed through the sawmill of them. And when he was almost there, the thrill of being crushed, just a little, made the tears squeeze out the corners of her eyes. She thought it was just the exertion of the moment. It was just tears squeezing out, maybe an excess of oxytocin, endorphins, or some other brain-altering chemical. Love melting out. It was different with him, how her body clamored after him. And it was a din she only wanted him to shutter.

* * *

No one was close enough to hear her guttural, "Mmm," as she sat there at his coffee shop gig, pencil paused over her paper, remembering their most recent time together. She had to set her pencil down then, overcome by the sensation of him, and the taste, that she couldn't begin to express with a pencil.

It was that night at the coffee shop that nudged her farther. They were together but separate. Not touching. He was singing, she was drawing. And for her to feel that sense of camaraderie with someone, that sense of working alongside, made her step over some hurdle that had been knocked to the ground. What would Jezebel say?

She got up to get a second coffee. And for that next set, her coffee was always the perfect temperature, even as it changed. Because her sense of perfect was fluid. First it was too hot, and she enjoyed the lingering numbness of her tongue. Because she was busy drawing, it rapidly flattened out toward cold, and the taste of bitter oldness edged the cup with a greenish hue. After the last sip, she popped her cardboard cup down on the shiny table. A veneer over beat-up wood, glossy. The gleam became a glare. She bit the corner of her lip before a ragged exhalation.

She hadn't heard him do that "So in Love" since his Old Dog show. She remembered how it had coiled around her. But she didn't want him to play it tonight. Those words should not get said yet, because they were on the cusp. And thankfully, he didn't sing that song, but she swore it hung in the air between them that night at the coffee shop. Everything lovely and haunting about it.

Twisty History

She was working part-time, had a beautiful growing girl, was mentally consumed with this new relationship, and yet she found it easy to work on her art. She found the time. She was pulled to the things she loved. *Five Women* was finished over the course of the next couple months. She hoped it was okay that it had a little whiff of the Nina Simone song. Although hers was obviously not about racism, it was about stereotypes of women. It was about being stuck.

Clover had crawled across the room early on and grabbed the corner of one print. It was the print of herself on the end, ironically, and she had chewed a little tiny piece on the corner. Juniper had been so upset at first. Clover's mobility took her by surprise. To leave your sweet pudgy baby with a cloth book on her activity blanket in a corner of the living room, only to turn around from the kitchen to see her on the other end of the living room with a corner of your artwork in her juicy hands, leaving a soggy print, was startling. Seeing Clover essentially roll, scoot, or crawl all over the trailer to get into anything she could was like watching someone invent the wheel. That was Juniper's brilliant girl. Of course, sometimes Juniper would find her lodged up against the bathroom door, crying and stuck, unable to find her "reverse." That was damn funny.

Ultimately, Juniper liked the idea of Clover's portrait having a chewed corner. A little independence to do what she wanted seemed appropriate.

She had painted a singular background that spanned the five portraits. It represented the local landscape and further unified the pictures. She ended up painting right over the blue flower quilt behind Clover but liked knowing it was there. The landscape image she painted was striations of a setting sun over a gray November cornfield, stumps of ochre brown cornhusks marking the ground.

She wondered where she would hang this installation of prints. It was Gobles. She could go to Kzoo and find a place where her work might be seen by more people. Or she could find a spot here in her speck of a hometown, where everyone would know who they all were. Where folks could speculate what it was about till the cows came home. It'd be good for them. Juniper was leaning toward the wagging tongues. Why be brave if you weren't going to see it through?

She rocked Clover that night, giving her milk, going on an imagined tour of her town, thinking of a place to hold her idea. The library was barely more than a shaggy little storefront. Downtown was a row of limping brick shops. Not the gas station, probably not IGA—maybe the high school? She and Clover both dozed off in the rocking chair, and the cold air on her nipple actually woke her up. There was a drop of milk hanging from her breast, almost midair, and Juniper remembered one of her classes where the teacher talked about surrealism and the story of Dali's creative thinking technique. Dali apparently set himself up to fall asleep sitting with a spoon perched in his hand, a plate on the floor. At the first moment of dozing, the spoon would fall to the plate, clattering him awake amidst his uncensored, unconscious surreal ideas. March air, milk cold dropping onto her absorbent shirt. Something about the flap of her nursing bra and the drop of milk reminded her of *The Persistence of Memory*, the melting clock. Ahh, she was teetering with imbalance, the ideas flitting around her, sinking into her, emerging from the very essence of her. She was jumping ahead to her next idea. She lay Clover down in her crib and watched her sleep like all mothers do. In silhouette from the hallway light, she saw the round and curving lines of Clover's face, like a path to follow.

Falling asleep that night, she mentally haunted through each street and park of Gobles, thinking of where or how to display five large squares in the light of day.

Morning light shone in her high window. And she thought of a space that met all of her criteria. It was odd, but she had to go see it. She zipped Clover into a warm fleece sweatshirt, buckled her in to her seat, and drove over to the downtown. It was a block of old bricks that really didn't have much meaning anymore. Early spring just exacerbated Juniper's urge to look away or to look over the tops of the squat buildings. But instead, she looked afresh at the faces. The sidewalks ghosted little girls in dresses with yarn bows. Grandmotherly types with plastic bonnets over their set hair, fresh from the salon. She superimposed images she'd seen of what downtown used to look like. Trim men used to wear tucked in, button-down shirts. Mothers carried paper-wrapped chunks of meat for that night's dinner. The immediate needs were celebrated, maybe as easy as ticking items off a list. There was a time with less distraction and more near-sighted purpose.

But today was a reminder that dirty snow in melting Gobles hardly seemed hopeful, just soggy and patchy. Forgetful.

She parked on Van Buren Street. Thriving businesses had long since been replaced by sad ones, even sadder in their hope. In an sagging community with no art, if it wasn't gas or snacks, failure was nearly destiny.

The ice cream shop was front and center. Juniper had called ahead, not sure they'd even be open yet, but Mr. Pasternak had answered the Tastee Twist phone. He seemed to remember Juniper from his last few years teaching math at Gobles High.

With one hand she held the stroller while the other knocked on the screen door that had been retrofitted into the bricks. The shop had been part of a furniture store at one point, and maybe a flower shop before that; her memory was fuzzy. But it was a weird privilege to step inside this place she'd driven by thousands of times and see if her memory served her right about how perfect the space might be. She liked the feeling of knowing this town on a micro-scale. Not just buildings, but corners of unvacuumed, pebbly carpets. Dead bugs in windowsills that stayed for years. A light that was out on the gas station sign. The exact color of varnish on the library chairs. The way one tree would fill out during the spring, and another would reach upward. These were all sticky photo album pages to her.

Mr. Pasternak seemed mayoral as he opened the screen then stepped out to hold it as she jiggered the stroller down the wide hallway where folks could wait in line out of the weather, whatever it might be.

"Miss Kowalski. Look there, you've got a little one. Well, isn't she a doll." His face aligned in the way nearly everyone's does in the unexpected presence of a baby. It tended to backlight folks' faces, Juniper had been noticing. Seeing Clover seemed to add symmetry to years of living that was spread crookedly on most peoples' faces. The lines on Mr. Pasternak's forehead didn't become smoother, just parallel. The wet gray shadows around his nose and the whites of his eyes lightened as Clover looked into him and the space around him, her presence giving *him* an aura.

"Mr. Pasternak, how are you?"

"Trying to enjoy retirement, staying connected to the goings-on here with the shop." Mrs. Pasternak had passed away a few years before, and that was the kind of thing everyone knew, so they let that set between them.

"So. I have this odd request," she said as she admired the space. Clover chewed the face of her cloth doll.

"You hinted," he said while leaning against a chair in the broom closet at the end of the hall, which served as his office.

"Yeah, I have this art that I created. It's actually five portraits. And I've been looking for a place to hang them in town." He was just leaning, arms folded. He didn't nod or smile. It reminded her of how she felt growing up in Gobles all along. Different. People thinking she was different. Typical small-town stuff, but ugh. "And you have that big chunk of brick wall there." She gestured behind her. Clover hurled her doll down the hallway. Juniper picked it up.

"I never thought of doing anything like that, hanging up some art," he finally said. The space in question had a high, grubby set of windows on one side, and as they spoke, some fledgling rays of sun showed up in the wide hallway, casting themselves against the brick.

"Can I show you?" she asked. "I've got the pictures in the car. I'll get them right now."

"Okay, I guess," he said. She was uncomfortable leaving Clover sitting there, but it was the only choice. She made a few trips out to the car and back then placed the squares in a row on the floor, where they now looked like bodiless ladies waiting in line for ice cream. She worried about how much explaining she'd have to do. This might be considered a little avant-garde, she thought. Or weird. It might be considered weird. She had a quick couple of sentences explaining the history of the matriarchy in her family. But she didn't get a chance to start in before he said, "That's Jezebel Kowalski there. I miss that lady." He walked up to the portrait and leaned over a bit, looking into Jezebel's eyes. Then he looked left over at Carol. "Oh, and I remember that one." His tone changed. "She was stern, Jezebel's mom." But then he smiled. "Juniper, this is some Gobles history you got here." He was approving. "Well, and some current events." He chuckled at his own joke and winked in the direction of Clover.

Juniper hadn't expected this positive response. She had to reroute her plan. "I have some words on the history of the women in our family I'd hang with it," she dared.

"Hm. This could be real neat to see while folks are waiting in line," he said. Without saying anything, he strolled up and down his own hallway, looking up at the dirty windows on one side, then across to the expanse of brick. The brick wall was as plain and empty and bland as Gobles itself.

"You'd need to figure how to hang 'em without drilling," he thought out loud.

"Yeah, I planned to get some clips that go into the grout. I heard they work great." She was getting excited, allowing herself to examine the grout with a scratch of her fingernail.

"Yeah, I don't see why not. This seems kind of neat," Mr. Pasternak added. He gazed at all five portraits. "So it looks like you're taking one

element from each generation and putting it in the next portrait." He
nodded thoughtfully. "Yes!" Juniper was pretty much elated at that
point. "You got a title for this?" he asked.

"Well, the title is *Five Women*. But there's a caption I want to include:
Here shines the mothers who are."

Mr. Pasternak took that in and let a puff of air out of his nostrils as
he seemed to contemplate. He was mumbling something to himself,
and she started to worry. More audibly, he said, "What was that
saying out there to the cemetery? That fake gravestone to fathers?"
Juniper felt suddenly as nervous as she did at her sixth-grade spelling
bee, nearly panicky. But she spoke slowly and clearly: "Here lies the
father that could have been (as good as dead)." She paused before she
added, "That's what was carved on the stone."

Mr. Pasternak took in the heaviness. But then his head twitched
up, and he kind of squinched one eye shut as he really looked at
Juniper for the first time that day. "Well, I'll be damned if I'm not a
Sherlock Holmes here." He chuckled. Clover laughed. And that made
both Juniper and Mr. Pasternak laugh.

This time it seemed like there was news in the paper right away.

> Twisty History? Five generations of Kowalski
> portraits up at Tastee Twist. Local artist, Juniper
> Kowalski, makes her statement about Gobles
> women, and the shackles and gifts that one
> generation gives the next. From left to right:
> Carol Taylor, Jezebel Kowalski, Cora Kowalski,
> Juniper Kowalski, Clover Kowalski.

The short paragraph accompanied a blurry black-and-white photo
of the newly adorned brick wall. Mr. Pasternak had actually allowed
her to paint her caption right on the brick, and she loved the added
integration, like her work was a real part of the town. She knew
the paper must have talked to Mr. Pasternak right away to get that
quote about shackles and gifts; those were her words. But the part she
couldn't stop reading was two other words: local artist. Like stepping
into a pair of shoes at the back of your closet that finally fit the way

they were supposed to. The local artist smiled and held her baby with kisses while reading the paragraph over and over.

* * *

"Dammit, June." Cora stomped out her cigarette at the sight of her daughter and granddaughter opening the front door.

"Ma, please don't smoke inside."

"Yeah, but dammit. Why'd you do that again?" Cora asked while opening the kitchen window.

"That's why I'm here," Juniper offered. "I wanted to clear the air with you if you were mad." She tucked Clover into her high chair with some blueberries splayed on the tray.

"If? Come on now. I got my face plastered downtown. Them backgrounds you painted look amazing, though." Leave it to Cora to say something sweet about Juniper's work amidst her own embarrassment.

"First of all, thank you, Ma, that's nice. And second of all, do you understand my intention?" she asked. Cora didn't respond. She tended to doubt her own reasoning and never was one to raise her hand.

"It's meant to honor you and the love you've given unconditionally. And it's meant to show how our past can keep us anchored. But as much as I needed to cry out about Dad, I needed to shout joy about you, Ma. And Grandma, Great-Grandma, and Clover."

"God, Junie." Cora started to cry. "I won't pretend I'm not mortified. But you are a good girl to want to honor your family like that."

"Plus Mr. Pasternak thought the history was cool," said Juniper gently. Neither had said too much about Cora destroying the father's gravestone. Juniper was careful around the subject and figured or hoped it would all get resolved in time. Anger seemed to be put on hold.

Cora said, "Well, it's ice cream season coming up now. This should get interesting."

* * *

Juniper got calls of support from Bethy, Manny, and Jo-Jo. And her old art teacher sent her a note in the mail to her mom's house. Her cursive was florid, and she wrote her words lined with a ruler on the bottom: *Juniper, it is amazing to see your work, and your voice in this town! I am so proud of you! Keep it up. Sincerely, Ms. Schwarz.*

All the positive response made her want to fling her art. She was getting urges to go out and start tagging things with images and words. Not spray paint; that wasn't her medium. She had heard about this Banksy guy when she was in Chicago. And she got that whole thing. He wasn't just a graffiti artist, anyway. His work was beautiful. How he integrated surroundings into his work was just brilliant. He had so much to yell with paint for the world to see. It occurred to her as an afterthought that her *Five Women* was possibly aligned with the social realism she'd learned about in school. Diego Rivera's Industry murals in Detroit had crossed her mind. Both of those artists were using a medium that was large simply by being public. She had to think. Where was she headed here with her art? She had to think about what more she wanted to say. The fact that she could just keep going, she really *wanted* to keep going, thrilled her. She too wanted to yell, holler, shout, announce, question through her work.

Dahl had gone with her to see her finished work at Tastee Twist. He told her the portraits were great. He said he was impressed and had loved her concept from the get-go. But after reading the article on her dinette, he surprised her by standing up and going around to her side of the table where she was feeding Clover. He took her face in his hands and gently turned her head so she would have to look at him.

"Juniper, your work is fantastic." Then he kissed her forehead and sat back down.

She smiled. She was high on everything. She loved that he had been there for the very first inspiration of her project and that he had helped her with it by giving her the framed canvas prints. No doubt his generosity had helped her get there faster. His generosity of spirit kept her in awe.

Gobles IGA

Clover was sitting in the front kiddie seat of the grocery cart, enjoying her worldview. Juniper felt like a big ol' hypocrite that she was using the mesh bag with a couple strawberries inside for Clover to gnaw on while they shopped. The stupid mesh bag she'd thought was totally frivolous but was now grateful for. Well, that was motherhood. A little hypocrisy never hurt anyone.

Juniper was in the cereal aisle, frankly enjoying the outing. They both were. Clover was so pretty in her dark pink jumper, with her shiny hair that looked like golden wheat. It was almost Easter, and Juniper got sucked into the happiness of cute little baskets and thought of the fruit puffs that Clover adored, fitting nicely in some plastic eggs. Sometimes she would lean over and whisper a little song in Clover's ear. She'd whisper-sing, *"We need pasta, we need oatmeal, and little sticks of cheese for you,"* and tickle Clover's round belly.

Juniper was always proud these days. Proud to be a mother. Proud of her sweetest little girl. Even proud to be such a young mother, energetic and capable. She had nursed Clover before they left, but she started fussing like she was still hungry. Must be a growth spurt, Juniper thought. She got out a baggie of Oat-ohs, which was both sustenance and entertainment. She kept one hand on or near Clover, tethering her as she leaned down to reach for a cylinder box of oatmeal. As Juniper stood up to put the box in the cart, she was startled by Kirk's grandmother, Carol Tomasz. Juniper was sure it was her. She was using one of those motorized wheelchairs with a basket that they provided in the front of the store. Her best friend from elementary, Jessica Green, had Mrs. Tomasz for fourth grade, and they used to giggle about her hair that looked like it could take flight. That was before she needed the wheelchair. For some time, Juniper had been paying extra attention to the extended Janoski family around town. She would cross paths with an aunt or see a cousin having a yard sale and be sure not to stop, even if they were selling baby girl clothes.

Mrs. Tomasz was comparing two boxes of granola bars, reading labels. Her back was to Juniper, so Juniper hustled out of the aisle. She was figuring which way she should go to escape. Juniper turned left and figured wrong.

Her face blew right past embarrassed to ashen. She panicked in the single second she had to register who was leaning down, looking at the shredded cheese. She hadn't seen him in over a year, but the hair. The vee of his back. She should have quickly turned right, but she stupidly stopped completely. He turned around with his bag of cheese, clearly returning to his grandma's basket. Juniper was still stuck as he stood up fully and walked straight toward her. She got to look at him full-on as he went from cheese-selecting mode to recognizing ex-lover mode.

"Juniper." His voice still resonated her "r." But he looked older, even when the lines around his eyes smoothed out as he finally registered the shock of a baby in the cart. "Juniper, wow." She just stood there, Juniper-style.

Clover said, "Bzzzzz," with spittle bubbling all over her face, which helped Juniper pull herself together enough to say hello.

Kirk said, "I thought I might possibly see you when I was in town. It certainly crossed my mind." He nodded sheepishly, as if to himself. She hadn't asked anything.

"Well, here we are," she said.

"A baby, huh?"

"Yep. Clover."

At this, his face softened. "Clover. That's so nice. And pretty, like her mama." Juniper's heart clenched. He had always said things like that. Things that made her shaky and exuberant at the same time.

But wasn't he doing the math? Maybe guys were bad at that kind of stuff. Clover could be six months, she could be a year. He'd have to stop and think to realize her age was suspect. But his face was sad and resigned. He didn't look like he was doing calculations in his head. He didn't look like he noticed Clover's thick blond hair and blue eyes. Maybe Juniper was going to get away with it. She was also sad and resigned.

He said, "Yeah, so. Um, me too." Juniper looked at him quizzically. "I mean, Jody and I have a brand-new baby boy."

Juniper was immediately stunned and hurt. "Wow," she said. She shouldn't be hurt. But she was *so* hurt.

"I know, Juniper," he said. "I know."

He looked at her with such sadness, and what she thought was love and regret. She knew that what she had felt was real, and it would always be there now, because it was inextricably linked to Clover. But they would not have worked together. She knew that. She realized then that maybe he didn't know that. He was with his wife and new baby, and maybe running into her hurt him too, especially if he saw her baby as coming from someone new. It would have been someone new right away. He wouldn't need math to figure that much out. Maybe that was why he didn't even ask.

"I'm going back to my grandma now. And I'm not supposed to say this, but I don't know if I'll see you again. I miss you. I've missed you. And I'm sorry." He didn't wait for her response. To be fair, she always took too long. She did sort of want to shout out after him, "Me too!" But she was too quiet and too late. So, to his twisting torso, she whispered, "*Me too.*"

Clover babbled as Juniper drove the cart straight to the checkout. She zipped out to her car in the parking lot, barely using her peripheral vision to get there safely. She just didn't want to see him again.

But like a slap in the face, there was his blue car, parked right next to hers. He wouldn't have recognized her Toyota. She didn't even have her car when he knew her. In his back seat was an infant car seat, facing backward, with a sweet, tiny boy, soft and lovely, sleeping with a paci in his mouth. And next to him, with her hand protectively on the baby's head, was the baby's mother. Jody. His wife.

Juniper buckled Clover in, all the while feeling a projected sensation of being a fleet-footed boxer that her grandpa might have watched. The dancing-dodging. The recoil sensation of being hit. The spraying sweat, flying off with each punch. Shiny silk reflecting the obscene lights. The narrowed vision of eyes swelling shut. And being hit again. And again. The floor made of a rubber that smacked and smelled. Relentless pain.

Clover grabbed a fistful of Juniper's hair and yanked. Juniper yelled out. Loud enough that from inside the blue car, Jody turned her head and looked at her. And she smiled from the back seat of the Subaru, right at Juniper. The mother code of understanding. Juniper was TKO'd

Yes

It was exactly one week later when Juniper's phone rang. She could almost tell who it was going to be. She felt it coming. Life could sometimes be confusing with time, where the past seemed to loom up ahead, and the future, this phone call, had been sitting around ghosting every room Juniper entered for the past year and a half.

"Kirk."

"Yeah, Juniper. It was good to see you last week. Weird, but good."

"Yeah, you too. I won't lie, I was pretty stunned to see you. I've always kept my eye out for you, but when you were there, I was pretty freaked out."

"It's been weird, and sad, and just confusing."

"For me too," she said. "I saw your baby. And your wife."

"Huh?"

"You parked your Subaru right next to my car. I saw them in the back seat."

"Oh geez, okay."

"Your boy is adorable." This was the small talk. But why had he called? Clover was down in her crib, napping. Juniper had been thinking about trying to work when the phone rang and it was finally him. "Kirk, why did you call?"

"I saw you, and it just hit me hard," he said. Her heart was starting to jump around. What, he just missed her? She waited for him to say more, because if she opened her mouth, she knew she would yell something permanent.

"June, I actually had a dream about you. But it wasn't just you, it was you and Clover." He said her name. "Seeing you with a baby really hit me," he reiterated. "I don't have any business asking, I know, but I can't stop thinking about this. Are you with someone new?"

Juniper just wanted to run away from this conversation, but her heart wanted to run toward it all. "No," she said and waited for that to sink in for him. Of course she was with someone new. *Now.*

"So what then? What happened?"

"Kirk." Even she was annoyed at her own minimalistic way of talking, but she couldn't just blurt it out. She had to lead him to it, that's all she could do. She didn't have the courage to state the facts plainly.

"Can I just say something?" he asked. "I was really struck by Clover. She's such a pretty girl. Like you, of course." Some weight was added to the room. "She has this little cleft in her chin," he said.

"You noticed."

"I noticed, June. Is there something I should know?" His voiced edged higher when he asked. It wasn't going to get any easier, and the time was presenting itself.

"Yes," she said.

"Yes? Yes, what?! God, Juniper, yes *what?*"

"Yes, she is yours."

Juniper fell apart with a sob. She sobbed with a loss of control that she had not experienced since her grandma died.

It seemed Kirk had set the phone down, because his voice seemed farther away, and he was yelling and swearing. She heard him yell, "Jesus fucking Christ," and slam or throw something. She was scared. She pictured him walking down a hallway in his house, moving away from her and the phone, like a coyote pacing. He came back and picked the phone up. Then her fear turned to something else, because then he was crying. She could hear him, and his tears and his face, and she wanted to hold him. But that wasn't allowed. This all was a horrible thing that wasn't allowed.

Juniper thought to speak first. "I'm sorry. I'm so, so, sorry. I didn't know what to do, and then it seemed too late, and I wasn't going to give her away, or anything else like that, and you were done with me." She pushed a little of the blame over to him so he would have to at least taste it. "I love her so much, Kirk. I love her." She was pretty sure he was still crying. "And I loved you."

"June, I need to think. I need to process this. I've got a wife and baby here."

"I know," she said, still scared at how he would end up reacting, what this would all mean. "I'm so sorry," she said again. When they hung up, she went right to Clover's crib and picked her up. She'd never woken her up deliberately, but all she wanted was Clover in her arms. They settled on the couch. She lifted her shirt and flap, and through closed eyes, Clover drank.

* * *

She went out to check the mail a few days later. Taking in the ochre yellow of weeds at the end of her gravel driveway, Clover bouncing on her hip, she saw a personal envelope. Rare. Scratchy blue ink that she didn't recognize. She saw his face every day in Clover's, yet she didn't know his handwriting. She walked back up the driveway, clutching the weight of what might be in that envelope. Inside, she set Clover down on the floor and tore it open. It was five thousand dollars and a letter.

Dear Juniper, You are wonderful with Clover. I am so happy she is doing so well. She is beautiful. You have never ceased to impress me. My feelings for you run deeper than I can process and deeper than I can act upon. My son is doing well, and my home life seems to be back on track. My commitment here has to come first because Jody came first, and I took an oath that I must uphold. Please understand. I will be sending checks when I can. Please know that I care. Love, Kirk.

The fact that he wrote her name, Jody, just further sealed the already sealed deal. He would be someone who had changed the course of her life and then left. Another male following some cruel but seemingly prescribed rule of behavior in her life—their lives. She heaved air from the very bottom of her lungs and picked Clover up to change her diaper. She hoped Clover wouldn't notice that Mama was crying. She got her dressed in a pair of leggings and frilly T-shirt, and they drove to the bank. She deposited his check and swore she heard a clunk when the teller filed it, like hitting the bottom of a piggy bank. There. It was finished.

* * *

Clover was free to turn one. She ate Funfetti cake and chocolate ice cream with Cora and Juniper and Bethy and Jo-Jo and Garret. She grabbed fistfuls of icing with an adorable earnestness. She hugged a stuffed kitty still in its wrapping paper, loving the crinkle. She slapped Garret right on the face, and Juniper yelled "No!" and they all laughed, except little Garret, who screamed. They had balloons and joy. They put on some wholesome Raffi and watched Clover bounce like a crazy person, holding her Crinkle Kitty. Garret mostly cried. The ladies ended the afternoon with shots of Jägermeister, which Bethy pushed on them. But it was the only grown-up fun they'd had in some time, so Juniper and Jo-Jo said yes as Cora lined up the glasses. Clover fell asleep in her play yard for the night, tightly hugging her still-wrapped kitty with one fuzzy ear now poking out. Some of the paper had dissolved beneath the onslaught of slobber. It was messy happy.

Juniper had told no one about seeing Kirk. About his rejection in the form of five thousand smacks. It was a new feeling then, not being offended at being rejected herself, but rather absorbing the blow of the rejection of her daughter. Juniper had to absorb the rejection until Clover would be old enough to absorb it herself.

Subdivision

She found herself comparing what was becoming incomparable. At one point, she had avowed a certain love for Kirk because of their life-creating bond. But with Dahl it wasn't a generous, benevolent feeling of love of man through love of mankind. She was growing to love Dahl by listening to him slowly. Like a tear in a canvas, she would step inside and see an entire world that she never could have imagined. In her amazement was love. In her surprise was love. In his eyes that turned up when he wasn't smiling was love. Then she would step back out of the canvas and tend to life. This went on easily for a while.

Cora was totally supportive of this, Juniper's first real relationship in like, forever. And Cora loved Dahl. She aggressively volunteered to watch Clover. Juniper tried to bring up her doubts, like about that early introduction of Glossy Melissa and some other questions she might've liked answered. Or maybe not. She could admit that she didn't like his mysterious ways. She hated mysterious ways. She tried to cajole out his secrets with her quiet understanding, and every time she thought she might be getting a clear, full, picture, his big silences would crowd their space again.

And Cora would say, "Settle down now, you guys just started dating. Don't make the man tell you all his secrets right away."

It seemed like sound advice. But it was from Cora. They were both floundering in the dark here. Dahl seemed to have a past that met no expectations. There was something about him, and even them together, that seemed timeless. It was both beautiful and mysterious.

The biggest mystery was the most simple. He didn't invite her to his place after they started dating. At first when she asked about going there, he said he liked her trailer, it was homey, and reminded him of his grandma.

"Duh," she said. "It's a grandma place."

After two months, she insisted. Turned out he was living at home in the basement of his parents' split-level. But when she finally went to visit and saw his room on the lower level, the whole house was eerily silent. After her second visit, she said, "Well, where are your parents?"

"They aren't here," he said. "Want something to eat?" He pulled some cream cheese out of the golden wheat-colored fridge and some Triscuits out of the varnished amber cupboards. The large, ornate, circle handles were in the center of the doors. The amber from the cupboards must have flown into her subconscious, releasing an invisible fly, niggling its curled antennae. Amber was a preservative.

She realized that his place, his family's place, had a similar feel to her own place. It seemed misplaced by a generation. Dahl was thirty-two, but the home looked like it was really still stuck in the eighties or nineties, not unlike Grandma's. No cars but his Accord were ever in the driveway. He spoke of his brother, who lived down south in Indiana. So he lived in his parents' house. But it would gradually dawn on her that his parents didn't actually still live there.

They were going out that day, to a local farm that hosted ice skating and sleigh rides. She had never been on such a date. He was in the upstairs shower, and she perused the photo gallery in the hallway linking the bedrooms. There was Dahl, with his light brown hair of youth, feathered back, his glasses big and owlish. His face was smooth and sweet and not yet manly, as it would become. His older brother, Casper, had darker hair and a stern look about him. Dahl had said he always strived to be as smart as Casper, as thoughtful as Casper.

There were Sears-type photos of four of them, featuring velour and pointed collars. There were other relatives and a rotating roster of dogs. At the end of the hall, displayed in a silver frame, were his mom and dad, holding hands on their wedding day. His mother had glorious blond, cascading hair, undulating in waves down her shoulders. His father had that same stern look as Casper. They were under an arch in front of a green field, surrounded by an abundance of daisies. They were a gorgeous couple.

Dahl came out of the shower with a towel around his waist, looking every part the Viking stock he must have hailed from. There were droplets of water on his shoulders. He looked at her with a light in his eyes. To see him there in a towel, sturdy and large, the appeal for Juniper was animalistic. Their contrast was a constant reminder of her own femininity. He was so clear about his attraction to her, by how he always stood too close and looked greedy. It was so easy between them. He let his towel fall to the floor, and she thrilled at the sight of his skin and his body. Sturdy and bold. His arm slipped around her waist, which she loved. He guided her over to the couch, practically pushing, and she was smiling. His fresh, showered smell evoked a swell of timelessness that overtook her. His lips were full and soft. He lifted her shirt, unbuttoned her pants. He took her. He gave to her. It was joy with him. It was nearly blinding joy. Except. The wallpaper had swirls of feathers from Asian birds in blue and gold patterns along all four walls. There was no respite from the aviary assault as she threw her head back on the arm of the couch. The weight of him. God, she loved the weight of him.

The motion of ecstasy jarred her into a reminiscence of Kirk on her own couch. Somehow then, she was able to connect the silence in his house to a logical conclusion. The blood rushed away from her head, then rushed back as she stayed upside down for a minute or more, dizzy, blank, filled. He dripped out of her. The house smelled like old dust. Almost a linger of perfume. But not from Glossy or something recent, she was sure. It was more powdery and old-smelling. She waited until she was sitting up, and he placed his towel beneath her in a chivalrous gesture that both protected the couch and let her lie in peace. But it wasn't peaceful as she felt a wave of panic for no logical reason other than the silence was becoming cloudy. The blue and gold birds flew in and out of pagodas in a way that made no sense. She pulled a silken throw pillow in front of her chest so she could ask, "Dahl. Where are they? Where are your parents? Why aren't they here? Ever."

"Hey. Let's get dressed," he said. He kissed her head and went downstairs, plunking out a left-hand chord on the family upright as he passed it on the landing. She watched him skip down, holding the white wrought iron bannister. She smiled that he nearly flounced in his nakedness, unconcerned, proud. She followed him to the lower level, where she now suspected was the only place he could talk.

"Okay, Juniper." He was sitting on his own bed now, wearing jeans and a t-shirt. His sheets were printed with a laser-beam pattern. She joined him, cross-legged, and waited with worry.

"I was sixteen." He took hold of the hem of his sheet and ran his thumb up and down repeatedly, trance-like. "My dad was sick. He had MS." At this, he looked up. "Do you know what that is?"

"Kind of."

He explained enough so he could go on. "Well, he got worse. And it seemed like all of a sudden. One day I was a dumb kid, then he got his diagnosis, and I remember feeling like, 'Well, this is it, time to grow up.' My dad had been a carpenter, and he had to give that up almost immediately. He'd just started to have trouble walking, and I remember my parents talking about us having to move." He shook his head. "I was a little shit, because I fought with them both over it. I didn't want to move from my childhood home." Dahl didn't live in Gobles. Their house was on the outskirts of Kalamazoo, and to Juniper everything about it was better than what she'd had. She got the appeal of a home like that. The middle-classness of it was downright magical.

"Anyway, we hardly had time to process his decline when he fell down the front stairs there." He pointed up to the stairs that went from the front door to the main floor of the house. "He fell, broke his hip, even though he was only fifty-two. He got pneumonia in the hospital and died. It was so fast."

"Oh. Dahl. I had no idea. I'm so sorry." She reached out and tried to hug him, but he flinched and pulled away.

"No. No, there's more." He went on. "So, after the funeral. That very night. I guess my mom was upset, too upset to handle it. Someone, I still don't know if it was her doctor, or whoever, had given her some pills just to help her cope, I think. I mean, we barely got through the funeral. So she took some pills, apparently, but also had a lot to drink. She must have taken too many pills, and Casper and I both know that it wasn't on purpose. We know it with every ounce of our being. But he, Casper, found her the next morning in her bed. She was gone."

At that point, tears were streaming down Juniper's face. She was shocked and couldn't process how a family had been through so much. Dahl wasn't crying. But he looked ashen. He let her hug him, but only briefly.

"I need to get up, okay?" he said. They went for a walk in the cold around his old neighborhood. She thought knowing this secret meant she knew everything about him. She had felt her first love for him that was devoid of lust while they held hands through the depressing, aging subdivision.

Speaking to Everyone

Despite the tapestry of grief presented by Dahl, she would need to weave in the bright goodness from her own life, because it was emerging in colorful threads that needed to be integrated. In fact, something amazing happened. Something all those bike rides to Walmart, layering sweaters, and toilet scrubbing never prepared her for. She got a call.

"Oh, hi. Is this Juniper Kowalski?"

"Please take me off of your calling list," she said firmly, as usual. They had to take you off if you did that. She waited for the response.

"No, my name is Candy Reagan. I'm from Channel Three down in Kalamazoo." Her accent was so neutralized that her last name sounded like ray gun. Maybe she wasn't local. Maybe this was a scam.

"We heard about your artwork around Gobles, the tribute to fathers and mothers," said Candy.

"It's not a tribute to the fathers," Juniper corrected.

"Yes, well, you know. Your pieces about fathers and mothers," Candy amended diplomatically. Juniper waited. "So we just wanted to see if we could come out to talk to you about them."

"Am I in trouble? I got permission for the portraits."

"Oh, goodness, no. We want to *interview* you, Juniper. Would you be open to that?" And she said "that" with such a flat "a" sound that

Juniper decided she couldn't fake their local, strident "a." She might be from Channel Three. It might be real.

"Okay."

"Okay? Good!" Candy chirped and made an appointment to come see her the following day. They were going to meet out at Gobles Cemetery, if the weather held. She wondered why the cemetery. All that was left was a jagged edge of Walmart paver sticking out of the dirt.

* * *

Juniper didn't know what to wear to such an interview. She didn't think about news equaling cameras equaling all of the greater Kalamazoo area. She was just wearing her good jeans. She was going with her mom and Clover. She needed the support, and by default they had to bring Screechy.

She pulled up to the cemetery. It was an overcast day, spooky really. Moody with that old Michigan panel of gray wash overhead. They got out of the car, and behind the biggest maple was a white van with a satellite and News 3 logo. There was a lighting umbrella making the day shine on a person she assumed was Candy. Between her blinding hair and fuchsia lips, Candy hardly needed any help with light. The initial hubbub of vehicles and people slammed Juniper with a sensation of cold jelly in her stomach and then a line of dotted sweat on her forehead. She hadn't had time to imagine what this interview would entail. And there was still no time, because an assistant-type person came up to her with a smile and handshake.

"You must be Juniper. Glad you're here," he said. "Do you need any water?"

Juniper was juggling Clover and handed her over to Cora. "We might keep her in the frame," the assistant guy said, maybe to himself.

That wouldn't work. How could she juggle Clover and answer questions thoughtfully? Then she felt something touch her head, and she whirled around to find a woman with a hairbrush touching her up, apparently. Then a tiny brush for her face, which also must have needed some help. She had worn a bit of makeup, but there were professionals bustling around her. She felt whisked about, even though she had barely moved from the spot where she stepped out of the car. Then Candy strode up to her with a startling smile that looked like her face had been pulled outward, eyebrows up, chin down, cheeks wide. She would have almost looked frightened if there wasn't the requisite smile beneath the hyper-opened eyes. "Juniper! So glad you're here. We're excited to talk to you." Candy shook her hand then gestured to the remnants of her stone, just as Cora had left it. Juniper had a realization that no one but her knew how it was destroyed, and for the sake of her mother, for the *honor* of her mother, she'd keep that secret.

Candy said, "I saw the news photo of your stone while it was intact. Your statement. It's bold, and I can't wait to get your thoughts on camera."

She briefed Juniper on what would happen and walked Juniper over to their umbrella-lit spot by the tree. Cora was occupying Clover on a muddy patch of melted snow. Juniper had rare opportunity to feel nervous but was pretty sure that was the feeling that had taken over her body. She was surprised at the physical manifestations. She couldn't get the rhythm of her air right, and she felt clammy on her face and on the backs of her knees. "Can you give me a sec?" she asked Candy.

"Oh, yeah. Sure. I'll be right over there." Candy pointed with her clipboard. Juniper stood in front of the rubble, her back to everyone, and reimagined her words. What it meant to her: fathers that could have been, had they chosen to show up, be present, love their people instead of licking their wounds. She nodded to herself. She gulped in fresh pockets of wind then felt like a sieve through which the air could pass freely. The air was honest, and the constrictions left her.

She turned around, and Candy gestured for her to join her in the empty director's chair beside her. They were artificially lit, with the cemetery that she'd only previously experienced with haunts of grief or angst or a quiet ear toward the birds settled in behind them. Candy had told Juniper that the close-up newspaper shots of both her pieces, "Mothers" and "Fathers," would be featured, so she needn't explain how her pieces looked.

"Just tell us what they mean to you, and your thoughts about what they might mean to many of us," Candy explained. "Explain why you thought your stone was so inflammatory that someone was moved to destroy it," she added.

Every single person hushed on cue, and Juniper and Candy were left alone, a couple of girlfriends chatting art and family. A couple of women chatting about not enough jobs around this part of the country. No equal access to higher education for those trailer-dwelling, Walmart-working folks that made up the immediate surroundings. Candy knew all this; she was working in Michigan. But she asked anyway.

"How do you, Juniper, think the lack of jobs in this area affects fathers who might leave their families? Do you think they might become frustrated and ashamed about their inability to be good providers? Did this affect why your father may have left your family?"

Jeez, this Candy wasn't just a piece of pink sweetness.

"Yeah. I think the whole socioeconomic piece is knotted up. Not enough jobs, not enough money, not enough education. You can go from one to the other in any order and back again, and there's hardly an escape. These things all get knotted together with this coiled-up ball that has become our culture. You can't separate." Juniper felt like she was exhaling her exasperation in words. "On a more personal note, I can't blame our culture for alcoholism. That's everywhere, I know. It's touched our family too. But I can blame our culture somewhat that my father left without hardly trying. That is somehow okay here. That's practically a sanctioned path—to give up on family without hardly trying. And I speak about this as my Michigan culture, because that is what I know. I am speaking what I know." Juniper paused as Candy nodded.

"Wow, Juniper, you touch on some important issues. Important enough to inspire anger, it seems." Candy gestured to the rubble. And here, Juniper followed through on her decision not to address the broken stone. She knew Candy had brought it up in her intro of their talk. She wanted to step back, be the old Juniper and not say a word. Let the stone in both of its iterations do the talking.

"Yeah, and my art is not proposing a solution, just acknowledging a problem. And honestly, some personal pain on my part."

"I think many families can relate to what you're saying about these struggles and the fragmentation of family." It was Juniper's turn to nod. She now saw Candy as a beautiful woman. Candy wasn't just a pretty bright face. It was almost like she was talking to Bethy, but oddly more personal. For once, she wasn't worried about offending anyone, because she was speaking to everyone.

"Juniper, how about your portraits? Is that a continuation of the same conversation?"

"The flip side, sure." Juniper explained her concept of integrating one aspect of each woman's portrait into the next generation that was meant to symbolize her new catchphrase—the shackles and gifts one generation gives the next.

"I love each of these women. That's the foremost reason for these portraits, a gift of thanks. They represent something personal, of course. But I also hope they represent something more archetypal. I hope they represent the passage of time and the varied shape family trees might take. In my case, a straight line of strong women." Juniper smiled for the first time. "And not everyone has the good fortune to have one generation after the next of girls." She smiled wider, and like magic, Clover was placed in her lap. Juniper wrapped her arms around her girl, smiled over at her mom, and felt she was finished. But something made her look over at her grandma's grave. It was like she could feel Jezebel's approval. Men were bad, women were good. *Yes, I believed in you, I believed you would end up here. Here, so different than you thought, young lady.* Juniper's eyes burned with threatened tears, but she held back, held the moment.

All These
Phone Calls

That night, Clover was in the play yard, fussing about her teeth pushing through her gums. Her hair stuck to her face, all sweaty, and she grunted like she was actively working to get those back teeth to emerge. She'd whimper, then grab the frozen washcloth Cora had made for her and suck for a moment before throwing it out. Cora or Juniper would lean over from their spot on the couch and hand it back to her. But mostly, they were leaning forward into the TV, in and out of the fan whir.

"Ma, turn it up. Please. The fan is loud. Clover's loud." The box held so much power in those minutes before the six o'clock news. They thought they'd get a little snippet or preview of Juniper's interview. And sure enough, the announcer teased the next hours' news, which included Juniper's art. There it was. They flashed images of her "Fathers" gravestone and then the "Mothers" portraits, then her sitting beneath the giant tree!

The waiting through commercials and every other story was nerve-wracking for both of them. Juniper had never seen herself on television and was surprised that she didn't seem like a wisp of a girl. She was surprised that her tone was kind of commanding. She was surprised that she was happy about the segment and felt a warm thankfulness toward Candy Reagan. And she was surprised at the part she liked the most, when they gave her Clover, and she could witness the love in her own eyes. Clover's pudgy hand rested on the skin of Juniper's arm, and she felt it anew, how Clover's hand felt like soft powder. Juniper looked happy. Like she was happy to be a mother.

When the news was over, Cora's phone rang, and she jumped up to get it. Juniper listened to Cora saying, "Thanks. Yeah. I am proud, yeah." Then she laughed. "Okay, I'll tell her, thanks Mary Ann." It was Bethy's mom.

"That was sweet of her," Juniper said. They didn't have a moment to talk about what they'd just seen. The phone rang again. It was Cora's cousin.

The fact that Juniper was on TV changed Shelly's tone from suspicious to impressed. Juniper could gather that Shelly might have been saying something about Juniper's grandpa, because Cora said, "I know, Shelly. I was glad when Ma protected us. Juniper just needed to have her say about the whole thing, I guess." She could sense Cora being tense at the mention of such a painful subject. "Thanks Shelly, I will."

Then the phone rang *again*. This time it was a coworker of Cora's. Juniper was absently playing with Clover while she half-listened and half-daydreamed about what had happened. She had an image of the cemetery and realized with a sour taste in her mouth that what she had created might upset Jo-Jo somehow. The gravestone and father reference might hit too close to home. She had to reach out to her right then.

"Hey, Jo-Jo. I wanted to call you. I don't know if you saw the news?"

"I didn't. Why?"

"It's just about that fake gravestone at Gobles Cemetery."

"Oh, that. I know about that," Jo-Jo said.

"Well, I didn't want you to be upset by it or anything. You know I think the world of you, and you're doing such a good job with Garret, and Gary was a great guy, and I was just worried."

"Juniper, don't worry. I'm good. I didn't think anything negative. Plus, you know I got my own MIA dad over here. Even though I'm grown up with my own kid, I can relate."

"Oh good," Juniper said. They chatted baby stuff and promised to get together with the little ones. Juniper had called Jo-Jo on her cell, and meanwhile Cora was still fielding a ringing phone. But Juniper didn't have time to eavesdrop, because then her cell rang.

"Juniper, it's me. Kirk." The bottom dropped in Juniper's stomach. Her voice snagged in her throat. Kirk. Holy. "Yeah, this is weird, I know. I'm sorry I haven't been in touch for a little bit here. I know we left things weird. I'm sorry." He just kind of rambled, and Juniper was too taken off guard not to let him. "So this is some coincidence, I guess. We're here at my grandma's again, and the news came on. What are the chances? I saw you on Channel 3. I was blown away. Nice, nice work."

She could hear him fidgeting with something on his end. He was clicking and scratching at something. "Juniper, I just felt simultaneously kicked in the gut and really impressed. I'm guessing you might've been referring to me on the gravestone. But your portraits are stunning. They just talked about the meaning of your work, which is pretty cool. But your concept and execution were something else. The way you linked the backgrounds from one portrait to the next is gorgeous, and the sunset-like colors behind each person are rendered so cleverly." He paused again. "Juniper, are you there?"

"Yeah. I'm here," she said. "Thanks."

"I just had to call you. It was impulsive, I know. I didn't mean to freak you out," he said.

"How's your boy?" Juniper asked.

"Oh, Jack is great. Just great."

"Good." Juniper let the silence hang. What was it to her? She thought she could hear the nighttime crickets that might possibly be heard between the two homes if she stepped outside. Maybe they were listening to the same crickets, breathing the same Gobles air.

"So, how is," he paused like he didn't want to say her name, "Clover? She's grown. She's beautiful."

"Yes." He shouldn't be able to compliment her so objectively. Juniper felt a torrent of pain, then a bolt of anger at him spoiling her moment. He shouldn't have called like that. "Thanks for that check before," she said. "And thanks for the call. I'm glad you liked the work. Okay, I have to go, glad your baby's good."

She just wanted to get off the phone. She knew she was being abrupt. But she was done. And anyway, she was about to cry. She actually threw her phone down on the couch. Cora said, "What? Who was that?" And instead of answering, Juniper started bawling. Cora set Clover back into the play yard, which made her scream. Juniper checked that Clover wasn't upset by her mama's crying. But Clover did seem confused and concerned. Juniper picked her up, hugged her, and felt a surge of comfort from having her baby in her arms. *Her* baby. Not his. She sobbed and rocked with Clover, petting her curls and rubbing her back. Her sweet baby.

"June, who was that? You have to say." Cora looked worried. "I'm so nerve-wracked, I need to go outside for a smoke. You have to tell me. Wait. Was it him?" Juniper looked up, still crying, and nodded. Cora looked furious, like she was taking cues from her daughter. "Really? Right now he needs to chime in? I know shitty timing, and that is shitty timing," Cora spat. She sat down next to Juniper, holding Clover, and wrapped her arms around the two of them. That pretty much summed up the whole thing, thought Juniper. Right there on the couch, they summed up the whole damn thing.

Run-on Confession

In June, Dahl had some crummy-paying gig outside in a park. For thirty-five bucks he would sit in the gazebo and be the headliner of "Sundays at Lakewood Park." Everyone who knew Juniper was so happy for her now that she was with Dahl. Bethy couldn't believe that she'd snagged the singer from the Old Dog, even after Juniper astounded Bethy with the Kinko's back story. His voice, his presence, and generosity toward Juniper over the past months had given him a bit of cult status in Juniper's world. Cora had had him over for dinner right away and saw how he was with Clover. Cora had doubts at first. Juniper knew enough during that first dinner that Cora was watching for the other shoe to drop. She wasn't sure what to do with a guy who seemed to be *nice*. Juniper wanted to freeze that first evening so she could scoot around to Cora's side of the table and tell her to knock it off. *Stop giving Dahl that look*, she wanted to say. The fact that Dahl was also a good listener just about threw Cora right off her game.

At the park, she felt like they were on a field trip as she helped him load his amp and mic stand and guitar stand into her car. The day was all pollen and flitting birds, sun bouncing off Clover's gold hair that was finally starting to be laced with earth tones. Clover was in the stroller next to the gazebo, and Juniper could see her as they made the fifty-foot lug back and forth to his car to get all his gear.

He was sweating a little already and started in again, as if they had been still talking about his past.

"So, anyway. Then I met Melissa." This got Juniper's attention quick. "I know she's not so fun to hear about," he said kindly. "But I wanted you to know everything. I credit her for helping me clean up. We were together for like five years."

This had the odd result of leaving Juniper feeling slightly relieved. Any girl he didn't marry or at least stay with after that much time, there must have been something wrong with her. "She's a nice girl. Really." Juniper hated hearing him defend her against nothing. Juniper stayed quiet. "She was nice, and a good person, and helped me out a ton." He paused here to unfold his chair and started unwinding the cords to his amp and mic. He looked up at her from that slot of space above his glasses as they slid down his nose. He shoved them up and said, "Yeah. She was nice, but damn, it wasn't like when I met you."

Everything he had said before that was okay after that statement. "Her family was who I loved. I loved them all, and that's what I've been struggling with. June, I was never in love with her." He didn't add "like I'm in love with you" or anything like that. "I don't know whether to tell you this, but I'm talkin', so I might as well finish."

He sat down in his folding chair while she stood on the grass in front of his stage, Clover in the stroller, flinging her back against the seat in a protest to get out. "She was kind of expecting me to propose. They all were. When I met you. So I did have a little trouble extracting myself from that. From her family." It was the end of that part of his story. An older couple had set out lawn chairs, and she stepped back, not angry, not happy, really. Just ready to be done with his never-ending back story.

It wasn't like with Kirk, she reminded herself as she pulled Clover out of her seat and onto the blanket. Clover said, "Yes!" and started scampering off toward Dahl and the stage. It was okay; she wasn't in anyone's way. Juniper sat as Clover toddled around the stage, circling around Dahl, who was warming up. The sun shone, and people came, and then the mahogany sound of Dahl rang above them, as pure as birds lacing the air. She thought he almost didn't have to tell her all that stuff, his voice was so laden with the layers that can only be created by wading through thick pain. He exuded love, of all things. She found him to be a beautiful man, and whether his stories had been only heroic or only failures, she wouldn't have seen him differently.

Clover bounced around while rattling an empty potato chip bag, drooling with delight, sometimes crooning along. Dahl would glance up at her antics and truly smile. But for Juniper his look was more penetrating and serious. When he sang something that was sad or soulful, he would sometimes glance into Juniper's eyes, and she almost always had to look away. His look was so powerful, tilted up corners, wisdom stepped up and down the arpeggios of his guitar lines, and faded against the summer trees.

* * *

"So, June," Dahl said on the drive home. "What are you going to do now that you're famous?"

"Ha," she said.

"Ha," Clover said from the back seat.

But Dahl didn't let it drop. He waited until she made a successful left onto Lake Street.

"You know there's this contest or show or something in Kzoo every August, right? You know 'bout that?"

"Yeah. Maybe. I've heard of it."

"June. I. Per. You. Should. Enter."

She laughed. "Stop!"

"Dude. Girlfriend dude. You're really good. You've got to keep this momentum."

"Stop! I'm trying to drive!"

"You can multitask here. Tell me you'll do it."

"I'll think about it."

"Clover—" Dahl turned around to the backseat. "Clover, tell your mama she's stubborn."

"I'm going to drop you off right here on the side of the road!" Juniper got unusually animated, which just egged Dahl on.

"We'll revisit this later, young lady," Dahl said as he placed his hand on her thigh.

Juniper was smiling. She didn't realize she loved being teased. She liked being called out. Encouraged. At the next light, she turned to Dahl. He was looking out the window, singing along to the Ben Folds disc he had brought.

"Geez. This stuff is dark when you start listening," Juniper said.

"Yeah, but spot-on." He sang along, "Give Judeee. My notice."

And Juniper nodded. She nodded at his unselfconsciousness. She nodded at his low resonance channeling a high voice. She nodded in time to the music in her car, hoping Dahl and his voice were soaking into Clover.

* * *

Juniper dropped him off, and once they got home, she put Clover down for a nap. Juniper lay down on her couch. Her trailer cocooned them. The rooms were small. The light, dark. With eyes closed, she recalled that walk around Dahl's subdivision. How gray it was, and how he had continued to open up.

"So, Casper was nineteen, and we got to stay in the house. It was weird as hell. I ate Cap'n Crunch every day for months. I hobbled through my junior year."

Juniper had felt like she was in the background, there to absorb everything he might say that day.

"Hey, you know how I got my job at Kinko's?" he had asked.

"How?"

"I literally took it over from Casper. He graduated from Western, and I was piddling around. Well, that's a separate story. Yeah, and he just told the manager that his little brother wanted his job, and boom, that was it."

"But weren't you like, twenty?"

"Nineteen, yeah."

"But does that mean you've had that job for over a decade?" Juniper was alarmed at that thought. Of course he was too good to be true. This had been established on the evening she was introduced to artichokes, or maybe even before then, when he didn't call right away.

"Oh, hell no. I've been around. Part of that separate story that I'll tell you at some point here. Soon." Juniper wasn't sure how many more revelations she could handle. As selfish as that sounded, his life had had too many twists and turns and pain and loss, and it scared her. But then she'd look at his eyes or hear him sing and realize it was a focused pain. It was a suffering meant to be shared. He had loved his family, and it was the light that shined through his pain.

But then, two nights after the park gig, in her trailer, again with no preamble, he said, "So I did finish school." She guessed he was continuing his story. The candles she had lit in her living room flickered on the back of his head as he sat at her dinette. "High school. Worked at Kinko's for about a year before the reality of everything became too relentless, if that makes any sense."

She had made him spaghetti with meat sauce. It was one of the few things she could cook really well, and he seemed to love it. It made her happy to feed him. And something about Clover in the back room sleeping added a secret thrill for her. The evening had been laced with a little family fantasy that gave her a rush. She bustled around her tiny kitchen, hovering over his refills and seconds. What was so primeval about the domesticity?

"And I had a group of music friends who played the Kzoo circuit, like me." He hardly mentioned his playing in all of this. "We did some drugs, nothing fancy. Just plain, voluminous drugs." He swallowed a bite of meat and looked up at her with his eyes, gauging. Everyone knew that for an artsy girl, she was squeaky.

And she did return his look then with a bit of a scolding glance, meant to be both chastising and understanding. "Go on," she said.

"Well, I was stupid and young and just started drinking too much. Too much beer after a show that I played, or friend played, or a show we went to see. All those nights out equaled a pretty constant state of inebriation."

He sat back in his chair and wiped his mouth, with his surprisingly gentleman-like manners, with the paper towel she had set out under his silverware. "One night I thought I was being responsible after I was too drunk to even see straight, and I spent the night in my car." She was uncomfortable again, thinking, when was this confession going to stop? His whole life seemed like a run-on confession. She didn't want her opinion of him to decline with each piece of news, and she was still reeling from the one about his parents to even process the severity of his life as a totality.

"It was July, and one night in the car turned into two, then three. I'd go back to the house to clean up and get a change of clothes. But I'm ashamed to say, I was mostly living out my car, drunk, for an entire summer."

Juniper sighed. She sat down. It was a lot. She wanted stability. This was a man who was floundering. Who had floundered. She couldn't stop sighing, and he said, "Juniper, I know this is crazy. I'm not trying to scare you off. I just want you to know what my deal was."

"It's a lot to take in, that's all."

Something in his story was backlit by his strength of spirit, though. He had not once used his family's tragedy as an excuse. He just told his story. But how could every moment of those early years not be swallowed and regurgitated by the uniquely painful grief of a boy for his mother? And a mother like that, golden and loving, from everything he had said. And his strong father rendered weak, and their precious family of four that was obliterated in a stunning fashion. Nothing but raw compassion and sympathy welled up in her at that moment. His choices most certainly were guided by grief, and she blamed him not an ounce. She got up from the table to clear their plates.

"Dahl, I don't know how you've survived through everything you have. And I don't fault you for a moment for your self-medicating journeys. Who are we to question your path of healing?" She spoke for anyone who may have judged him along the way. She wanted him to know that she saw him climbing out of the pit of pain. She wanted to be the one holding out her hand. She did not see him continuing to slide backward. His future was upward, she thought that night.

She meant every word, and in a twist of selfishness, she admired him all the more for bringing out the best in her. She had never felt such compassion and understanding. And for a man, no less. Her hair tickled her neck as she leaned over him to kiss him on his whiskered cheek. When she leaned in, she could see his round nostrils, his breathing like a satisfied dragon. His eyes glittered behind their glass. His hands clasped and tucked over his belly as he leaned back, giving thanks in a reverse grace, after supper. There was humble supplication in his gesture.

Artist's Showcase

To retell it, to rethink it, was painful. But there was something there that asked to be looked in the eye.

She had gone into Vacation Express early. She went in with her courage, and a coffee, and hopped up on the stool to start looking. It was right there, the Kalamazoo Artist Showcase. August 2006 Application. She had brought the disc with high-resolution photos Dahl had helped her with. School of the Art Institute of Chicago, Bachelor of Fine Arts, 2003. She listed her best works, along with the photos and reference to her newspaper articles and interview. She listed the work she was submitting for entrance into the showcase: *Gary's Lungs*. She thought it looked great. She was still thrilled with how it had turned out. But the process of pressing the "send" button took so much courage. That day she sent the application in was actually when the process became painful. Well, that wasn't totally true; there was some deep-seated pain that got prodded right during that conversation in her car. The discomfort and pain certainly didn't wait until the actual rejection itself. But that came too.

* * *

She had no choice but to let the insecurity wash over her. They wouldn't let her know if she got in until sometime in late July. That was so long. She should just be proud that she entered, she told herself. But that day, she didn't want to tell Dahl that she'd actually done it, in case she got rejected. She spent that day folding sheets, vacuuming, and reliving the feeling that she wasn't good enough, even though the world had been telling her otherwise. She couldn't stop thinking of Kat. She was embarrassed that she never reached out to her. They had been such good friends, but she was too cowardly to repair the rift, which would likely have been as easy as a phone call. She thought of how Kat would be shocked that she had a baby now. Or maybe not. Her face burned as if that ugly last month at school had just happened.

She went to the computer first thing before each shift. And the email came several weeks early, saying that her work would not be included in this year's showcase. Thanks but no thanks. Good luck next time. Under a steamroller on a hot summer day. Flattened. Crushed by the news like steaming asphalt. She sat on the stool in the office center of Vacation Express, no windows, facing the computer and the off-white wall and that sucky, shitty email. But she thought her work was good. She was humiliated. All that outside validation, and she still sucked. Still wasn't good enough. She was shaking and sweaty. Her vision was narrow, and she could honestly barely open her eyes. She didn't know how she'd get through the day. Thankful that she'd told no one was how she'd get through the day.

She hopped down from the stool but felt clumsy and heavy as she landed. She went over to the fridge behind the front desk and stole a bottle of water. Everything felt harder and heavier. She avoided the ladies in the break room and just grabbed her cart. She got through her first few rooms. It wasn't even lunchtime. She was alone, scrubbing out a tub. Manual labor wasn't exactly therapeutic if you did it everyday. She tossed the white towels and washcloths into the bin on her cart then pushed it down the hall to her next room. But instead of starting in on 205, she took the stairs to the office center. She pulled up her email and wrote Ms. Showcase back. It was the director of the showcase herself who'd sent the email. Podunk operation. She asked why she didn't get in. She might as well have driven down there and asked her in person. She was that on fire, that upset.

After each room, she'd run downstairs again to check her email. Ms. Showcase wrote back before the end of her shift. *Dear Ms.*

Kowalski. Thank you for your inquiry. We found your work to be a topic we had seen before and slightly too derivative.

What the fuck. That was not an answer. So she wrote back, *Thank you for your response. I understand the competitive nature of this showcase. I was wondering if you could tell me how this piece is derivative?*

Dear Ms. Kowalski. Sure. We thought the internal organ was too reminiscent of da Vinci.

Juniper guffawed then looked behind her to make sure no one was watching. *Jesus.* That was the stupidest thing she'd ever heard! *Da Vinci, what the fuck.* That was it: she went from mostly ashamed to completely pissed off. Who were these people anyway? Unbelievable. Her shift was over. She hung her smock up in her locker.

"Hey, Juniper, what's up," Bethy said. "You okay? You look all hot and bothered."

"Ugh! It's nothing!"

"Okay, if you say so."

Only Bethy could get away with any comment at that moment.

"Look, I promise I'll tell you later. I just need to get home. Everything is fine. It's good. Just rough day." Juniper avoided actually looking at Bethy.

"Okay, talk to me later, 'k?" Bethy sounded concerned. It would have to wait.

Because it was Dahl she wanted. She wanted to drive over to his house, but she needed to get Clover. She needed to relieve Cora. But after all that, she called him, and he came right over to her place. She fed Clover while she told Dahl everything about the Kalamazoo Artist Showcase. She was all fired up, and he just listened at first, until she started crying when she told him about not actually applying to grad school because she was afraid of getting rejected. Now here it was, confirmation of her inferiority.

"Hey, hey." He put his arm around her. She didn't know what to think about that. If it was patronizing or what.

"I'm fine. I'm okay," she said, not fooling anyone. "But they have to be total idiots to say my work is derivative of da Vinci! That makes no sense."

"Listen to what you're telling me," Dahl said.

"What?"

"That what they're saying makes no sense. Do you think your painting is good?"

"I *did*."

"No, come on, you still do, right?"

"Yeah. I think I do."

"Juniper, you can't let a couple of little voices drown out your own."

That stopped her cold. That stopped her hamster wheel of shame. That was something to think about. That was something clear. She looked at him, sitting on her couch with a beer, easygoing, kind. Just a giant ol' pause button right there on her couch. Stop and think. Stop and listen. Pay attention to what's true.

Eye Level

She just felt so angry. This was new for her, any kind of lingering anger. Yes, getting rejected from the Showcase was a kick in the gut. But that stupid derivative comment just ate away at her. Maybe she needed to be soothed, because she found herself at Cora's. She brought her bin of watercolor supplies. Clover was toddling up and down the hallway. Juniper set up at Cora's kitchen table, put on some coffee, and just started talking.

"Ma, can you just hold still, there for a bit?" Juniper gestured for Cora to take the chair facing the window.

"Oh, I look like crap, not now, June."

"No, you look fine. Just hold still."

"Can I smoke?"

"Um, *no*."

"Just one?"

Juniper thought of the picture it would make, and went over to open the window over the sink. Then she opened every window in the living room. "If you must."

Then they talked as they always did. Some customer had been coming into Subway all the time, and Cora was convinced he was flirting with her. Cora wanted to go to one of Dahl's gigs at the park. She was warming to the idea that Dahl might not be a one-hit wonder.

Juniper talked about Clover's newfound love of the sand pit behind the trailer. Juniper drew. She felt the soft scratching of the pencil on the watercolor paper. The softness of the charcoal leaving the pencil. She couldn't be angry, at that moment.

She watched the emerging lines of her mother, cigarette dangling in a somewhat masculine way. Exuding a gruffness that was cultivated through humble cynicism. That mind-your-place culture present in the set of her shoulders. Juniper drew and drew, layering so that an outline was fleshed out and built upon. They were quiet together as Cora flipped through a magazine, and Juniper thought about how if their family had indeed built off of one another, instead of just holding even, if they'd *built* each generation to be higher than the last, where would they be? Would each generation be *derivative* of the next because they had learned something? Copying and building off of one thing to better the next iteration? Or at least to grow. You have to know what comes before. Right? Clover was fussing for a snack. Juniper peeled a banana and gave her half. She thought of one of her favorites, Egon Schiele. She went to her old bedroom, and found the right art history book. He was there, in charcoal and watercolor. His empty backgrounds. The magnificent hues of watercolored skin. For Cora's skin, she relished using the greys and blues and greens that she saw. Could you paint a missing color? The missing pink from Cora's cheeks, or add a little to the whites of her eyes. Clover was now under the kitchen table, stacking some wooden puzzle pieces, her presence softening the look on Cora's face.

It was a small piece, and finished over a couple sittings. The image of Cora spoke, just as the real one did when she walked up and down the aisles at IGA, or stood behind the Subway counter.

* * *

The next time Juniper went to the library, she brought along three new pieces that she had done, including Cora's portrait. They had spilled out of her. The work was spilling out of her. She wanted to give her ideas away. The works themselves were small, meant to fit in between the pages of books. She thought that spreading them out, in a public space, even if it was covertly, felt right. Her idea was to place them amongst the pages of something important.

She settled Clover by grabbing a "Wheels on the Bus" book from the Children's section. She could feel librarian eyes following her. There was always something about her being such a young, single mother that made the eyes follow her to see if she was doing it right, or if she was just another part of the problem. There was no red juice in Clover's bottle. She didn't even have a bottle. There was a book in her hands for pete's sake. But still the silent judging.

"Can I help you find something?" The boy librarian said.

Or not so silent. "No I think we're all set. Thanks." Juniper wanted Clover to absorb her sentiments about the library and its pulse-soothing quiet. And today, that meant moving away from the scoldy Librarian Dude. She could hear the plastic wheels on the stroller make the softest crushing sounds over the flat-woven carpet. She had to lift up on the umbrella handles to scoot into a right hand turn into the fiction stacks. She loved the idea that she was really just among reconfigured trees. Sliced trees with every sentiment imaginable, etched and inked, obscuring the rings of years, rendering them timeless. Her cloth book bag hung on the back of the stroller filled with three drawings pressed into *The Shipping News*, which she needed to return. In the first aisle she saw the "A" she needed. She slid out *Pride and Prejudice*, and carefully pressed the thumbnail sketch of Cora into the book. It was Cora lit eternal by her own kitchen light. Her real light was quiet and stifled under layers. The watercolor paper had dried rippled. Juniper paused for moment to admire the shape of the novel's pages interrupted by her intrusive paper. Even the paper itself seemed rebellious in its thickness, not allowing the book to close smoothly. But the old grey cover shouldered its secret once it was slid back into place. It was so weirdly satisfying.

Her second slip of art was a more realistic piece: a depiction of the Vacation Express façade, including its purple and green logo. With oil pastels the colors maintained their opaque denseness. The sign colors were set off against that creamy fake stucco, which she thought somehow smeared the green and purple off course, so that all three colors were hideous. A building, a still life, in mocking colors.

She took the corners hard to make Clover giggle, and did an extra zigzag through the first half of the alphabet until they got to the "R's" of Rand land and Atlas Shrugged. Damn these small libraries. They only had paperbacks of Ayn Rand. Once Vacation Express was placed inside the book, this small picture interrupted not only the pages, but the stance of the books surrounding it, like her ideas were elbowing for real estate.

And finally, a self-portrait. It was a close-up drawing, with her skin's imperfections. Her pores. A blemish even. A scratch near her eye from Clover's nails that needed to be clipped. She wanted to hide this version of herself somewhere comforting. The place seemed silly, but it was her idea, and she could be silly. James and the Giant Peach it would be. Back to the children's section. She unbuckled Clover who bolted like a clumsy Ferdinand straight towards the beanbag chair. Juniper had a moment to slip over to the 'big kid' books, which she could physically remember from her own childhood. These were books she could remember holding in her hands. She felt like there might still be her smears of chocolate on the Judy Blumes. She found James, and in she went, as if into the peach itself. Now *that* was a color that was perfect, at least in her imagination. Psychedelic yellow-orange tinged with red. So juicy that the wetness was a bright white, creating splashy slashes. The blue-green of its stem and single overgrown leaf.

"Ah, excuse me."

Juniper whipped around. Her face flushed ahead of what might be coming.

"Ah, what is that paper you put in that book." Not a question, an accusation.

Juniper literally had nothing to say. She was trying to form a thought to present to the librarian. The boy librarian. Lean—no—lithe. Late twenties, an actual sweater vest, which was likely meant to be hipster-ish, but was totally librarian-ish.

"There—" he pointed. At James and the Giant Peach, tipped, and all cattywompous on the shelf.

"Mamama!" At this point she was saved by Clover toddling over. Clover didn't have any books in her hand, but she did have a raggedy triangle of a page corner. All Juniper could think, was *oh no, not again*! And she scooped Clover up, and said, "Sorry," to the librarian. A sort of blanket sorry. Sorry we're here, sorry we're loud, sorry I'm littering my artwork in these lovely books. Sorry my kid tore one of these books.

But then Librarian Dude walked over to the shelf and picked up James. He fanned the pages like he was shuffling a deck, and there it was. Her charcoal face.

"Ummm?" He finally asked. All his faux-cool unraveled. He just seemed uptight. "You can't do this." He took out her drawing.

"Okay," she said.

He handed the drawing back to her. He didn't even really look at it, and it was good too. She wanted him to at least look at it, and see it was her. But no. Her real face flamed. She felt stupid, she supposed. Busted doing something pointless. She clicked Clover into her stroller, deposited *The Shipping News* in the return slot near the main entrance, and held the front door with her butt as she pushed the stroller out.

Her car was parked right there on the street. She buckled Clover in, put the stroller in the trunk. But she didn't want to leave without leaving herself there. She wanted her face to surprise somebody. Maybe they would recognize her. It was Gobles, after all. She wanted to be seen. She picked her self-portrait up again, and strode back toward the library. The front door was within eyesight of the car, and she kept an eye on Clover sitting Buddha-like, waiting for their next adventure. She stepped in the lobby as the screen door slammed behind her, and faced the community bulletin board. Babysitting, odd jobs, fix your computer. And now her face. She stole thumbtacks from an outdated flyer for the school musical, and squarely put herself at eye level. There, now she could stare at everyone as they came and went. Making her face so visible, not by luck or accident, but totally on purpose, helped her to realize that she had changed. She was hanging up her coat of shame. At not being worth it. Fuck grad school. Fuck the stupid Artist's Showcase. She was as good. She was equal. Separate, here in Anonymous, Michigan, but equal.

Red Flags

Life-altering events should be flaw-altering, or so Juniper thought. She had this flickering idea that when she and Dahl were thrust in front of Cora as an example of happy/good love, Cora would be altered. She too would be able to accept and participate in good love. Why could Cora not experience this? Why she could not choose, from the world of good people, a man that would be kind and attentive, would puzzle and pain Juniper for always.

The next one was named Johnny. He had a job. He had a house. He had four kids. And that was where it got questionable for Juniper. Four kids, three different moms. Red flag for Juniper, but not for Cora, who would have to actually acknowledge he had three ex-wives for it to be a red flag. Cora was attracted to very manly men with tanned skin and black t-shirts, like Johnny. Men with a toughness about them, with dirt under their fingernails and a cigarette actually dangling from their lips as they tried to fix something. Second red flag—attempts to fix things that ended before said thing was fixed. When Juniper met Johnny, he was in the driveway (which Cora also seemed to be attracted to—men who spent time in driveways), his head under the hood of Grandma Jezebel's beast of an Olds. He was wiping off the dipstick, and Cora was delicately smoking her own cigarette, watching him.

"Hey, June." Cora's voice scratched. She was eager, as usual, in these situations. Juniper lugged Clover and the diaper bag out of the back seat and slammed the door shut with her hip.

"Gimme that four-leaf Clover!" Cora called. But her arms were crossed.

Right then was where Johnny's head should have emerged from the hood, but it did not. He did not. He most certainly would have heard Juniper's Toyota, which had an exhaust system that liked to announce itself before it arrived. He would have heard the slamming doors. She held Clover for a moment before setting her down, assessing the situation. This whole visit was so that Juniper could casually meet Johnny. It was certainly casual to keep your head out of view, thought Juniper impatiently.

Clover started in with her latest run of vocab words. "Gamma! Gamma! Moke!" This last one always made Cora and Juniper laugh, even though it was a sore spot. Plus, this Johnny here also had "moke."

Clover's helium-filled voice scooped and swooped. Johnny did pull his head out from under the hood and stood full up to his middling height. And still he didn't say anything. Clover was as cute as they came, and he didn't crack a smile. Unbelievable.

Cora's eagerness fixed the problem. "The lasagna should be about done babe," she said to Johnny, like they were an old couple.

At that point, Juniper was too fascinated with his oblivion or rudeness to say anything. Cigarette haze was everywhere. Juniper could barely contain her exasperation at all of it. Inside, she buckled Clover into the high chair and gave her a chunk of cucumber to gnaw while she sliced the rest. She saw that her mom had a package of frozen garlic bread and went to put that in the oven with the last few minutes of the lasagna. The voices of Cora and Johnny were in the hallway, a low mumble, then a lower mumble, back and forth. She just kept up with her salad-making, waiting.

"Juniper," Cora confronted from behind while she was finishing the salads. "This is Johnny."

Juniper turned around and waited for him to say something. She was not going to say hi first. He finally said, "Hey," which allowed the evening to begin.

Would he like Italian or ranch, Coke or beer? Cora pulled the lasagna out, bubbling, brown spots on the tinfoil. Juniper felt sentimental about her mother's effort. They ate sliced garlic bread together, each taking a piece from the same plate. And he ate with an earnestness that was just about the only thing Juniper could think of to like about the dude.

She couldn't wait to be home in her own trailer and drove carefully, thinking of Clover in the back. She thought of Dahl. That whole visit made her want to run to him, drive right to where ever he was. She had felt so uneasy around Johnny. But not Dahl. Dahl made her feel safe. In her stomach, she felt warm thinking of him. After all that time—riding her bike to work in sleet, after giving birth and raising a baby with only the help of her mother, after becoming a "local artist"—after all that, she was a little sheepish to think that Dahl made her feel protected and safe. But the feeling was glorious and bewitching. Indeed, like a spell had been cast.

Almost Done

They pulled into the driveway, laughing and flirting. They just wanted to scoot in to get Clover then rush back to Juniper's to keep on with all that good feeling between them. Stupid Johnny's truck was there. Dahl slapped Juniper's butt as she floundered for the right key to Cora's door. Juniper squealed and swatted his hand away.

Through the closed door, they heard yelling. Juniper panicked, worrying about Clover. She unlocked the door, with Dahl right behind. But it wasn't Clover crying or yelling. It was clearly Johnny. His mad voice. His pushy, mean voice. Instead of rushing in, Juniper and Dahl paused at the doorway, keys dangling from the knob. They listened, but then Juniper foolishly stepped down the hallway toward the kitchen. With each step his words came into focus.

"What do you mean *almost done, bitch*? I been at work all day, and you still got to check on the food? It should be steaming off my plate by now." Johnny was ranting. "You need to be on the ball, pay attention. See what I'm telling you? See?" He was too loud, and as Juniper stepped fully into the kitchen, she was horrified to see Johnny down on his knees, firmly holding Cora's head in the oven. The red light was on.

Juniper could only see half of her expression. The side of her face, squished under Johnny's dirty hand, looked terrified. Cora was silently crying. Her stomach was heaving with the force of her sobs.

Dahl shoved Juniper out of the way. He lunged for Johnny's waist and pulled him up off Cora, who fell oddly limp beside the open oven door. Juniper used all of her strength to yank her up and away from the heat. "Ma! Are you okay! Ma! Answer me!"

They were all on the floor, lava hotness chasing them, rolling into the room. Cora seemed to be working hard not to slip into a mute state of shock. But she did nod to Juniper. She looked horror-stricken. Juniper hated it. Hated her mom's face like that.

Dahl was kneeing Johnny's back, into his right kidney, and holding his face to the floor. Juniper could see that Cora was blinking. She was okay. Sort of. But as soon as she stopped crying, Juniper started crying. She grabbed strands of Cora's hair that seemed to be singed. Blackened bits fell off in her fingers. Juniper wanted to straighten the crackled up light-bulb filaments. Cora's hair should be straight. Juniper smoothed it and smoothed it, hating the ugly smell. It seemed a casserole was burning now too, despite the open oven door. Juniper could see fleshy white egg noodles brown and black around their edges, peas dark and shriveled. She had to focus keenly on turning the oven off and shutting the door.

"June, 911. Call 911." Dahl now had both knees digging into Johnny's back. His size and anger ensured Johnny wasn't going anywhere. But Johnny wasn't fighting back as Dahl now smooshed his face sideways and into the linoleum. Johnny didn't appear to be totally with it, maybe drunk or high.

Juniper followed instructions and called 911, although she didn't remember if she spoke to a man or woman, or what she said. It was going to take ten minutes for any cops to get there.

Juniper panicked full throttle again as she thought of Clover. She ran down the hall to the crib, yelling "My baby! My baby!" When she got to her old room, she flicked on the light to see a perfect, sleeping Clover, belly rising and falling, rising and falling. Juniper picked her up, and Clover whimpered in her sleep.

"Take Clover and your mom out to her car," Dahl instructed loudly from his frozen spot on the kitchen floor.

Juniper said, "Ma, come on. Now."

Cora did get up and started crying again, this time with sound. She followed Juniper to the car. By the time Juniper buckled Clover in to her seat in back, and Cora was in her own passenger seat, the flashing lights were trumpeting the arrival of safety. Juniper didn't follow the two policemen back into the house. She sat in the driver's seat, even then thinking about the fact that they were in Jezebel's car. She turned around in her seat, checking on her sleeping Clover and waiting for Dahl.

He came out and got in back next to Clover. All he said was, "They're gonna come to your house, Juniper, later tonight for a statement."

She started the engine, and REO Speedwagon came blaring out of the radio. The opening synth of "Ridin' the Storm Out" grew like it was gonna swallow her up. The song catapulted her back to childhood. She reached to turn it off, but not before it was seared into the moment.

As she backed down the driveway, she saw Johnny being taken out in handcuffs. They all saw it. Stunned and quiet, Clover still asleep, they drove the two miles to Juniper's house. Jezebel's trailer.

Dahl found sheets to make up the couch for Cora to sleep. She curled into the back of the couch, and it was Dahl who covered her. Once Juniper knew Cora was actually asleep, she felt she could let her overwhelming fear and horror out. She was sitting at her dinette with Clover, also surprisingly asleep, and on her lap. She was unable to put her down. Dahl came over to them and wrapped his arms tightly around them both as tears fell down Juniper's cheeks. She felt the strongest sensation of love she'd ever felt for anyone besides Clover. Out of all the anger and fear and horror, she knew it was inappropriate timing to finish falling in love. Yet she leaned into Dahl. She leaned into his warmth and wisdom and inhaled his smell, timing be damned.

Rash Pursuit

Johnny was gone forever. Juniper was irate, and it showed in all of the angles of her body. Knuckle whites, elbows perched, cheekbones and nose flaring. The label "protective mother" was no longer a size too big. Cora had no one professional to talk to. She needed to talk to someone about the abuse. Her attraction to abuse. Someone had to help her. But for now, Juniper went with her to get a haircut from a beautiful woman whose eyes had oodles of knowledge. This woman asked no questions at all, not one, about how Cora's hair got burned. She must have seen the Kowalskis' stricken eyes. The scissors glinted in a very welcome way. And Cora came out looking clean, with shorter, smooth, flat hair. She didn't quite look free yet, but her tawny eyes were raw on their way to healing.

"Ma, you look so nice," Juniper said after they left the salon.

"New chapter, huh?" Cora reached over to grab Juniper's hand, which was only slightly out of character. But it really upset Juniper. Like what people did at funerals, invading or avoiding personal space in uncharacteristic ways. Cora hadn't held Juniper's hand like that since she was a little girl.

Juniper took Cora out to lunch, and Cora was chewing a chicken sandwich, getting her strength, she said, "That Dahl. Geez Juniper, where'd you find him, huh?"

They were eating as a means of moving forward, sharing the sentiment of fleeing something that had already gone. But Cora's tone was something she had never heard in her life. Well, at least not from Cora. She sounded jealous. It couldn't be. And yet it made sense. Cora's man was a psycho, and Juniper's was a savior. Juniper thought before she spoke. This was gonna be tricky to navigate.

"Yeah, Ma. I know. He kinda surprised me there." But underneath her acknowledgment of Dahl's heroic acts were her fears about where he was now. It wasn't a great way to begin a loving relationship—saving your new girlfriend's mother's head from her abusive boyfriend holding it in an oven. Juniper was kind of confused about how to feel about it. Ashamed, embarrassed? Cora seemed to be continually on the verge of flinching. Juniper wanted to be gentle and thought self-deprecating might be the way to go. "Yeah, I don't even really know what's going to happen with us or whatever. He had a girlfriend. I don't even know where things stand."

"Well, you know as well as I do how guys can be. Cut and run," Cora said.

This stung Juniper that Cora would dare lump Dahl in with this broad category of "guys." And it stung her more that it cut right to her deepest fear. Cora looked like she could stand to light up right then. Her fingers flicked out an agitated beat on the restaurant table. Her nails were too short to make any sound, so her fingers thudded, padded with yellow-stained flesh.

"Well, I hope I didn't screw that up for you too bad."

"Ma! God, stop. Come on. We're just glad everyone's okay."

Cora snorted. "Not really okay. You know—" She let the useless words hang. Wait a minute. Cora was pissed. What a relief to see this bubbling up.

"Ma, you're just angry. And frankly, I'm glad. Don't take this the wrong way, but it's about time." Juniper was secretly cup-half-full at this and thought maybe it could mark the last time ever that Cora got hurt. Hurt so bad and invaded one too many ways and times, she would stand taller and speak louder, and no one would do this to her again.

Juniper encouraged her. "Go ahead. You *should* be mad. You've gotten mixed up with some grade-A assholes." It was like she was provoking Cora instead of offering platitudes.

"Well, Juniper. Dad wasn't my fault."

"You mean your dad? God, Mom. I know that. Everybody knows that. Why would you even feel the need to say that?"

"Just. I don't know. You didn't trust me when I went to the hospital."

Juniper sighed. That was complicated. "But come on. You get the nuance of that. It was never, ever your fault. But he had a pattern of behavior around you. And you had a pattern of behavior around him. I was afraid for that. And rightly so, I guess." Juniper said this gently, very careful to not sound accusatory.

"Yeah. I know."

"So, you know, I've had this thought that maybe that's why you end up with men who are abusive." Juniper said the word. "You did love your dad. And that sucked. Everything about it sucked. But that's where you learned what loving a man was like."

Cora actually looked a little surprised, like she hadn't thought of that. "Geez, you got a point there." She ate about five French fries right in a row, like she finally realized she was really friggin' hungry. "Your theory makes sense," she said after a long pull on her Coke. "But it don't make sense why you up and get a man like Dahl. I mean, you got the same shitty background as the rest of us." Meaning her and Jezebel, at least.

"I don't know, Ma. I don't know." Juniper had to pause at that. Why did she deserve real love? What did she do right, or was it dumb luck?

* * *

The week after everything had happened with Johnny, Juniper felt like crushed scrap metal. Crushed from all directions. Good from Dahl. Horrific on all the other sides. Then the constraint would relax into an ooze of sadness. She oozed from the severity of this aftermath they were slogging through. The revelations and emotions were kaleido-scopic. Shifting daily, only to have some original horror come back around through the viewfinder. Shards of burned peas. Mirrored oven door glass. Red light dots. Skin-colored egg noodles, hard past cooked. Black t-shirts. Sharp heat roiling. Glowing hair filaments.

Dahl finally stopped by that evening, after her lunch with Cora. He came in Juniper's trailer door and looked around for Clover while hugging Juniper. But Clover was tucked in bed.

"Hey you," he said.

"What's going on?" Juniper asked. Like, where've you been, I've been worried about you never showing up again.

"Yeah, I know. Didn't mean to be scarce. How's Cora? She okay?"

"I took her to get her hair cut and out to lunch," Juniper said.

"That's so nice of you, June bug." He used her favorite nickname. She was jolted back to those odd comments a couple of years ago from Kirk. *You were patient...I was impressed with your kindness.* And the comments reignited an uneasy feeling. It was a compliment that didn't seem to give.

"You want a beer or something?" she asked.

"No, thanks. I actually can't stay long."

She zipped around to see his face. What? Why?

"Why?" she asked, afraid to sound desperate but unable to let it be.

"Yeah. I just wanted to see if you all were okay. And to maybe chat for a sec."

Juniper just leapt right over fretful, nervous, and worried. Her eyebrows went first. Then some very honest tears. "Okay," she said very quietly.

"Hey, there, no. Don't do that," he said. He even reached over to brush the tears off her face. "Hey." He was trying to lighten things up or something, because he said, "I just felt like I jumped from one crazy frying pan into a crazy fire." But he immediately took a gasp in. "Shit, Juniper. That was a bad choice of words. I'm sorry. I just meant, I got overwhelmed. Shit. Sorry."

Her stomach was quivering with impending sadness, her head with anger. She pressed her lips sealed. Clover cried from her crib, and Juniper got up to tend to her coldness and wetness. The balled-up old diaper trapped Clover's warmth. Footsy jammies zipped all the way up. She ran her hand over Clover's hair, her face. It was fortuitous that Clover needed her for that moment. The reprieve gave her perspective. She could handle what he might be about to say. Everything was right here, dammit.

He was sitting back in her couch, clutching her cross-stitched pillow in front of him. She stood in her hallway, only three steps from where he was. She looked down, searching his face, thinking about how wonderful everything had been, except that one thing that wasn't even her fault.

"I was just so taken with you. I rashly pursued you when I was already taken," he started. "I never felt like what I did was fair to Melissa." There it was, her name. That was not a thread she was interested in tugging on. And she was growing more mad. Anything to smear a cover over how much this was going to hurt.

"Yeah. What, you need to figure this out?"

"I don't know. Yeah, I think so," he said. Maybe what had happened at Cora's jolted him back to his realer reality. Maybe he didn't like the view of what a future with the Kowalskis might look like.

"I got asked to play a club in Chicago," he said.

"Why didn't you say that first!" Juniper softened. "Geez, Dahl. That's great."

"I'm opening for The Wrenches. I'm really excited," he said. And immediately, she was sorry she was going to miss it. "I just need to figure myself out a little better. I don't know what I want any more."

"You want your music," Juniper said.

He set the pillow back down on the couch, stood up, and hugged her with his big hairy arms. He rocked her a bit. It felt like he was singing to her, but he was just breathing in her ear. His beard and the air coming out of his nostrils pushed into her space. His shirt smelled like outside and old car. His look pierced her. Then she realized he was saying goodbye. Goodbye forever? Goodbye for now? Either way, she would hold every last tear back until the aluminum clunked behind him. He gave her this closed-lip smile of gratitude, likely grateful that she wasn't screeching like his ex. Grateful that she was letting him slip away so easily. Of course she was. She figured the only tether she might have at this point was to be the one that was so easy. He could miss her effortless pull and release.

He pulled the door open and just walked out. She had to give a push so that it was sealed. She faced the door and was startled to taste the metal. She thought, *Oh here we go.* But then she realized her tears were falling backward, into her eyes, into her head. She was holding her tears, and they were falling backward, she was pretty sure. Behind her eyes, into her sinuses, onto the back of her tongue, and she swallowed them deeper. And that tasted like salty metal.

She did not watch him drive away. But if his windows had been down, he would have heard a loud, grieving, spilling voice filled with the pain of loss.

Reimagined

The next day, he sent this long, winding email using the words "adore" and "passionate" and "love." See, he wasn't a bad person. Possibly the opposite. Maybe a great person. His email was lovely, until the end, where he said, *So look, I just need some time to figure out what I want.* And of course all she read was *...time to figure out who I want.*

He was so clearly confused. But dammit if she hadn't been jerked around by that sentiment before. She had issues too. She couldn't stand to be with someone again who was unsure. *God, Dahl,* she wanted to yell through the computer. *I am not unsure! I haven't been unsure about you since I heard you sing. No, since you framed all the women in my family.*

She had been holding Dahl up as a man who was great because he showed up; he had been truly generous with his presence, which was no small feat in her mind. But now she was that much more let down precisely because she had grown to expect this brand of greatness from him. She had thought he'd be sticking around. The disappointment felt like too much.

She had barely eaten all day, but after her shift, she grabbed her swimsuit from her employee locker. It was a weekday evening in July, and the pool was beyond empty. Well, the water was full. It was always full. She stepped into the antifreeze color, thinking of the irony. The water was actually not warm at all, and the goose bumps zipped up her spine and back down her arms. She would move slowly and take the pain of shivering discomfort. The control it took to inhale smoothly was an achy feeling. It hurt to step on her numbing feet. She hated it.

She took a gasp of air and layered her fingers in a chevron to dive into the water. Below, she opened her eyes and nearly screamed when an image of Gary flashed in front of her. It was his face, underwater in the deep end. She knew it wasn't real; he was wearing his dark uniform, and she could read his name patch, which would be impossible. She jumped up, gasping. She felt spooked by the emptiness and how every little drop of sound created an echo. She placed her hands in a neat chevron again and dove toward Gary's liquid ghost. With her eyes open, she could see the rectangle boxing her in. She took another gasp and dove again, and this time she cried. Underwater tears silently trailed behind her. There would be no echo underwater. She continued to gasp, dive, and only underwater would she cry. She was sure her tears were voluminous, even though there would be no proof. Pain flooded out with her tears and seared into her thoughts of turquoise, aquamarine, blue-green. She was leaving behind salt in this sort-of fresh water. She was swimming in her own salt. Her own ocean. In Michigan, surrounded only by fresh water, she was creating an ocean to save herself, to swim away.

* * *

Three weeks felt like a year when he emailed her again. This one read, *I decided I want to move to Chicago. The gig went great. They asked me back. And we both know they got Kinko's everywhere.* She thought that such an odd turn of phrase: *we both know.* She couldn't respond right away. She wanted to think about what to say. She didn't want to sound the way she felt, and she wanted to control what she put out there into his world. *Forget this heartache crap,* she thought as she cleaned the rooms that day. She was still cleaning rooms. Funny, when some admin duties came up, she hemmed and hawed just enough that Manny said, "You want to keep cleaning, it's fine by me." It was just that she wasn't fooled that printing address labels or filing was any more purposeful than cleaning mirrors and vacuuming. She wasn't feeling like learning anything. She just wanted to listen to the Windex and the soulful streaks. She could smear that showy turquoise into oblivion. That was gonna be more cathartic than the random paper cut.

Maybe Bethy could help her. It was her first crushing breakup, in a way. Kirk wasn't a breakup, exactly. He was a separate category. But she felt so forlorn, missing Dahl, and there was no ambiguity in her pain. She took her break by wandering the halls looking for Bethy. She could take an educated guess that she'd be around the lobby or front desk, but then again, she might be in her own Narnia in the back of someone's room. Juniper wasn't sure what was going on now that Bethy was manager. Did she still take those "side jobs"? She was likely supposed to be at the front desk, but it was Manny there as usual.

"Hey, where's B?" Juniper asked.

"She's doing me a favor today. There are only two of you. Karen's out sick. Bethy's cleaning down the hall as we speak." Manny pointed down past the computer alcove. She thanked him and easily found Bethy's cart hanging out of 110. She was sweetly humming "Like a Virgin" to herself while she swirled the toilet bowl.

"Are you trying to be cute and ironic at the same time?" Juniper asked as she squeezed past the cart and leaned into the white-tiled bathroom.

"Junie baby! Look, we're working together!"

"Uh-huh. You're in the trenches today, boy oh boy."

"Oh puleez." Bethy was swirling away. Then Juniper noticed that as she flushed the toilet, she stuck her brush in one more time and swirled counterclockwise, backward.

"Beth! What are you doing?" Juniper asked.

"Oh, the backward swirl?"

"Um, yeah."

"So you know that water swirls *counterclockwise* in the southern hemisphere, right?"

"Okay?"

"So. I met this guy, Rodrigo from Venezuela, and well, I'm thinking about flying down to see him. We met online."

"Beth. What in the southern hemisphere does that have to do with cleaning toilets backward?"

Bethy hesitated. "Well, we've Skyped a few times, and he's amazing." She gauged Juniper's acceptance. "I just do this thing, it's embarrassing okay, I forgot you might *judge* me. I just twirl the water left, and then, for like five seconds, I can pretend I'm in Venezuela. And I'll kill you if you tell anyone." She puffed out her cheeks and squinched her eyes shut.

Juniper lost it. She bust out laughing and couldn't stop. And every time she thought she'd calmed down, she'd picture some guy named Rodrigo swirling down the bowl.

"Stop!" Bethy begged.

"You're crazy!" Juniper said, while finally catching her breath and wiping her eyes. That was like ten minutes, maybe, that she forgot about him. Ten blessed minutes.

"Dahl broke up with me."

"Shut the front door. What? Why?"

"It's been like a few weeks—"

"And you're just telling me now?"

Juniper knew that was a mistake. Her biggest ally. Well, besides Cora, usually. But Cora was out for now. No matter what Cora said, it would sound like *I told you so*. She should have been crying on Bethy's shoulder this whole time.

"Aw, Juniper. That sucks. I'm sorry."

Juniper nodded and tried not to lose it right then and there.

"God, you know. I'm just a dreamer. But you, you're an artist. You've got to get this out. Get this angst on canvas or something."

Bethy was right. She had some easygoing wisdom that people missed sometimes.

* * *

At home that evening, Juniper was helping Clover feed herself, which mostly entailed catching things that fell. Bethy had left her with a solid feeling of sisterhood, like she had someone to lean on a little. She remembered Bethy's sweet Madonna. It wasn't really all that ironic. It's like her soul was virginal or something. She was a good lost soul; the other part was just a technicality.

"Clover! No!" Juniper watched as Clover two-fisted some mashed sweet potatoes until it all squished out between her fingers. Her face was pretty much orange already anyway, and she smiled, showing her handful of shoe peg corn-shaped teeth.

"Haha!" Clover added. "Haha Mama. Ha. You Mama."

Juniper chuckled. "You little—" She poked Clover's belly and tickled under her arms. "Haaaa!" Clover laughed and smart-mouthed her way through the rest of dinner. Juniper got some spoonfuls of sweet potatoes and rice into her, thinking about bath time next, when she heard a fist banging on her door. It scared her. It wasn't a knock, but a firm, side-fist bang.

"June! Open up! It's me! Bethy!"

"Oh, geez," Juniper muttered.

"Geez," said Clover.

"June!" Bethy yelled again.

"I'm coming," Juniper said and wiped her hands on the dishtowel. At least Clover was still buckled into her chair. "What?" Juniper asked as she opened the door to see Bethy with mascara in all the wrong places.

"God, honey, what is it?" asked Juniper. Bethy went right to Juniper's couch, flumped down, then leaned over with her face in her hands, renewed crying. Juniper handed her a paper towel.

"Just tell me when you're ready," Juniper said. But Bethy couldn't seem to speak. "Look, I gotta clean Clover here." Juniper went to her bedroom to get a box of Kleenex and brought them back out to the couch. "Let me give her a quick bath and get her ready for bed, and we can talk. Is that okay? Can you hang?"

Bethy was still face-down in her hands, furled over in her blue puffy coat, and she nodded, her blonde hair looking dirty and tangled from behind.

Juniper made quick work of a bath. Clover liked to try to climb out of the tub, and Juniper would just pick her up under the arms and set her back down. Clover thought that was very, very funny, until she didn't. Then she started screaming. There was soap in her eyes. It was baby shampoo, but still, she screamed. "Aaaaah! No, no!" And Clover slapped at Juniper while she rinsed the little rebel. Juniper started to sing, "Hush little baby, don't say a word, mama's gonna buy you a mocking bird."

This gave Clover pause; she loved to hear Juniper sing. But hearing her own voice made Juniper sad about *her* favorite voice. Thoughts of him laced her words as she sang the verses, over and over, and toweled Clover off. She could hear Bethy sniffling in the living room. She came out to check on her, carrying a nudey Clover in the towel.

"Hi!" Clover said to Bethy.

"Hey there, cutie patootie," Bethy said with a wet face.

"Look, give me ten minutes. I've got to get her to bed. Then I'm all yours."

Bethy nodded again and shuddered like Clover did when she was about finished crying. Juniper felt bad, because she felt like she was juggling two kids. Was this how it would be with more than one? Being divided, the back and forth, she imagined, then felt guilty.

She zipped Clover into her pjs and sat in the rocker wedged into a space in front of her dresser that she had to move anytime she wanted to open a drawer. She lifted her shirt to give Clover a hit before she went to sleep. It honestly calmed both of them down. As the chemicals or hormones were released, she could feel her own heart rate slow and see Clover's eyes flutter. Juniper worried about when she'd be weaning Clover and didn't want to give up a single moment. They were down to this once a day before bedtime. Clover reached her hand up to hold a snip of her mama's hair, which wasn't comfortable, but Juniper indulged her. So much had happened lately, it seemed these things, these touches, were very, very important. Within minutes, Clover's eyes rested, and her arm fell backward in abandon. Juniper pulled her shirt down and hefted Clover up and over into her crib. She stayed sleepy, if not asleep, and let Juniper cover her up. Juniper kissed her. She whispered, "Kisses. Mama loves you," as she inched out of the room.

"Bethy. What is it? What happened?" She sat down next to her friend.

"June, I screwed up worse than ever." Juniper waited for her to go on. "You remember Rodrigo?"

Juniper smiled softly. "Of course." Just a few hours ago they were laughing about a five-minute trip to the southern hemisphere.

"You know those Skype calls?" Juniper knew enough about Skype but hadn't thought about all the possibilities, apparently. "Yeah, well he *recorded* them." Juniper cocked her head like she didn't understand. "We were *doing* things."

"Okay? What do you mean?"

"*I* was doing things for the camera!" she said. "For him!"

"Oh, shit." Juniper got it.

Bethy started to cry again. "It gets worse." She was clearly hating every minute of this. "He posted two videos of me online."

"Oh, no. Beth."

"What do I do? What can I do? God, this is awful." Bethy began to freak out more. "I couldn't figure out how to remove them from his post on this horrible site. And now he won't respond to my calls or anything."

"Did this just happen? How much have you tried to get the videos off that site?" Juniper asked. Maybe it was good that Juniper didn't have a computer at her place. There was nothing they could do at that moment but let Bethy cry and be horrified at something she likely couldn't take back.

"What have I been doing?" Bethy asked the room. "What I am I doing with all these losers!" she yelled.

She looked stricken, and Juniper imagined her tallying up her history. Maybe rethinking her path. Juniper let her rant some more without contradicting her. Because how could she utter platitudes? This wasn't good. But Bethy did admit that her face was not really recognizable in the videos. It had been kind of dark in the bedroom, and her hair had covered most of her face, she said to Juniper. And that was enough to prevent her from going further ballistic. The realization that maybe she could deny it was her. Like she would ever be confronted. But just in case. Her golden hair had come incidentally to the rescue. They figured they could get Manny's boyfriend to take a look. One, he wouldn't care. And two, he knew computers better than anyone else they knew. Maybe this would turn out okay. Bethy could calm down for now. Her face changed from stricken to resolute. "I can't keep doing this," she said. There was no need to qualify what "this" was.

Juniper said, "Yeah."

"God, what was I thinking?" Bethy seemed like a princess who woke up, stretched her arms in pretty yawn, and said, "oooh, where am I?" Like she had a bad dream with some bad wolf, and thank goodness she was safe here in this castle, wearing some damn fine frock. But the fairy tale was reimagined, as they say. The prince was nowhere.

"Shit. I am quitting this. Never again. Ne-ver."

"Quitting boys? Quitting stupid men?" Juniper asked.

"You know what I mean!" She furrowed her eyebrows, but then her shoulders sagged. "Quitting whoring myself out," she said more quietly. She sat there and let that thought sink in. Then got up and hugged Juniper. She just kept nodding as she clutched her car keys and said thank you several times. Juniper closed the door gently behind her and was left wondering what to do about her own missing prince.

Three Columns

Something about Bethy's downward spiral, Cora's posttraumatic state, and Dahl being gone really got to Juniper. It was that all this stuff had happened, and yet things were still the *same*, that scared her. It really scared the shit out of her. She didn't move back to Gobles to morph into some shadowy version of Cora. She felt so guilty for thinking that. But they weren't the same kind of person. They had different needs. Juniper knew that she was an artist. That was not a choice. But whether or not she created, of course, was a choice. She knew something about the power of choices.

When Juniper was at the art institute, they had to take a few classes that weren't art-related. She had gotten to take an elective about music. Really just an appreciation course based on classical music. They had learned some about musical forms, which Juniper had loved. She was surprised there was such a math to it, and she really took some useful facts away about balance and growing and releasing intensity. The painting she had done after that class was even titled *A Study in Sonata Allegro Form.*

She thought about that class and liked to draw parallels to her life and music. And the sameness of Vacation Express and motherhood, and static poorness, made her feel like her life was going to be a rondo that never frickin' ended. The hotel, home for dinner with Clover, hotel, bowling with Cora, hotel, hanging with friends, hotel, and on and on and on. She was deeply afraid that she would never be able to compose a life that would escape that main theme: shitty, meaningless job interspersed with the types of things you tuck around a shitty, meaningless job. Not enough money, depression, wondering if you were doing it wrong, not enough money. Nobody ever mentioned fear, but Juniper was learning that fear was heavy. There is a weight to fear, and Juniper didn't want to say the next part, even in her head. But her subconscious whispered *and it will crush you.*

"Now that's different," Mrs. Dee had said about Clover's name.

Librarian Dude had said, "Ummm? You can't do this."

"It's pretty late in the year, we've given most of the scholarships out by this point," Professor Quinlan had said.

"You didn't even apply!" Kat had called her out.

"I'm not sure I get what you're doing here," Kirk had said about her living in Gobles. About her trailer.

"Too derivative."

People said things. Their voices echoed. But what about Dahl? What about all the things he said? "Juniper, you are one radical dude. You are so beautiful and stunning with all that pain and love. Your art amazes me. And even more because I can see you're just getting started here. You are getting better and better at speaking your heart."

She was dividing her life into these two sets of people: one column for people that got her. Another for people that didn't. And she watched with a little shock as she placed each person into their appropriate column: Cora, Bethy, Manny, Mr. Pasternak, Dahl, Kat, maybe Karen and Jo-Jo in the first column.

Mrs. Dee, Ricky, Rob, her dad, Grandpa, maybe Gary, asshole librarian, Professor Quinlan, and Kirk in the second column.

God—maybe even Grandma Jezebel belonged in that second column—maybe she *didn't* really believe in her. But Juniper had to take that right in the gut. She had to take it, because Jezebel was just being honest—what had Juniper proven by the time Jezebel died? That she could get into some fancy art school? Grandma was right not to be impressed by that. But Juniper had to create a third column here: people she could change with her own actions. Grandma Jezebel would most certainly be at the top of that new column. *Because if she could see me now, Juniper thought, she'd fucking love what I've done. She'd love my anger and passion and voice. She'd wanna nestle right into that shit.* And she felt her grandma's imperfections and love so tightly right then that it brought Jezebel back for a moment.

Now Juniper was all fired up about that third column. She thought of being in the newspaper, and being on TV, and all those moments represented the third column. The third column was every fucking body else that could see what she'd done and *think about it*. React to it. Talk about it.

Of course, at the bottom of column three, because who knew for sure, was Clover. She'd be watching real soon here and deciding what she thought too. And if she got her mama. If she believed in her.

Ding-Dong

It certainly seemed to take a while, at least to Juniper. But Cora's house phone rang, and Juniper heard her talking to someone she clearly didn't know well. It was formal, with a "Well, thanks for letting me know. Okay. Okay. Yeah. Sorry for your loss."

Juniper's ears perked up at that. Sorry for your loss? Who died? A mild panic approached but was squelched by Cora hanging up and her eyes immediately overflowing.

"Oh, June. It happened. It's done. He's gone." And Juniper put two and two together: the tears plus the "he" equaled Grandpa. She paused real hard so as not to exhale in a revealing way. Or smile even a little, in a ding-dong the witch is dead kind of way. What a thing, to reconcile your own joy with someone else's sadness. But damn if this wasn't the best thing ever.

"Aw, Ma. I'm so sorry." She reached out to hug Cora and held her for a long time. It hurt to see her mom wrecked. But Juniper knew, or at least suspected, that she wouldn't be wrecked forever. *Just cut the cord, already. Let. Him. Go.*

When Cora asked, "Please June, will you do me this one favor. Please come to the funeral with me?" Juniper said of course and thought about buying a new dress. A new dress for a new era. A new dress for a fresh start. Juniper hardly even wore dresses, but it was, indeed, an occasion.

They were just sharing dinner that night. Clover and Juniper and Cora, just spending time together, and Juniper thought maybe it was good that she was around while her mom processed both her parents being gone. Juniper made tacos while Cora was building block towers that Clover would whack down with delight. Cora was laughing, although her eyes were still puffy and rimmed with red. But then, abruptly, she stood up. Clover looked up to Cora, standing now like a tower herself, and giggled at Gamma. But Cora was standing rigid.

"Ma?" Juniper asked from the kitchen. She had been keeping an eye on them the whole time, and it was like a cold front was passing through the living room. "You okay?"

Cora was looking off into the distance, but there was no distance. Juniper wiped her tomato juicy hands onto a dishtowel and went over to her. She was aware of Clover now attempting to emulate Cora's towers and was distracted by that millisecond of pride. Then she asked again, "Ma?" That was like a gentle cork pull.

"How in the fuck was that woman just calling me now?" Cora said that her dad's girlfriend had called to let her know that Carl Kowalski had died the morning before. A day and a half before. The infection had got the best of him, and the family had planned the funeral to be on Tuesday, in two days. The family. Juniper heard that. The family did not include them. Cora then practically growled with a voice that came from some previously bricked-up well. "What about *my* fucking loss?"

Juniper wanted to say *don't swear in front of Clover*, but honestly it was the sentiments flying around their heads that would hurt her more than an errant fuck.

Cora was getting louder. "I said to *that woman*, 'sorry for *your* loss.' Sorry for your loss! Who's sorry for my loss?" Juniper nodded. Cora continued. "We're goin' to his funeral. I'm gonna see his name etched in stone, if they weren't too fucking cheap and actually got him a stone. I'm gonna see his name. Kowalski. And thank god I already smashed something. 'Cause otherwise I'd haul that sledgehammer right on over there during some stupid prayer and haul off and smack his head so hard, he wouldn't know what hit 'im!" Cora was laughing, but it was maniacal. "Plus. *Plus!*" she yelled, "he couldn't fuckin' hit me back!" And she laughed and laughed and plopped down on the couch and started hacking through her guffaws and tears. Juniper was holding Clover by this point.

"Okay, Ma. It's okay. I'm going with you. We can get through this." Juniper was a little scared. She honestly couldn't remember Cora ever flying off the handle like this, except that one time she wasn't there.

They both must've had that thought at the same moment, because Cora said, still growling, "Now, June. I'm sorry about your stone. I'm sorry I did that. But damned if it didn't feel good. I'm sorry. But what you said, no offense, just wasn't enough to me. Wasn't strong enough. You were a little gentle, for my tastes. And well, that just got me a little pissed." She felt around the coffee table like a blind person for her pack of smokes. She lit and inhaled, clearly righting herself, and said, "Really, because he couldn't 'have been.'"

Juniper looked at her, waiting for her to elaborate.

"I mean, Carl could not have been a good father. You cannot reach down your daughter's panties and be a good father."

Juniper raised her eyebrows and started crying. Finally. Clover was nestled into her mama's neck, probably so as not to see too much. Juniper felt sick hearing those words that she already knew. They all sat and tried to calm down by thinking about the only uplifting thing they could think of: things being smashed and gone.

* * *

But more than that, *Dahl* was gone, and heartache was changing her in ways she did not appreciate. She wasn't surprised that she couldn't stop thinking of him, but she was surprised that she couldn't stop worrying about *her*. His ex. She had an agenda to stalk Glossy Melissa. It was not something she was proud of, obviously, but her biggest fear was that Dahl up and got back together with her. Pretty or not, Glossy was a whiny mess as far as Juniper was concerned. Well, maybe that was mean. Juniper was a mess too, now that Dahl had dumped her as well. Juniper was really not at her best. How about if she just drove by the Iverson split to see if anyone was there? She had an inkling that Glossy worked in Kzoo at some real estate agency. Well, more than an inkling. Dahl had maybe mentioned it when he discussed the possibility of selling the family home. She could just drive by the agency and see if Melissa was there. See if her hair was a mess, at least. Juniper was driving her own self crazy. *No. There has got to be a better way than this. I have got to channel,* she thought.

She went to the back room of her trailer and like a squirrel started scavenging and rustling through her supplies. *Fuck this,* she thought. *Don't swear. I can't stalk this girl. She did nothing wrong.* Juniper slapped a big piece of scrap up onto her easel. It was the shape of a large triangle, cut off from something else. The paper was yellowish-white from being old. She grabbed a charcoal pencil and started in, scratching, scribbling outlines. She hardly knew what Melissa looked liked anymore. She had only googled her that one time at the library and found some random pic of her as a bridesmaid in a dusty rose dress. Her hair had been done up, and her lips matched her gown.

Juniper was drawing a picture of a girl that was reminiscent of the black-skirted stomper that nearly ruined her fancy wine and maybe ruined her good thing with Dahl. This girl was comprised of hard, angry scratches. This girl's hair was like an otter's backside, sleek, slidey, slick. Her face was raised in that accosting way she had pointed at him. Her eyebrows were accusatory. She was accusing Dahl of falling for *her.* She was accusing Dahl of choosing Juniper.

Melissa's mouth was turning out great, with contorted lips and flashing teeth. She could leave this part of the paper its natural color. Melissa would have old, yellowish-white teeth. Juniper's whole body was moving around her easel. She was leaning into the paper, then away, one arm using large gestures, the other swiping tears. Stupid. She went to find some watercolors and mixed a nice washy pink. Melissa's cheeks and bloodshot eyes would be a nice finish. Juniper could hardly see at this point through her own tears. Stupid girl. What did Melissa have to do with any of this? He had chosen Juniper. He had chosen *her.* But then he chose not to.

* * *

Her head bowed next to her mother's as a minister talked about Carl Kowalski's life. Juniper was satisfied that the minister said little. He didn't say Carl was a funny man, or a good provider, or liked to enjoy a sunset. None of those things were true. He'd lived and left a trail of hurt. She saw it even in his new wife's eyes. His grown step-children were respectful by being quiet. The event was hardly remarkable. But Cora needed it, needed to be there. She was hurting, and Juniper was sure to be strong. She was ready if Cora needed to lean. And then in the receiving line, Cora did it again, said, "Sorry for your loss," to her. The woman who was technically her stepmother, but they'd barely met.

And this portly woman with a curly perm and a polyester drapy shirt held Cora's handshake. "It's your loss too, hon. Don't think I don't know that."

At that, Cora lost her shaky composure and nodded as tears streamed hard down her face. She nodded again, then leaned onto this woman, leaned into a hug. Juniper was right there in all of it, so she could hear Cora as she whispered to the woman, "Thank you for that."

"Oh, hon. We all know what he was like." This woman let Cora hug her as the line backed up.

* * *

If she could just get unstuck and unobsessed. If she could just stop wishing for Dahl and his vibrance. But her subconscious was so unruly and threw tantrums of memory. How else to describe the flashes of sex, of him strong and throwing her off the stage to protect her from some imaginary fire? Up against a wall, pushing her into everything she was surprised to scratch and claw for? The dynamic of submission was now delicious. How else to think of a man who looked at you like he was hungry?

She finally had to firmly decide that the only way to combat the black hole of gravitational heartache was to relent and relinquish. More Radiohead and Nirvana to push the emotional slivers out of her swollen skin. She let it all swirl freely, haphazard. She just wanted it spent already so she could move forward. Even if moving forward eventually meant being stuck first, bent over the desk of remembering him.

Change Jar

As Juniper continued to get over her breakup and Bethy her break
out, they sought each other's company and differences. This
manifested in Juniper harboring Bethy at her trailer while sketching
her portrait. It was soothing for both of them. Their talks circled
around the future, mostly. Dreams, hopes, and all that jazz. Although
Juniper had already cut to the chase with the motherhood part, that
didn't mean she didn't want to go back and collect her fortunes of
lasting love and artistic fulfillment. It was good to name things while
they were still young, she thought pragmatically. They discussed
Bethy's situation and how it could be a relief anyway to be sitting
right there on your answers.

Bethy was a pleasure to draw, and Juniper felt stupid for not
thinking of it sooner. The light was crap in her living room, but the
drawing could be a basis for a painting or something later. She was
doing Bethy in profile first. Juniper was enchanted by her perfect nose
and the roundness of her cheekbones and how they exuded a rosy
beckoning. The shape of Beth's face was both sharp and soft, like the
curved wood in a boomerang.

They were interrupted by Cora banging on the door. Juniper could
hear her muffled voice saying, "Come on Juniper, lemme in."

Juniper unlocked, and Cora stepped in and closed the door behind her. "Oh, hey, Bethy, how are you?" Cora turned and said, "June, you won't believe this. I've had the best day. Well, maybe. You've gotta come with me to dinner. It has to be Subway."

Bethy had to go home anyway. Juniper grumbled a bit but sensed a reason behind the insistence. Maybe Cora had gotten a raise or something.

Twenty minutes later, Juniper was buckling Clover into the brown plastic booster seat in the booth at the Walmart Subway.

"Do you think this new haircut I've been getting makes me look different?" asked Cora.

"Sure. What do you mean, Ma?"

"Like professional, or something?"

Juniper nodded. "Oh, yeah. It looks good. It's more sophisticated, I think. It gives you a put-together look."

Cora wore a very satisfied expression at that answer. "Right?" She sat with an expectant look.

"Why, Ma? What's up?" Juniper was squeezing the honey mustard dressing onto her salad. Clover had already deconstructed her ham and cheese. Cora had gotten a milk with Clover's kid's meal, but Juniper insisted that she have water. She had to explain to Cora that because she was still nursing, that it was the cows' milk that was redundant, not hers. She already had been frustrated to have to explain to Cora that juice was jive. Liquid sugar. All these facts were in the news and in papers and magazines everywhere. Maybe it was a generational divide. But when she had been over to Jo-Jo's, Garret was chugging something bright blue out of his bottle, so who knew what people were thinking.

"This dinner here is celebratory," Cora said.

"Tell me already!" Juniper smiled now. Something good—anything good—was a relief. And a celebration dinner, even at Subway, was reason to smile.

"I was in the parking lot last week." Cora's hands were in her lap, scraps of lettuce scattered around her untouched sandwich. Juniper always got caught up on the shape of the wrapper, its diamond or squareness dependent on its orientation. "And Jim Kojeck comes up to me."

Juniper thought, *Here we go.* Then she felt immediately sorry. She just assumed that ol' Jim Kojeck thought her mom's new haircut looked good too and asked her out. What with her diet of cigarettes, Cora had maintained her slender figure, and that fact wasn't lost on the middle-aged dudes around them. Juniper was chewing and listening.

"We just start chatting. He's asking me what I'm up to. I tell him about working here." She nodded up to the "Subway" marquee over the menu. "You know I don't like to bad-mouth nothing, even though this isn't my favorite job. Well, I musta hinted. But I was nice about it." Cora picked up her sandwich to take a bite but set it back down. "He starts telling me about his new business, and I'm like, 'Good for you Jimmy, good for you.' He has some commercial coating business, so I just nodded. I didn't know what that even was." Cora's voice had ramped up, like she was getting to the good part. Juniper raised her eyebrows while she chewed in a "get to it, already" kind of way.

"He says things are going well, settling in. And now he doesn't have time to answer his own phones. Or do his filing, or pay his bills." Cora was beaming by this point. Juniper was smiling still, hoping beyond hope that this story was going to end how she wanted it to. "Long story short, I went in, he showed me around, asked me a bunch about my availability, if I wanted full-time. June, he gave me a job! A job I never asked for, I might add. I'm the new secretary at Great Lakes Commercial Coating!"

Juniper squealed, slid out and over to Cora's side, and gave her mom as big a hug as the booth would allow.

"I start next week. I'm gettin' health insurance. And dammit, this is the last meal we're eatin' here!" They raised their paper cups and hit them together. They made no sound at all, but the ice shuffled inside, close enough to a clink. They laughed.

Juniper figured she had a week to sort out a childcare situation for Clover that wouldn't drain the well that was about to fill up.

* * *

There was no doubt that any kind of change could be jarring. Sameness sometimes equaled soothing, comfortable. Familiarity was good. So here the Kowalskis were, all up in a tizzy. Cora needed some new clothes for her new job. This definitely classified as a need, too, because you couldn't start an office job in holed-up jeans. Money was going out before it came in. This must be what they meant by "You gotta spend money to make money." They'd had meetings over coffee in Cora's kitchen about what was best for Clover.

"June, she's ready for daycare. Let's just try something out. She'll be happy making some little friends."

"But the cost is nuts, Ma." She slid a brochure for Little Tots over to Cora and showed her what three full days would cost.

"Jeezus." All they could do was sit there and explore one dead end after another. Juniper had received WIC till Clover was one. And the only reason it lasted that long was because she was breastfeeding. (At least someone knew something, she thought.) But she had thought she was done with that, done with assistance.

* * *

Back over at the library, Sweater Vest was sitting in Children's, so Juniper glided past him and grabbed a couple books for Clover, then they walked over to the computers.

"'Puter!" Clover pointed.

"Yes, honey. Good job! Computer." She hated what she had to look up—"financial assistance single mother Michigan." Two hundred thousand hits. There were options. There was help. She realized that Kirk had never sent another check. She thought it odd that she had forgotten about that possibility. In her focus on Dahl, she had lost sight of her past with Kirk. It just faded. But she thought of him now, and the feelings were overshadowed by other sadnesses. She was sinking into a pit of black hole muck, feeling bad for herself. *Fuck that. That's right*, she thought, *you heard me.* Talking to herself in her head, because she was in the library with her little girl. But the sentiment. Oh, the sentiment was there. She was not about to get sucked down by the fact that she needed. Everybody needed. She started printing applications to take home. This was happening, and they were gonna get through. And besides feeling like she was still healing paper cuts of heartache all over her skin, they were happy, dammit. Cora's new job, Clover's shiny light, Juniper's art.

Juniper recognized this transition. They were on a path from here to there. And asking for help was going to get them there better and faster. She gathered her pile of documents then headed back to the Children's Room to check out those books and a few more. Sweater Vest handed them back to her, indicated the slip with the return dates, and Juniper looked right into his squirrely eyes, and said, "Thank you." He gave an insincere smile.

She grabbed Clover's hand, and Clover said, "Tank you." Juniper's head was spinning, and she felt a little teary. The freedom of saying fuck-you to the world will do that to you. "Tank you, Mama! Tank you!"

She scooped Clover up to carry her down the sidewalk to the car. Once the bag was nestled on the floor with the books and papers, and Clover was buckled in, she kissed her and said, "You are welcome, sweet girl. You're welcome."

What We Feed Our Daughters

She was seeing the world through Clover-colored glasses. It wasn't such a bad way to view choices. Babyhood had been all about urgency, clamoring, fists in grip, screaming for food and love. Wants were needs was what Juniper learned.

Clover was spindling upward, and Juniper had to act as lookout. Juniper had to stay a step ahead, a rung above, to watch out and warn.

What she saw was the big girls, older than Clover. Just girls, but they had clearly been fed a line that they swallowed. Good girls emulate. And too often, they held large vats of clear, hard plastic. A two-fist grip showing caramel-vanilla-hazelnut-chino inside. Right on display, the mothers would rumble up to drive-thru windows, low rumbles mimicking largeness itself. And they would order something that in its caloric volume, with frequentness, would steal away their daughters' beauty. It was a crime. "Here, drink this." Like another fairy tale where the older woman is threatened by the young girl's burgeoning beauty and just has to fix that problem. Today's modern version: feed your daughter sustenance out of crinkly packages. Give her caramel liquid from a plastic cup. There. Now she looks middle-aged like you. There. You powerful woman, you stole her time in the sun. Oh, that's not what you meant to do? You didn't know? She can't get that back. Can't get the perfect blossom of fifteen back. Can't get a jump-start on twenty-five with the weight of something stolen holding her under, holding her down, like a pillow over her beautiful face. As beautiful as it will ever be, stolen from her.

* * *

Clover was kicking the back seat with her muddy rain boots. They were driving to the IGA. Something in the rain streaking over her clear windshield, the constant disruption from the wipers, refreshing her thoughts every second. Food. Wipe. Daughters. Wipe. Choose. Wipe. It was a left-hand turn into IGA, so there was the clink-clink turn signal, thud-thud of Clover's kicks. Juniper could sit back and let it all wash over her. The ideas would just come with a clean mind.

She checked the yellow line on her left as she opened the car door. She could see the Tim Hortons drive-thru across the lot, and Juniper was struck by the people in the line of cars doing what they always did. It wasn't just a jealous wish to be in line with them, in a big warm vehicle, buying the sweets to wash over you. It was the mindless consumption that in excess could steal your health. It wasn't like that particular shop was to blame.

On her trip to the grocery store that day, she daydreamed with Clover perched in the front of the cart, right in her face, sharing her air. Sometimes your child was separate from you, but not always still. It was an ebb and flow kind of thing. As Clover got older, she watched her ebb and thought of her farther and farther away, the nature of things.

It was a sea of food around them. The juice, the meat, the packages of granola laced with chocolate bits. What did they need? What were they told they should want? How did it come to be that the color of an orange wasn't enough? How did that neon not beckon enough? What was the advantage of this? She passed by the Hamburger Helper, the hand-face waving, and she did not pick up the box. She paused. Down the aisle, she saw the pasta and rice and grains. She picked two of those instead. They both enjoyed the shake-a shake-a sound of the elbow pasta, the shh-shh of the falafel in its box.

At home, unpacking her thoughtful fruits and vegetables, she felt a shift. She leaned her hand on the back of her dinette chair. She felt off-balance, dizzy, and went to grab a cup of water from the sink. Then another. The dizziness continued as she felt an ooze of ideas. The beginning of the creative process was like a medicine that did you good, eased your way, but had off-putting side effects. It was a messy feeling, a little chaotic. If she figuratively stood back, got out of the way without censoring anything, her next project might emerge. She would regain her balance. But not yet. Now, she could taste the oak color of the legs on her coffee table just by looking over there. The yogurt was getting too warm from the summer day. The plastic grocery bags passed through her hands as she emptied each one, they felt like melted petroleum but sounded like a broken snare, loud rattle. The kiss of the fridge unsealing. Mundane became large and life became endless as she looked over to Clover running up and down the hallway. Toward herself in the full-length mirror, and away from herself. Ebb and flow. When Clover got to the end of the hall, she would quickly turn around to see if she could catch herself, or whoever that little girl was, by surprise. She giggled.

Juniper took each plastic bag and tied it in a knot, something that was habit by now. The knot would prevent Clover from putting the bag over her head. Her dizziness settled quickly this time. The sounds faded and the colors rose up. The textures and lines lay in wait.

She was stuck on the family motif. The most striking thing for her now was motherhood. She was daily bowled over by how this was going so differently than she thought it would. How differently motherhood seemed from the inside. The daily sweat and ever-presence. No one ever said. No one ever told her that through this total exhaustion and overwhelming love, she would be granted a new perspective, and the weight of meaning would increase for some things and disappear for others. She didn't doubt that being a mother made her a better person. Stunned that it made her a better artist. She wanted to do some mother and child painting, but with the roles reversed somehow. Child and Mother. On the back of the scroll of grocery receipt, she wrote her thoughts:

Single, unwed mother
A million in one in a million.
I held out my arms for baby to shackle me,
But she took my hands and set me free.
This way, mother, she pointed
As she drank my milk and exhausted my love.

This time, her piece started with where she wanted to paint it. She wanted it to be big and public, like Banksy hiding in plain sight. When she was in Chicago, kids were really talking about his street art in London and using stencils to tag urban places. She loved his aesthetic. She loved his aggressive sentiments grasping for or demanding peace. And preparing for her next idea, she couldn't get his image of "Girl With a Red Balloon" out of her mind. She thought about tagging and immediately thought of how it would feel to wear handcuffs. She didn't need to be a rebel to get heard. She was going to ask first, just like at Tastee Twist. Then she could take her time and work in the light.

Ladder Up

Sav-Mor was a local food store right on the edge of Paw-Paw. It was old-school in that the linoleum was brown, the lights flickered, and the weekly fliers in the window were clearly made with a super-large permanent marker. Someone had decent handwriting, but the name of the store drove her crazy. Just add the "e's" already! She worried the bad spelling lowered her chances of receiving an open mind toward her proposal. How would she argue that a large-scale mural depicting something obnoxious, like a baby with an iced coffee, would be a great asset to their storefront? Well, store-side was the best she hoped for. And their side was perfect, with a nearly uninterrupted expanse of blond brick.

She had driven down without Clover; she needed full use of her vocabulary and thoughts. She walked over to the customer service booth. Rolls of stamps and lottery tickets displayed, a flashy show of cigarette packs, looking like a row of lights in a casino ballroom. A young girl with lots of black eyeliner, chewing gum, was standing sideways at the window.

"Oh hi, what can I get ya?"

"I just had a question for your manager, is he or she around?"

"Um, okay. Can I tell him what it's for?"

Juniper had an answer prepared. "Sure. I'd like to talk to him about some advertising." Total lie, but simple. The girl ran up the steps to get him. Those mysterious steps. Nearly every grocery store seems to have this secret office, and Juniper was being beckoned up to the top. There was a thirty-something guy in a brown smock sitting behind the desk with a thick meatball sandwich open and the suspected fat marker. He was drawing the guidelines with a metal yardstick and was quick and efficient. He was the man behind the curtain. Or at least the man behind all those nice signs. It could be a good omen. He seemed like a smart guy, she judged by his demeanor and handwriting.

"Aw, man, I don't know. I don't really think my dad'll go for that," he said when she explained the idea of a mural on the side of their store. She had complimented his signs. And he had been appreciative.

"I did something similar over in Gobles. The ice cream shop there let me put up a photo installation. But inside. On their brick." He had the marker open now, and the toxic smell, which she loved, was wafting like hookah smoke.

"That was you? I know those pictures! I took my kids to get ice cream there this summer. Cool concept." He was nodding. He put the marker cap back on. "Yeah, that was cool. So, is it going to be—"

"It's going to be very different," she interrupted. "But it will be similar in that I hope to make a statement." Something in the conversation was shifting. She didn't know whether to talk more or less.

"How big?" he asked.

"As big as you'll let me," she said. "I'm thinking the north side of the building, so not right up front."

He was thinking, eyebrows furrowed.

"It would be a way to support local art. If you don't like it, we can remove it?" She was getting desperate to get a "yes."

"Look, I gotta talk to my dad. Leave your number. I'll let you know."

She smiled and reached out to shake his hand. He gave her a firm shake. "Supporting local artists. We need more of that, huh?"

"Yeah," she said. "Yeah, I think we do." And she turned on her highest wattage smile. It was no Bethy, but she was trying. She strolled back out to her car, faded smile still on her face, "local artist" ringing in her ears.

* * *

He called the next day. "Look, I have a deal for you. My dad says okay as long as you speak favorably about us with any publicity you get. *And…*you paint the other side of our building, the south side, with our Sav-Mor logo, then you can use the space."

"Wow." She didn't have to think for long. She loved sign painting and found confining assignments meditative. It'd be a lot of work, but she wanted to be heard. "Okay," she said. "But I don't know about publicity."

"Yeah, well, my dad looked you up online and saw that TV clip and newspaper stuff. He just wanted to be prepared."

"Huh," she accidentally said out loud. "I mean, yes. Great, sounds good."

* * *

She had to tell Cora what she was up to this time.

"Obviously, there's no stopping you now," Cora said. "You know how I been helping you with Clover since you went back to work?"

"Yes," Juniper said, nervous about what might be coming next.

"Well, honestly, June bug, I consider this your real work. And I want to help you. You know I got my nine-to-five, which starts at eight. But I'm regular. So we can work around my schedule, and I can take her when you wanna paint."

By then, an assistance check had indeed come in. There wasn't a ton left over after Clover's two days a week at Little Tots, but they had some money. Juniper felt horrible about spending assistance money on more art supplies. But women spent it on career training or whatever. Well, this was going to *be* her career. She wasn't sure how yet. But to Juniper, it was important. And she just didn't have to tell anyone.

Juniper collaborated with Trevor, the manager with good sign skills, to create a "Sav-Mor" that would do the store, and his dad, proud. She felt like she was just starting to get the hang of painting on brick when she had finished the caption underneath *Five Women*. She knew how to get the brick cleaned and primed. She used a grid to outline the template with a fat pencil. The paint was going be red for the letters, with black outlining.

She was wearing overalls and a tank top, and her shoulders looked sprinkled with cinnamon after a single afternoon. By the end of the week they were singed a little, her overalls a mess and her hair a sticky ponytail of sweat and paint. She could see in Trevor's look that there might be an appeal to her disheveled state. Maybe he was just admiring her work. But it didn't feel like that as she climbed down from the ladder and he shielded his eyes, following her down each rung. "Nice work," he said.

When Trevor's dad came out to see the finished sign, he beamed.

"Well now, that is something!" he said, admiring the six-foot-tall black and red Sav-Mor.

Trevor said, "Told you, Dad."

* * *

When she got to Cora's to pick up Clover, she was all happy and proud, giddy about the finished sign, how good it looked, and the positive response.

"I know it's just some sign. But Ma, I'm so happy. I'm doing my thing here." Juniper was overflowing with energy, excited to start her own mural. But Cora wasn't reflecting that good feeling or seeming happy for her.

"Ma, why're you acting weird?"

"I'm not. Why are *you* actin' weird?" Cora was just being silly, but Juniper was serious.

"Come on, something's up. You're not telling me something. You're all shifty."

Cora sat down. "Fine. But, just for the record, I didn't want to get into this now and ruin your good mood."

"What?"

"Your friend there, Dahl, stopped by yesterday." Cora waited for Juniper to react. "Aren't you gonna say something?"

"Why don't you tell me what the heck he was here for, then I'll know what to say. I mean, why'd he come to you?"

"He wanted to know if you were mad at him. He just stopped by. It sounds like he's gonna be back in town for a bit. Then he's going on tour with that group he was opening for."

"Well, I'm not mad at him."

Cora looked at her sideways.

"What! I'm not," Juniper said. "Unless he got back with Glossy Melissa."

"Who?"

"His perfect ex."

"I doubt she's perfect, hon."

"Well, gorgeous or whatever."

Cora rolled her eyes. "I'm just the messenger here." She got up, went to her room, and came back with a book. "He brought you this." She handed it to Juniper. It was the latest edition of *Master Paintings in the Art Institute of Chicago*. Inside was a note: *Hey Juniper. This is in case you miss Chicago. I brought a piece back for you. Hope you like it. Love, Dahl.* The book was large and heavy.

"Pretty nice gift, huh?" Cora said.

Juniper thought the gift was really nice. But seeing the note and his "love" brought back the pain. What if he was actually back with Melissa and just wanted to give her some lame pity gift? She was jealous of something she was making up, but just the possibility of it drove her crazy. She had no idea what she wanted to do. It was tempting to want to get in the car and drive to his house. But she needed to think for a bit. Plus, she wanted to get to work on her own mural. Her focus could be stronger than this distraction. And for that, she was proud of herself. Plus, it wasn't long before she heard from Bethy, who heard from some Old Dog server, who said Dahl had already left for his tour, which made it even easier to focus.

So with a little effort, the good feeling from her successful Sav-Mor sign segued onto the north side of the building, and she began her new grid. She had prepared by drawing several sketches of her idea. It was Clover sitting in the grass holding a large iced coffee with two chubby hands. She was really thinking about her approach. She had thought about her lungs and realism. She thought about pop art used in advertising. The social realism of Diego Rivera seemed pertinent, especially as she was embarking on a mural that had a blatant social comment. The public splash of Banksy.

She loved the pressing down of a deadline. And she really just had what was left of early fall until cold came. That was her deadline. It felt like a nice chunk of time, with more useful days than not. But she still had shifts at Vacation Express and life in general to contend with. So the times she could paint the side of a building, out in the elements, were limited. Yet she secretly loved every part of the challenge. She was constantly in this heightened state of working or thinking about her work.

When she was a kid, she liked feeling squashed into tight spaces any time the next door kids played hide-and-seek. She was always tiny. And she loved seeing their stunned faces, by the time dusk fell, when they finally found her under an overturned box that looked too small to hold a ball, let alone her. She could out-hide, out-squeeze any of them. She was good at tight spaces. And this tight space just happened to be time.

In the beginning, she mostly worked on her days off, priming her space, her canvas of brick. And when she was home in Gobles, her mind was always one town over, flanked by the faded asphalt of Sav-Mor and the new space she was creating. Then she found herself looking for any chunk of time to drive over. Some days, just to check on it, see her idea blossoming after a fresh night's sleep. She found she couldn't stay away from that wall.

The humongous sketch was complete, and it was time for color to start going up. Juniper was giddy. Clover woke up at the crack of crack anyway, so it was easy to pack them up for an hour or two before Juniper even needed to start her hotel shift. Morning sifted light a little after 5:00 a.m. and was full-throttle glowing by seven. She'd get a lot done before the heat struck, and Clover seemed to like the adventure of it. Plus, it was great to have her there for Juniper to gauge the giant Clover against the real one.

September was more than a calendar threat. It seemed one day she was avoiding the heat, and the next day she was seeking it as summer flipped to fall overnight. But then, mid-October, she was blessed with a run of Indian summer, a blast of three hot ones right in a row. She had actually switched two shifts with Karen to make use of the nice days. Out came her tank top and overalls. Out came Trevor to watch. But he got more than he bargained for, seeing Clover there jumping in her play yard.

"Hey, now. Who's this?" he asked.

"Clover, meet Trevor," Juniper said, and she continued trying to find a mix of paint for the pink base of Clover's skin. She tucked a little more white into her pile of paint, knowing the acrylic was going to dry darker than it looked now. She wanted Clover's skin to be cherub-like.

"Um. How do you two know each other?" he asked Clover. Oh, he was funny now. She stopped with her brush in the air.

"Trevor! She's mine."

"No way. I don't believe it."

What didn't he believe? That she was old enough? Juniper was too busy to respond to his curiosity. She was toying with different blue shades for the undertones.

"I mean, how old *are* you?" he asked Juniper. Clover was watching the two of them volley from her play yard.

"How married are you?" she shot back. That shut him up. But he smiled. She felt a little thrill of power slip through her.

Coppers

The coppers were out. It was the afternoon of devil's night, the afternoon before Halloween. Copper leaves. And the po-po. Juniper enjoyed the festive atmosphere. Folks coming out of Sav-Mor with bags of candy. Folks stopping by to see what she was up to, there on the side of the store. That night marked a grand shift: she would find that recognizing an exact moment of change is a gift to be savored into old age. She would replay that moment throughout her life, and it usually brought a sense of purpose and peace.

The night marked a permanent shift in her balance as she perched there on the ladder overlooking the Midwestern flats of home. She felt, ironically, that she had to let go, that she had to hold her arms out to maintain any sense of balance—particularly disconcerting on the second-to-last rung of that ladder. The grays that exemplified her Michigan sky felt limitless. Gray was the black that encompassed everything, swallowed everything, plus the white that reflected it first. She thought how frustrating that gray had been, like a lid on a pot, holding everything in, everything down. But the gray was mist that expanded upward into obvious infinity of sky. You cannot be confined by a mist.

Leading up to that day, Trevor had become a daily fixture as her blank wall had grown a face. He had asked, "What exactly are you painting? What is that, a baby? What is he holding?"

"Baby's a she," Juniper would correct.

Then one day he came out and said, "Hey, that's your little girl!"

From that point, Juniper started smiling, because it meant she hadn't lost her painting chops. She had game. Precision was key. Not that the mural was realistic, exactly. There was certainly some creative license she took with her Technicolor choices. She wanted people to see it fast. If they were driving by, she knew she had to be as flashy as a neon sign. It was large. It was bright. She wanted the piece to stop people and arrest their thoughts and purposeful errand-running.

Bethy and Mary Ann had come by earlier in the week to admire her work and ask, "Why is Clover holding a giant iced coffee?" It was nearly done. Daily, she had to focus extra on anything nonessential in her life, because she was really amped up. She had found joy.

She could follow each new work like pebbles through this forest of life, and along with motherhood, that would be her purpose and happiness. It was her own quiet wisdom, she thought. She was so damn excited, perched on the ladder, overlooking the parking lot and grocery store and gray sky. Birds and electrical wires. She had laughed. Well, it might not be wisdom, and she certainly wasn't quiet.

* * *

It had gotten to this point where she needed only a couple more hours to finish; it was the home stretch. She had been working all day, that devil's night with that one thing on her mind. She could go home for an early dinner, feed Clover, and get back to Sav-Mor before it was totally dark. Or she could leave her headlights running if she needed them to get the last touches finished that night.

But when she got to Cora's, the first thing she saw was Clover whimpering in her sleep.

"Ma, what's up with Clover?" Juniper reached down into the play yard to feel her forehead. "She's hot."

"She's been fussy all day," Cora said.

Juniper checked her temperature. Clover had a slight fever. Juniper was frustrated. She had wanted to work, and now Clover was sick. "Did she eat lunch?" Juniper asked. Instead of getting a list of what she had that day, they watched as Clover heaved up her last meal.

"Oh no! Ma, get a towel please!" She plucked Clover out of the play yard. There was throw-up everywhere, and now on her. Clover heaved again, and Juniper rushed her to the linoleum in the kitchen. By the third time, they had made it to the bathroom, and they were both dripping, hot, and crying. Juniper sat down on the edge of the tub and held Clover, waiting for a possible next round. But Clover's belly settled down; she was just upset.

"Let's get you cleaned up, little girl," Juniper said. She ran a bath, tweaking the hot and cold until it was perfect. She stripped Clover and rinsed her down. Then she drained the tub, wrapped Clover in a towel, and ran a second bath. This time she used soap and shampoo and got her nice and clean. Cora had taken all the clothes and towels down to the washer.

Clover was worn out and dozing in her pjs on Juniper's lap on the couch. "Ma, I'm just gonna stay here. I don't want to load her into the car and drive her home right now."

"Okay," said Cora. "I'm gonna get some dinner and take a shower." She made a ham sandwich. Juniper ate some hummus and crackers while Clover continued to sleep on her lap. While Cora was in the shower, Juniper thought of her mural. She thought of the piece of shading she wanted to fix around Clover's nose. She thought of the light that would be fading soon. She thought of the grass detail she wanted to add. She thought of her name at the bottom. She was debating whether or not to sign it. It wasn't like her other stuff. Everyone had seen her working on this one.

Clover seemed to be comfortable, and Juniper lay her in the crib in her old bedroom. She tossed her own throw-uppy shirt in the washer and put on an old paint-splattered sweatshirt and a winter hat. The temp was okay. She could finish if she just went over there now while Clover was sleeping. She could finish by tonight.

It could be done. Cora stepped out of the bathroom, toweling off her hair.

"How is she?" Cora asked.

"She's okay. I laid her down," Juniper said. She was uncomfortable asking, but she had to. "Ma, I just want to run over to Sav-Mor. I planned on finishing tonight. I'll try to be quick. You can call me on my cell if she wakes up upset or sick." She trailed off, wanting the go-ahead, wanting to rush out to her work. Not wanting to actually have to ask. Cora raised her eyebrows. But Juniper gave one more little push and finally asked outright. "Can you just watch her while I finish? I really want to finish."

"June, your baby is sick. Do you really think it's the best time to go work on your art?"

Juniper knew it wasn't the best time. But it lured her. And it wasn't just her work that lured her, but also the promise of what might come after. It was the home stretch. She was salivating for the response. Positive, negative, she knew her work itself was good. She knew the craftsmanship was there. She welcomed the controversy of the subject matter, and pride over the response to the project overtook her better judgment.

"I'll be quick," Juniper said. "Just call if you need me, if Clover needs me."

Cora looked disapproving, but even that couldn't stop Juniper. She headed toward the door. Her hand was on the knob, but then she had to go back into the bedroom to check on Clover. She leaned over to kiss her.

Her supplies were in the trunk of her Toyota. The ladder she had left was tucked next to the building. Somehow with getting home from work, Clover being sick, and grabbing crackers for dinner, it had gotten late. She missed the last of the best light just driving there. She got out, started hauling the few things she needed out of the trunk, set up her ladder, and got to work. She completed the grass. She sealed up that paint. But it was too dark to really see. She wanted to check the grass colors better. She pulled the car right up to the mural, her headlights creating false shadows that she didn't appreciate.

If she could be done in an hour, the headlights would likely be okay, if she could just angle them right. She felt sad finishing. She stood back to check that shading on Clover's nose and climbed back up the ladder to see it up close. Before she could focus, the yellowish-white light from her headlights was splashed out by pulsing red and blue. Whoop, whoop!

Juniper whipped around, her first thought actually being an ambulance. But no, devil's night cops. She could barely see through the flashing. She wondered why they were stopping in front of her, T-boning her car in place. Whooop! Whoop, whoop! The cop stepped out with a megaphone and started talking at her.

"Get down," he said.

What the hell?

"Cute prank, but I wanna see your hands." Juniper stepped down and turned to face the guy. She squinted. "Hands up already." His mouth was right up in the grill of the megaphone, and he was hard to understand. She put up her hands, which were empty. "Young lady, you're trespassing on private property. You are vandalizing." She wanted to defend herself, but man, he just kept going. He stepped closer to her and put down the megaphone to talk in his real voice. "Folks have had enough with this devil's night crap. And I'm afraid you was in the wrong place at the wrong time."

"But no, I'm supposed to be here," she said. She wanted to strike the right tone of not deferential and not defensive. She could do this.

"No, young lady, I don't believe you are. I know Mr. Piotrowski, and he don't strike me as the kind of guy that likes a joke painted on the side of his store."

"No! He gave me permission, I swear!" At that moment, a call crackled over his speaker. It sounded like he was needed somewhere else.

"I've just been told we're doing zero tolerance tonight. Officer O'Brien just got some kids tossing firecrackers at him out their sunroof. I gotta bring you in."

"No!" she said. "No! I'm not vandalizing, this is my work!" She was yelling; she couldn't help it. She realized she was yelling, wearing a paint-splattered hoodie and black chucks, looking about eighteen. He wasn't even listening to her as he pushed her head into the back seat. She pulled off her hat and held it in her lap. He was on his two-way, totally preoccupied with the news coming in for him about all the goings-on. She surprised herself by not starting to cry. He was just talking and talking over that thing, driving her around with one hand on the wheel. It was navy blue out. It was a little unbelievable to see what appeared to be an orange harvest moon. She turned away from it, as she always had a weak spot for complementary colors. But the judgmental moon followed her with its shine. She leaned her head against the back seat window and looked sideways into his face. The moon's eyebrows seemed furrowed downward in disapproval.

"But I'm a mother," she said. "I'm a mother," she whispered. Those words stayed put in the back seat with her, behind the Plexiglas. Thinking of Clover at home sick, maybe needing her right that very moment, she felt like she might just be exactly where she deserved.

Angel's Night

Something must have been happening behind the scenes, because she was on a bench, no handcuffs or anything. She was thinking she'd get to call her mom. But all she got was a front-row seat to the underbelly of her sad old town. Forget the scrappy kids coming in for pranks—the whiskery old drunk men and ladies with too many dimples in their thighs to wear those pleather skirts were what really tugged her. Then some medium-aged guy with medium brown hair and plain everything flung himself onto the cement floor of the station, seeming to incite a seizure of some sort. If that wasn't sad and scary enough—watching him twitch and flail, practically gasping for life—it was watching her officer and the receptionist lady ignore him.

She wanted to cry, but she couldn't. She was struck dumb. And then she felt her milk letdown. Clover was almost one and a half, and she was still nursing her. Another fucking thing about motherhood people could have been more clear about. What it meant to sustain another living creature was so much more than that physical sustenance. Nursing Clover for all that time had given them both something that cut right to the quick of what it meant to be human. It was exhausting to give your energy and essence to someone every day. But that, as much as giving birth,

was the gift of life. Clover's very independence was a result of
that original bond, still going strong. Vitamins, minerals, love,
antibodies, suggestions, help, dreams, confidence. Yes, confidence. Someone could have told her about all that, just to ensure
she would stick with it. But luckily, her mothering instinct was
strong. She could, so she would, and didn't have to think past that.
She hoped she would not end up weaning her only daughter due
to bars that she couldn't fit through. Her exhausted mind just
wandered around at that point. She was so tired from the day.
So tired.

She looked up at the front desk to the ignoring receptionist. And
that was what finally made her cry. In front of her was Dahl. The
back of Dahl, as he filled out some papers, no doubt on her behalf.
She sat rooted to her seat and memorized him there with his flannel
shirt-shaped cape.

What happened to that woman she thought she had become? She
felt like a little girl as he turned toward her and smiled sadly. "Hey
there. You alright?" She couldn't really answer. She was crying like a
waterfall, so she just hugged him.

* * *

The whole thing was a mistake, of course. Her cop had called Mr.
Piotrowski, Trevor's dad, and woken him late that night, devil's night.
He immediately assured Officer Pultz that Juniper was sanctioned to
be there. Both Mr. Piotrowski and Officer Pultz called Cora to tell her
what had happened. And Cora, alone with Clover, cried with relief.
She had been worrying so hard, after she had tried to call Juniper
repeatedly, with no answer. And with Clover in her arms, awake again
with a heightened fever, Cora was stuck rocking her and fretting the
night away. So she had called Dahl. And he showed up.

After the station, he drove Juniper back to Sav-Mor. Her battery
was dead from the headlights being on too long. He T'd right up to
her like the cop had and charged her, red to red, black to black. But
once she was in her driver's seat, he held the car door ajar and gazed
up at the sipping Clover. He said, "Now that's something. You've got
a lot to tell me. Is that your best public work yet or what?"

"Thanks, Dahl." She loved that he loved her work. "But why are you here? Why are you really here?"

"Your mom called me, looking for you. And when the cops called her, I told her I wanted to come get you myself." It was like Cora and Dahl had been having some secret communication without her. "My tour is done for now. And I wanted to come back. I wanted to see you."

"But I thought. I worried—" Juniper had trouble. *You can do this,* she said to herself. "I thought you maybe were gonna get back with Melissa."

Dahl was still standing next to her car, and he leaned in so his face was next to hers. "I was never going to get back with her. When I told you it was her family I loved, I realized that family in general was going to be an emptiness I would always be looking to fill." She had turned to face him, and it felt like he was looking right into her heart. He went on, "I have to admit maybe I did freak out a little with the whole Johnny thing. But I got some time to think in Chicago. I had a really beautiful thought."

Morning was rising. The smell of dry weeds and browning leaves colored the air. "I thought about having my own family someday. How that could bring more healing and joy than anything else I could imagine." He reached in and stroked the back of her head.

She felt a burst of warmth and smiled. Her face was still wet from the on-and-off tears. But she knew how to rock a quiet moment, she was sure of that. And there was no doubt of the love that was reignited. She had missed his touch more than she'd missed anything in her life.

"I can't wait to hear what people say," she finally said, looking up at her painting.

He closed her car door. And through her open window, he said, "Well, I know what I say." He leaned his head in. "I say you're amazing. And I'm sorry it took a night at the po-po to tell you."

She laughed.

"I love you, Juniper."

He followed her to Cora's. Juniper hurried inside to see her baby girl. Dahl walked in behind her. She rushed to the living room and scooped Clover up from Cora's arms. She sat in her favorite corner of the couch and propped a pillow under her arm. She unzipped the paint-splattered hoodie, lifted her t-shirt, and reunited with her girl. The relief nearly echoed in the room. She looked up to see Dahl and Cora, smiling at a joke she wasn't in on.

* * *

Juniper never did sign her mural, and the shading on Clover's nose was off just a little. It bothered Juniper a lot, but she also found it important to keep it that way. Slightly off. She had never thought about the momentum of her work. The fathers, the mothers, her daughter representing maybe a cautionary tale, maybe a social commentary on food as sustenance or entertainment. Maybe it would just be a portrait to some. That wasn't for her to decide; It was for the viewer. All those shoppers at Sav-Mor who maybe took the time to walk over to the north side of the building and see what all the fuss was about. It was on the news, it must be important. It must mean something.

What did matter was that they became a threesome. A family. Dahl grafted on and added a branch to the family tree. His music was welcome, and the ABCs never sounded so sweet.

"You know that was Mozart who wrote that melody?" Dahl asked. Clover was wrapped up in his songs and learning. She danced to his strums. Up and down was her favorite means of expressive movement, and bouncing up and down she went. Dahl sang right into her eyes, teaching her the words and love. The love of a man. *Next time won't you sing with me.*

* * *

Two pink bunny eyes looked up at Juniper before long. This time Dahl sat in the daddy chair, Cora on the couch at home, waiting with bated breath. The technician came in, and Juniper felt this swell in her heart. It was *her*. From a few years before. Juniper was following the technician's distracted eyes throughout the dark room, wanting to catch them, and say "It's me! Remember me?" This woman had marked a transition in Juniper's life, and for her to be here again was just something else.

"Hi, hon. Looks like you were here a few years ago, and now you're back." Juniper nodded. The tech finally looked at her. "Hey," she said, "I think I remember you. You were young."

"Well, yeah, kinda," said Juniper. "Mostly, I just looked young."

"How's that little girl doin'?" The tech read from her chart. Dahl interjected his man's voice into the room.

"She's just a firecracker, and we love her to pieces. Pretty like Mama." The tech looked at Dahl and smiled; he had that effect on women. She got to work, lifting Juniper's tissue paper smock and splurting the goo. Juniper felt sensitive in her belly area, with all the pulling and stretching, and she felt a nick of the tech's nail. Her nails! They were magenta this time but still long and magnificent. In the darkened room, the silver paisley accents swirled and glowed. The magic wand ran over and over her belly, her baby. *Their* baby. The tech clicked and clacked the measurements, a familiar sound to Juniper. But Dahl was a nervous wreck under that charm, and they were both watching every twitch of the tech's face. It was her teeth Juniper noticed first, bright white reflecting the computer screen.

"You wanna know the sex, right?" she asked.

"Yes," Dahl and Juniper said together.

The tech was smiling, better than any words. "Well, he sure looks big and healthy to me," she said.

Juniper started crying and looked over at Dahl, whose face was crumpled like the tissue paper gown.

"A little man," he said. The tech knew to hand it to him—the photo printouts of his baby boy. And Juniper thought ahead to when he would cut the cord and leave the twine.

Acknowledgments

I would like to thank my husband David for his endless hours of listening to me read the early drafts of this book aloud. Your ear was invaluable and your insight so often spot-on. And to my wonderful sons, your presence has brought more joy and inspiration to my life than you will ever know. You have all fueled my writing by nourishing my soul.

Sarah Cypher is the wonderful freelance editor and author who first saw my work. My writing is better because of her talent, and my gratitude for her guidance is enormous.

Thanks to my dear friends, Maria Martellucci, Danielle Poupon, and Beth Finley, for cheering me on every step of the way. Your encouragement is priceless.

I am deeply grateful to Deb Bertges for her support and wisdom, always.

I was overwhelmed by the kindness of this community of authors who took the time to give a new writer advice and encouragement: Elizabeth Atkinson, Dana Alison Levy, Tracy Mayor, Holly Robinson, and Mark Karlins.

I am so lucky to have met all of my Muse and the Marketplace buddies who inspire me with their ideas about writing and keep me laughing with our shenanigans.

And the deepest gratitude to everyone at Crowsnest Books for being so wonderful to work with: Lewis Slawsky, Alex Wall, Adam Mawer, and Allister Thompson. What a fantastic experience, thank you.

About the Author

Monica Duncan is a writer of literary fiction, musician, wife, and mother. Originally from Michigan, she finds herself continually drawn to the hidden richness of the places she comes from. Now living in Newburyport, Massachusetts, she is still at home by the water.

Monica holds music degrees from Michigan State and Indiana University and is active as a freelance musician and teacher in the Greater Boston area.

She's pretty sure she'll always be in love with the soundtrack from "O Brother, Where Art Thou?" and has discovered that her favorite skill as a writer she learned from her life in music: Be a good listener.

Reading Group Questions

1. Juniper is an artist. What gives a person the right to call themselves an artist—how they think and see the world, or only what they have produced? Do you in any way consider yourself an artist?

2. You know that Dahl is a good guy. You know Johnny is a bad guy. What about Kirk? What do you think?

3. There is a chapter in Twine entitled "Sub-Rural" and the term "subrural" is used to describe the area surrounding Gobles. What do you think this means? And is it more than just geography that defines a place as sub-rural?

4. What is great about the relationship between Cora and Juniper? Is it ever okay that a child (even a grown-up) behaves as more of a parent, upending the parent-child dynamic?

5. What do you think about Five Women as a celebration of Juniper's "family tree that don't fork?"

6. At one point Juniper is debating where to install Five Women—if it should be displayed in Kalamazoo where many people would see the work, or in small-town Gobles where fewer people would see it, but where it might be more meaningful. She ultimately chooses Gobles; do you think that was a good idea? Should a place like Chicago be the ultimate goal for Juniper?

7. There are many short chapters in Twine (as opposed to fewer, longer chapters). Was this too

abrupt for you, or was it perfect for an author wanting to hold your attention in today's—hey, where'd you go?¡

8. What did you think of the title? What does it mean to you?

9. Juniper experiences motherhood in ways that surprise her. She had heard stories of women who "lost themselves" when they became mothers. But Juniper becomes voluptuous of both body and mind. She is moved to create art and life in tandem, and begins to truly find her voice as an artist during her pregnancy and and after Clover is born. In what ways did Juniper's mothering surprise you?

10. Juniper is her own hero. "Empowerment" gets so much lip service, but how do we become empowered?

Our hurts and pains can really inhibit our ability to act freely and in our own best interests. For Juniper, empowerment is not just being strong and powering through external obstacles, but also having the courage to dive in and work and wade through her deepest internal obstacles to find freedom and love and joy. Do you relate to Juniper's empowerment?

11. Alternately, how do we become disempowered? Gobles, Michigan is filled with people characterized by their wanting. There are not enough jobs, so there isn't enough money, without enough money there isn't enough education. These three factors in combination créate a trap for people born into this environment. Who created the socioeconomic climate of subrural Michigan that is responsible for the disempowerment of its people? Are we each

individually responsible for our own disempowerment? Is there a character in Twine who clearly
feels disempowered?

12. One of the bigger conflicts in this novel is not the
overt obstacles, but the assumptions of the reader.
We assume that poor is bad, we assume that a place
like Gobles is bad, we assume that a child like Clover
is behind before she even starts her life. What is it
about Juniper's choices and attitudes that thwart
our assumptions?